ANCIENT LONGINGS

IMMORTAL LOVE BOOK 6

MEG M. ROBINSON

Arcane Crow
— PUBLISHING —

ALSO BY MEG M. ROBINSON

DEDICATION

This one is for everyone who has dealt with depression and fought their way to their own happy ending (or is working on getting there).

TRIGGER WARNING

I don't normally do trigger warnings (but I also don't write anything too dark). In this case, I felt it necessary. One of the main characters deals with depression and thoughts of suicide. It is referenced throughout the book, so if that's something that bothers you, unfortunately there's no good way to skip just the parts involving that. But, as with all my books, she does get her happy ending.

CHAPTER I

Aelia had been twenty-two the first time she died. She'd been staring in horror at Lemuria as it crumbled and burned, disappearing beneath the waves before those same waves dragged her under, holding her beneath the surface until she drowned. After reviving only minutes later, she'd died again before ever seeing land, this time victim to hungry sharks. In the thousands of years that followed, she died hundreds of times in dozens of ways, but she always came back to life, whole, healthy, and with barely any sign that she'd ever suffered an injury. Hanging, stabbing, burning, beheading...none of them seemed to take, nor did divine intervention. In a low moment, she had goaded a god into killing her, but within an hour, her body fully recovered. That death hadn't even left a scar.

If only she could forget the pain as quickly as the signs of it faded.

Being an immortal human had been difficult. In the beginning, she didn't have the magic or community to help her hide her lack of aging from the humans, because she wasn't truly Arcane. She was other, a unique being in the universe. And knowing she would come back from anything didn't prevent hunger pangs or illness. Nor did it grant her any kind of protection from magic, which was why she was now sleep deprived. It had been a week since she'd had a full night's sleep, all because of nightmares inflicted on her by a group whose purpose was to protect the Arcane.

Clearly they felt no responsibility toward her since she was biologically human.

She sat on a hill overlooking the small village that the new Lemurians had claimed as their own. It had once been a thriving place, and far more advanced than other societies of the time. The Lemurian gods had ensured it was comfortable and safe, which was why, over six thousand years after it had been lost, the buildings below her were still in good condition. They had needed cleaning, of course, but the structures themselves had mostly been sound. And with people living in several of them, the village no longer looked so sad and abandoned.

The original five that had landed on Lemuria in a life raft had grown to twenty-one—including a new Lemurian baby and a half-Lemurian goddess no one had known existed. All in less than a year.

It was truly amazing. Thousands of years ago, the Lemurian gods had disappeared along with almost all their people when the land they'd called home was destroyed. Over the years, the few who had survived the destruction had perished until only one had remained, hidden away in a tomb. When an archaeologist named Seth had found that last Lemurian, he'd set off a chain of events which had led to Lemuria's rediscovery. Within hours of reaching the forgotten land, he'd become a Lemurian god, and one of the old gods had been brought back from wherever their enemies had sent them.

At first, the joy of rediscovering Lemuria had pushed the darkness from Aelia's mind. She'd enjoyed a small measure of peace from the depression she'd suffered from for more years than she could count. It hadn't lasted, so she did what she could to distract herself.

Two months ago, she'd helped some friends save a magical library from a force more ancient even than Lemuria, and that library—the Athenaeum—was still recovering, which was why she was on the phone with the woman in charge of it.

"They finished all the upgraded protections, then?" Aelia asked, absently watching people moving around on the stone streets below.

"They did," Sophia said with a sigh. "Athena and Thoth finished the last of them yesterday. I think all of them went overboard, but given how close Peter came to basically ruining the world, I can't blame them."

"At least you've got the gods to make it so that can't happen again."

Sophia made an indistinct sound in her throat, clearly not convinced. "They won't be able to get to the Miasma, no, but there are still plenty of ways for people to ruin the world, and most of them aren't in the Athenaeum."

"No, but no one, not even gods, can prepare for every eventuality," Aelia said, shrugging as she watched someone head for the stream. Kara, she thought, though she couldn't be sure from that distance. But since she saw a small black and white creature following her, she was probably right. The shade cats that called Lemuria home loved stalking Kara for some reason.

"True. But it still had a lot of people spooked. Including Death."

That caught Aelia's attention, and she literally straightened. "Death?" she asked, careful to keep her voice casually curious.

"Oh, did you not hear about that?" Sophia gave a short laugh. "I'd been here for about a month when this couple teleported into the Athenaeum. Something you know shouldn't be possible except for the patrons, and they can only manage it because the wards are their magic."

"Right. Seth was thrilled when he realized he could teleport in and out once he became a god and joined the patrons," Aelia said, nodding absently.

"I'll bet he was. But anyway, Blanche had gotten a spell from my grandfather that would allow her to summon Death. The real thing, not just a death god."

"I wasn't aware there was a literal embodiment of death," Aelia murmured, her mind starting to consider and reconsider ideas.

"Most people don't, and he seems to like it that way," Sophia admitted. "But Blanche got the spell and used it. I won't go into all the details because they're not mine to tell, but apparently she and Death hit it off. Though a necromancer marrying Death does make sense, I guess. Who else is he going to marry? Though she lives in the freaking underworld, and I don't know how any living person can deal with that."

Aelia could, but then she had an entirely different viewpoint on death and the underworld than anyone else on the planet. "Interesting. I've met a few necromancers, and even spoken to a couple of ghosts, but I've never actually talked with anyone who's been to the underworld. Do you think I could get her number?"

"To talk about the underworld?" Sophia asked, surprised.

She fought back impatience. If this Death really was the ultimate authority over who lived and died, surely he'd be able to do something about her immortality. She craved mortality. The chance to live, grow old, die, and be reborn with a clean slate? She wanted nothing more. Reincarnation was a fact, she knew that, and would give everything to experience it. "You know I'm human and immortal, which means the underworld is the one place I'll never go. As someone else who seeks knowledge, can't you understand why I'd want to talk to someone with firsthand knowledge of it?"

"If she likes you, she might actually take you there," Sophia said. "She did that to me once. Except it was a surprise, and I didn't leave the castle she lives in, so I can't tell you much about it." She made a thoughtful sound before saying, "Yeah, I suppose she wouldn't mind me giving you her number. It's not like I'm sneaking you into her house or anything. I'll text it to you."

"Thanks, Sophia. I appreciate it."

Sophia laughed. "I'm glad, because I still owe you and everyone else who helped with the Miasma."

"And like we told you back then, we were saving the *world* from the Miasma, not just the Athenaeum, so there's nothing to owe. Helping you helped us all."

"Still, without you and everyone else?" She sighed heavily. "I don't like thinking about it. But as much as I love talking to you, I should probably get back to work. There's still a ton to do. A lot got screwed up in the short time we were out of the Athenaeum."

"I understand. Let me know if you need anything."

"I will. Bye, Aelia."

"Bye," she echoed before hanging up the phone. A few seconds later, it dinged with a text. Checking it, she saw it was just Blanche's name and phone number. But despite her desire to be mortal, she didn't call Blanche right away. Instead, she found herself standing and wandering down to the village. It was odd. Before she'd gotten Blanche's number, she would have said there wouldn't be any hesitation before calling, before making her request, but now that she had it? Something was stopping her. Responsibility for the nearly two dozen people who now called Lemuria home, maybe? Except why was it her responsibility? She wasn't a Lemurian, god or otherwise. She wasn't even Arcane. Nor did she have any real attachment to anyone here. No one was family or even a close friend. In fact, she'd done what she could to keep herself as detached as possible. It wasn't as easy as she would have liked, since she did genuinely like everyone she now called neighbor.

People called out to her, and she responded with friendly words and a pleasant smile she'd perfected lifetimes ago. One that looked pretty but was empty. No one had seen through it in longer than she could remember. Proof, she supposed, that she'd mastered the poker face.

For the next few hours, she went through the motions, all while her mind kept going back to the number now in her phone, and what it could mean for her. That night, she joined the rest of Lemuria in the square. Given that they were such a small community, they had opted to have what they were calling family meals every Saturday. Potluck dinners where they could not only socialize, but discuss the next steps in bringing Lemuria back to some semblance of its former glory.

Aelia would have loved to skip it, but knew that would draw more questions than she cared to answer.

Carrying the dish she'd prepared to the new pavilions that were off to one side, she set it down on the table and took her place near one end of a table off to the side. It was the best she could do to distance herself from the other Lemurians—not that it did much good. They always did their best to include her, whether or not she wanted included. Tonight, they seemed to sense her mood, though, and the conversation flowed around her more than toward her. Tempest—who had been the last Lemurian—tried to engage her, but that was normal. She and Tempest had known some of the same people back before Lemuria had been destroyed. Aaron did the same, and more diligently than Tempest, but that also wasn't a surprise. The tiger shifter had helped them get to Lemuria, so there was history there. And she'd made the mistake of sleeping with him once, right after they'd found what remained of the island. It had been...amazing, but not something she'd allowed herself to repeat. It would have meant a closeness she wasn't willing to accept.

The others mostly left her alone, which she was grateful for. These dinners hurt. Though there were some single people like Aaron and Kara, there were also several couples and families who now called this place home. It had begun when Seth and Tempest had learned they were expecting a baby and Seth's dad had moved to the island, then others had begun immigrating to Lemuria. It was painful to see, especially when she looked at those who had kids.

She missed her children, even if their faces had long ago blurred in her memory.

"Can you hold Katrina for a moment?" Tempest asked, offering the month-old baby to her. "She likes her Aunt Aelia, and I need to run home for a minute."

Aelia started to argue, to ask where Seth was, but knew such a protest would just draw questions she didn't want to answer. Smiling, she accepted the tiny halfling. "Of course." Tempest seemed to disappear as she transformed into air to run her errand, and Aelia turned her attention to the infant staring up at her. Against her will, she found herself cuddling Katrina and kissing the top of her head.

Automatically, she began to sway, falling into habits she thought she'd broken after deciding she'd never have another child.

The weight of the baby in her arms was both comforting and overwhelming. And when one of the new mers commented on how adorable she looked holding Katrina, it became too much. Fortunately, that was when Tempest returned. Aelia rose as quickly as she could without jostling the baby and walked to the elemental. "I'm sorry, but I need to go," she told Tempest, handing the baby over.

The woman looked surprised but cradled Katrina to her chest. "Of course. Is everything okay?"

Aelia forced a smile. "I just need to go." She turned and left before she could be asked anything else. It was hard for her to keep her pace to a walk when she wanted to hurry, and when she was out of view, she broke into a run. She didn't head for her house, but aimed for the orchard, moving as fast as she could, like putting distance between her and the happy couples and families would ease the emotions watching them caused.

It didn't work.

She ended up in the midst of the fruit trees, well out of view and earshot of any of the Lemurians back in the square, even the gods. She hoped. Several Arcane races had excellent hearing, but the orchard should be safe.

Aelia wasn't sure exactly what had broken her. Holding Katrina? Seeing Delilah and Rose showing casual affection? Watching Veronica and Ezra play with their daughter, Kelly? Maybe all of it. None of it. She wasn't sure it really mattered. She'd reached her breaking point. True, she'd reached it years ago, but she always found a reason to keep going. Until she hit that breaking point again.

Pulling her phone out of her pocket, it slipped from her fingers and hit the grass. She knelt and picked it up, aware she was breathing more quickly than normal, but that didn't matter either. Nor did the slight trembling in her fingers as she unlocked her phone and went right to the text where Sophia had sent Blanche's number. She called before she could stop herself.

"Hello?" a woman said when the call was answered, her voice a little gravelly, but not unpleasant.

"Blanche?"

"Yeah. Who's this?"

"My name's Aelia. I'm a friend of Sophia. And several other people you know, it sounds like."

"Aelia? Yeah, I've heard of you. From Erasmus, though, not Sophia."

"Not surprising. I've known him for years longer than I've known Sophia."

"Makes sense. What can I do for you, Aelia?"

There was no suspicion or hesitation in her voice, just honest curiosity. Normally, that might make Aelia feel bad, but not today. "How much has Erasmus told you about me?"

"Not that much, really," Blanche admitted. "He said you were an amazing source of information on the Arcane and humanity, and probably knew as much as most of the knowledge deities, but he was pretty evasive on anything else."

Aelia nodded to herself and thought quickly. She could beat around the bush, lead up to her point, but she was through doing the safe, sane thing. She got right to it. "I'm immortal. Completely human otherwise, but immortal. And not like gods or vampires are. I literally cannot die. Or rather, I can, but it never lasts long. I've drowned, hung, been beheaded, burned, and much, much more."

Blanche was silent for a minute before she responded. "Erasmus definitely didn't mention anything like that," she said slowly, unable to keep the surprise out of her voice. Aelia expected it. No one suffered from her affliction but herself. No one had ever suffered from it. She would know. She'd been hunting for another immortal since she first realized what had happened to her, and had never found even an inkling that one existed.

"He doesn't know all of it. The immortality, yes, but he keeps that quiet. He knows how to be discreet."

"He definitely does," Blanche agreed. "I wasn't aware that it was possible for anyone to die and come back without outside help, especially not a human. If I ask how it happened, are you gonna tell me?"

"The details? No," Aelia answered flatly. "Let's say it was a case of someone young and dumb playing with things she didn't understand. And it isn't something that can be repeated."

"Uh huh. And why are you telling me this if you haven't even given Erasmus these details? What do you want from me?"

From her tone, Aelia had a feeling Blanche knew what was coming, and she felt a sense of anticipation and foreboding as she drew in a breath to ask the question that could finally give her peace. Except she hesitated, staring up at the sky as her emotions warred within her. No, she finally decided, she had to ask. She couldn't keep living like this.

It was time she became just like everyone else.

CHAPTER 2

Aelia had been acting increasingly odd the last few months. Or maybe it was just her norm. Aaron couldn't really say for certain, given they'd only known each other for less than a year. But the woman he'd watched for the last few weeks was far different from the one he'd traveled to Lemuria with. Definitely different from the woman he'd spent a night with after they'd found the island and found Tempest after she'd been kidnapped by one of Zeus's sons. Distant, like she were a puppet without a purpose.

Tonight, when she'd run out of the dinner like she was about to break down, he'd followed her. Maybe it was a little pitiful how easily he noticed everything about her, but it didn't matter. Something was clearly wrong, and he wanted to make sure she was okay.

Normally, she might have noticed a muscular six foot two man trailing after her. His black shaggy hair might blend into the night, but his tanned skin wouldn't allow him to completely disappear. Then again, neither could she, given he could shift into a tiger and had some of the night vision felines enjoyed. And his alternate form did give him an edge on moving silently, and practice had only made him more stealthy, so she never realized she was being followed. And maybe he should have let her know he was there, but something told him not to.

To follow, to watch. To wait. Eventually, she stopped in the orchard and pulled out her phone, so he leaned against a tree and studied her.

Aelia was a stunning woman. She looked like she was in her early-twenties, though he knew she was far, far older. Closer to Tempest's six thousand something than his own few hundred. But whatever age she'd frozen into had left her slim, with gentle curves he wished he knew far better than he did. There was something appealing about her petite form, though in the past he had never gone for women more than a foot shorter than him. But her topping out at five feet hadn't been an issue during their one night, nor any night that had followed. Not in his dreams, anyway.

Her hair was creamy blonde with gold highlights that hung straight to the middle of her back, and he knew it was as soft as silken thread. Her skin was almost as pale as her hair, which set off eyes that were actually purple. Other than contacts, he'd never seen eyes that shade before, and he loved them. Especially when she smiled. Or they went dazed during sex.

Aaron knew there were scars on her smooth skin—maybe from her many deaths, maybe from normal injuries—but they didn't detract from her beauty. Nothing could, and since he'd seen her freshly revived after drowning and being shot, he was pretty sure he knew what he was talking about.

"Sophia tells me you're married to the true Death."

Aelia's words brought his worries back to the forefront of his mind, and he frowned, fighting to keep his nails from shifting into claws.

"Can he make me mortal?"

He lost the fight, his claws digging deep into the tree, and he was sure his muscles had bulked up a little as his emotions tried to force a shift. But he couldn't properly intervene if he couldn't speak, so he forced himself to remain human.

"Then can he kill me?" Aelia asked, more desperation in her voice than he'd ever heard from someone before. It simultaneously enraged and scared him. She should never sound like that.

Snarling, he stalked forward, no longer caring if she heard him, and he snatched the phone out of her hand. "Forget it," he snapped at whoever was on the other end, barely managing to end the call rather than smashing the phone against a nearby tree. In all honesty, part of him wanted to beat the shit out of whoever she'd been talking to. "You're not dying," he told Aelia.

Though he was on the verge of shifting into a half-tiger form, she wasn't scared of him. Her eyes were hopeless instead, and he nearly lost his resolve, but he couldn't stand the thought of losing her. Seeing her die was hard enough when he knew she'd come back within minutes. Hearing that she wanted to make it permanent? It was the most terrifying thing he'd ever experienced.

"It's not your choice, Aaron," she said, extending her hand for her phone, but he lifted it out of her reach. A dick move, probably, but he didn't care. Everyone knew he could be a dick.

"Maybe not, but why would you want to die? Do you know how many people would kill to be in your shoes?"

Her eyes narrowed at him, and she rested her hands on her hips. "Do you know how many people are absolute imbeciles who have no idea what it's like to never die?"

"Then tell me," he demanded. "Tell me what's so fucking bad about being an immortal living on Lemuria. Tell me what would make you call who I think is the Grim fucking Reaper and ask to die. Tell me why you'd make everyone here mourn you!"

"Oh, so it's better if I have to mourn all of you instead?" she shot back, getting as close to in his face as she could manage, but she didn't even reach his shoulder. Despite that, the fierceness on her face was nothing to sneer at. And honestly, under normal circumstances, he wouldn't want her to be mad at him. She might be small, but he didn't doubt her capabilities. "I'm older than dirt, so do you know how many people I've had to bury? The friends, the family? How about lovers? Wives and husbands. Do you know how many children I've had to watch grow old and die? And I don't just mean humans, either, Aaron. The first person I lost wasn't just Arcane, she was a Lemurian, just like Tempest. She should still be alive, and I still lost her. But maybe it's okay if it's only one person suffering?"

The emotion, the raw grief in her voice, was hard for him to hear, but it was the words themselves that threatened to stagger him. He knew she was old, and no one that old escaped loss, but it sounded like she'd dealt with more than most.

And he hadn't known she'd had kids. How had he not known that? He should have, but then again, she didn't often talk about her past.

"No," he said, calmer than he'd been before her rant. "I don't want you suffering, Aelia, but I think you're missing something important."

"What's that?" she asked dryly, folding her arms over her chest. Instead of looking casual, it looked like she was closing herself off. That was the last thing he wanted. No, the second to last. The last thing he wanted was to bury her.

"Immortality doesn't have to be all bad." He shook his head to stop her retort and plowed on. "Lemuria has been rediscovered, and no, it might not be as big as it was once, but there's still a lot to explore, to learn, and to rebuild. And there are others here who aren't going to die of old age, ever. Vazi and Seth are actual gods, Aelia. And Tempest? She's a true Lemurian, so no old age for her, either. And from what I hear, they're not alone. Julian? Wade? Those demon twins? None of them are going to die of old age."

"That's the thing, Aaron," Aelia said, shaking her head, "they might not die of old age, but they can still be killed, just like Selana. And before you even think of mentioning how Seth and Vazi are gods, remember that they're the only two full Lemurian gods around. They might be difficult to kill, but difficult isn't impossible. Gods, even Lemurian gods, have died before."

He couldn't really understand her point of view, since it was so far from anything he'd experienced, but he understood fearing loss. "There has to be another way than talking to a god of death."

"Aaron, my immortality isn't natural. And according to Death's wife, even he can't undo it and make me mortal. If he can't make me natural again, then what chance does anyone else have? Besides, even if you discount all the people I've lost and will continue to lose..."

He'd known there was something bothering her, but it sounded like it wasn't just future grief. "What? What's been bothering you so much that it's driven you to this?" he asked, wiggling the phone in the air.

Aelia sighed and turned, pacing away from him before she turned back to him. "I assume you want the short story?"

"I'm fine with the short or long story, as long as you tell me what the hell's going on. Stop leaving us all in the dark, honey. We're worried about you."

She nodded and sank down into the grass, drawing her knees to her chest and wrapping her arms around them. "I've had run-ins with the Ekklesia over the years."

He frowned and walked over to her, sitting just within arm's reach. "Why would the Ekklesia..." He sighed. "Don't tell me they've given you shit because you're technically human and their whole job is to keep humans from learning about the Arcane."

"No, it's not that," she said with a shake of her head. "You know they're more concerned with humanity as a whole rather than individuals. Otherwise, there wouldn't be thousands of demis out there. Even Seth's mom was human, and she was fully aware her husband was a shifter. The Ekklesia doesn't care about that."

"True, but then what's the problem?"

"My immortality. Again," she said with a tight smile. "A while back, a *long* while back, I was killed and came back to life, but it wasn't Arcane around me at the time; it was humans. So I inadvertently exposed the Arcane. Sort of. I had a choice between helping the Ekklesia on demand, or being imprisoned, and a lifetime in jail for me would last a very, very long time. Since I had no wish to spend eternity in a cell, I chose to work for them."

Aaron hadn't dealt too much with the Ekklesia. Occasionally he'd turned relics over to them—before he'd learned of the Athenaeum—but he'd also never done anything that could expose the Arcane. That said, the fact that they'd treat Aelia like that royally pissed him off. "Are they pressuring you to do something you're not comfortable with?" he guessed.

"It's more than that. They somehow found out I was associated with Lemuria and want the location and any intel on it I could give them. Except, since they can't physically reach me, they've been using other methods to try to persuade me."

His eyes narrowed and a small growl slipped out. "What methods?"

She rested her cheek on top of her knees, gaze fixed on the grass behind him. "They must have a dreamwalker. He or she has been in my dreams every night for the last..." She sighed. "I don't even know how long. Lack of sleep is starting to get to me. Essentially, they're torturing me to try to force me to cooperate."

Again, his body tried to shift, and he barely managed to resist it. "Are you fucking kidding me? Those pricks! They're supposed to keep all of us safe, not abuse anyone to...what? Increase their own power? What would they even gain from knowing about Lemuria?"

She shrugged. "I'm not Arcane, so I'm not one of those they're sworn to protect. And from what I've heard from Erasmus, they tried to take control of the Athenaeum years ago. Supposedly, they claimed it would help them hide the Arcane better to have access to the relics and knowledge Erasmus's predecessors had collected. Maybe they think Lemuria can do the same thing. But does it really matter why they want the information?"

It really, really mattered, but he could shelve it for now. "Have you told anyone?"

"No," she admitted. "Seth and Tempest have the new baby, and Vazi's been focused on helping Dania recover. Not that I can blame him. No one had any idea a half-Lemurian goddess was out there, and he has so few members of his pantheon. They have other priorities. Besides, I'm handling it."

"I don't think you are, not if it's pushed you toward suicide," he said, tone more blunt than he'd intended.

"Then what the hell do you expect me to do? I don't have a lot of options here! Yes, I know a lot of sorcery, but it's not really going to help. Trust me, I've tried every spell I know, and there are a lot of them."

"And you're determined not to go to Vazi or Seth?"

"I am."

Aaron had always loved being a tiger. He'd never regretted that he didn't have magic beyond his ability to transform. Right now, he wished he had true magic. Then he remembered something he'd heard when they'd gone to take the Athenaeum back from a possessed madman. "What about that Hall the Athenaeum people were talking about?"

"Hall?" She lifted her head, brows lowering. "Sozu? What they were calling the Hall of Records?"

"Yeah. Wasn't it like an even more ancient version of the Athenaeum? Maybe it could have some answers. You wouldn't even need to tell Sophia about this, since you seem to want to keep it as quiet as possible."

The look on her face wasn't hopeful, it was angry and suspicious. "You just want to get inside the fabled Hall since they wouldn't let you poke around the Athenaeum. It's the same reason you wanted to find Lemuria. It wasn't to help Tempest."

"Hold the fuck up," he said, back stiffening with indignation. Yes, he could be an asshole, and he was ambitious, but he *never* manipulated his friends. "I didn't even know about Lemuria until after I agreed to help Tempest. Hecate asked me to help, I said yes, and then I found out about Lemuria. But I'm not going to apologize for wanting to find and explore Lemuria, anymore than I'm going to apologize for wanting to see what information the Athenaeum and Hall have. I'm an archaeologist. It's kind of what I do. But that doesn't mean I don't genuinely want to help you. Don't insult me by confusing the two. And if you don't have any better ideas, then the other option is to tell one of the gods who happen to be our friends. Or see if the Athenaeum has something. Both ways require actually sharing something of yourself with people."

The true offense on his face made guilt bloom in her chest. It had been a cheap shot, and she knew it, but the thought of returning to Sozu filled her with mixed feelings. On one hand, she'd once loved the place. On the other, the last time she'd been there, Lemurians had still roamed the world, and she'd not yet suffered all the loss she'd now experienced. Still, it wasn't a bad idea. Grovek—the god who'd created the haven of knowledge—had collected information on anything and everything. It likely did have something that could help, but she couldn't simply commit to going. Not yet.

"I'm not sure. I'll think about it."

It obviously wasn't the answer he'd hoped for, but he nodded. "I'll give you a few days. But if I see you spiraling, if I get even an inkling that you've called the Reaper back, I'll go straight to Vazi."

Irritation replaced the guilt. "I'm not a child, Aaron."

A slow grin curved his lips. "Oh, I remember that very, very well. But if I have to play dirty to keep you with us, then I will. So spend the next few days actually thinking about it—or thinking about other options."

"Fine," she snapped.

He offered the phone to her, and she snatched it out of his hand. "And in the meantime, Aelia, if you need anything, you really can talk to me," he told her as he got to his feet. "I'm just worried about you."

Sighing, she nodded and accepted his hand when he offered it, rising. "I know. Sorry."

"Not a problem. Just try to remember you're not in this alone."

She was afraid she'd be very much alone in the end.

The altercation with Aaron had left Aelia exhausted. Honestly, she was used to being emotionally worn out, given how often it happened. Depression might not have been spoken about for most of her life, and at times had actually been seen as something that could land a person in an asylum, but it didn't change the fact that she'd suffered from it for longer than she could remember.

So after he'd left her alone, she'd gone straight to her house. To her surprise, it actually felt like home, and that had nothing to do with being surrounded by the things she'd collected over the years. She was more pragmatic than sentimental—now, at least—so they were simply things. Some of them ancient, expensive, or powerful, but still just things.

Tonight, she didn't let herself think too hard about why the ancient stone house felt like home.

Too wound up to sleep, she wandered through the rooms. It wasn't a large home—no bigger than a modern two-bedroom house, really—but it had a few aspects she enjoyed. Unlike modern bathrooms, which often had tubs too small for most people to fully submerge themselves, this one had a small pool. She could easily stretch out in it with two friends and have plenty of room. Then there was the library, which was a requirement for her, given all the old books she had. Important ones, in some cases, since there were few copies of them left—if any. And lastly, the square-shaped house was open to the sky in the middle, and there was a beautiful garden there, complete with a stone fountain.

It was the garden she headed to now, sighing as she sat on the edge of the fountain. There was only the tiniest sliver of moon above her, but she didn't mind the darkness. There was nothing in the deep shadows left for her to fear. But the darkness did make her feel even more alone than she normally did, but maybe she needed to be reminded of that after Aaron's words.

She'd been there for twenty minutes when she sensed she was no longer alone. Frowning, she straightened and let her eyes skim over the darkness. The woman didn't make her look hard or long before she stepped closer, hands held up to show she was unarmed, but Aelia knew that didn't always mean anything. Not in a world full of magic.

The woman was just a few inches shy of six feet, with straight black hair and pale skin. She was pretty, even beautiful in a goth kind of way, though it was only the black clothing that made Aelia think goth.

"Who are you?" Aelia asked, not moving from her spot, though she was extremely concerned that someone had managed to get onto Lemuria without Vazi or Seth assisting them. It shouldn't be possible. Even the gods couldn't manage it, and she knew Zeus had likely been trying since the day most of the land had sunk. No, he'd probably been trying since the day he'd learned the Lemurians were more powerful than the Greeks.

"Blanche," was the answer, accompanied by a smile. "When we were cut off so abruptly, I got concerned."

Aelia relaxed a little. Death came to everyone—except for her—so of course he'd be able to get places others couldn't. It wasn't much of a stretch to assume his wife would have similar abilities. "Why would you be concerned about me? We've never met."

"No, we haven't, but there are a couple of reasons," Blanche said, shrugging as she sat a few feet away. "One, I recognized the tone of your voice, and I can't just ignore it. I've had that tone a time or two, and so have people I care about. Two, I like both Erasmus and Sophia—though I know Sophia better than I do her grandfather. And I know she appreciates what you did for her."

Aelia shook her head. "I didn't do that much. I was just one of many."

"The one who knew how to get inside a ward even a couple of magic and wisdom gods didn't know how to break," Blanche pointed out. "Not something just anyone can say."

She could only shrug because she couldn't argue. "You could have just called back."

"I could have," Blanche agreed, "but I wasn't certain your phone hadn't been destroyed, and in case you were in trouble, I wanted to help get you out of it."

A quick laugh trickled from Aelia's lips. "I promise you, Aaron can't hurt me, even if he wanted to. He was more...upset that I was hoping to hurt myself, in any fashion."

Blanche arched a brow. "There something going on between you two?"

"No," Aelia said, then nearly cursed herself for answering too quickly. "We went through hell together getting here, but we're just friends."

Blanche nodded slowly, studying Aelia for a long moment. "Can I ask you a personal question?"

She frowned. "I suppose."

"Why do you hate your immortality so much? And before you answer, let me add that I've got my own brand of immortality."

That caught Aelia's attention, but she doubted Blanche could understand exactly. "What do you mean?"

"Long story short? My husband and I were once some of the first humans on the planet. He died—was the first ever to die, in fact—and became Death. Not understanding his powers, he accidentally killed me. After we were reunited not that long ago, I died again. He resurrected me and ensured I couldn't die again. Though unlike you, I won't ever actually die."

She thought about that for a moment, but only came to a single conclusion. "Because he controls death and doesn't let it happen?"

"Basically, yeah. Where death is reversed for you each time, for me, it just doesn't happen. And okay, I was a little pissed about that at first, but I came around pretty quick. I never have to worry about losing my husband or our friends. Plus, I live in Cindatha—the Underworld—so even if someone I care about dies, they're not lost to me."

"I think you already know why I hate my immortality," Aelia said, smiling wryly. "None of my spouses have been impossible to kill, I've lost all my children, and I don't have the option of seeing them in the Underworld whenever I like. Or ever, since I can't ever die and go there myself."

Blanche nodded knowingly. "I get it. And I won't push you, or stay any longer since I am basically a stranger, but can I give you one piece of advice before I go?"

Aelia wasn't sure what Blanche could say that she hadn't already experienced for herself, but nodded.

"I won't go with that bullshit about better to have loved and lost, or any of that darkest before the dawn crap, either. But I will say that sometimes? The chance of being happy is worth jumping feet first into the fire and risking the burn."

With that, she disappeared without any of the usual signs of teleportation. Aelia stared at the spot where she'd sat, and thought about those words until dawn began to lighten the sky.

CHAPTER 3

I t had been almost two days since Aaron had followed Aelia to the orchard, and his mind hadn't eased any. She had been just as distant, interacting with the other Lemurians on only the most superficial of levels. Until today, but he wasn't exactly sure the interaction was her choice. Seth and Tempest had asked her to babysit, and it wasn't exactly the easiest thing to say no to a god, even if said god had been barely more than human a year ago.

That was still a major kick in the ass for Aaron. For years he and Seth had been rivals, and not always friendly ones. Not that he begrudged Seth his elevated station in life. Being the Lemurian god of mountains somehow suited him. And while the power might be cool to have, Aaron didn't think he wanted the responsibility that went with it. Never mind that he—along with Seth and the others—was doing everything he could to help build Lemuria up. When he wasn't still doing his old job, anyway. A job he'd put on hold after hearing Aelia's phone call. Technically, he was supposed to be joining his team in the Mediterranean, but he'd put it off indefinitely.

Aelia was more important.

That left him with nothing to do, so he'd stripped back at his house and shifted into his tiger form. One of the big draws of Lemuria was that he could shift whenever and wherever he wanted. Since everyone here knew about the Arcane, there was no need to hide what they were, so anytime he needed a run, he went for a run.

But today, it wasn't letting him work out his frustration and fear. No matter how far, how fast he ran, he couldn't escape the replay of Aelia asking to be mortal. Essentially asking to die. He couldn't get the image of the last time he'd seen her die out of his mind. To think that one day it could be permanent? It was unthinkable.

He snarled under his breath, which prompted a soft gasp. Pulling up abruptly, he looked over at the source of the sound, seeing Dania sitting on a fallen tree.

The half-Lemurian, half-Greek goddess was almost as petite as Aelia, and they actually resembled each other, at least in facial features and stature. Both were pale, but where Aelia had violet eyes, Dania's were dark blue. Where Aelia's hair was blonde, Dania had dark tresses. She'd been painfully skinny when she'd been found imprisoned, but had filled out during her two months on Lemuria. The wary look in her eyes wasn't quite as prominent as on her first day here, but it still came entirely too often, especially around men. Since she'd been the captive of Zeus for thousands of years, he couldn't blame her.

No one on Lemuria liked that particular god much.

She wore a dress, but had shunned any white clothing since she'd gotten a choice. Today it was a teal blue sundress, and he was pleased she was starting to find herself. Having her mother, Rhea, visit often helped, but he had a feeling just being away from Zeus did even more. That didn't prevent her from staring at him wide-eyed, with electricity crackling around her fingers, strands of her hair lifting slightly from the rest.

Startling the goddess of natural destruction was never a good idea.

Trying to make himself look like less of a threat, he sat down and ducked his head. That helped her understand that he wasn't just an animal, but the relief was marginal.

"You're one of the Lemurians, aren't you?" she asked, her voice soft, sweet, and nervous. When he bobbed his head in a nod, she relaxed a little more, but frowned. "You can shift if you want. Or go. Either way is fine with me."

Like Aelia, she hadn't interacted with people much lately. Again, he couldn't blame her, but she was never going to acclimate to this time and place if she didn't speak with people. He might not be the best option since he was both male and occasionally an asshole, but she pulled at his protective instincts. Not quite like a little sister, since she was several thousand years older than him, but it was a close enough approximation.

He doubted she realized that shifters were nude after making the transformation, so moved behind a bush before he returned to his human form, so his lower body was hidden from view. He had absolutely zero modesty, but even he wasn't enough of a dick to let it swing in front of someone who might have trauma that could be triggered by the sight.

"You're Aaron, right?" she asked once he'd transformed.

"I am, yeah. Sorry. Didn't mean to startle you."

"It's all right. I just didn't think many people came out here," Dania told him. "There aren't many people here. I like that."

"They don't. Or not often," he said. "Shifters are more likely to, since we feel the urge to run in our animal forms, but there's only a few of us here. Beyond that, this area has been explored, so it should be safe if you're just wanting a place to be alone."

"I'm not sure if I do," she admitted.

"That's good. Because basically everyone on Lemuria is trying to grow this little community of ours. Did you know there were only five of us when we first found this place again?"

Dania shook her head before she lifted her hands to fiddle with her hair. "No. *Matera* told me that most of Lemuria was destroyed and it was thought lost for many years, but she didn't tell me anything about how it was found again."

"Would you like to hear the story?" He wasn't much of a storyteller, but she was starting to relax, and it was good for her to know the history of this place.

"I would, but why are you hiding behind that bush?"

Unable to help himself, he grinned, but stayed firmly behind the foliage. And just to be safe, he covered his groin with his hands, just in case gaps between the leaves kept him from having sufficient coverage. "Because I've yet to meet a shifter who keeps their clothes on when they shift, and I didn't figure you'd want to see me in all my naked glory."

Her cheeks pinkened, and her gaze dropped to the ground in front of her, though there was nothing to see. It made him happy that he'd chosen modesty. "No, I wouldn't. But I...ah...I think I can help?"

"Help? With clothes, you mean?" He shrugged. "Sure. I mean, I don't mind hiding behind a bush, but I'm sure you'd be more comfortable if I had clothes on, so go for it." She was a goddess, so it should be an easy thing for her, but he also wasn't exactly sure how god abilities worked, and according to her mom, she was a goddess of nature, just the destructive part of it. When imprisoned, she'd been forced to cause earthquakes, hurricanes, and volcanic eruptions. Hopefully, she didn't accidentally explode him or suck him up in a tornado or something.

Dania nodded and lifted her gaze to him. After a moment, he felt cloth settle over his skin. Glancing down, he burst out laughing. He was wearing a dress not dissimilar to the one she'd been wearing when she'd been found—an ancient Grecian gown. His was a lovely shade of purple. Actually, it was about the same color as Aelia's eyes.

"What's wrong?" she asked, frowning in confusion.

He stepped out from behind the bush, grinning as he leaned against a nearby tree, careful to keep distance between them. "Just can't say I've ever worn a dress before, but I think it suits me," he joked.

"Oh!" Confusion shifted to embarrassment, and her frown deepened, her eyes worried. "I'm sorry. It's the only thing I wore for many years, but I can—"

Aaron waved a hand absently. "No, it's fine. All the important bits are covered, and a dress is just a piece of clothing."

"Are you sure?" she asked, playing with her hair again. Nervous tic, maybe?

"Yeah, I'm sure. I am who I am. Clothing isn't going to change that. Besides, aren't you more interested in the story?"

Her fingers paused for a second, then she nodded. "I am."

"So, Seth found Tempest in this tomb in South America about a year ago. She'd been there since Lemuria sank. Turns out, Vazi knew something was coming and put her there to protect her. He just didn't realize he'd disappear and not be able to get her out." He frowned and cocked his head. "Not sure how Seth found her," he murmured before shaking it away. "Anyway. She woke up and they immediately got attacked." Dania gasped, but he just nodded and continued talking. "They managed to get back to America and went to Kara," he said, referring to the half-witch, half-elemental who had been Seth's best friend for years. "She'd heard of Aelia as someone who knew lots of bullshit other people had forgotten, and when they learned Tempest was from Lemuria, they didn't know who else to go to who might know anything useful."

"Because she's immortal?" Dania asked.

"Yep, though we didn't know that back then. She was around when Lemuria was whole," he explained. "Once the four of them met up, I had a goddess ask me to help them. We all got together in Hawaii—a group of islands not really that far from here—and started looking for Lemuria. Obviously, we found it." He left out the murderous god who had met them here, and Seth's adventure back in time, not wanting to overload her with too much.

"And then you just started bringing other people here?"

"Basically. Started with Seth's dad, then friends or friends of friends we knew we could trust. Obviously, we don't want just anyone to end up on Lemuria. We want it to grow, not get destroyed again."

"I agree. It's beautiful here. And peaceful," she said, letting her eyes roam around the forest.

Since it looked like Hawaii, but even less touched by man, he agreed. It was a true tropical paradise. "It is. And for someone like me who's made a living learning about the past, it's a treasure trove. Not of riches, but of history."

"Then why do you seem sad?"

The question surprised him. For someone dealing with as much as she was, she was still perceptive. Or maybe her past had forced her to pay such close attention to others. Trauma victims tended to be exceptionally observant, he knew. "I'm worried about a friend," he admitted.

"Why?" she asked simply.

It took him a moment to figure out how to answer without revealing Aelia's secrets. He'd absolutely spill them all if it meant saving her life, but it would probably be to Vazi or Seth. Dania might be a goddess, but from what he'd been told, she had no more experience with life than a preteen. And she had her own issues, so he wasn't going to add to them. Again, he was an asshole, but he wasn't completely selfish.

"She's sad. Not just normal sad, but really sad, in a way that doesn't go away. You can't get cheered up or anything. It's called being depressed." At least that was his best guess as to what had pushed her from immortality to her current state of mind.

"Oh. If you can't get cheered up, how do stop being depressed?"

He smiled sadly and shrugged. "That's a question people have been asking themselves since you were a little girl. Sometimes it passes, if it was caused by something that happened to you, like losing someone you care about. Sometimes people take medicine that can help, at least for a while. But there's no surefire, permanent cure for depression." Though he really wished there was. Aelia wasn't the first person he'd cared about who had suffered from it, but he had to admit it bothered him more now than it had in the past.

"That sounds horrible," Dania said quietly.

Aaron nodded and went to tuck his hands into pockets he didn't have. Instead, he folded his arms over his chest. "It's definitely not fun, but that's why I'm worried about her. I can talk to her, try to distract her, but I don't know that there's anything I can really do to help her."

Dania's face went serious, thoughtful, and she went back to playing with her hair. "I don't know if I'm depressed, but I know there's nothing anyone can do to make me feel better. My mother has tried. So have Seth and Vazi. But I can say that it helps when people…" She hesitated, struggling for the right words. "When they listen and give me what I need, even if it's not what I want."

Curious, he cocked his head. "What do you mean?"

"Well, explaining things to me helps. I spent most of my life locked up on Olympus. I don't know what a lot of things are, and it makes me feel like I don't belong. And I'm not entirely sure I do, so that makes me feel worse. But I like knowing about things, even if it makes me feel dumb sometimes. And I like it when people give me space when I need it." She smiled a little, and it struck him as shy. "And I like it when people talk to me like I'm not an abomination or someone so fragile the wrong word might break me."

He immediately shook his head. "You're not fragile. Someone fragile would have broken a long ass time ago. The fact that you're still kicking and able to have conversations like this tells me you've got a spine of steel. If you were fragile, you'd be curled up in a ball somewhere, damn near catatonic."

Dania blinked a couple of times, but kept smiling. It even looked more real now than it had. Good. He'd meant every word. No one could be Zeus's prisoner and not suffer. A lot of people would have retreated into themselves, or worse. "Thank you."

"No need for that. Just telling the truth." He jerked a thumb back in the direction of the village. "Trust me, any of them will tell you I'm not really what you'd call a kind man. If I say something nice, I mean it. Of course, if I say something dickish, I mean that, too."

She laughed and shook her head. "I don't think I mind if you're...dickish. A lot of people here have been overly nice to me." Her humor faded. "It makes me feel weak and like an outsider. So, having someone be blunt and...dickish...makes me feel more normal. Which probably sounds odd, but it's the truth."

"Again, spine of fucking steel," Aaron said, shrugging. "As for the outsider? Other than Vazi and Tempest, you're the only other one here who was born on Lemuria. You've got more right than the rest of them to be here."

She frowned lightly. "Seth is a Lemurian god. He wasn't born on Lemuria?"

Shit. So no one had explained that, and his shortened version of the story had left that out. "No, he wasn't born on Lemuria. His parents are actually a shifter and a human."

Her frown deepened. "How is he a Lemurian god, then? That's not something that can just be...changed."

"Not normally, no," he agreed. "But when you stab a murderous god with a special Lemurian knife, apparently that's the exception. And don't worry," he said quickly when her eyes widened and lips parted, "the god he killed really needed it. And if he hadn't done it, none of us would be here. Vazi would still be wherever the other gods are, and Tempest, Seth, Kara, and me would all be dead." Aelia would still be alive, but she'd have been trapped on an island with an insane god, which might be worse.

Before she could think of a response, there was a shift in the air. In a fraction of a second, she went from relaxed to tense again, but to his surprise, she immediately calmed. "*Matera*," she said, smiling and getting to her feet.

Aaron followed her gaze to see a goddess who had become a regular visitor to Lemuria; Rhea, the mother of the gods. Not just Dania, but also Zeus and his siblings. He'd never spoken to her, but everyone could recognize her on sight now. About the same height as her daughter, she had a curvy figure. Her black hair was curled and pinned up in a style that would always say Greek to him. Where her daughter was fair, her skin was lightly tanned, and where Dania had blue eyes, hers were brown, and they lit up upon seeing her daughter.

"Dania," Rhea said, but her gaze fell on Aaron and narrowed. The wary expression lasted only a moment before confusion took over. "Why are you wearing a dress, tiger?"

"His name is Aaron, *Matera*," Dania answered before he could. "And the dress is my fault."

"How is it your fault?"

"I was running as a tiger when I ran across Dania. She was kind enough to give me clothing. I'm not going to complain that it's a dress," he said, working to make his tone respectful. He might mouth off to Vazi and Seth, but he knew those gods. Seth was too laid back to really get pissed, and Vazi had what might be considered a soft spot for the original five. But he wasn't going to risk treating Rhea the same way. The goddess of motherhood was extremely protective of her daughter.

"I...see."

"I'm not used to creating men's clothing," Dania explained, but she wasn't embarrassed about that now, and smiled instead. Good. She was getting more comfortable.

"And like I said, I don't mind. It covers my junk, so I'm good. But since your mom's here, I'll get back to my run."

"All right. Thank you for talking to me, Aaron."

"Anytime," he said, and he meant it. "It was nice to properly meet you," he said to Rhea, inclining his head to her.

"And you," she said, though she sounded distracted.

Instead of shifting, he walked away from the goddesses, heading back to the village. It was time to check on Aelia again. But when he came across a patch of flowers, he picked some on a whim. Flowers might not cure whatever ailed Aelia, but maybe it would make her smile. Sometimes, the little things were the only ones that mattered.

CHAPTER 4

When Aaron entered the village in a dress and with a handful of flowers, he expected to see people, and really expected to get ribbed about his fashion choice, but didn't see anyone. He considered running by his house to change before he went to Tempest's to check on Aelia, but opted not to. Hell, maybe the dress would give her a giggle, which would be a win, too.

Except when he knocked on the door, it wasn't Aelia who answered; it was Tempest. She didn't giggle, she just laughed.

"Aaron? Why are you wearing a purple dress?"

"What?" he asked, using two fingers to partially lift the skirt. "Not my color?"

That made her laugh harder. "The color's perfect, but why are you wearing a dress?"

He shrugged and dropped the skirt. "Naked tiger after a run, nerved-up goddess who only knows how to make dresses. You do the math."

"Ahh. Yes, I suppose a dress is better than running around Dania naked. Especially if her mother's around."

"Oh, she showed up, and was very confused. Then again, that might have been the only thing to save me after being alone with her daughter."

Tempest grinned and shook her head. "Only you, Aaron. But what are you doing here? I'm guessing you're not looking for me since I can't see you bringing me flowers."

"Nah, though I might sometime, just to see Seth's head explode."

She rolled her eyes. "When are you two going to drop the act and admit you're friends?"

He feigned an offended expression. "Friends? With that asshole? Never!" he said dramatically.

"Uh huh. Aelia's gone home."

"Yeah, I figured when you answered the door."

Tempest smiled. "Want to come in anyway? Tell me why you've been watching Aelia like a stalker the last few days?"

"I'm not stalking her," he said, no trace of humor left in his voice.

"I know," she agreed, "but you've watched her since the day you two met, and that attention has gotten even more intense the last day or two."

That gave him pause. "Shit. Is it really that noticeable?"

"To me, yeah. I don't know about everyone else. I didn't say anything because it's honestly kind of cute. Asshole tiger getting all starry-eyed over an ancient sorceress? It's sweet. I'm just not sure what changed a few days ago."

Aaron shook his head. "I'll admit to having a thing for her, but the change is between me and her." For now.

Tempest watched his face closely until a cry from inside the house made her sigh. "I'd push, but a crying baby trumps your love life. Just don't hurt her, Aaron?"

"That's the last thing I want," he promised. "Go, take care of Katrina."

She kissed his cheek and smiled. "You may pretend otherwise, but you're a good man, Aaron," she told him before going to tend to her daughter.

He stopped by his house to change on the way to Aelia's. The dress might have made her laugh, and it was definitely less constricting than his usual clothing, but he was ready for pants. Except she didn't answer when he knocked. He was debating whether to leave the flowers when he heard another cry. This one was definitely not a baby, and it sounded pained rather than sad.

Fortunately, with such a small, exclusive group of people living in an isolated location, there was never any need to lock doors. Most houses didn't even have locks. Without hesitation, Aaron opened Aelia's front door, and went to stop whoever or whatever was hurting her.

It had been a bad idea to lay down for a nap when she got home after babysitting, but Aelia was just so tired. She'd averaged only two hours of sleep a night for the past week, and caffeine just couldn't keep up.

Almost as soon as she'd fallen asleep, the nightmare had begun. Whoever the Ekklesia had targeting her had clearly just been waiting for her to fall asleep. Worse, they were very, very skilled at imagined torture. She'd witnessed such things in the waking world, but it was somehow worse in dreams. Her sorcery didn't work. She couldn't pass out to escape. There wasn't even the brief respite death could provide. It was simply never-ending pain and demands to give up all the information she had on Lemuria. Where it was, how to reach it, who lived there, what gods were protecting it. Anything, everything. She was sure they'd expected her to give in days ago, but protecting the people on this island had become her sole purpose in life.

She just wasn't sure how much more of this she could take before breaking.

She was being flayed alive when the dream went foggy around the edges. There was a sound hidden beneath her screams, but she couldn't make out what it was. Her body jolted, and the pain dulled some, letting her hear the sound more clearly. Was it her name? The dreamwalker had used her name several times in demand, but this tone was different. Scared? That didn't make any sense. Angry would, and she could hear a tinge of that, but it wasn't the primary emotion.

Another jolt and her eyes flew open. She was staring into tiger blue eyes and a concerned face, but it took her a few seconds to recognize Aaron's features and the hint of a drawl he retained from his childhood in Tennessee.

All her good intentions about keeping an emotional distance from the Lemurians flew out the window. She could still feel the echo of the knife on her skin, and she needed someone, something to comfort her, and he was right there. Shoving herself into a sitting position, she flung her arms around him and pressed her face against his shoulder, holding onto him, anchoring herself to reality as she tried to wash away the memory of the dream.

He shifted until he could wrap his arms around her in return, his hold tight as she tried to push the remnants of the dream out of her head. Instead of fading like normal dreams, these nightmares stayed fresh and clear. Just another way of tormenting her and trying to convince her to give in.

"Aelia," Aaron murmured, rubbing a hand soothingly over her back. It felt good, but it didn't really provide any comfort. His presence, oddly, did.

"Yeah?" she responded, her voice muffled by his shoulder, but she wasn't quite ready to let go of him yet.

"Was it the Ekklesia?"

Her answer was slower in coming this time, but she nodded. "It was."

His hand paused for a second before he resumed rubbing. He gave her another few minutes before drawing back. "You remember our deal?"

She nodded and shifted, swinging her legs over the edge of the bed. "Not likely to forget you screaming at me."

"I didn't scream, I just spoke firmly. Not my fault if you didn't like what I had to say. But your time's up."

Her head jerked up so she could look into his face, his serious eyes.

Reading the mutinous look on her face correctly, he added, "You do something about this, today, or I will."

"You have no right to dictate what I do or don't do," she snapped, shoving out of the bed, wanting some distance between them. "It's my life, my problem, and my choice of how to deal with it."

To her shock, he grabbed her bicep in an unbreakable grip. It didn't hurt, but there was no way she could pull away, even when he dragged her across her bedroom to her full-length mirror. As soon as he released her arm, she tried to jerk away, but he caught her shoulders and positioned her in front of the mirror, facing it. "Look," he ordered. "Take a look at yourself."

"I know what I look like," she said, trying to move away, but he wasn't letting her go.

"I don't think you do, because you wouldn't be this much of a pain in the ass if you did. Look. At. Your. Face."

Giving in because it was easier than fighting him, she sighed and looked at her reflection. Honestly, she didn't look her best, but she had just woken from a nightmare. Her hair was mussed, her clothes rumpled, and she looked irritated and tired. Nothing she hadn't expected. "I'm looking," she said impatiently.

"You're not," he disagreed. "If you were, you'd notice that there are bags under your eyes, you're even paler than normal, and your eyes look haunted as fuck. You've even lost weight, just in the last few months. You're almost as skinny as Dania was when she first came to Lemuria, and Zeus had barely fed her."

She wouldn't admit he was right, but she could see everything he had mentioned. She hated that. "Aren't you a charmer?" she asked sarcastically. "I thought you were supposed to be some sweet-talker when it came to women. Spewing compliments to get them naked."

He met her gaze in the mirror and stepped closer, so she could feel the heat of his body against her back. "If you want me to charm you, I absolutely fucking will. I'll seduce your mind and body and spend hours making you feel beautiful and sexy. I'll spend days making you come more times than you can count. I'd love to do just that. To fill the air with the scent of your pleasure and tasting your skin anytime I'm not buried as far inside you as I can get."

Those words and the tone they were spoken in got to her. Sleep deprived or not, she could feel her body responding. It didn't help that she knew for a fact he could make good on his promises.

Aaron leaned in closer, so his lips brushed the shell of her ear as he spoke in a seductive whisper. "But I'm not. Not until you're back to your old self." It didn't stop him from kissing the side of her neck, so her pulse leapt. Stepping back, he continued in a normal tone. "And I'm just being honest, Aelia. You're still beautiful, but you look like you've been through hell. So you do something, today, or I do."

Aelia couldn't break his gaze, even reflected in the mirror, and after several minutes of a silent battle of wills, she sighed. "Fine. I'll do something."

"Good. What?"

Frustrated that he kept pushing, she stepped away from him and ran her fingers through her hair, fighting not to tug at the blonde strands. Ignoring him, she went over her options. She could tell Vazi, but he'd probably just kill the Ekklesia. Not the best option, since they really did help hide the Arcane from humanity. No, she hated a lot of their methods and definitely couldn't stand their ambition, but their purpose was sound.

Contacting Sophia or Erasmus at the Athenaeum was another option, but it wasn't a guarantee. Dreamwalkers were just witches with a rare affinity for dreams, so there might not be anything about blocking their influence. The Athenaeum had a lot of information, but it didn't have everything. And it would mean letting someone else in on her problem, which meant risking getting close to someone else.

Glancing back at Aaron, she had to admit her best option was probably the one he'd brought up two days before. Sozu. The Hall of Records. Except she wasn't sure she wanted to set foot in that place again. She'd basically spent a year of her life in the sub-realm that Grovek—the Lemurian god of wisdom—had created. It, more than anywhere else, held memories for her.

"I don't want to tell our gods. Vazi would just kill the Ekklesia, and we need them."

"Yeah, he's pretty protective of everyone who lives here," Aaron agreed.

"Which means...I think I need to go back to Sozu."

"The Hall, right?"

She nodded and sat on the edge of her bed. "But I don't know if I can."

"Why not?" he asked, moving toward her, but he didn't sit, just stood in front of her, watching.

"Ghosts."

He seemed to accept the simple answer and nodded. "Would it help if you didn't go alone?"

Aelia actually had to think about that. Not just if it would be easier for her, but how Grovek would have felt about having strangers in his sanctuary. Then again, Sophia and her allies had already been inside. Smiling inwardly, she decided he wouldn't have minded that, since it had helped save the world.

"Yes, I think it would help."

Aaron nodded again. "What do I need to pack?"

She frowned at him. "What makes you think you're coming with?"

"Does anyone else know you've been having problems?"

"No."

"Do you want anyone else to know?"

Sighing, she shook her head. "Not really."

"Then it's gotta be me, doesn't it? What do I need to pack?"

"It might take a couple of days to find out what we need, so food and water, changes of clothes. There are bedrooms with bathing facilities, so you don't need to worry about that." She thought for a moment, then added, "And something for taking notes, if you want it. Nothing can be taken out of Sozu."

"What do you mean?" he asked, sounding more curious than disappointed.

"Grovek put protections on the library. Basically, anti-fire, anti-theft, things like that. So you won't be able to take any pages or tablets out of there. You should be fine taking pictures with your phone, but if you do, I ask that you ensure they're kept safe."

"I can do that. I'm particular about anything on my phone anyway," he said, brushing that concern off. "It's habit. Don't want other archaeologists like Seth getting someplace before me."

She smiled faintly. "Fair enough."

"So...how do we get there?"

"Since you're going with me, we'll take the shortcut. We can leave from here."

"Shortcut? Cool. How long do you need?"

Aelia shrugged. "Not long. Just long enough to grab the same things I told you to grab."

"You get started on that, then. I'll be back in half an hour. Just...maybe don't take a nap before I get back?"

She shuddered lightly and glanced at the bed. "I can agree to that."

"Don't worry. We'll figure out how to block them—without killing everyone in the Ekklesia."

He turned and left the bedroom. It was only then that she noticed the flowers on her nightstand. Both touched and surprised, she walked over to the small bouquet and picked it up. She recognized the flowers as ones native to the island. Sweet-smelling ones, so she lifted the blossoms to her face and drew in their scent.

It had been a long, long time since someone had brought her flowers. Even longer since they'd taken the time to pick them personally. Damn him.

Setting the flowers down and attempting to put them out of her mind just as easily, she started packing.

CHAPTER 5

Instead of going straight to his house, Aaron went back to Tempest's. This time, he was hoping to find Seth. Luckily for him, it was the god who answered the door.

Instead of the animosity that would have been the norm only a year ago, Seth said, "Hey, Aaron. What's up?"

"Got a minute?"

"Sure. What's going on?"

Aaron glanced behind him, and though he didn't see Tempest, he took a step back. "Out here? In private?"

Curious, Seth stepped outside and closed the door behind him. "Something wrong?"

He hadn't really promised not to tell Seth anything, but he found himself reluctant to break Aelia's trust, especially since she was making an effort to remedy the situation. "It is, but I'm working on it. And no, I can't say much."

"Not really what I wanted to hear," Seth admitted. "If there's a problem, I want to help."

"I know." And he really did. He'd never actually disliked Seth, though he was pretty sure that didn't go both ways. On his side, though, it had always been more of a competition. Okay, maybe it hadn't always been friendly, but he'd never seen Seth as an enemy. "I promise it's being worked on, and I hope it'll be fixed soon. Just wanted to let you know Aelia and I are going to be gone for a few days."

Seth's brow furrowed. "Gone where? Exploring Lemuria? Are you going somewhere dangerous?"

"No," Aaron assured him. "I promise it's safe. And it might only be a day or so, but I didn't want to just disappear and have people worry."

"You're sure there's nothing I can do?"

There probably was, but he had to give Aelia the chance to fix it herself. Taking the decision out of her control wouldn't help her. "Not right now. But if that changes, I promise you'll be the first to know," he promised.

Seth looked reluctant to let it drop, but he nodded. "All right. Be safe."

"We will."

He only took a few minutes at his house, but he was used to packing for various digs and other expeditions, so quickly had the supplies loaded in a backpack, including a tablet, camera, and notepad. And a gun, because he never left Lemuria without it. Screw what the rest of the Arcane thought about firearms, he wasn't going to out himself or die because of pride.

When he got back to Aelia's house, his pack on his shoulders, he found she was ready and waiting for him. "You said we were going to use a shortcut to get there, but what is this shortcut? And is there anything else I need to know before we get there?"

"You know the big thing—no taking anything out of Sozu—and you're not the sort to try destroying knowledge, so you're good there,"

Aelia answered, putting her own backpack on. "As for the how, it's not a way you can replicate. You would have to find a hot spring to get there."

"You know you're not making me less curious," he pointed out.

"I'd apologize, but I really can't help it. I'm not the one who set this all up. And you're about to experience my way firsthand," she said with a ghost of a smile. "Are you ready?"

"Eager, actually."

She nodded and stepped closer, taking his hand. A moment later, they stood in a large round room illuminated by torches. The structure was made of stone blocks, more perfect than anything else he'd ever seen, even in modern construction. They stood on a round platform with a open, vertical circle behind them, a shimmer inside it hinting that it was magical. A portal, maybe. Surrounding the platform were four statues—two women, two men, each of them winged and with some sort of snake integrated into the art. On his right, there were stairs circling up the wall to the next floor. On the left was a single archway leading to another room.

"Holy shit," he whispered, marveling at the construction and artistry of the place, and he'd only seen the entrance. He turned to Aelia and saw grief on her face as she looked around. "You okay?" he asked, placing a hand on her shoulder, though he wanted to take her into his arms.

"It's just been so long since I've been here," she whispered, emotions thickening her voice. "The last time, there were other Lemurians on the planet, and Grovek's other apprentice, Akila, was still alive. According to Sophia, they found her tomb beneath the Sphinx. They didn't know how long she'd been there."

"There's a tomb beneath the Sphinx?" he asked, momentarily distracted.

"Apparently," she said, stepping off the platform. When she did, the ghostly image of a woman appeared just within touching distance. Slim, Aelia's height, with black hair and blue eyes lined with kohl.

Even as he wrapped his hand Aelia's arm and pulled her back, the woman began to speak, her voice accented. It was almost like Vazi's, but different. A blend, perhaps.

"Aelia, I had hoped you would return to Sozu. Grovek would have appreciated knowing his apprentices were continuing his work," she said, and though she was facing Aelia, even appeared to be looking at her, the words sounded recorded. "As you may know, I have been killed, but I've left this imprint of myself to help you in any way I can. All you need to do is call out, and I will appear." There was a pause, and grief flickered over her face. "I'm sorry I can't do more."

As suddenly as the image had appeared, it disappeared.

"Aelia?" he asked, gentling his hold on her arm and looking at her face. It was the same but for the tear sliding down her cheek. He brushed it away with his thumb. "Who was that?"

"Akila," she answered. "I'm not sure how she managed that, but she'd been his apprentice for a long time before I met either of them. She could have learned a great many things in that time."

"You going to..." He trailed off and frowned, glancing toward the stairs. "You hear that?"

Aelia cocked her head and listened for a moment before her gaze followed his and her eyes narrowed. "Are those voices?"

"Could it be the crew from the Athenaeum again?"

Slowly, she shook her head. "Sophia promised they were going to reach out to me before coming here again. Besides, they're still fixing things that got messed up when they were dealing with the Miasma. That's a bigger priority than investigating this place."

"How did they say they found this place?" he asked, easing the backpack off his shoulders and setting it down.

"Clues in Akila's tomb, I think."

"Under the Sphinx? So someone else could have figured those clues out?"

Aelia shrugged, but she looked just as disturbed as he did. "It's possible. Intelligence and knowledge aren't limited to the Nasaru."

He quickly got rid of his boots—in case he needed to shift—and drew his gun before heading for the stairs. Though he wanted to tell Aelia to stay there, he knew it wouldn't do any good. She'd just argue that he was the only one who could die and stay that way.

He wished she wouldn't have a point about that, because he hated seeing her hurt, even if it was always temporary.

They crept up the stairs, and she at least stayed behind him. The second floor was pretty similar to the first, though instead of a platform, statues, and a portal, there were tables and chairs. He paused, listening, then headed for the arch rather than moving further up. He was impressed by how quietly Aelia moved for a human, making barely a sound. Most humans were noisy creatures, even those who prided themselves on being quiet, like hunters and soldiers.

He paused at the opening, but didn't need to listen this time. He could see several people moving around in the room directly across the hall. They were taking items off shelves, glancing at them, then tossing them on a table or onto the floor. At least one item—it looked like a clay tablet—broke. Easing out of view, he whispered to Aelia. "At least three people. Looks like they're ransacking it."

She didn't look scared, she looked outraged. "We have to stop them."

He agreed, nodding. "Want the gun? I can shift, but you'd have to do the talking."

She shook her head. "If it comes to a fight, I've got my own magic."

He didn't doubt that. After the Athenaeum, he'd heard a few things. She was probably the most capable person on the planet. And yet he continued to worry.

Easing forward, he stopped at the next doorway, careful to keep most of his body hidden by the wall, so only part of his face was visible. The room they were in was full of shelves and a single table. Sheets of what looked like papyrus, along with stone and clay tablets, were scattered around the room, as if they'd been discarded. "Stop what you're doing," he barked, but when the three men turned, his mouth went slack. "James? What the hell are you doing here?"

One of the men drew a pair of knives, another held his hand in a way that suggested he was a witch preparing to throw magic or something. James—Aaron's brother—just shot him a killing look. "None of your fucking business, Aaron."

Stepping out from behind the wall, he had enough presence of mind to wave to Aelia to remain hidden. He hadn't seen his brother in decades. While part of him missed having a relationship with his only sibling, James had made choices none of his family had approved of or been able to live with. "It is my business when you break into someplace you don't belong and seem to be trashing the place."

"Who is this guy?" the man with the knives asked. "Is there a reason why we're not killing him?"

"If he gets in our way, wound him, but don't kill him," James said entirely too casually. "He's my brother."

Aaron heard Aelia's soft intake of breath, but he didn't look at her. If he could keep these three from knowing she was there, he would. Especially if his brother was now okay with random violence. "What are you looking for?"

"I don't care if he's your brother. Get him out of here or kill him," the potential witch asked.

James said nothing for a long moment before he nodded. "If we let him leave, he'll just come back with others. We can't afford the delay." When the witch started to gesture like he was about to conjure and throw something, James lifted a hand in a signal to wait. "Before you take care of him, I think he should know why we're here. Give him proof that his baby brother isn't the failure he thinks I am."

"Whatever. Just make it quick," the witch said, looking like he was all too eager to kill Aaron. That one had killed before. And often, if Aaron had to guess, but he stayed quiet. They weren't going to die, and he needed to know what James was up to. It couldn't be good if he was hooked up with men who acted like mercenaries.

"Fine," James said, waving away the man's concern. "You want to know why I'm here?"

"I do," was all Aaron said. James had always been volatile, and he didn't want to set him off before he knew what he was dealing with.

"Do you even know where you're at right now?" James asked, grinning and spreading his arms wide. "The Hall of fucking Records. And do you know what's in here?" This time he waited for an answer.

"A lot of things, I imagine," he answered carefully, though he was wondering how James had not only found the place, but knew what it was.

"The secret to immortality! Hell, we've already found information on it."

Aaron was genuinely surprised. "You what?"

"That's right, big brother!" He tapped on one of the pages on the table. "Some guy named Grovek wrote about it. He knew of two people who were immortals. *True* immortals," he emphasized.

The thought of his brother becoming as immortal as Aelia honestly terrified him. He didn't want to see James dead, but neither did he want him to be undying. "Why are you looking for it?" Monologuing was supposed to be for bad guys, but it seemed his brother counted.

His parents were going to be heartbroken if he told them.

"Because your screw up brother isn't such a screw up," James said, smirking. "I've been working for the Ekklesia for more than a century, while you're still just a boy who digs around in the dirt."

Fear gave way to anger. Not at the insult to his profession—he didn't care about that—but the rest of what he'd said. James was working for the very people Aelia was being tortured by? He knew their ambition was great, but he wouldn't have thought they'd stoop to the acts they'd committed just in the last few days. And now they wanted to be immortal? Hell. No.

"I'm not letting you leave here with the secrets of immortality," Aaron said, and though he hated it, he lifted the gun. If he had a choice, he'd deal with the two mercs and take his brother to someone to erase his memory.

He doubted he was going to get that choice.

"We're not asking," the man with the knives said, but it was the witch who acted first, throwing a fireball at him. His feline reflexes let him duck out of the way, but he felt the heat of it as it passed by, harmlessly hitting the stone wall behind him.

Aaron aimed at the witch, firing, but with a wave of the man's hand, the bullet veered off course and buried itself in a wooden shelf. James hung back, which surprised him, but it seemed that while he was okay with watching his brother die, he wasn't as okay doing the job himself. And none of them were aware of Aelia's presence. Yet.

He kept firing as the man with the knives rushed toward him. He missed the witch, but one bullet buried itself in the other man's arm, effectively eliminating one of the knives he held. That was the last shot he was able to get off before he had to dodge the other knife.

Partially shifting, he slashed out, catching the merc across the belly, just before the man slammed into him. It knocked them both back into the hallway. Worse, it let him catch sight of Aelia.

"There's another one!" he yelled, even as he tried to stab Aaron in the gut. The tip of the blade pricked against Aaron's stomach, but he managed to grab the guy's wrist, preventing it from sinking deeper.

With her presence known, Aelia didn't hesitate to jump in and start helping. He didn't know how she did it, but without her moving, the man on top of him was thrown off, slamming hard against the wall. When his body hit the floor, he didn't move, so Aaron dismissed him for now.

"Kill him!" James yelled before he shifted, his body morphing into a large orange and black tiger. Since James's attention was on Aelia, Aaron started for him, but before he could even get to his feet, the witch started blasting him with magic. The first hit knocked him back so he landed hard on his ass. Fine, he didn't need to be on his feet to shoot, and he raised his gun, firing and struggling to remember how many times he'd fired. This time the witch wasn't able to block all the bullets. The first and second he got. The third was altered slightly, but grazed against his side. The fourth, though, that one hit right where Aaron intended, hitting the witch square in the chest.

The witch looked mildly surprised as he glanced down at his chest, at the red blooming over his pale blue shirt. Then he fell to his knees and started to fall to one side. That was when Aaron forgot about him and turned his focus to his brother.

It was already too late.

The tiger was standing over Aelia, her neck in his throat, her eyes blank. He'd killed her, using a tiger's favored method.

"No!" Aaron yelled, turning the gun on his brother, something he never thought he would do. "You bastard!" he snarled before firing. James dropped Aelia and twisted, but the bullet lodged in his back leg. Letting out a roar of pain and anger, he glared at Aaron for only a second before he turned and raced toward the stairs.

There was no doubt Aelia was dead, and though he hated to leave her, Aaron scrambled to his feet and started after his brother, but he'd only gotten to the doorway before James was heading down the stairs. He still followed, but James dove through the portal before Aaron could reach him.

"Godsdammit!" he screamed, his voice echoing off the stone walls. They'd come here hoping to help Aelia with the Ekklesia's nightmares, but instead she'd died. Again. He was doing a fantastic job of making things better for her.

CHAPTER 6

Putting on his boots and snatching their bags up, Aaron stalked back up the stairs to where Aelia still lay, a small pool of blood beneath her damaged neck. He sat down beside her and pulled a shirt out of his pack, rolling it up and sliding it beneath her head. He couldn't do anything about the damage to her throat, but he could ensure she'd be comfortable when she revived.

Pulling a bandana and bottle of water from his pack, he dampened the cloth and began wiping the blood off her skin, fighting not to look into her lifeless eyes. He might not be able to help her, but he could erase as much of the signs of her death as he could.

Gods, he really hated when she died. Knowing she would come back never helped, because there was always the fear that this time, she wouldn't. Not knowing how she was immortal, or its limits, it would always be a fear.

He sat there for thirteen minutes, watching her. For every second of those thirteen minutes, she looked exactly like a corpse. It might have been easier if her wounds had slowly healed until she revived, but that wasn't how it worked with her. Her brand of immortality meant she was dead for a variable amount of time, then all at once her body healed and she was back.

This was the longest he'd had to wait. He wasn't sure what dictated how long it took her to come back, and he had a feeling she wouldn't want to talk about it.

In a rush, the bones in her neck aligned and the punctures in her throat closed. Life came back into her eyes as she drew in a breath.

She shoved at the floor to sit up, and he reached out to help her.

"I really fucking hate it when you die," he told her, his hand on her back to support her until she was fully recovered.

"It's not a lot of fun on my side either," she said, voice a little rough. She winced and rubbed her throat before she smiled faintly. "First time a tiger's killed me. Wasn't sure I had a lot of firsts left."

Not finding that at all amusing, he only clenched his jaw and gave her time to relax.

"What happened?" she asked.

"I shot the witch as James was killing you. Chased him, but he made it through that stone ring and disappeared. Where does that go anyway?"

"Back to wherever you started from. When we go through it, we'll be back in my house." She frowned and looked up at him. "Did you know he was working for the Ekklesia?"

"I had no fucking idea," he admitted, shoving to his feet to go check on the man she'd knocked off him. He should have done it as soon as he'd gotten back, but had forgotten about him, too concerned with Aelia. It took only a touch to learn he was dead. Apparently, he'd broken his neck when he hit the wall. Fitting, since that was also what had killed Aelia. "Don't suppose you know of an easy way to dispose of dead bodies, do you? The other option is to toss them through the portal, but if we don't know where they'll end up..."

"I do, actually." She started to get up, but he saw she wasn't quite steady yet, and walked over to pull her to her feet. She walked to the first man and knelt, resting a hand on his shoulder. She said something, and the body dissolved into dust. The process was repeated on the witch's body.

"That's kind of terrifying," he admitted, though he was also impressed.

"If it helps, it only works on the dead. Won't do a thing to the living."

"That's reassuring." Not that he thought she'd do anything to him. She wasn't a cruel person, and he had to believe she liked him at least a little.

"What's not reassuring is how they were able to learn anything from the materials here."

He frowned. "What do you mean?"

"Last time I was here, everything was written in Lemurian. It's not exactly a well-known language. So how were they able to read enough to learn about immortals?"

"It might not be well-known, but that doesn't mean it's completely dead," he pointed out. "One of them might have spoken it. Or Akila might have translated some stuff before she died. What's stuck in my head is how they said there were two immortals."

Aelia went still and looked at the table where the trio had placed several items. "I was wondering about that, too," she admitted quietly. "Grovek never said anything about another immortal. I wasn't even certain that he'd known about me." She looked at him, adding, "It happened right before Lemuria's destruction."

"I know we came here to find something to block dreamwalkers from getting into your head, but...."

She nodded and walked over to the table. "If there is another immortal, we need to find them."

"I was going to say we need to make sure my brother and the Ekklesia can't become immortal," he said dryly. In all honesty, he wasn't sure he wanted to find another immortal. It might help Aelia, knowing she wasn't alone, but he wanted to be that comforting person for her. If there was another immortal, that was who would be her go to. Wouldn't it? But if finding this other immortal was what she needed, he'd suck it up and do it. "We can look for both?"

"We can," she agreed. "I think we should start with the things here that they earmarked, then go find Grovek's journal."

"His journal? Why?"

"Grovek had a system, one he insisted his apprentices follow, which is why I know it," she began, sitting at the table and beginning to sort through the sheets and tablets. "When he was researching something...mundane, for lack of a better word, the notes just got made and filed wherever they belonged. Learn something new about dragons? It goes with information about other magical creatures. Find a pretty new rock? It's cataloged with other geology information. But if it was something more important, it was journaled first."

"Important how?" he asked, though part of him wanted to go hunting for that dragon information.

"Like the Miasma the Athenaeum was dealing with. That's something big, important, and dangerous. It was journaled first, then, depending on what it was, it might be duplicated for the library."

"So even if there's stuff about immortals here," he began, gesturing at the table, "there might be more in his journal?"

"It's very likely, yes. It might be more fragmented, as he would have made notes as he learned things, but we can deal with that."

"Do you know where his journal is?"

Aelia made a low noise in her throat as she shrugged. "I know where it should be, but his last day wasn't exactly a normal one, and we don't know what your brother and his friends disturbed." She glanced up at him. "I got the impression you two aren't close?"

"Even less now that he ordered his friends to kill me, then actually killed you," Aaron said in a low tone. "But no, he's basically been shunned by my family for a while now. He wasn't exactly a good kid, but then he hurt someone—badly—to get what he wanted, and wasn't the least bit remorseful about it."

"I'm sorry," she said, letting it drop at that, which he was grateful for. Instead, they both focused on sorting through the writings. They were in Lemurian, which was unfortunate. Aaron had begun learning it, but he was far from fluent, so it took him longer to get through a document than it took her.

After they'd looked through everything on the table, Aelia shook her head and pointed to one sheet. "That's the only thing I found containing anything about immortality, and all it says is that it happened twice."

"I didn't find anything either. Though one of these days I'd love to come back and read through all this. When I can read the language a little better."

She smiled faintly and nodded. "Ready to go find Grovek's journal?"

"Sure."

Picking up their things, they headed back down to the first floor and out the door. Aelia went straight into the room across from the doorway. It looked like it could be a modern-day study—other than the stone walls, torches, and lack of true books. Oh, and the jars of things he wouldn't even try to identify.

Instead of a desk, there was a round table in the center of the room, with tablets and sheets of papyrus on it. Shelves lined the outside of the room, full of those jars, more tablets, and random objects. Except it looked like someone had wrecked it. Nothing was broken, but it was a mess, with sheets on the floor, jars shoved haphazardly aside, and a modern-day notebook and pen on the edge of the table.

Aelia made a distressed sound and ran her hands through her hair.

"You okay?"

"He would have hated seeing his space like this," she answered absently, starting to straighten up. Aaron didn't actually know where anything went, but did his best to help. When she was content with the state of the room, she went to one of the shelves and pulled what looked like a crude book down. Upon closer inspection, he could see it was multiple sheets of papyrus that had been lashed together with what looked like sinew. It was a crude book.

"I have to say, that isn't what I expected when you said his journal," he admitted.

"That's because you were born well after the first book was invented," she told him as she sat down. "They would have appeared sooner if the Lemurians hadn't disappeared," she went on, taking a breath as she ran her fingers lightly over the sheet in front of her.

Aaron moved closer and glanced at the writing, grimacing when he saw it was also in Grovek's native tongue. Which was okay. He had a feeling she needed a few minutes alone. Resting a hand on her shoulder, he said, "I'm going to go see if they messed with anything else, or left anything behind."

She nodded and looked up at him. "All right. I'll call if I find anything."

He left the room, closing the door behind him. Pausing a moment, he scrubbed his hands over his face. It had been a hell of a day. He just had to hope it would end up being worth it.

The hallway went in both directions, curving around the central room. Probably circled all the way around. Randomly, he went left. There were pedestals and statues lining the hallway, and he glanced at them, but forced himself to focus on the task at hand. If he didn't, he'd get distracted and forget about why they were here.

He came across another door on his left. Opening it, he was surprised to see a bedroom. More medieval than he was used to, but a bedroom. There was a bed, wardrobe, and bathing facilities, including a stone tub. And the bed looked slept in, with a bag sitting on the foot of it. A quick look told him it probably belonged to one of James's companions. Knife guy, since there were another four of the weapons.

Collecting the bag, he went out and continued around the hallway until he came to another door. This one was the same as the first, just with a different bag. Thing one was definitely his brother's. He could smell James on the canvas. There was a gun inside, a tablet, and some other supplies. The tablet could certainly come in handy. If they could get into it.

When he left and went to continue around the hallway, he did a double take, stopping and staring at one of the statues. He didn't recognize the ones in the entrance, or any of the other ones on this hallway, but he recognized this one.

It was Aelia.

The statue was done in marble like the others, though it was cream colored, like Aelia's hair. She wore a dress that screamed ancient world to him, though it didn't match any particular culture. Or maybe it had been Lemurian. Her hair was curled and pinned up, exposing her face. And the detail on it was exquisite. The others were, too, he supposed, but this was a face he knew intimately, so he could truly appreciate the craftsmanship that had gone into making it. It didn't even matter whether it was magical or mundane, it was still amazing.

Stepping closer, he trailed his hands over the stone cheek and wondered. There were other statues here, sure, but he had no idea who they were of, or why these people had been immortalized in stone. Under other circumstances, he might dwell on that, but not right now. He wanted to get back to Aelia before anything else happened to her, so continued down the hallway.

The third room was the same as the first two, including having a bag. On his way back to Aelia, he came across one other statue he recognized—Akila—but he only noticed it in passing. They might be searching the past for an answer, but it was the present that worried him.

CHAPTER 7

Aelia wasn't sure if she was happy Aaron had left her alone or not. She did need a moment, but she was surrounded by her past without a buffer. Gods, she could really use a buffer. But since she refused to call him back, she focused on the journal in front of her, trying to move past the ghosts in her mind.

She had read a chunk of the materials in Sozu, though far from all of them. There were simply too many for her to have read them all in a year. The journal in front of her was one she'd never even touched before. Grovek fully believed in sharing information, but this journal had been the one thing he'd refused to allow his apprentices to touch. It felt like a betrayal to be looking at it now, but she thought he'd understand. Though she didn't hold out any hope that she'd ever get the chance to ask him. It was a miracle Vazi was back, and how often did the same miracle happen twice?

She and the other apprentices had always wanted to know what he kept in this book. They'd speculated many times, often delving into the absurd, but Grovek had never confirmed or denied anything. So it took a great deal of willpower to skip past the information that wasn't relevant to her current situation and skim for any mention of herself or immortality.

She didn't find anything until the last sheet. Some of it wasn't news to her. She knew exactly how she'd gained her unfortunate immortality. What she hadn't known was that there had been another before her.

When Aaron returned, she was leaning back in her chair, staring at the page, a frown on her face.

"Did you not find anything?" he asked, setting three bags down by the door.

"No, I found something," she answered, not looking away from the journal.

There was only one chair in the room, so he leaned against the wall, tucking his hands in his pockets as he watched her. His eyes were more intense than anyone else she'd met—at least as far as she could remember. Sometimes—like now—they made it difficult to meet his gaze. Most of the time, she could admit, she actually liked the intensity. "Anything useful?"

She considered how much to tell him. It wasn't all necessary, not really. He didn't need to know how she'd become immortal. In all her years, with all the lovers and spouses she'd had, it was the one thing she'd never told another soul. She hadn't even spoken to Grovek about it, and wasn't sure she would have even if he hadn't disappeared. But if she was honest with herself, it was a burden to never speak of it. To never share it with anyone else for more than six thousand years. And why? Why had she always insisted on carrying that weight by herself? Punishment for having brought it on herself? Maybe.

Drawing her gaze from the journal, she let it settle on Aaron. There was faint curiosity on his face, but she wouldn't expect anything less from someone in Sozu, especially not someone like him. He also looked concerned. For her, she knew. It both pleased and pained her to know he cared for her. To others, he came off as a playboy, a very love 'em and leave 'em sort of man. She'd even thought that herself at first, especially after they'd had their one night together, but now she thought that first impression was very wrong.

Maybe it wouldn't be such a bad idea to share the load with someone else...if it was him. Or it might just make things infinitely more complicated. But if she was ever going to take the chance, she supposed now was the time.

"Most of what I'm about to tell you needs to stay just between the two of us. The personal parts," she clarified. "It's not anything I've ever told another soul, and I'm not really sure if it's a good idea to tell you now, but I do *not* want anyone else knowing. Not even Vazi or Seth."

Both curiosity and concern only strengthened on his face, but he nodded as he shifted, almost coming to attention. "If it's something that affects only you, I won't breathe a word to anyone," he assured her. "If it affects Lemuria—or your safety—then I make no promises. I will yell it in the square if it saves people."

Aelia couldn't find fault with that, so nodded, tracing a finger over the words in the journal. "I'm going to tell you this in order, so some of it is from the journal, some of it is what I experienced," she explained, drawing her hand back, clasping them together in her lap.

"That's fine," he said, staying where he was, which she was grateful for. She wasn't sure what she'd do if he touched her right now.

"Years before I was born, a man named Navid was the first to become immortal. Grovek found out—he doesn't say how—and took care to make sure no one else could do it again. He didn't believe anyone needed to be both blessed and cursed that way, and I can understand that. So he brought the source here, to Sozu." She smiled weakly. "Then I became his apprentice. I was young, eager to learn anything and everything. I was obsessed with Lemuria and the Arcane, so being here?" she said, spreading her hands to indicate the whole of Sozu. "Well, you know how that is."

He nodded, giving her a faint smile. "Yeah, I know. I'm focused on what we're doing, but I'd love to come back and just read for a few years."

"I know I gave you a hard time for that back on Lemuria, but I understand. I was the same way once." She drew in a deep breath, exhaled slowly. "When I was exploring, reading, learning, I came across a tablet. I've never seen anything like it before, then or now. It wasn't chiseled on stone, or like the clay tablets, where the words are formed before the clay is hardened. This was on some black stone I couldn't identify, and I've never seen anything else made of it since. It was smooth, but it didn't reflect light. It absorbed it somehow. And if I were to see it now, I'd say the letters looked like they were lasered into the stone; they were that perfect and precise. Not something easily achieved back then, as I'm sure you know."

"I do. What'd it say?" he asked, voice calm, but his eyes told her he wasn't as relaxed as he appeared.

"I don't remember," she admitted. "I've never been able to remember."

"What do you mean? How could you not remember back then?"

Aelia shook her head. "I was stupid and, without knowing what it was, I read one of the lines." He tensed, but she didn't wait. If she stopped now, she'd never tell him the entirety of it. "As soon as I did, a couple of things happened at the same time. Whatever I spoke was wiped from my mind, and I was hit by…" She sighed and pushed her chair back, needing to move. "It wasn't quite pain, though it certainly didn't feel good. It was like my blood turned to molten metal and spread through my body. Heat, but no burn, I guess would be the easiest way to explain it. Intense enough to hurt, but no actual pain, which I know doesn't make sense." She shrugged as she paced. "Whatever it was, it dropped me in an instant, and I passed out."

"What happened when you woke up?" he asked, and his voice proved he wasn't really calm. There was a hint of his tiger in the tone. Just a little growl, but for a shifter to let even that into their voice meant they were more than a little worked up.

"I was in my room here, and the tablet was gone." She glanced back to the journal. "Grovek found me. He knew what had happened and made sure I was safe. Then he put the tablet somewhere literally no one but him could access. Another dimension, kind of like this one, from what I can gather." Looking back at Aaron, she gave him a sad smile. "Two days later, Lemuria was destroyed, and I had no idea what had happened to me until I drowned and revived."

Aaron's head jerked in a nod, and could see him struggle with something. "Did he say who the other immortal was? Could my brother have found that information?"

"I don't know if he could have found it, but yes, Grovek named the first immortal. Navid."

Another nod. "Even if he didn't find the name, I think James is going to be looking for him. Both immortals, but since I never used your name, and he has no way of knowing you're the other, you should be safe."

"That isn't necessarily true," she said grimly. "Remember, the Ekklesia know I don't stay dead. It's what brought me to their attention in the first place. If your brother really is working for them, it's entirely possible they may give him my name and description. Though as far as they know, I haven't left Lemuria since we found it again. Then again, I don't know how they found out I was there in the first place."

"So we need to find this Navid first, while keeping you well out of the Ekklesia's hands."

"That would be ideal, yes," she agreed.

"Which brings us to the toughest question yet." He inclined his head toward the journal. "How do we track someone when we only have a name, and don't know where he's been for the last few thousand years?"

Aelia blew out a breath and sank back into the chair. "There are tracking spells, of course. Sorcery, even, so we wouldn't need to involve any witches. But generally, more is needed than a name, especially if you've never met the person in question. A personal item, a blood relative, something like that. If he's the only Navid alive and he's still going by the name, it might be possible, but I doubt our luck is that good."

"Could we use you?"

She frowned and blinked at him. "Excuse me?" She didn't like the idea of being used in any capacity.

"Didn't mean it like that," he said. "You two share the same brand of immortality, and it sounds like some kind of spell caused it. Couldn't we use that? You're not a blood relative, but isn't it kind of the same thing? Just instead of tracking common DNA or whatever, we're tracking a common spell?"

Not for the first time, Aelia wished she knew more about what had caused her to be immortal, though this time it wasn't in a hope of reversing it. Slowly, she nodded. "It's...possible. I'd certainly have to modify a spell to do that, but I know where the sorcery section is."

"Do you need any help?"

"If you were more familiar with sorcery, I'd say absolutely," she said, smiling to take any sting out of her words. He was definitely intelligent and capable, but she wouldn't ask a master electrician to do brain surgery. Asking an archaeologist to research sorcery wasn't really that dissimilar. "But it means you get a chance to explore Sozu, though I doubt you'll find any language but Lemurian on the texts here."

That helped with his soured mood, and he nodded. "When this is done and we're back home, remind me to put becoming fluent in Lemurian higher on my to do list?"

She laughed softly and nodded. "Absolutely. I'll even help. For now, you heard Akila. Call for her, and she can help you find wherever anything is. I'll be on the fourth floor if you need me."

Aaron nodded and watched her leave the room. Grabbing his tablet, he went up to the second floor, since the first floor seemed to be more living areas than library sections. Once there, he called for Akila. He knew Aelia assumed he'd dive right into trying to solve mysteries that had plagued him, but that wasn't what he wanted to research. Not now.

The image of Akila appeared before him. "How can I help you?"

This was a kind of magic he'd never seen before, and he was tempted to investigate it, but it was far from the top of his list. Besides, he wasn't a witch or sorcerer who could duplicate it. "Is there anything about Lemuria in here? The land, the people, things like that?"

"Of course. There's quite a lot. You will find most of it in the west room of the second floor."

He frowned. There weren't any windows to see the sun—if there was one—and he doubted a compass meant for Earth would function properly here. "Which way is west?"

She pointed at the stairs directly opposite the doorway. "That way," she offered before disappearing.

He went through the doorway and began walking the circular hallway, but stopped. The magic causing the image of Akila was odd, and he wondered if she was more like the woman had been, or a magical database. Maybe both, given she was speaking English. Or she'd died more recently than anyone had expected. Cocking his head, he called Akila's name again.

"How can I help you?" she asked again.

"You knew Aelia, right? You were both apprentices?"

She smiled, making him lean toward this actually being a part of Akila. "Of course."

This might be crossing a line, but he didn't care. As far as he knew, no one had known Aelia for more than a few hundred years, tops. This woman had known her when she was a mortal human. Before everything she considered bad had happened to her. "What was she like?"

"She was lovely, inside and out. Bright and cheerful, and intelligent, of course. Grovek never took an apprentice who wasn't exceptionally intelligent. I also found her to be empathetic, and she truly loved learning."

"Was it common for Grovek to take human apprentices? Or for them to be on Lemuria?"

Akila laughed. "While there were multiple humans brought to Lemuria by friends or lovers, Aelia is the only human who has ever entered Sozu. Grovek was very particular, and though he held no ill will toward humans, for the most part he believed their short lifespans made them poorly suited to apprenticing here."

Which meant Aelia must have really impressed him, since he couldn't have known she'd become immortal. Or maybe he had. The god of wisdom might have been able to learn some way to glimpse the future. At this point, he wasn't going to consider anything absolute.

He debated what to ask next, but he wasn't sure what she might know that would still apply. Aelia had changed a lot since she'd last been here. Instead of asking about her past, maybe he should be asking about her present. "Is there anything here about blocking people from entering dreams? Like if someone was attacking someone in their dreams?"

"All the information about dreams is in the south room of the third floor."

"Thanks," he said, heading back to the central room. He was partway up the stairs when Aelia appeared at the top with her phone in hand. "Hey. You found something?"

"I think so, but I need a few things," she said, continuing down the stairs.

"Like what?" he asked, reversing direction to walk down with her.

"A few things I have at my house, like claws and bone dust. The tricky item is going to be the unicorn horn. I'm not sure any still exist."

He caught her arm and came to a stop. "Hold on a second. Unicorn horn? As in, from unicorns? Horses with a horn on their forehead? Those unicorns?"

She arched a brow and nodded. "Yes, that's generally what's considered a unicorn."

"Holy shit," he said, shaking his head. "I didn't know they were real. I knew about dragons, but unicorns? I thought they were just stories."

"I think they are now," she told him sadly as she continued down. "I haven't seen or heard a hint of any still alive since...I don't know. The first century BC, maybe."

"Tell me about them?" he asked, wanting to know what was real and what was just exaggerated.

"They were beautiful. Not all white, like some of the myths say. They were black, white, brown, multicolored...just like horses. Their horns were colored like their coats, too. A black unicorn might have a black horn, a brown unicorn a brown horn, but they all had a shimmer to them." She paused, a little smile creeping over his lips. "I rode one once. A long time ago, but I still remember it clearly."

He forgot all about the Ekklesia and his brother at that statement, and just stared at her. "You did what?" he asked, not quite sure he'd heard right.

The smile grew. "I rode a unicorn. Took ages to get it to trust me, but it was well worth it."

"Well...shit. I think I'm a little jealous," he said, shaking his head as he started walking again. "So how much of the stories about them are real?"

"The virgin thing is a myth. They don't give a damn whether someone's had sex or not. They care more about personality." She glanced at him. "You know how people talk about not trusting someone if a dog doesn't trust them?"

"Sure."

"It's like that, but unicorns were much more perceptive than most dogs," she explained. "Unfortunately, their horns and tails were useful in a number of spells, especially healing ones." She sighed and shook her head, her shoulders drooping. "Which is why they're gone. Greedy, ignorant people killed them for their tails and horns. It's sad that it's happened again with rhinos. And they don't even have useful magic to attempt to justify those deaths!"

"And they're kind of unicorns themselves," he murmured, nodding.

"Mmhmm. But," she said, striding across the room toward the doorway, "since their horns were so useful, it's possible Grovek might have one in his workshop."

Aaron frowned. "Really? He didn't sound like the sort to have killed an animal just for its horn."

She shook his head. "He wasn't. But if one died of natural causes?" Her shoulders lifted in a shrug. "Let's just hope he does have one, or I'll have to go back to square one on this tracking spell, because I haven't even heard of a genuine horn since England was just a baby country."

Her reference to England put a curious thought into his head. "Can I ask you something?"

Her gaze flicked up to him. "You can ask me anything. Doesn't mean I'll answer."

That was fair, so he nodded and asked. "Where are you from? Before Lemuria, I mean. Where did you originally come from?"

Aelia's steps paused in the doorway of Grovek's study, her hand resting lightly on the doorframe. "I was born in Egypt, though my parents came from what's now Denmark."

"That's quite a journey for back then," he said, unsure if he should have brought it up, based on the haunted look in her eyes.

"It was," she agreed before going inside. "Do you know the Lemurian word for unicorn or horn?" she asked.

"No, can't say either of those words have come up yet," he said, relieved she was moving on, distracting herself from his ill-advised question.

She nodded and grabbed a notebook out of her bag, writing out the words for both unicorn and horn, with the English translations next to them. He still loved the way Lemurian writing looked. Swirls with random straight lines. He and the others who had moved to Lemuria had found that the language felt familiar to them if they had any Lemurian blood in them. Namely, shifters, witches, sirens, and elementals. Those four species had originated on Lemuria, so literally all of them were descended from people who had spoken that language. Which meant it was a type of genetic memory, though he did wish it had come with a download of the language instead of a familiarity with the look and sound of it.

They split up, looking for either a horn or a powder labeled as unicorn horn. The room wasn't that big, but it still took several minutes before he found something horn-like, except it looked like it had been cut. "Is this one?" he asked, lifting it off the shelf and turning so she could see it.

Brow furrowed, she walked to him and took the object from his hand, examining it for a moment. Still not looking certain, she rested it in one palm and used a finger of her other hand to draw a symbol over the surface while she muttered to herself. After a second, she smiled. "It is." She walked back to her bag and knelt. Pulling out a shirt, she wrapped the horn inside the cloth and tucked the bundle in his bag.

"What are you doing? Don't we need to bring the other things here since we can't take anything out of this place?"

Aelia smirked and shook her head, zipping the bag up. "You can't take anything out of Sozu. I can. Same way you have to find a hot spring and know the password to get in here, and I just need to say the right spell."

"You could have mentioned that sooner."

"Why? The tablets and sheets that are here belong here. I wouldn't smuggle anything out for you."

"I'd return them," he muttered. "Any chance you'll teach me the password?" he asked, scooping up his bag as he followed her back to the circular room.

"Probably. Sozu wasn't meant to be abandoned, and you're one of the people I know who won't abuse it. Besides, I know you and the Athenaeum aren't going to wreck the place like the Ekklesia wanted to."

Anger and guilt toward his brother welled up again, but he said nothing as they strode through the vertical ring and appeared back in Aelia's house.

CHAPTER 8

As soon as they were back in Aelia's house, she started walking toward what had once been a second bedroom. She'd clearly turned it into a workshop, though, as it was filled with books, notebooks, a computer, and all sorts of what he imagined were spell components. Animal, vegetable, and mineral, judging by the look of them, though he could only identify about a quarter of them. And there were relics from various time periods and locations, like the Lemurian statue he'd seen months before at her old house.

She set her bag on the floor by a heavy wooden table and removed the horn, setting it on the surface. A folded piece of paper was pulled out of her back pocket and set beside it. Her next stop was a cubby full of rolled-up papers. She selected one and unrolled it, spreading it out on the table. A world map, he saw as she weighed down the four corners.

"You need any help?"

Aelia shook her head as she began gathering items to place beside the horn. "Not really. Look around if you want, just don't break anything, and leave the computer alone."

Now he really wanted to get into her computer, but she was trusting him to be in this room, so he opted to satisfy his curiosity in other ways. The horn was cool, but she had all sorts of cool things in here. Including a pouch of what was labeled red diamonds. Opening the pouch, he was stunned to see there were eight of the damn things. Only two were cut, and of those, one was about a carat, while the other had to be at least ten.

He nearly dropped them. Very, very carefully, he put them back in the pouch and placed it back where he'd found it. No way was he going to risk losing one of those. He might not be a jeweler, but even he knew there were millions of dollars worth of stones in that bag. Immortality clearly had some perks.

Glancing back at Aelia, he saw she was shaving part of the horn into a bowl, so he continued to look around. There were dozens of types of crystals and rocks, dried plants from all over the globe, all kinds of minerals and other substances, and a couple of things he was clueless about, even with labels.

He didn't pay attention to what she was doing until he saw her pick up a large claw and aim it toward her arm, obviously intending to use it to cut herself. In a moment, he was at her side, his hand around her wrist, stopping her from pressing the tip against her skin.

"What are you doing?" he demanded.

She sighed but didn't fight his hold. "Part of the spell requires me to not just draw my blood—as that's an ingredient for the spell—but to do it with the claw of a predator. This is the claw of a lion, so it qualifies."

There were two things wrong with that. One, the tip of the claw was far from as sharp as it had been when it was attached to the animal, and two, he hated the thought of her being in pain. "There isn't any other way?"

"I've already altered the spell to the point where I can't guarantee anything. If I alter it anymore, I can promise it won't work. Which means we won't find either your brother or Navid."

They needed to find James. He wasn't as certain about Navid, but he knew it was important to her. Which meant they needed to do this. But they could be smarter about it.

Nodding to the claw, he said, "That's dull as fuck. It might break skin, but it'll do more damage than necessary. Tear rather than cut. More pain, more chance of infection, just...more risk."

"Then what would you suggest? Go find a live lion?" she asked dryly. "Or are you going to do it?"

He didn't like the idea of her being in pain, but he absolutely despised the thought of being the one to cause that pain. Still, it was their best option. Releasing her wrist, he said, "Fine. How deep do you need it and how much blood do you need?"

"Depth doesn't matter, but I need enough blood to wet the powder and ash in the bowl," she said, offering her arm to him.

Grimacing, he shifted one hand and flexed it, extending his claws. Unlike the one she had in her hand, his were razor sharp. Using the hand that was still human, he cradled her arm. Saying nothing, he quickly pulled one claw across her perfect skin, then let his hand shift back to normal. As soon as blood welled, she pulled her arm back and held it over the bowl so it would drip into the powdered mixture inside. Once she had enough, she began mixing it quickly, then poured the thick contents onto the center of the map.

Confused but curious, he moved closer and they watched the red and gray mixture. For a second, nothing happened, not that he was sure what he'd expected, but then the blood crept away from the solids.

It slithered across the paper, moving from the Atlantic where it had landed, and coalescing in the southwest portion of Norway. There was too much liquid to indicate a specific city, but it was a starting point.

"Don't suppose you're familiar with Norway, are you?"

"Not in this century," she said, shaking her head. "But don't worry, I speak the language," she assured him as she grabbed a cloth and held it over the cut. "We need to find out who can take us to Norway."

"First, we should get some sleep." She started to say something, and he had a feeling it was a protest, so he went on before she could get the first word out. "You haven't been sleeping, and we don't know what we're going to find there. Besides, my brother isn't going to have gotten this far yet. He doesn't have you to help him narrow anything down. Tomorrow, we can hitch a ride to Norway."

Her jaw clenched, but she nodded. "I don't know that I'll get much sleep, but it's not a bad idea."

"I'll go talk to Seth, make sure he can take us tomorrow, maybe add some stuff to my bag, then I'll be back."

She frowned. "Why are you coming back?"

"You've been having nightmares, Aelia. I'm not going to let you suffer alone."

Her head cocked, but he couldn't read her face. "What can you do about the nightmares?"

"Probably nothing," he admitted, "but if I hear you having one, I can wake you if it gets bad. And if it gets really, really bad? Grab one of the witches on the island. Hell, I'll talk to Seth and make him find a dreamwalker to ward your dreams or something."

It took a few seconds, then she nodded. "All right," she said quietly.

"You need any help taking care of the cut?" he asked, not particularly wanting to even look at it, even though it had been productive pain, and something she'd all but demanded.

"I've tended to plenty of cuts. I think I can handle it," she said, smiling faintly.

He hesitated only a moment before he nodded. "I'll be back soon," he promised before leaving the house, not bothering to collect his bag. There was no point if they were just leaving for Norway in the morning.

He went to Seth's house first, but instead of knocking, he shot the god a text, asking him to come outside. In only a minute, Seth appeared in front of him, his face impassive, but his eyes were concerned in the fading light of dusk.

"I expected you to be gone longer," he said, looking Aaron over for injuries.

"It feels like longer than one fucking day," Aaron admitted, dragging his hand through his hair. "Got a couple of favors to ask, and before you bitch about being left in the dark, I'm bringing the light this time."

"About damn time," Seth said, folding his arms over his chest. "What the hell is going on?"

"I won't get into all the details, because it'd just take too long, but basically, the Ekklesia has been blackmailing Aelia into working for them for centuries. Somehow they found out she was here or associated with Lemuria or something, and they've been bombarding her with nightmares to try to get her to give up information on us."

"Motherfuckers," Seth spat, instantly switching from concern to pissed. "That's why you've been watching her lately?"

Aaron faintly smiled, but instead of answering, he continued to fill Seth in. "We went to Sozu—the Hall of Records—to try to find some way of blocking them from her nightmares, but it didn't go smoothly."

"There wasn't anything there?"

"We actually never looked," he admitted. "There were already people there when we got there."

Seth paused. "The Nasaru? Sophia's people?"

Aaron shook his head. "No. The Ekklesia's people. And one of them was my brother."

"Your brother?" Seth repeated, frowning.

"Yeah. Apparently, he's been working for them for a while. No idea how they got into Sozu, but they were there looking for the secrets of immortality."

Seth's gaze shifted in the direction of Aelia's house. "They know about Aelia?"

"No, but my brother killed her, so if they meet again face to face, he will," Aaron admitted. "The problem is, Aelia wasn't the first. Immortal, I mean. There was another man made immortal before her. Again, long story, but James—my brother—knows, and we're pretty sure he's going to try to find him. Well, them, because he just wants to know how, he doesn't care about who."

"No way he's going to find Aelia while she's here."

"No, but he could find the other one. Guy named Navid. We found him—or at least narrowed it down—but we used Aelia's blood and immortality to do it, and that's something he obviously doesn't have access to."

Seth shook his head. "Let me see if I've got it all straight. The Ekklesia are tormenting Aelia, there's another immortal like her who just won't stay dead, your brother and the Ekklesia are looking for him, and you and Aelia found him? That's what you were holding back?"

"Hey, to be fair, I didn't know about all the immortal stuff until we got to Sozu," Aaron said, shaking his head and shrugging. "But we can't let anyone else get a hold of the secret of immortality. Aelia obviously hasn't abused it, but there are a ton of people who would."

"And the Ekklesia are definitely some of those people," Seth agreed. "Did Aelia tell you how it happened?" he asked after a moment.

"The basics, but it can't be replicated."

"Why not?" Seth asked with another frown.

He hesitated, but decided he could partially answer. "It required a physical component that Grovek hid."

After considering for a moment, Seth nodded. "Good. I'm glad I have friends who are as immortal as me—including my wife and daughter—but there are a shit ton of people I don't want to see live forever. But what do you need from me?"

"Two things. First, can you give us a lift to Norway in the morning?"

"I have my family because of you and Aelia. Taking you to Norway is hardly a repayment for that."

Aaron shook his head emphatically. "No, if you want to repay that favor, then find some way to stop the Ekklesia from getting in her dreams," he said firmly. "You know how tough she is, but yesterday she was screaming in her sleep and didn't wake up until I shook the shit out of her. *That* is my bigger priority. It's not like James can make himself or anyone else immortal."

Seth cocked his head. "Then why are you looking for him? Navid, you said his name was, yeah?"

"I did, and because it's important to Aelia." He hesitated, but couldn't bring himself to tell Seth just how much Aelia hated her immortality. Or how he was afraid he was going to lose her before he ever got her. Wouldn't she prefer being with someone she couldn't lose? That did seem to be her biggest fear, after all.

"Then we'll make it happen. But I'll take care of both issues. I've got an idea on the nightmares. Not concerned with them finding Lemuria, but I like Aelia, too. Maybe not the way you seem to, but she's a friend."

Aaron was known for being sarcastic, often to a fault, but he didn't make any jokes this time. "She's more than that to me, even if she doesn't know it yet."

Seth grinned and nodded. "Yeah, that's what I figured. I'll do what I can."

"Thanks. And...can you not let Aelia know I told you all this? I mean, if you find a way to help with the nightmares, she'll know about that, but not the rest?"

Seth nodded. "I can. Shoot me the location you need, and I'll drop by in the morning to pop you guys over."

"Will do. Thanks," he said, before leaving to pack. They might be in Norway for several days, and he wanted to make sure they were prepared for anything. And since they were flying Divine Skies, he could afford to take a suitcase.

She might always come back from death, but it was his goal to make sure she didn't suffer that pain anymore than necessary.

Seth watched Aaron go, both amused and pleased. He and Aaron hadn't gotten off to the best of starts, but he'd warmed up to the guy. They weren't best buds or anything, but they were friends. To see him so far gone over Aelia was nice. The fact that it might give him ammunition to rib the guy didn't hurt.

But Aelia? Everyone on the island loved her. He didn't like knowing that she'd been suffering like this for gods only knew how long without telling anyone. Teleporting himself to the Athenaeum, he paused for a moment, then began walking toward Olivia's office, where he sensed she was.

He passed a few people and they nodded in greeting. The other divine patrons didn't spend too much time in the Athenaeum, but the Nasaru—the people associated with it—had gotten used to him. Mostly.

While he might be a god, he was still a new one and lacked the arrogance of most, so when he reached her door, he knocked.

"Come in."

He pushed the door open to find Olivia sitting behind her desk, frowning at her computer monitor. She was a woman of average height and slim build, with shoulder-length red hair. Her skin was fair and she had light blue eyes ringed by a darker shade of the same color. And while she was currently covered from the neck down in black clothing—including her hands—he knew she was covered in tattoos.

She was the newest head curator of the Athenaeum. While Sophia was the boss of them all, the curators tended to the Athenaeum and its people. They were the librarians, the cooks, the armorers. While the venatores collected new books or relics, and the nasaru guarded them, the curators took care of them all. And Olivia was in charge of the entire branch.

But that wasn't why he was standing in her office. She might be a fabulous resource for research, and have a memory surpassed only by memory deities, but she was also a literal nightmare. Dreamwalkers were just witches with an affinity for dreams, but Olivia was part of a race whose powers revolved primarily around them. That made her perfect for his current request.

"Got a minute?"

She glanced up and smiled faintly, leaning back. "For you, sure. Though I won't argue if you want to stay and help for a bit after."

"Depends on what you're working on."

"Cataloging all the crap Sophia and Lucas found before we had to run a few months ago. And making plans for returning to the Hall of Records."

"Hard pass. But you are going to talk to Aelia about going back to the Hall, right? I mean, she calls it Sozu, but it seems like she's kind of the only living expert on the place."

"Definitely. We're eager and curious, but we're never going to turn down the help of an expert." She grinned. "That's how we got you as a patron, isn't it?"

"Basically," he agreed, sitting in the chair in front of her desk. "Can you protect a person's dreams even if they're nowhere near you?"

She shrugged and reached for a bottle of water, sipping at it. "Sure. I mean, it's easier if the person is nearby, but they're dreams. They don't exactly use the same rules as the waking world, so it's doable as long as it's someone I've met or have something belonging to them. I just need something to link me to their dreams."

"It's Aelia."

Her brow furrowed and she set the bottle down. "What's going on?"

"To keep it short and sweet, the Ekklesia are sending her nightmares to try to force her to reveal information on Lemuria." And just like that, his anger returned. Part of him wanted to go smite them all—or at least smack the shit out of them—but he knew that the organization was a necessary one. The Arcane might be powerful, but they were still vastly outnumbered by the humans. And there were a few who wouldn't hesitate to scorch the earth to rid themselves of magical 'invaders.'

She grimaced and shook her head. "I know a lot of people would go right to blaming one of my kind, but honestly, dreamwalkers give more nightmares than actual nightmares do. Besides, as rare as dreamwalkers are, nightmares are rarer."

"I know, and I was thinking basically the same thing. But does that mean you'll help her?"

"Abso-fucking-lutely. I hate it when our powers are abused. Besides, you're a friend and our patron, and I liked Aelia. From the little I spoke to her, anyway."

"And the fact that you're hoping to get a guided tour of the Hall doesn't play into it?" he asked dryly.

"Oh, it's a factor, but a small one," she admitted without shame. "I'll start working on it tonight."

That wouldn't help Aelia now, since night was falling in Lemuria while it was early morning in Greece. Still, he had faith she could hold out for one more night, especially with Aaron there. "Thanks. I owe you one."

She waved that off. "I think at this point, we all basically owe everyone involved for the rest of our lives after that whole Miasma bullshit. We're good."

"Thanks," he said again before heading back to Lemuria and his family. At least he'd taken care of one problem. The others were going to be more complicated.

CHAPTER 9

elia was still packing when Aaron returned. He didn't even knock before coming in, but she couldn't decide if that annoyed her or not. She had known he was coming, and he was helping her, but it was also a little presumptuous. She was also too damn tired to really care. Lack of sleep coupled with a regeneration had taken a lot out of her.

He walked into her bedroom and set a suitcase against the wall. "Seth's good to take us in the morning," he told her, watching as she placed the last few items inside her own bag.

"Good. Did he ask a lot of questions?"

Aaron shook his head. "Not really."

She nodded and zipped her bag, setting it in a chair to the side. "I'm not sure why you want to stay here. It's not like you'll be able to hear me from the living room."

He smirked and arched a brow, as though she'd just offered a challenge. "First off, I heard you from outside yesterday. It's why I came in and woke you up, remember?"

She did, so just sighed and nodded. "And second?"

Aaron didn't say a word, just held her eyes as he stripped off his shirt, took off his boots, then pushed his pants off. She didn't blush—it had been centuries since she'd blushed, and besides, she'd seen him nude on several occasions—but she did frown in confusion. What exactly did he think was going to happen? Okay, so she had to work to keep her eyes on his face, but that wasn't the point. She wasn't going to just jump into bed with him, and sex would hardly do anything to prevent the nightmares.

He shifted into his tiger form, which she had to admit was beautiful. He was the only black tiger she'd ever seen, either shifter or animal, and she'd always thought tigers to be lovely creatures. Even her earlier death didn't change that. His fur was black, but she could just make out the darker stripes in the light from the candles placed around her room. Some of the others had opted for solar power and electricity for their homes. She'd lived most of her life without it, and used electricity only when necessary. So the only electric lights in her house were in her workshop. She did go for a few modern conveniences, though, such as a fridge and electric stove. They were just so much more efficient.

Aaron stalked toward her, brushing lightly against her legs before he curled up on the floor beside her bed. Frowning, she put her hands on her hips. "Fine, but I don't want to see your bare ass first thing in the morning."

He huffed as if he didn't believe her, then laid his head on his paws, watching her.

She debated leaving the room to change for bed, but again, he'd already seen her nude, had touched her everywhere she could be touched, so it didn't actually bother her. And like shifters, nudity rarely bothered her anyway. She'd once been modest, but her long life had eroded that part of her. Changing into a soft tee-shirt and pair of shorts, she extinguished the candles, stepped over the tiger, and climbed into bed.

As she lay there in the dark, she realized she hadn't thought about becoming mortal since Aaron had woken her from her nightmare the day before. She wasn't sure if it was because she had a problem to focus on, or Aaron himself. But she really hoped it was the problem, because Aaron was just another person who was going to die and leave her one day.

One of the reasons why Aaron had wanted to sleep in Aelia's room—though the floor hadn't been his first choice—was that he was a light sleeper. A lover shifting in their sleep wouldn't wake him, but the sounds of a woman whimpering in her sleep absolutely did.

It took only a second for him to rouse, and another few seconds to shift back to his human form. Though his clothes were in a pile only feet away, he didn't take the time to grab even his pants before he was rising and moving to the bed.

"Aelia, wake up, honey," he said, gently shaking her shoulder. She just moaned in a way that was definitely caused by pain rather than pleasure. "Aelia," he repeated, voice louder, the shake harder. Still nothing, proving the nightmare had its claws dug firmly into her.

Sitting on the edge of the bed, he cupped her face. "Aelia," he said sharply.

She woke, gasping like she'd just surfaced after minutes under water. "Stop! No more!" she cried, kicking out at him and grabbing for his wrists.

Before she could get a good hold of him, he jerked her upright and wrapped his arms around her, pinning her arms to her sides. "Aelia, it's me. It's Aaron," he told her, voice pitched to carry over her protests. "It's Aaron. You're safe. You're on Lemuria and you're safe."

It took a few moments before his words penetrated, and she went still in his arms. "Aaron," she whispered, curling into him.

He shifted and pulled her completely into his lap, his arms remaining around her. There was no telling what they'd inflicted on her tonight, but it had clearly been rough, whatever it was. He wanted to find and beat the shit out of each and every person who'd done this to her, even if it meant kicking the ass of every member of the Ekklesia. But vengeance could come later, after she was settled and they'd gotten rid of the nightmares entirely.

Her life had clearly been hard enough without nightmares being used as blackmail and torture.

For several minutes he just held her and stroked her back while she trembled against him, gasping softly, almost like she'd just had a crying jag. Most people would have, but her eyes had been dry. Wide and wild, but dry.

"Do you want to talk about it? Or would you prefer to go back to sleep? What can I do to make it better?" he asked, keeping his voice soft and gentle.

"I don't want to talk about it. I don't want to remember any detail of it," she whispered, her face pressed against his shoulder.

"Okay," he agreed easily. "So what can I do?"

It took her a minute to answer, lifting her head so she could look up at him. "Would you...hold me until I fall asleep? Might help me not feel as alone," she said.

This was the first time she'd ever appeared even remotely vulnerable, and he decided he hated it. She was too strong to be made to feel vulnerable by some power-hungry dicks who wanted access to a land they had no claim to. "Whatever you need," he said, realizing he meant it very literally.

She shifted to climb off him so she could get back under the covers, which was when he remembered he was naked. Not that she seemed to notice, even when she pulled the covers back over her. He started to stand, to at least put on his boxers, but she made a small sound of distressed protest, and he backtracked. Instead, he pulled the bedspread back and laid on top of the sheet, so there was that bit of fabric between them. It might not bother her, having him nude against her, but in the condition she was in, it didn't feel right to make that decision without her input.

Once he was settled, he put his arms back around her and pulled her close. She settled easily against him, using his shoulder as a pillow. It was both dream and torture for him, as he'd wanted to sleep beside her again since their one night together. The fact that he could do nothing but hold her was frustrating, but he'd accept the frustration if it meant she could rest a little easier.

"Thank you," she murmured, her pretty purple eyes closing.

"You're welcome."

Despite the nightmare, it was only a few minutes before her breathing evened out and she slipped back into sleep. This time, she slept quietly, without any hint of a nightmare.

It took him longer, and this time he was the one plagued with nightmares, and his arms only tightened around her, wanting to comfort her even while unconscious.

When Aelia woke, she was in bed alone. Aaron's bag was still by her door, but there was no other sign of the man himself. Letting herself wake slowly, she thought about the night before. Not the dream—she'd been serious about not wanting to remember it—but how he'd taken care of her after bringing her out of it. It didn't really match the Aaron she knew, but she kind of liked it. A soft side of a man who appeared to be all charm and sharp edges.

The scent of coffee wafted into her bedroom, and she forced herself to get up. She started to go out as she was, but wasn't sure what time Seth was coming over. He might even be out there now, for all she knew.

Sighing, she changed into a pair of cargo pants, boots, and a tee-shirt, pulling her hair into a ponytail before she went looking for Aaron and coffee. She found him alone in the kitchen, preparing breakfast. Two cups were already full of coffee, and a bowl of cut fresh fruit sat beside them. One of the benefits of living here was the orchard full of fruit just outside the village. A few were found in other lands, but a couple grew only on Lemuria. She'd missed them. Lastly, a plate of sausage sat beside the stove, while he finished up the eggs.

"You didn't need to cook," she said, heading over and picking up the full cup, sipping from it. Black and just a little sweet. It was perfect, but how had he known?

"Sure I did," he said, glancing over his shoulder at her. "Wasn't going to ask you to cook for me, and after the night you had, I figured you could use more than a piece of toast or something. Besides, we don't know what we'll find in Norway, so figured we could both use a good meal."

He was being sweet. It was a little weird. She wasn't sure she liked that. Still, she ate and had to admit she felt better with a full belly.

"When is Seth supposed to be here?"

Aaron glanced at his watch and shrugged. "Anytime now. Eager to leave?"

"Eager to find this Navid before the Ekklesia does. If they've treated me like this, I can't imagine they'd treat him any differently. And we don't even know what he is. Human? Arcane? Does he know any sorcery to protect himself?"

Aaron nodded as he ate the last of his sausage. "Fair enough. And yeah, I can't see leaving anyone in their care. I just hope every single one of those pricks gets what's coming to them," he said darkly.

Honestly, she was with him there, especially since they'd pretended to care about her, to be her friend, then slowly transitioned their relationship until it was what it now was.

Someone knocked on the door and Aaron pushed his chair back. "That should be Seth," he said, going to answer it.

She frowned at his back, but took another drink of coffee before she went to grab their bags and joined them in the living room. "Hello, Seth," she told him with a smile.

"Hi, Aelia," he said, glancing at Aaron in a way that made her immediately suspicious.

"What?" she asked, looking between the two men.

"I know you didn't want this spread around, but I told Seth about your nightmares," Aaron said bluntly.

She went still and narrowed her eyes at him. "Why?"

"Because we never looked for a solution in Sozu, and I'm sick of you dealing with those. There's no fucking need for you to suffer like that," he said, his tone mildly pissed. Well, he could get in line if he wanted to be mad.

"He's right," Seth quickly interjected. "And I found a solution."

That distracted her from her irritation at Aaron. "What solution?"

"Do you remember Olivia?" he asked. "From the Athenaeum."

Aelia nodded. "Of course."

"She's a nightmare."

She hadn't known that, or she would have contacted Olivia after she'd realized what was going on. It wasn't an answer she'd considered, because she hadn't met any nightmares in far too long. Most had to be dead, and she had no way of contacting the others. Besides, there weren't many nightmares running around. "She agreed to help?"

"She did," he confirmed, nodding. "Tonight, you should be able to sleep soundly."

"Tell her I said thank you?"

"I will. Now, are you two ready for Norway? Bergen, right?"

Aelia frowned and glanced at Aaron. They hadn't discussed specifics.

"Bergen works. We don't have a specific location, just a general region, and Bergen's right there in the area," Aaron explained.

"And it's the largest town in that part of Norway," Aelia said, nodding as she understood. "That makes sense. And yes, we're ready," she said, offering Aaron's bag to him.

Seth nodded and teleported all three of them to the outskirts of Bergen, away from any eyes or cameras. Before leaving them, he asked, "Do you need any help? With anything?"

Aelia shook her head. "Not right now, but I'll let you know if there's something we need help with."

"You sure?" he pressed. "I know neither of you were born on Lemuria, but you're both Lemurians now. Since I'm one of the very, very few Lemurian gods, I take that seriously. I'll do what I can to help."

Aelia set her bag down and gave him a hug. "I know. And thank you for that."

Seth sighed and patted her back. "You're welcome. Just...seriously, let me know if you need help. Of any kind," he told them before disappearing.

"Since we may be here for a few days, I'm thinking we should check into a hotel first. We can use it as our base of operations while we're here," Aaron suggested.

Aelia nodded. "That's a good idea."

They started toward the town to check in, and Aelia had to wonder if this was going to be a gigantic waste of time, or if they were actually going to find another immortal like her. Either way, she had a sense that something was about to change.

CHAPTER 10

They checked into a hotel, and though neither of them would normally go for anything fancy when it came to hotel rooms, they opted for a suite so they'd have room to work. And honestly, she needed the separate bedroom. If he was going to keep being so sweet and considerate, she'd need the distance.

Once in the room, they got settled and got out their computers—a laptop for Aelia, a tablet for Aaron. "You know I'm not the investigator between us, even though you investigate the far past, so how would you recommend we begin?" she asked, cracking open a bottle of water as she sat cross-legged on the couch, computer in her lap.

"Divide and conquer," he decided, settling in a chair, his legs stretched out, feet propped on an ottoman. "I know you said we don't know what he is, but if this guy was on Lemuria back then, chances are he's Arcane. At least it sounded like humans were rare?"

Aelia nodded. "We were. When I was there, I think there were only half a dozen others. And that was in the midst of thousands of Lemurians."

"Then one of us starts looking for unusual events, another for unusual people. Most Arcane move every couple of decades, but I know some of the longer-lived can..." He trailed off and seemed to be struggling for the right word.

"Go crazy?" she asked blandly.

"Basically," he said with an apologetic shrug. "Honestly, I'm shocked you're as sane as you are."

"Sometimes I think I'm not," she said quietly.

"You're as sane as the rest of us," he said before continuing on. "My point was, an Arcane who's going a little nuts is going to mess up here and there. Maybe not enough to out the Arcane, but enough to make the papers now and again. Hell, I wouldn't be shocked if all the alien and Nessie sightings were Arcane whose minds were slipping a little."

She hadn't thought of it like that, but it made sense. "I'll look for unusual people," she decided, though she wasn't sure this was the right way to go about things. If Navid was like her, he'd done his best to keep a low profile. She couldn't be absolutely positive, but she was fairly certain she'd never made any papers. And she moved at least every ten years, so no one had even started to wonder about her lack of aging. A few comments about how she looked so young, but even normal humans received that kind of attention now and then. Weren't there a couple of actors that the internet was constantly saying never seemed to age? Then again, for all she knew, they were Arcane. It wasn't like there was a comprehensive list of every Arcane on the planet.

For the next few hours, they worked, speaking little and noting anything they found that was out of the ordinary. He seemed to have more luck than she did, as the 'unusual people' she was finding all seemed to be the mundane sort. People with unusual but non-magical talents; a woman who lived several years past the century mark, and of course, the drunks or insane who made wild claims that couldn't be substantiated.

"Not finding anything?" Aaron asked, his eyes glued to his tablet as he tapped and swiped at the screen.

She shook her head, lips turned down in a frown. "Nothing worth spending much time on, no."

His gaze flicked to the top of his tablet, then over to her. "Break for lunch? Well, dinner here, but lunch for us."

"Couldn't hurt. Come back to it fresh," she said, nodding. "Besides, sitting in one position for so long has made me stiff."

Aaron's lips twitched. "Me too," he said in a low, intimate tone.

"Pervert." But she didn't actually mind the extremely mild double entendre. "Room service, or do you want to go out?"

"Let's go out. We might be here for business, but that doesn't mean we can't enjoy the area. Besides, this is my first trip to Norway."

"Really?" she asked, closing her computer and setting it on the table.

"Really," he confirmed, setting aside his tablet and standing so he could stretch. No one could blame her if she happened to look when his shirt lifted enough to reveal a slice of toned abs.

"Unfortunately, I haven't been here in a while, so I don't know any good restaurants," she told him as she stood, hand on her lower back as she stretched as well.

"That's fine. We can ask at the front desk. I'm not picky, so wherever is fine with me."

She did the asking since he didn't speak Norwegian, and they found a very nice restaurant just a few blocks away. After helping him with the menu—again, it was in Norwegian—they ordered, and she decided to include a shot of aquavit. As she'd told Aaron, it had been years since she'd been here. Might as well enjoy some of the local spirits. She might push herself to be pragmatic, but she couldn't help the occasional bout of nostalgia.

"So what were you doing before Seth and Tempest asked you for help?" Aaron asked, surprising her.

"What?"

He smirked and shrugged. "Just curious. Obviously you've been to a hell of a lot of places and learned a lot of things, but what were you doing a year ago? Did you have a job? Did you invest in Microsoft when it was a baby company and are living off stocks? Were you babysitting all the neighborhood kids? What?"

"Oh." It had been a while since anyone had shown interest in her as a person, and she had forgotten how to react to it. The fact that it was Aaron made it both better and worse. "I did make some investments that allowed me to live comfortably, but I'm not the sort to...sit idle," she began, shrugging. "So I freelanced. Translations mostly, though some historical research."

His lips turned up. "How much research did you really have to do?"

"Not as much as they thought I did," she admitted. "Though before modern technology, news didn't spread like it does now. Something major in one part of the world might not be heard about in another for months, if not longer. So some research was still needed."

"And the translations? Just how many languages do you speak?"

She blew out a breath and slumped back in her chair. "I honestly don't know," she told him after a moment. "Quite a few, but I haven't sat down and counted in a long time. I'm not even sure how fluent I am in a few of them anymore. If you don't use a language, it's very easy to get rusty."

"It is," he agreed. "Tell me you know Italian, though."

Her head cocked. "I do. Why?"

He grinned in a way she could only describe as suggestive. "Because I don't speak French, and languages like Latin and Sumerian aren't really the best for whispering dirty things in a pretty woman's ear."

She blinked slowly at him, not having expected the blatant flirting. When they'd first met and had spent days on a boat together, he'd flirted heavily, but over the last few months, it had toned down to almost nothing. Even with his promise a few days before, she was caught off guard. Surprised or not, she didn't blush, but she did feel a gentle heat beginning to build. "I don't know...Sumerian spoken right can be extremely suggestive," she found herself saying, rather than shutting him down. That too was a surprise, but she didn't attempt to take it back.

Aaron leaned forward, resting his forearms on the table as he held her gaze and continued grinning. "Is that so? I might have to convince you to give me an example later," he said in a low purr. And when he purred out words, it was literal. Normal tigers might not be able to purr, but tiger shifters could. Unfortunately, that gentle vibration added to his words only made them that much more appealing.

"I might just let you convince me," she said before she could think better of it, but the moment the words were out of her mouth, she realized she actually meant it. She still wasn't prepared to allow her heart to get involved, but her body? It was primed and ready for some serious involvement with this man. Her life had been long, and she'd had hundreds of lovers, but he was certainly among the best. She wasn't even sure if it was really skill, or just the passion he'd shown when he'd been with her. Whatever it was, it had certainly branded itself on her body and her memory.

Their flirting was stalled when the server returned with their food, and though they spoke little while they ate, the eye contact was shockingly intense. It wasn't anything as crude as thinking he was just imagining her without her clothes, it was more than that. Intimate in a way simple eye contact rarely was. That should have made her feel uncomfortable, but it didn't. She felt wanted. Maybe more, but she was afraid if she let her mind go down that path, she wouldn't enjoy the moment so much.

When they'd finished eating and had paid, they headed back to the hotel in silence, but that also wasn't uncomfortable. There was no need to fill the silence with meaningless words like there was with almost everyone else. Yet, the moment they were back in their room and the door closed behind them, he moved. Not slowly, but fast and graceful, just like the predator he was. Before she could react, he had her back against the door, his arms caging her in. She was trapped, and her heartbeat quickened, but in that moment, she didn't want to be free.

Aaron didn't touch her, but kept his palms pressed against the door as he leaned down. Her lips parted slightly in anticipation, but he paused with his mouth a fraction of an inch from hers. She expected him to say something—that Italian he'd mentioned earlier, maybe—but it seemed he just expected her to wait and to want. She did both.

Only a few heartbeats passed before he was kissing her. No build up, no sign that he was about to move, just a hard, hot kiss that scorched her nerves and fried her brain. Aelia moaned and arched up toward him, wanting more. He complied, but still didn't touch her with anything but his mouth, though that was enough. Her eyes slid closed and she reached up, wanting to feel his body against hers. Yet as soon as she touched him, he stepped back, just out of her reach.

Blinking her eyes open, flustered from the abrupt change, she could only give him a confused look. Fortunately, he looked no less affected by the kiss than she felt. Retaking one of the steps he'd given up, the tips of his fingers trailed over her cheek before he slid a lock of hair that had escaped her ponytail behind her ear. Somehow he made the brush of his finger along the top of her ear sensual.

Bending again, he whispered in her ear—in Italian, just like he'd promised before. "I know you want more. So do I. But if—no, *when* we find this immortal, I'll give it to you. I'll strip you down and spend an entire night making you moan again. I'll savor every inch of your amazing body and let you use me in any way you want. Because do you know what I remember, Aelia?"

She shook her head, but it was the smallest of movements, not wanting to break the mood. "What do you remember?" she asked quietly.

"I remember exactly how you taste. I remember the way you felt around me. And best of all? I remember how you looked when you came for me." His lips delicately brushed against her ear, making her shiver. "I want to see it again, so let's find this immortal soon, okay?"

"Okay," she breathed, unable to even think of the reasons why she'd kept her distance from him for so many months.

He leaned back so she could see his face, and he smiled, giving her one last kiss, though this one was short and sweet, rather than long and hot. "Then let's get back to research," he said, switching back to English. "I don't want to waste a single fucking second. And I've got a damn good incentive to find him."

Though he turned and walked back to where he'd left his tablet, she leaned against the door for a minute longer. Not just to catch her breath, but to try to force her legs to move again. But since she also didn't want to wait any longer than necessary, she made her way back to the couch and picked up her laptop.

It was a while before her mind was fully clear and focused on her mission.

CHAPTER 11

Aaron fought not to smile when he caught Aelia sneaking multiple glances in his direction. It might have been mean, teasing her like he had then not even touching her, but he hadn't done it to be cruel. He'd done it to distract her, to interest her in something other than her missions. Hell, to get her out of her own head. Because while he might understand her need to find Navid, he still couldn't understand the desire that had made her call the Grim Reaper's wife. If he could make her feel alive, make her feel like life had something more to offer, then he would, even if all he could offer was his body. Whatever it took. She didn't need to know that he intended to get a great deal more than just an exchange of pleasure by the time he was done. He could be a very patient man when he wanted to be. It was the nature of predators, and she was the sweetest prey he'd ever chased after. And the one who meant more to him than any other.

The big problem was he didn't just want to be a walking sex toy. He'd promised they'd end up in bed when they found the immortal, and he meant it, but he didn't want to just be a living antidepressant. It might be selfish, but with her, he didn't want it to just be sex, no matter how enjoyable it might be.

Shaking his head slightly, he got back to the research. An hour before, she'd switched gears, joining him in trying to find events that might point toward magical events, since focusing on people hadn't gotten her anywhere. And they'd found several stories that had traits that could be Arcane, even if some were normally considered harmless. Strange lights off the coast could be witches, or even mers. Freak weather to the east of town could be either witches or elementals. Several people had reported fairy circles in the nearby forest, though both agreed that could simply be a natural occurrence. They'd still check it out, just in case. A church was rumored to be haunted to the northeast, then there was an area to the southeast where a local had been claiming, loudly, that animals avoided like the plague. He said he hadn't seen a single bird, deer, or insect in months.

"If Navid was on Lemuria back then—and we have to assume he was given that Grovek knew about his immortality—then odds are he was Lemurian himself," Aelia said, frowning at her screen.

"Agreed," Aaron said, resting the tablet in his lap and focusing on her, wondering where she was going. But he recognized the tone of someone talking something out to get from point A to point B, so said nothing else.

"And if he's Lemurian, then he's either a witch, siren, elemental, or shapeshifter," she continued, tapping one nail lightly on the cushion beside her. "Maybe a halfling, but he'd have the powers of one of those four. And if one of these events is his doing, then shifter is the least likely of the four, witch the most likely."

"Also agreed. I know anyone can learn sorcery, but most shifters don't bother, so the lights and weather are almost definitely not a shifter."

She hesitated before going on and finally looked away from the screen to focus on him. "You mentioned immortals going crazy before, and you weren't really wrong to say it."

"I wasn't meaning you," he began, but she shook her head and lifted a hand.

"But I was, for a while," she admitted.

His brow furrowed, and he had to force his body to stay in the chair. She wouldn't appreciate sympathy right now. "You were?"

She made a low sound and nodded. "In the beginning, even knowing I couldn't die, I made a family for myself. Husband, children, grandchildren, and so on. But life back then was difficult, especially for humans, and my family was all mortal, with human lifespans. When I lost the last member of my family, when I saw my last grandchild die of old age while I still looked twenty-two, it broke me a little." She didn't pause, didn't give him time to decide if he wanted to give her a hug, but hurried on. "It's entirely possible the same happened to Navid. Maybe not the same trigger, but too long a life wears on a person."

He nodded slowly. "And the point of him potentially going crazy?"

"Sane Arcane take care to be discreet about their magical abilities. We all know what happens if the Arcane mess up and the humans find out about you. If it's just a few people, you get no more than a slap on the wrist and the humans' memories wiped. More than that? Someone is likely going to die, so why risk it unless it's life or death? Or you're insane."

"And these events can potentially be explained away, but if someone looks too closely, digs a little too much, they might find out it's a witch or elemental and expose us."

"Right," she agreed with a nod. "If he has gone insane, there's no telling what he's doing or why he's doing it. Fun, boredom, a misguided mission... The list really could go on and on, and the reason why honestly doesn't matter. Not to the humans, and not to the Ekklesia."

Aaron nodded and picked the tablet up, looking at their compiled list. "I think we should check a few of these before it gets really dark. If they don't pan out, we've still got tomorrow."

"Agreed. I'm thinking that the area that animals avoid should be at the top of the list."

"Same. Then the weather." He glanced at the window and the position of the sun. "It'll probably be full dark by then, so we can check out the lights. And tomorrow we can check the stuff in the forest, because I don't want to be wandering an unfamiliar forest at night. I could probably get us out, especially with GPS, but I know I didn't pack for a long hike." But now that it was in his head, he wouldn't mind going camping with her. Just the two of them alone in the woods, sharing a tent? Sharing a sleeping bag? Didn't sound like a bad deal to him.

"No, it doesn't seem like a wise move," she said. "You have the locations on your tablet?"

"Yep," he said, getting to his feet. He grabbed his backpack, just because he wanted to be as prepared as possible for anything that might pop up, and slid the tablet into it. "You ready?"

Setting her laptop aside, she put her shoes back on then nodded. "I am," she told him.

They rented a car, relieved it had built-in GPS, and put in the first address. It only took half an hour to reach the first location, and less time to find out that it was a dead end. The source was most definitely

Arcane, but rather than anything nefarious—or caused by Navid—it turned out to simply be a witch with a passion for gardening, and a hatred for animals eating his flowers. He'd tried all manner of mundane things to try to keep them out of his flowers, but they hadn't worked, so he'd created a ward that repelled the pests. He really could have—and should have—been more discreet about it, but there was nothing that could really out the Arcane to humans. And he definitely wasn't an immortal.

The second location was also a bust, also Arcane, but it was even less nefarious than the gardening witch. An air elemental had come into her powers, and they were strong. Because of that, she occasionally had some difficulty controlling them. The teenage years were difficult for everyone, but when you had strong powers like she did, it made it worse. Fortunately, her parents—also elementals—were working with her. They were also more than a little embarrassed that someone had actually come looking into the issue. Aaron and Aelia assured the family that they weren't in any trouble, then drove to the coast.

By the time they got there, the sun had fully set, and the lack of a full moon meant there was very little light. After parking, they walked down to the beach. Aelia took her shoes off, carrying them in one hand as they wandered the shore, searching for signs of the lights. It was relaxing. They had beaches in Lemuria, but he didn't often take the time to walk across the sand. No reason to. No one to walk it with. Though he might try to change that when they were done with Navid and the Ekklesia. He might be a man who found it easier to seduce a woman's body than to romance her mind and heart, but the effort seemed worth it when he saw the stress start to fade off her face. The tightness around her eyes loosened, and her shoulders relaxed. He was tempted to take her hand, but thought it was too soon for that. She might be coming around, though. He had to hope she was, anyway.

It was a little more than an hour when they saw the lights mentioned in several blogs, but the moment Aelia spotted it, she smiled and shook her head. "No Arcane's to blame for that. A god with a sense of humor or eye for beauty, maybe, but not an Arcane."

"What? Why?" he asked, studying the lights as they shifted in the gentle waves.

"Bioluminescence," she explained. "That's completely natural."

"Pretty, though," he said, though he felt the same disappointment he heard in her voice. They were oh for three, and he didn't like it. It didn't feel like a total waste, though. She was keeping busy and finally letting go of some of her stress.

"I guess we should go back to the hotel and see if we can find some more potential events to look into tomorrow."

They could do that, maybe should do that, but he had an idea. "Mind if we stay out here for a little longer?"

Curiously, she looked back at him. "I guess? Why?"

He tilted his head back, studying the clear sky. There was just the small crescent moon and twinkling of dozens of stars. Not even a hint of clouds to dim their lights. "I've never really spent time this far north, which means I've never seen the Northern Lights," he explained. "Since we're here and out at night, it might be nice to wait and see them."

"Oh." Her gaze followed his upward and she shrugged, but she didn't sound put out. "We can do that, though there's no guarantee we'll see them at this time of year."

"Maybe not, but I get the feeling that if they do appear tonight, they'll be more spectacular out here than back in town."

"True. That is one thing I miss about ancient times. No light pollution. You could see so many more stars." She was quiet for a moment, then nodded and sank down to sit in the sand. "Might as well sit. We could be here for a while."

He really hated sand. It got everywhere and was impossible to fully brush off, but in this case, he'd deal with it. Not only did he genuinely want to see the Northern Lights, but this was another way of trying to show Aelia the beauty that was still in the world, no matter how much of it she'd already seen. It might be a futile attempt, but he wasn't sure how else to go about helping her. And he wasn't a man who gave up. Some might call it stubbornness—and they weren't wrong—but he preferred determination.

"Have you seen it before?" he asked, scanning the sky as he sat beside her and braced his hands behind him.

"I have," she confirmed. "I lived in Iceland for a few years."

He smiled and glanced from the sky to her. "Is there anywhere you haven't lived or visited?"

She nodded without hesitation. "I've never been to the North Pole. No reason to, really. At least none that I've found. And there are a handful of countries, too. And yes, I'm meaning the land itself, not the political nation, since countries, kingdoms, and whatnot have a habit of changing. Sometimes rapidly and repeatedly."

They did, so he just nodded, and kept watching her as she watched the sky. "Is there anywhere you've wanted to go but didn't have an excuse or chance to visit?"

This time she took a moment, then gave two slow nods. "Actually, yes," she said, though she sounded surprised at the answer. "A few remote locations that have only really been made accessible in the last century or so. And Antarctica."

It was his turn to be surprised, and he stared at her. "Why the hell do you want to go there? It's just ice and penguins and even more ice, isn't it?"

She smiled and shook her head. "Not exactly. Even if you only go back a few centuries, there have been expeditions. A few that were lost and never found. A couple of them are underwater. And millions of years ago, Antarctica wasn't as far south as it is now. It actually had trees—rainforests, I believe—and I'd love to see that. Then there are all sorts of interesting features not found anywhere else, like the Blood Falls and lakes that have been isolated because of ice."

"Now that you mention it, that sounds familiar. The forests, I mean. But aren't they buried under a fuckton of ice?"

"I didn't say it was likely to happen anytime soon," she pointed out. "But anything is possible with magic and advancing technology."

He nodded and they lapsed into silence for several minutes. This time, she broke it. "You seem to love your job, and I know you have family—other than your brother—somewhere in America, so why did you decide to move to Lemuria?"

Aaron managed to hide his smile. It might just be casual conversation to pass the time, but instead of talking about innocuous things, she'd chosen to ask about him. It was progress.

"I do have family in the States," he confirmed. "Tennessee, but I think I've mentioned that before. It's where I was born, and they moved back a few years ago. And I'm close to them, and to my various aunts, uncles, cousins, and all that. I love them. I definitely love my job, too, and it's actually that job that was the deciding factor."

"How so?"

"I'm an archaeologist. I know Seth likes to joke that I'm just a treasure hunter, and don't get me wrong, I like a shiny gold idol as much as the next guy in a fedora, but I like the mystery of it. Specifically, solving the mysteries, finding the answers. You never know when you're going to find the one inscription, the one artifact, that rewrites part of history."

Her head cocked. "Is that why you do it? The glory of being the one to rewrite history?"

He fought irritation at her assumption. "No," he said curtly. "Don't get me wrong, I won't mind if the world has heard of Aaron Fischer, even if he'll 'die' in another couple of decades and be replaced by another identity, but that's not the point. Fame or glory or whatever you want to call it is more a potential side-effect. A welcome one, I guess, but it's not the goal. The goal is to find out what actually happened, despite it having been forgotten about for centuries." He arched a brow. "I would think you'd understand wanting to learn something new."

"Sorry," she murmured. "Yes, I do understand that. It's a large part of why I went to Lemuria the first time, and the entire reason I became Grovek's apprentice. But what does your job have to do with your decision to move to Lemuria?"

"Because it's one big mystery. Yes, you, Vazi, and Tempest were all there back in the day and know a lot about it, but can you honestly say the three of you know every single inch of that island?"

"Vazi actually might," Aelia admitted. "The man is the god of the sky. He can turn into literal air and move beyond fast. Besides, while Tempest and I may be a few thousand years old, Vazi is much, much older. And before you ask, I don't know just how much older, and though Vazi likes us, I'm not about to ask." She smiled faintly. "Besides, they didn't use calendars in the beginning. Days were simply days. They might notice the passing of the seasons, but Lemuria doesn't have major seasons. No winter, barely any autumn, and spring and summer are kind of combined."

"Fair enough."

They lapsed into silence again, so the only sound was the soft sound of waves sliding onto shore. It was peaceful, and he honestly couldn't remember the last time he had had such a calm evening. He actually started to doze off before Aelia's hand pressed against his forearm. "Aaron? Look," she said, her voice hushed, like she might do if she didn't want to startle a bird that had landed close.

Out of habit, he looked out over the water, but color drew his attention upward and instantly captivated him. He'd seen pictures of the aurora, of course—he wasn't sure there was anyone who hadn't—but pictures didn't do it justice, not by a long shot. Green dominated the shifting light in the sky, but there was a hint of pinkish-purple in it, too. It was one of the most beautiful things he'd ever seen, and he wasn't a man prone to stopping to appreciate beauty.

Transfixed, he did nothing but stare up at it for a while, though he had no idea how much time had passed. He didn't really care either. Despite his distraction, he didn't miss the fact that Aelia didn't remove her hand from his arm, and he wasn't about to do anything to remind her of its location.

"I don't know how many times I've seen this, but it never fails to impress," she said quietly, and he glanced over to see her staring with a look of wonder on her face. That lightened some of the worry he'd been carrying the last few days, though it didn't eliminate it, not by a long shot.

"I think I could see it a thousand times and still have to stop and stare for a while," he admitted. "You ready to head back to the hotel?"

For a second, he thought she'd say no, but then she got up, brushing sand off her pants. "We probably should. If we're going to be wandering through the forest tomorrow, we'll need to be well rested. And if Seth is right about Olivia's abilities, I should actually be able to sleep tonight."

She sounded relieved at that, and he understood. Still, he knew he was going to be spending a lot of the night listening for more sounds of distress. If Olivia could prevent that until they found a more long-term solution, he'd be forever grateful.

He did hate how many favors he was starting to rack up, but then he looked at Aelia and decided they were all worth it.

CHAPTER 12

By the time they got back to the hotel, it was nearly two in the morning. Not that it felt like it for either of them, given they were still on Lemuria time. And despite Seth's assurances, she wasn't looking forward to sleep. Olivia might be a skilled nightmare, but was she more powerful than whatever nightmare or dreamwalker the Ekklesia was using? She hoped so because she was very, very tired. Beyond that, she was frustrated, and though her current mission gave her momentary distractions from her depression, she still felt...crappy.

She watched Aaron move about the hotel room, admiring the play of muscles as he picked up his bag, as he stretched. When he bent over, she couldn't help but let her gaze drop to his butt. It wasn't the jeans making it look so good, either. The man might be a scientist, but he had an exceptional ass. She stared shamelessly as she thought about how he'd flirted when they were eating, and the kiss that had come after. The very hot, very memorable kiss.

Maybe if she exhausted herself with some intense sex, she'd be too worn out to dream. And it would definitely not be a hardship to enjoy his touch again. He'd planted the idea in her head earlier, and it was growing more and more tempting with each passing moment.

She walked toward him and he glanced up, though she didn't think she'd made a sound. His head cocked and he straightened, waiting until she reached him. When she grabbed his shirt in both hands and pulled him closer, he smiled. When she reached a hand up, cupping the back of his head and pulling him down for a kiss, he gave in without hesitation. He growled as he took control of the kiss, and the spark of heat that had begun with her thoughts was fanned into a bonfire.

Without breaking the kiss—because she thought she'd rather die again than end it now—she let her hands drop to his pants, undoing the button of his jeans. He shocked her by grabbing her wrists, stopping her before she could do more.

"Aaron?" she asked, suddenly feeling confused and embarrassed rather than aroused.

Releasing one of her wrists, he lifted his hand to her cheek, thumb brushing over her skin, her lips. "Don't give me that look," he said in a low voice, just a hint of his tiger's growl in the words. "Believe me, I absolutely fucking want you. I'd cheerfully kill to have you naked and beneath me again. Because as beautiful as that aurora was earlier, it doesn't hold a candle to you. And nothing has ever felt so good as it did when you came for me. And I've never heard a sound as sweet as when you moaned my name."

The bonfire was back, and stronger than ever. This man could make her feel things with words that others hadn't been able to achieve with hours of sex. "Then why did you stop me?" she asked, aware her voice had gone husky, but she didn't care.

Another brush of his thumb over her lips, and it shouldn't feel as good as it did. "Because while I know I have a rep for being a manwhore, and it's not entirely untrue, I've never, and will never, be with a woman if she doesn't actually want to be with *me*. And our last time together? Yeah, it was fantastic, and I get that it was a one night thing, but that was nearly a year ago."

"What's that have to do with anything?" she asked, finding it hard to focus with him touching her and talking to her like he was.

"Because a night rolling around in the sheets with a woman I barely knew was fine back then, but now?" He shook his head and slid his hand back to her ponytail, gripping it just tightly enough to tug on her scalp. The pressure drew a small sound from her throat and parted her lips. He leaned in, rubbing his cheek against hers. It wasn't often that he displayed feline characteristics in human form, but this particular one she liked, especially when it ended with him nuzzling at her ear. "Now I want more. I don't just want your body, I want you."

His last sentence was terrifying, but she was so turned on that the impact was less than it might have been otherwise. She couldn't give him herself. She couldn't give that to anyone. Not again. But that didn't mean she was willing to give up the promise of pleasure.

"I do want you," she promised him, slipping her hand beneath his shirt, fingers skimming over the hard muscles and warm skin beneath. "I can promise I really do want you. I want everything you teased me with earlier. I want everything your kiss hinted at."

Aaron smiled and kissed her throat before leaning back enough to look at her. "I believe you, but I also believe you're not ready to give me what I want. What I need. Desire isn't the only motivation you had for making a move, is it?"

She couldn't deny that, nor could she lie to him, which meant she wasn't sure what to say.

"I can't stand to see your face like that," he murmured, running a finger from her forehead down to her nose, as if he could smooth the wrinkle he saw there. "I also don't seem to be able to leave you horny and unsatisfied."

Hope flickered in her chest. "Oh?"

"Mmhmm. I'm still not going to fuck you, but I'll take care of you."

The frown was back, and she was a little suspicious of his intentions. "How?"

He chuckled softly and let his hand drop. "You'll just have to trust me. Do you want me to take care of you?"

Aelia felt a number of things toward Aaron, and a lot of it was conflicting, but there was one thing she knew with absolute certainty. She did trust him, without hesitation or reservation. He was one of the few people still alive she could say that about. Besides, if it meant an orgasm to relieve the need still filling her, she was willing to take a chance. "I do."

"Good." He scooped her up, and though she knew she wasn't a big woman, he still made it seem effortless, even when he carried her into her room. Setting her down beside her bed, he started working on her pants. "Kick your shoes off," he told her, and she complied without hesitation. As soon as they were gone, he yanked her pants and panties down to her knees, then lifted her and tossed her lightly onto the bed.

She automatically started to scoot up, but he grabbed her legs, halting her movement. When she stilled, he pulled her pants the rest of the way off, leaving her in just her shirt and bra. He sank to his knees beside the bed, and yanked her closer to the edge, until her ass was half off the bed. Pushing her knees apart, he shifted between them.

Understanding what he intended, she grabbed a pillow and tucked it beneath her head. She might not be prepared to give him all of herself, but that didn't mean she didn't want to revel in the sight of him. It might be easier, but she didn't want to block out the knowledge of who was giving her pleasure. This once, she could let her guard down, just a little. She would let her body feel, but keep her heart out of it.

At least, she tried to convince herself she'd be able to.

His eyes were hooded as he looked up the line of her body at her face. Hands skimmed over her thighs, and he leaned in, and though part of her wanted fast and done, he was obviously in the mood to play. His cheek brushed against her thigh, not just once, but repeatedly. It felt nice, but had the added benefit of letting his hot breath brush against her sex. That was probably the point, as it made her restless. But when she moved, to try to get contact where she most needed it, his hands gripped her thighs, holding her still. Even her sound of frustration didn't move him.

"Patience," he whispered, kissing her leg gently. "I said I'd take care of you. I meant it," he promised, his eyes too intense and caring for the moment. Part of her wanted to look away, but she couldn't break his gaze.

She didn't protest, which he seemed to take as agreement, but he also decided to put her out of her misery. He gently pushed her legs a little wider, then ran his tongue along her slit before teasing her clit. She gasped and arched toward him, silently begging for more. A lazy grin curved his lips before his mouth was on her.

Never in her life had she ever associated the word 'thorough' with anything even remotely sexy. Aaron was changing her mind. And fast.

He didn't try to rush her toward the finish line, but ensured he didn't miss a single nerve. At first he used only his mouth, and honestly, she could have reached her orgasm easily with nothing else. His tongue slid over her, his lips closed over her, and he even scraped his teeth delicately over sensitive flesh. Then he slowly slid a finger into her, causing her breath to catch. When he found her g-spot and rubbed, she couldn't prevent the moan, nor the way she ground against his hand.

Aelia felt her climax beginning to build, but moments before the pleasure would have hit, he backed off. Not leaving her, not even stopping, just shifting his focus. Unfortunately, while it felt good, it disrupted the climb that felt so vital at the moment.

Gritting her teeth in frustration, she pulled her shirt up above her breasts and quickly undid the clasp of her bra. Aaron might have said he wasn't going to be with her, had implied that this was going to be one-sided, but he wasn't unmoved by the sight, growling against her. A thought flitted through her mind that she should have done that sooner, because the light vibration was an added sensation layered above the rest.

She wondered if it would feel as good if he began purring.

Still holding his gaze, she began to tease her nipples, stroking, circling, pinching, though it was now as much for his benefit as her own. It might have teased him, but it didn't help her reach that peak. Twice more he brought her to the verge of coming, only to ease back. After the last time, she almost wanted to cry. "Aaron," was all she said, but something in the tone or on her face told him everything he needed to know. That was when he gave her the intensity she'd expected the moment her pants had come off and he'd parted her legs. He licked and sucked and rocked his finger into her like it was the single most important thing in his universe. Quicker than before, she felt the tension coiling in her belly, and she rocked her hips, determined that this time she was going to find the orgasm he'd denied her.

There was no easing back this time, just an almost feral growl as he rubbed at that spot within her until she detonated. Not normally an overly vocal woman in bed, she still gave a gasping cry as silken heat poured through her, leaving her weak, trembling, and more than satisfied. It might not have been what she'd asked for, but she couldn't deny his methods were extremely effective.

Aaron rose and leaned over her while she was still trying to recover, the tip of his finger trailing around her nipple. "Feel better?" he asked, his voice rough with obvious arousal. She didn't even need to look down and see the bulge in his pants to know at least part of him was regretting his decision not to fuck her.

"Much," she murmured. The release, coupled with her earlier exhaustion, began to pull her under. She clumsily tried to move up in the bed, but he took care of it as effortlessly as he'd lifted her before. She was asleep before he'd tucked the covers around her.

That had been a very, very bad idea, Aaron decided as he watched her beautiful eyes close and her breathing even into sleep. He didn't think of himself as an overly principled man—though he had a few lines he refused to cross—but not giving in now was killing him.

Assured she'd sleep for a while, hopefully without any nightmares, he grabbed a pair of sweats from his room and went into the bathroom. After stripping, he turned the water on and jumped in immediately. The initial blast of cold water made him hiss, but he was so fucking horny it didn't actually get rid of his hard on. There went that idea. Fortunately, the water warmed quickly, so he moved on to plan B.

One hand braced against the wall of the shower for support, he wrapped the other around his cock. Closing his eyes, he replayed everything from the last half hour. Stroking himself, he remembered how she'd tasted, how she'd reacted, the way her eyes had gone dazed when she came. In very little time he was groaning and coming on the floor of the shower. It wasn't as satisfying as being with her, but until she was ready to give him more, it would have to tide him over.

Cleaning himself quickly, he shut the water off and got out. After drying himself and pulling on the sweats, he went to check on Aelia. Still sleeping, and soundly, as far as he could tell. Kissing her forehead, he left her room, though he kept her door open. If she did end up having a nightmare, he wanted to hear it.

Getting into his own bed, he sighed and closed his eyes. He really hoped they found Navid tomorrow, so he could start working on convincing Aelia that she didn't have to be alone.

CHAPTER 13

As Aaron drifted awake, the haze of dreams was replaced by a distant confusion. He'd gone to bed by himself, hadn't he? So why was there a warm weight draped across his chest? Opening his eyes, he frowned as his mind struggled to catch up with what his eyes were seeing. Aelia was curled up against his side, using his chest as a pillow. At some point the covers had been kicked off, showing that she was wearing the shirt she'd fallen asleep in. Just the shirt, and it had ridden up to her waist, so he could see the curve of her ass and length of her toned legs.

His body woke up instantly, while it took his brain another minute. When it did, he was ridiculously pleased that at some point during the night, she'd come to his bed. He was a little surprised that he hadn't woken, but under the circumstances, he wasn't going to bitch. This was a hell of a step forward, and he didn't want to spoil it and make her retreat.

He also wasn't going to touch her, especially since she was still asleep. And since she was sleeping—and deeply, it seemed—he decided to leave her be. Carefully easing out from under her, he slipped out of the bedroom into the bathroom. The cold water on his face helped a little, but so did being out from under a half-naked woman.

When he was a little more coherent, he headed to the hotel phone in the other room. Given the hour, it wasn't likely she'd sleep much longer, so he ordered breakfast from room service. While he waited for the food and for her to wake, he picked up his tablet, hoping he could find more for them to check out.

He was just pulling the covers off the plates when she shuffled into the room, still wearing just the shirt and rubbing the heel of one hand against her eyes as she yawned. She paused when she saw him, blinking and trying to wake up. Hoping to help, he poured a coffee, added sugar, and brought it to her.

She gulped it down then looked at the tray of food. "Breakfast?"

"Yep," he said, moving to select one of the plates for himself. "Going to guess you slept well? Even though you snuck into bed with me?"

"Woke at some point and didn't want to be alone," she said without embarrassment, walking over and sitting beside him, her legs curling beneath her. "But yes, I slept better than I have in weeks."

"You know that's all my doing, right? Not Olivia's," he teased before he started eating.

She gave him a sidelong look. "Is that right?"

"Mmhmm. Told you I'd take care of you, didn't I?"

Her head cocked and she considered him before taking her own plate. "You did, didn't you?" she murmured. "I have to say, you did a pretty good job of it."

He shot her a quick grin. "Gotta take pride in everything you do." He bumped his shoulder against hers. "Especially when it involves saving a pretty woman."

Aelia just shook her head and they focused on eating. When she was done, she stood, and he had to resist the urge to run a hand over her bare thigh, then up, beneath the shirt. It almost hurt to resist, but he kept his hands to himself.

"I'm going to take a shower before we go."

Aaron might have resisted the touch, but he couldn't resist the tease. He rose to his feet, kissing her long and hard. "Do that. And think of me while you're in there. Of what we did last night," he whispered.

"Aaron," she breathed. It took her a moment before she managed to say anything else. "That's mean."

He only grinned and shrugged. "So was the fact that I had to use my hand last night," he told her as he sat back down to finish his breakfast. Her eyes narrowed, but he also noted her breathing quicken, so his grin widened. "Enjoy your shower."

She went into the shower, not quite stomping, and he heard the water turn on. He finished breakfast then picked the tablet up again, though he hadn't found anything new to add to their list. When she came out of the shower wrapped in nothing but a towel, there was a new scent in the air, and his head lifted, eyes zeroing in on her. He might not have the same sense of smell that bears and wolves possessed, but it was good enough to know that she'd absolutely thought of him in the shower.

Rising, he stalked over to her, caught her face in both hands, and kissed the shit out of her. She moaned and weakly placed a hand on his chest.

"I said to think of me, not get us both stirred up again," he growled against her lips before turning and putting some distance between them.

"Hard to do one without the other," she murmured, sounding dazed.

His steps paused and he glanced over his shoulder, the smile returning to his lips. He might be horny—again—but he liked that she associated arousal with him. "Good. Get dressed. We should get going."

She glared at him again, no longer dreamy from the kiss, and went into her room to change. Pity, but they did need to be focused. For now.

They drove to the edge of the forest and, packs in place, wandered in. It didn't take more than half an hour before they found the first fairy ring. He didn't scent anything but mushrooms, and Aelia did some kind of spell before confirming she didn't sense anything magical. Still, they went hunting for a second ring, and when they found it, it was also just a natural phenomenon. Unusual perhaps, but harmless. Besides, fae were Arcane, and they didn't live in mounds or other worlds like the humans believed. They lived on Earth, just like the rest of them. But since there was nothing to find there, they only had the church left to check.

The building was also in the woods, but as it was in the northeastern section, it was quicker for them to drive around than walk straight through. As Aaron was navigating the unfamiliar roads, Aelia spoke, voice thoughtful and a little hopeless. "We didn't find anything else to check into, right? Was just the lights, weather, animals, fairy rings, and church?"

"Right," he confirmed. "I looked again this morning, but nothing else looked promising. But don't rule this place out yet."

Aelia made a low sound and was quiet for a moment before she spoke again. "I know you said it was thought to be haunted, but what makes the locals think that? Norway isn't exactly short on old haunted churches after all, so what makes this one special?"

"True," he began, nodding, "there are multiple churches throughout the country that are believed to have some sort of spirit in them, but most of them have the standard stories attached to them, same as any other haunted structure. Odd noises, things moving or falling, shit like that."

"Exactly. And it's not really limited to churches," she pressed.

"No, it's not, but most of the churches—or other supposedly haunted buildings—don't have records of people going into the area and never being seen again."

She straightened in her seat. "What?"

He nodded. "To be fair, the last reported disappearance was almost fifteen years ago, but there were enough missing people prior to that to scare the locals from getting anywhere close to it." He shrugged. "All I'm saying is don't write this church off yet. Until we get there, we have no idea what caused the disappearances."

"You said the last one was fifteen years ago. When did they start?"

"Not sure, but I saw a couple of mentions of the disappearances going back a few hundred years."

"Okay," she said, rubbing her hands over her thighs as she thought, staring out the window. "These disappearances could be caused by anything. Predators in the woods or maybe the building itself is unsafe. Or it could always be some poisonous substance, like black mold but faster acting. It could even be an actual haunting."

"It could, but if it's a person causing the disappearances instead of a thing, then it would either have to be an Arcane, or a bunch of human copycats," he pointed out. "And honestly, I'm not really seeing the copycat thing. One person being fucked up enough to kill people? Okay, it happens. One copycat? Also happens. But enough people picking up the murdering thing to keep it going for several centuries? Not really likely."

"Depends on what they're doing with the people who disappear," she argued. "Could be a ritual, human trafficking, some secret society...Hell, it could even be Arcane, but not Navid."

"It could be a lot of fucking things. Is there any point in speculating when we're almost there?" he asked, pulling the car off to the side of the road.

"No, I guess not," she said, looking at the forest. He followed her gaze. With the sun up, it looked pretty and harmless. But while she was skeptical that they'd find anything, he had an entirely different feeling.

The church was only a twenty minute walk from where they'd parked. Unsurprising, really. Most churches were reasonably accessible, and that wasn't a new thing. Once, it had probably been in a large clearing, but now the trees, bushes, and other plants encroached on the structure. Only a few had made their way into or onto the church, though.

Stopping just inside the treeline, Aelia studied the church itself. It was made of stone, but she'd expected that. Wood didn't hold up as well or as long, especially without people maintaining it, and based on what she knew of architecture, she was estimating it was built in the sixteenth century. Could be later, but the exact date didn't really matter.

"I'm thinking this isn't a haunting," Aaron said from beside her.

"Why?"

"It's in too good condition. I know stone tends to hold up, but it almost looks like it's been cared for over the years. Since the locals avoid it like the plague, we know it wasn't them."

"Maybe, but with the forest closing in, it could have provided some protection from the elements."

"And could have caused issues with the roots instead, but it doesn't look like roots have compromised the structure."

She had to agree that was a point, and only nodded. Prepared in case there was a murderous Arcane inside, they started forward, but when they got about a dozen feet from the church—right where most of the plants ended—they ran into an invisible wall.

"Motherfucker!" Aaron snapped, rubbing at his nose. "What the hell is going on?" he asked, stretching his other hand out and pressing it flat against what looked like air.

Aelia's nose ached a little too, but she placed both hands on the invisible barrier. It didn't hurt to touch, it was simply a solid wall in front of them. Her head cocked as she murmured quietly—sorcery was her way of studying it, though she was fairly certain she knew what it was. It only took her a minute to confirm it and step back with a sigh. "It's a ward."

His eyes narrowed as they skimmed the empty area in front of them. "Do you know what kind?"

She shook her head. "It obviously keeps people out, but I'm not sure if it also keeps things in. Some wards are mono-directional. But I don't think it's as old as the church itself, just based on how strong it feels. And the plants."

"The plants?"

"They stop right about here, but there are some inside it. That makes me think it's newer. Much newer."

Brows lifted. "How much newer? Like it could be why the disappearances stopped fifteen years ago?" he asked.

"It's definitely possible." And it gave her hope. If someone was trying to keep people out of there, it was likely there was actually something in there. It could still be a ghost—a lot of them went insane and turned violent from what she'd heard—but it could also be something else.

An immortal would certainly be able to survive for that long without supplies being brought in. Then again, there were some who could conjure their own supplies.

"You can take it down, right?" he asked, glancing at her. "You told Sophia how to take that one down at the Athenaeum."

"I did, but there are a few problems with using that spell. First, I don't happen to have any dragon scales—and I mean at all, not just on me. Second, that spell has to be done from inside the ward. Third, it's actually the only spell I know to take down a ward."

He made a low sound and nodded thoughtfully, then smiled. "When we first hooked up with Seth, Tempest, and Kara, didn't they say something about Kara being good with wards? Like it was her witch half's specialty?"

"I...think you're right," she said, pulling her phone out. After selecting Kara's name, she put the call on speaker.

Kara's greeting was absolutely on par with the woman's personality. "Aelia! The hell, girl? You just disappeared on us. Where have you been?"

"It's kind of a long story, but to sum up the reason for calling, Aaron and I are in Norway, and there's a ward we need to get to the other side of. Do you think you could help?"

"Norway? Hell yeah! They have the pretty lights there, right?"

"Not during the day," Aaron told her, though his lips were curved in amusement.

"That sucks. But yeah, I'll ask Seth if he can bring me to you." It sounded like she was walking when she added, "And we really need to figure out another way of getting off this island. Seth and Vazi have got to be sick of playing taxi."

"When we get back, I'll talk to them about making a teleport relic or something."

"Good idea. If I can't get in touch with Seth, I'll call you back. Otherwise, see you soon!" Kara said before hanging up.

"I don't know why she thinks she wouldn't be able to get a hold of Seth," Aaron said as Aelia slid her phone back in her pocket. "He really seems to take being a god seriously."

"No, he takes being *our* god seriously," Aelia corrected.

He scoffed. "I don't worship the guy. But yeah, we live on Lemuria, so he does his best to take care of us."

They didn't have to wait long before both Seth and Kara appeared behind them.

"Whoa. You didn't say we were meeting at an old creepy church," Kara said, her eyes widening as she stared at the building.

"You didn't ask," Aaron pointed out.

"Fair point," Kara agreed easily.

"What in the hell are you two doing?" Seth asked as he studied the church. "And do you need me?"

Aelia glanced at Aaron, who shrugged. "Probably not?" he said. "We're thinking it's just a single person in there, so we should be good."

Seth didn't look certain, but then sighed. "Fine. But if that changes, let me know. Just call."

"We will," Aelia promised him.

He just nodded and disappeared.

"All right," Kara said, moving to stand beside Aelia. "Let's see what we're working on," she told them with a smile, lifting her hands and pressing them against the ward. Her head cocked and she made a thoughtful sound in her throat. "Well, this thing is made to keep people out, but won't stop anything that's in there from coming out. And it's been here for a while. Ten, maybe fifteen years." She looked over at the two of them as her hands lowered. "Why would they want to keep people out instead of in?" she wondered.

Aaron shook his head. "No clue. We're not even sure what—if anything—is in there. Or who."

"Who or what are you hoping is in there?"

He looked to Aelia, clearly leaving it up to her whether she filled Kara in or not. The problem was she trusted Kara. She trusted everyone on Lemuria, in fact, including the new people. But trust wasn't the problem. The problem was getting too close to them. It was bad enough Aaron was worming his way into her defenses, but he wasn't alone. If she told Kara what was going on, the woman was going to stick around, which meant there was a risk of her doing the same damage to Aelia's defenses. Her gaze slid back to Aaron, and for the first time in a long, long time, she wondered if that was such a bad thing.

"Another immortal like me," Aelia answered.

"Wait, what? I thought you were the only one. It sounded like it was some sort of fluke or something that made you immortal," Kara said, shocked.

"In a way, it was, but no, I'm not the only one. There's one other," Aelia explained. "And the Ekklesia are looking for him, so we need to find him first. The problem is, he's older than I am, but a tracking spell led us to this part of Norway. This," she said, nodding to the church, "is our last lead."

"Holy shit. Okay, yeah. Let's get this ward down." Her hands were pressed against the ward once more, and she began to work. To an outsider, it looked as though she was just standing there, but Aelia knew how much effort it could take to bring down someone else's magic.

Several minutes later, Kara stumbled back a few steps. She was obviously drained, but gave them a weak smile. "It's gone."

Both Aelia and Aaron helped her move back and eased her to the ground so she could lean against a tree.

"Are you okay?" Aaron asked, sliding one strap of his backpack off and swinging it around so he could grab a bottle of water.

Even as he opened it and pressed it into her hands, she nodded. "I'm good, just need to rest for a few." She gulped down some of the water, then leaned her head against the bark of the tree. "Go. Find out if the immortal's in there."

Aelia wasn't sure she wanted to leave Kara out here, especially defenseless, and it must have shown on her face, because Kara laughed softly.

"I'm fine. And I've got enough to hold my own against any human who might wander by. Besides, my scream can shatter glass and be heard ten miles away," she joked. "You'll know if I get into more trouble than I can handle."

Still not entirely sure, but desperate to know what was inside the church—if anything—Aelia nodded. "If you're sure, but definitely let us know if anything happens. This is important, but so are you." It was a little shock to realize she meant it. Dammit, these people had all gotten under her skin, and she wasn't sure how it had happened. Likely, she should not have chosen to move to Lemuria, but the land had been such a powerful draw.

"Of course I am. Now go. I want all the dish, and I can't get it until you guys check out that creepy ass church."

With that order, they turned and went to check out the creepy ass church.

CHAPTER 14

Aelia and Aaron approached the structure, and when they passed the spot where the ward had stood, they paused. "If the ward was just to keep people out, then why would anyone still be here? They could just walk right out of the building and go to wherever the hell they wanted," he asked, getting his gun out and settling it at his hip. She might revive from anything, but he still wasn't going to take any chances. Besides, when he died, he was just going to stay dead. Not his preferred state of being.

Her head cocked and she thought about that for a moment. "I can think of a couple of reasons. First, it's not a who, it's a what that's dangerous. Something that can't just get up and walk out. Or it could be a ghost that's bound to this location and can't be exorcised for some reason."

"Can people be bound to a location like ghosts?" he wondered.

"I don't see why not, it just wouldn't be an automatic thing. Someone would have to do it intentionally. But it's possible. And it could be that nothing in here is actually dangerous. Maybe there's something valuable someone was trying to keep safe, and they went a little overboard, killing people who got too close. Could be they either got tired of killing or someone else put the ward up to prevent more from occurring."

He nodded and studied the building. It wasn't huge, but it looked like it could have several rooms inside, plus the chapel. And that wasn't including anything that was underground. Northern Europe wasn't really his specialty, but he knew that a lot of old churches in general had crypts and stuff beneath them. "Well, we're not going to find out standing out here. You ready?"

"More than," she confirmed, starting for the front door. The wood wasn't as heavy as it should have been, and the hinges creaked loudly. If there was a person inside, they now knew they weren't alone, if they hadn't already detected them.

Aelia went first, though he wished she'd have let him go through the door ahead of her, and she stopped only a few feet inside. The abrupt stop had him hurrying in after her, and it took only a moment to see one of their theories had been right—there was definitely someone here.

Once upon a time, there had clearly been pews, all facing the raised platform where the pulpit sat. Now? The pews were almost entirely destroyed, the pulpit was gone, and most of the windows were broken. And on the steps to where the pulpit had once sat, was a man. His hair was dark brown and hung well past his shoulders, though it was beyond messy. He was bearded, and clearly hadn't had access to basic grooming, because it was scruffy and unkempt. His clothes reminded Aaron of those worn back in the fifties, and though they were clean, they were definitely well-worn but not well-loved.

Leaning forward so his forearms rested on his thighs, he cocked his head and studied them. He said something in what Aaron thought was Norwegian.

Aelia shook her head and responded in kind. Aaron frowned, wishing he'd taken the time to learn Norwegian at some point, though before now there hadn't been any need.

The man sighed and straightened, but remained sitting. "I have learned English," he said, though there was an accent to his words.

"Are you Navid?" Aelia asked.

The man frowned and slowly got to his feet. "Where did you hear that name? I haven't heard it in…" He shook his head and tugged on his beard. "I'm not even sure how long ago. I don't know what year it is, for that matter."

"We found it in a journal," she answered, and Aaron approved of her vague answers. "Does that mean you're Navid?"

"I am," he said, nodding and taking a step toward them. "But how could you have found that name anywhere? I stopped using it when my homeland was gone."

"Lemuria? It's—"

Aelia broke off when Aaron grabbed her arm. He wasn't sure it was the wisest move to let this man know Lemuria wasn't completely destroyed. Those who had seen the place back in the day spoke of it like it was a utopia, but he knew every society had its bad seeds. Until they knew this man wasn't one of them, he didn't want him to know anything important. He only hoped Aelia got the hint.

"You know of Lemuria?" Navid asked, his eyes narrowing. "How?"

Aelia glanced up at Aaron, and after a few seconds, nodded slightly. "Before I answer that, I need you to answer one more question," she said as she looked back to the man.

"Honestly, it's been so long since I had someone to speak to, I'll answer anything you like," he said, entirely too eagerly for Aaron's taste. Then again, he'd never been alone for more than a few days. If he'd been kept from contact with another person for years, he might be acting the same way. Either way, he wasn't going to trust this man without good reason to.

"If you're Lemurian, how are you still alive? They were all killed centuries ago, long after Lemuria sank."

Navid sighed and tugged on his beard again. "A mistake. And actually, I did die. Many times, actually. I'm the last of my people," he said sadly.

Part of Aaron wanted to assure him that he wasn't the last, but he kept that tidbit to himself. He needed more information, so asked, "Why haven't you left here? It sounds like you crave the contact of others, and there's a town not really that far from here." That was what he wanted to know. Was he trapped somehow, or was it by choice? And if the latter, what choice would have forced him to become a hermit when he clearly didn't want to be one?

Navid grimaced and shook his head, taking another couple of steps toward them, slow and easy. "It's a pity, really, that even the Arcane tend to dislike what's different," he began to explain. "They can understand the general concept of immortality—the kind gods, vampires, and such possess—but someone who does not stay dead no matter what is done to them is an abomination." He shrugged slowly before his shoulders slumped. "There was a group of witches that felt that way, and since they couldn't kill me, they felt imprisoning me was their only option," he finished, now just out of reach. "I am bound to this place, and I've been unable to reverse what they did."

Aelia started to speak again, but something about Navid's story rang false for him, and he stopped her with a gentle touch. "What about the disappearances that have been reported?" he asked. "The people who came to this church and never came out. What happened to them?"

"Oh, them." He shook his head sadly. "They couldn't handle it," Navid answered simply.

"Couldn't handle what?" Aelia asked, sounding as suspicious as he did.

He smiled, and Aaron had never seen an expression so unhinged, so full of unholy glee. Even the men with his brother had looked more sane than Navid at that moment. "This." He lunged toward Aelia, and Aaron used his feline reflexes to get between them. It worked, but only just. Instead of grabbing Aelia, Navid's hands closed around one of Aaron's arms and his shoulder. The immortal snarled and, before Aaron could fling him away without hurting Aelia, Navid's palm slapped against the side of his neck.

The instant skin met skin, both he and Navid screamed as agony poured through their bodies. Aaron's knees buckled, and he collapsed, but Navid went with him, never breaking the contact. It was almost like his hand was welded to Aaron's neck. He didn't know what was happening, just that it was the most painful thing he'd ever felt. His muscles wouldn't cooperate, wouldn't allow him to pull away or fight back. He couldn't even hold on to a thought long enough to try to think of a way of getting away from the man. Every time he tried, his mind was consumed by agony.

Another hand grabbed him, gripping his shoulder tightly. It took a little more time before he felt himself ripped away from Navid.

Aelia stared down at the men, both sprawled on the floor, only partially conscious. Aaron seemed to be the worse off, but he was breathing regularly, and a quick check told her his pulse was rapid, but not dangerously so. Rising, she stared at Navid, her hands clenched into fists, her eyes narrowed. "What in the hell did you do to him?" she demanded.

Rather than being upset at being pulled away, he laughed. It was winded and weak, but joyous. "It worked. It finally worked!" he crowed, stretching his arms out like he was savoring the moment.

"What worked?" she snapped, all patience completely gone.

Grinning broadly, his blue eyes shifted to her. "He asked about the disappearances."

That sentence chilled her. Had Aaron just become his next victim? He seemed okay, but was it just temporary? Was he about to die, too? "What about them?"

"For years I've sought a way to make myself mortal again, but each time, the person aged in seconds and died. But I learned from each one and got closer each time. The last one survived for fifteen seconds, which was a record until him," he said, barely managing to lift his hand and point at Aaron.

She glanced down at Aaron, but he didn't look any older than he had when they'd entered the church. That had to be a good sign, right? "Is that why you were really bound here? Not because anyone gave a damn about your immortality, but because you became a mass murderer?" she asked, horrified.

"It wouldn't have been murder if their bodies had been able to process the immortality," he said, pushing himself to a sitting position. Aaron was still prone, and she didn't like it. Why did he seem more affected than Navid? "Mostly, though, I tried on humans. I suppose they're not capable of immortality."

"Or you're just an egotistical psychopath," she said, her anger building beyond anything she'd felt in recent centuries. "*I* am human, but I'm just as immortal as you are."

"As I was," he corrected, cocking his head. "You're human, truly?"

"I am. And I understand not wanting immortality, I truly do, because I was around to see Lemuria sink, just like you, but it did *not* give you the right to kill innocent people in the hopes of escaping it!" she yelled.

"Of course it does," he answered easily as he pushed to his feet. He wasn't quite steady, but he didn't stumble or fall. "They were mortal and going to die anyway. After meeting me, they got to enjoy a permanent death. The chance to see the afterlife, to reunite with those they've lost, and potentially to be reincarnated. While I?" he said, slapping a hand on his chest. "I have to suffer through death after death after death! They should be thanking me!" he screamed back at her, spit flying from his mouth.

"And Aaron?" she asked, pointing at the still man. "What gave you the right to inflict our curse on him? He didn't get a choice, and now he's doomed to suffer just like we have!"

Navid smirked and shrugged. "At least it's no longer me. In a few thousand years, maybe he can pass it on to someone else, just as I have. Though it felt like he was a shifter, so I doubt it."

Aelia normally opted to avoid violence whenever she could, but she wasn't a pacifist, and she hadn't lived so long without learning how to fight, both as a human and a sorceress. Rarely had she ever initiated a fight unless it was to protect an innocent, but as far as she was concerned, Navid had just crossed all the lines.

Hissing out a few syllables, she flung her hand toward him, sending him flying back. He landed hard on the floor and slid several feet before stopping.

"Do you really think you can win against me? I was a strong witch *before* Lemuria sank, and I've only gotten stronger since," he warned.

She felt a cold, cruel smile overtake her lips, and she took a step toward him. "That might be very true, but you're forgetting one thing, Navid."

"That's highly doubtful, but do enlighten me."

A hand lifted, and she whispered a word, causing a ball of shimmering purple power to start growing above her palm. "I cannot die, and thanks to your selfishness? You. Can." His eyes widened with realization as she flung the magic at him. He tried to dodge, but he was still slow after the immortality transfer, and it grazed his side, instantly scorching fabric and skin both. There was no cry of pain, but she hadn't expected it. If his life had been anything like hers, he'd endured more than his share of pain. But she was by no means finished with him. He'd murdered innocents, he'd used people, and he'd forced his curse on Aaron. It was unforgivable, and she was fully prepared to be judge, jury, and executioner.

Navid wasn't going to go down easily, and proved himself a strong witch when he used telekinesis to levitate dozens of wood shards from the broken pews. It gave her just enough time to erect a shield, though it didn't stop them all. She hissed as a piece as long as her hand embedded itself in her thigh, and another, twice the size, impaled her stomach. It was just pain, though. It wouldn't kill her, not for good, so she didn't bother yanking either out.

As a witch, Navid might have the natural power, but Aelia had studied long and hard to perfect the sorcery she knew, and began throwing magic at him almost as rapidly as a witch. But as he'd claimed, he wasn't without skills either. He blocked or deflected most of her blasts, sending them into the aging stone, and even managed to return fire—literally. But she had one advantage over him, and while it should have been glaringly obvious, it seemed like it hadn't clicked in his mind.

He knew she couldn't die, but this whole fiasco had occurred because a large part of him was more than ready to do just that.

Relentlessly, she blasted him over and over again, and when he faltered, she decided she was done with this. She needed to ensure Aaron was okay, and Navid deserved no more of her time. Speaking a spell she'd tried hard to avoid using since she learned it, she made a twisting motion with her hands. Navid's head jerked sharply to one side, the crack of his neck audible.

It wasn't her first kill, but at the moment, it was the first one she'd relished. And hopefully the last.

When the former immortal dropped, she hurried back to Aaron, who was blinking at the ceiling, looking confused. "Aaron? Are you okay? How do you feel?" she asked, checking his pulse again. It had slowed and was still strong, so he didn't seem to be in any danger.

"Weird," he admitted, voice hoarse from when he'd screamed earlier. "What did he do to me?"

Aelia wasn't looking forward to telling him, so urged him to sit up, helping so he didn't strain himself if something was wrong. He wouldn't heal any faster than he had before, not unless he died first. Except his new position allowed him to see the wounds she'd taken, and his focus shifted from himself to her in an instant.

"What the hell happened to you?"

Angry with the entire situation, she knew she was just trying to punish herself for letting it happen when she yanked the wood shard out of her stomach. She gasped out a breath, the fresh pain a shock to her senses, but still, it wouldn't kill her. Probably. And if it did, she'd probably only be gone for ten minutes. When she reached for the wood in her thigh, Aaron stopped her.

"Aelia, what's going on? Where's Navid? How did you get hurt?"

"Let me take this out and I'll tell you everything," she promised.

He frowned and studied her face for a moment before nodding. "More gently this time?" he suggested.

Gentle would only prolong the pain, so she shook her head and just yanked it out, too. It hurt like hell, but she just tossed the wood aside. "Would have hurt more if I'd gone slow," she told him, voice tight, but she almost felt the apology she put in her voice.

"Is that all?"

Not really, but there wasn't much point in mentioning the bruises and other internal injuries right now. Not when she was about to change his world forever.

A scream from outside had them both scrambling to their feet and rushing outside, Aelia supporting him as he was still unsteady on his feet. But no matter what else had changed, they weren't about to leave Kara to fend for herself.

CHAPTER 15

James had found them.

Aelia had no idea how, since they'd only found this location by using her blood, which he definitely didn't have. He did, however, share blood with Aaron, so that was a possibility. She wasn't sure why he would have tracked his brother, though. There was no way he could have known Aaron would find Navid first. But the fact remained that he was there with three other men and one woman, all of them fighting to get to Kara. From what Aelia could guess, Kara had put up a ward to protect herself, but she was going up against five people, alone and weakened. Weakened because she'd helped Aelia. Aaron had already suffered irreparably for her mission. She wasn't going to let Kara be another casualty.

They ran toward the group, Aaron lagging just a few paces behind, but it turned out to be fine. As soon as James saw them, he stopped and his jaw went slack. "You," he said accusingly at Aelia. "I killed you."

"I remember," she said dryly, moving to stand in front of Kara. Though she was careful not to let James out of her line of sight, she studied his associates. Like the two in Sozu, these people were obviously not archaeologists, but trained fighters. Only two of the men were muscular, but the third held himself in a way that screamed fighter. The woman appeared relaxed, but Aelia knew better. There was a humor and excitement in her eyes that suggested she might be the most dangerous of all five. A killer rather than a fighter.

James glared at her and took a step forward, hands fisted at his sides. "You're one of the immortals."

"Obviously," she said, putting as much condescension in the single word as possible. "And you're too late," she said, forcing a smug smirk to her lips. "I killed the other, and you will not get the secret of immortality from me."

"Oh, please do resist," she woman said eagerly. "I love making stubborn people talk."

Aelia didn't even spare her a glance.

"James, don't do this," Aaron said, stopping beside Aelia, so Kara was behind them. "You're better than this."

"Seriously? You're going to try to pull the heartfelt speech to get me to realize the error of my ways?" James asked, sounding more disgusted than anything else. "We came here for an immortal, and we're leaving with one," he said, pulling a gun. He fired, and though they ducked, Kara's ward stopped it before it could reach any of them. That was also when the last of her power gave out and the ward failed.

Sensing that nothing stood between them and their quarry, James's four companions acted, two of them rushing forward, while the other two used their powers. No witches this time, but he had an air elemental and shapeshifter, since one started using the wind to pick up projectiles, and the other transformed into a wolf. The woman seemed to prefer up close and personal, because she drew a pair of knives as she raced toward them, while the last man's hands were empty.

Aelia lost sight of Aaron as she engaged the woman, needing all her focus to block the blades while throwing the occasional attack toward the others. To her surprise, James hung back, but when she got a glimpse of him, she saw he was watching her intently, the gun raised and ready. Waiting for a clear shot? If he knew she wouldn't stay dead, then killing her would be the easiest way to take her. Dead women couldn't resist.

She couldn't allow that to happen, especially since she knew Kara and Aaron would fight to prevent them from taking her.

The woman she was fighting was extremely skilled, and Aelia didn't have time to try to figure out a way around her defenses. So she cheated. Without stopping, she cast another spell. It took only moments for the woman's eyes to widen and for her to gasp as she tried to suck in air. It wasn't a pleasant spell, but there were very few beings who could survive without air. Whatever this woman was, she needed air.

To her credit, she kept trying to fight for a little longer until her body's need to breathe overcame everything else. Dismissing her, Aelia kept part of her mind on maintaining the spell as she turned to the others.

Before she could make a move, a gunshot rang out, and she sucked in a breath as a bullet pierced just below her shoulder. It was painful, and her arm was out of commission, but she'd been shot enough to know it likely wasn't fatal. It also reminded her that she needed to be more careful. She might resurrect, but she couldn't help Kara and Aaron if she was a corpse.

Ducking behind a tree, she flung out a hand toward the elemental, hitting him with the same glowing magic she'd sent at Navid. Unlike the ex-immortal, he wasn't prepared for it, so it hit him square in the chest, killing him instantly.

"Aelia!" Kara screamed, and she whirled to see what had distressed the woman. To her horror, she saw the wolf had hold of Aaron's throat and was shaking his head viciously. It took only that glance for her to know Aaron was dead.

For the first time, she prayed to all the gods that Navid had actually achieved his goal. Because if Aaron wasn't an immortal now, she'd just lost him. It sent twin flames of anger and sorrow spiraling through her. These people were going to pay.

Casting a quick shield spell, she stepped out from behind the tree and faced off against the remaining two enemies, as only the wolf and James remained. Aaron and Kara must have dealt with the other man before he'd died.

Looking directly at James, she told him, "You're going to regret that." She didn't give him time to retort, just looked back to the wolf and cast as she lifted a hand and twisted. He yelped and stumbled back, collapsing in a whining heap. Knowing he was just seconds from death, she focused back on James. "Do you see what you did?" she yelled at him, pointing at Aaron's lifeless body, even as Kara knelt beside him, looking grief stricken. "Because you chose to work for a group of power-hungry egomaniacs, you've killed your own fucking brother," she snarled. "Was your desire to find immortality really that important?"

"I didn't mean for him to die," James said, sounding defensive, but she didn't care. "But I have a job to do, and he got in the way."

"Your job is for corrupt people who abuse their positions! Their job is to protect the Arcane, not use them. And instead of helping, to just do their job of hiding us from the humans, do you know what they've done? Beyond the killing, did you know they've black-mailed me for centuries? And tortured me for weeks? If it were up to me right now, I'd kill every single one of them, including you." She meant it. In that moment, she wanted him dead. He'd killed the first person to wiggle his way through her defenses in centuries. He deserved death. They all had.

"You're immortal. You don't know what it's like to fear death!"

"And you don't know what it's like to fear living! I don't get the reset, the reprieve everyone else is entitled to," she screamed at him. "I've been everywhere, seen everything, done everything. There's nothing left for me, because I've seen every single person I love die, and I don't even have a chance of seeing them on the other side when I die, because I don't stay dead!"

"I don't think I do either. This is fucking weird."

Aaron's voice was groggy, but hearing it stole most of her rage. Part of her had been terrified that Navid had been wrong. For all she had known, he'd revived in the church, and Aaron would have never come back.

James took a few unsteady steps back, his gun lowering. "How?" he asked, stunned.

"Long story, and you honestly don't deserve it," Aaron said, sitting up with Kara's help. Turning his head so he could see Aelia, he told her, "I know he's fucked up, a lot, but I can't let you kill him, no matter how much he might deserve it."

She couldn't argue with him, not now, no matter what she might feel, and only nodded. "So what do you want to do with him?"

James started to run, but Kara said, "Nuh uh," and made a gesture. Judging from the fact that he appeared to hit an invisible wall, Aelia guessed it was another ward. Smart. As long as Kara's strength held, he'd be stuck.

"Call in help," Aaron said, leaning forward, like he was exhausted, and honestly, he probably was. Reviving didn't hurt, but it did tend to take a lot out of a person. And though she couldn't quite recall that first one clearly, she thought it had been more intense than those that followed. Then again, it might have just been the shock that had made her think that.

"What do you mean?" Aelia asked, moving toward him, though she was keeping a close eye on James.

He didn't say anything immediately, but thirty seconds later, the goddess Hecate appeared in front of him. It wasn't the first time any of them had met her, though she and Aelia went back much further than the others. She was tall and slender, and definitely looked like the goddess of witchcraft, necromancy, and poisonous plants. Long, straight black hair, skin as fair as moonlight, and pale, pale blue eyes ringed by violet. And of course she wore a black dress, this time coupled with a lot of silver jewelry covered in magical symbols. Hecate did like her shiny things.

The goddess took a moment to look around, noting both the dead bodies and the living people. "I'm going to ask what happened here, but I don't imagine you prayed to me for no reason," she said when she focused on Aaron.

He shook his head tiredly. "I didn't, no, and thanks for coming." Tipping his chin up in James's direction, he asked, "Any chance you can wipe his memory?"

Hecate arched one thin, dark brow. "How completely?"

Winded, he looked at Aelia, and she understood what he was asking. It didn't seem a proper punishment for what James had done, but this was Aaron's brother, so his choice. This time. She still wanted him to suffer for having caused all this. "Just all memory of Sozu—also called the Hall of Records—immortals, and everything he's seen in the last three days?"

"I can, but only if you promise that one of you is going to explain what's going on later."

"Please don't," James begged Hecate. "These people killed my friends and tried to kill me. Don't let them win. Don't wipe my memory!"

She cocked her head and walked over to where he stood, still trapped. Close enough to touch, she stared at him as if she were peering into his soul. For all Aelia knew, she was. Hecate had always been a little cagey about the extent of her abilities. "I have known that woman for almost three thousand years. She has never killed without cause. Do you really think I'm going to take your word over hers? Or over your brother's?"

James started to protest further, but she reached into the ward and touched a finger to his forehead. He went still, his eyes glazed, jaw slack. A few seconds ticked past, then she stepped back and dropped her hand. James disappeared.

"Where did you send him?" Aaron asked.

"To his home," Hecate answered as she turned back to them. "Now, what in the name of Hades is going on?"

"I honestly have no freaking idea," Kara answered, offering Aaron one of the waters from his own pack. "I helped break a ward and waited out here, then those guys showed up and started attacking. And one of the freakin' *killed* Aaron, but he came back, and that's really kind of freaking me out."

Aaron said nothing, and Aelia knew he wouldn't. It wasn't his secret to share. Or hadn't been. Now it was a secret they shared.

Sighing, Aelia sank down to the forest floor, her back resting against a tree. Part of her wanted to go to Aaron, but her emotions were too close to the surface to allow her to be near him without doing something foolish. "I was having nightmares and went to Sozu to try to find a way to block them. When Aaron and I got there, his brother was already there—the man you just sent home. They were looking for immortality and mentioned finding a journal—Grovek's journal, not that they knew it was his—that said there were two of us."

She shrugged and leaned her head back. "We used my blood to track the other immortal here. He'd been trying for centuries to get rid of his immortality. Namely, by attempting to transfer it to someone else, except they all died when he tried it. Some years back, a group of witches bound him to the church," she said, absently gesturing with her thumb. Then her gaze met Aaron's and apology was in her eyes as she told him what he had to have already figured out. "He tried the transfer again today, and this time...it worked."

Gods weren't often surprised, but Hecate was absolutely shocked. "I...can't say I'm surprised you weren't the only one, but I never would have guessed it could be passed on like that."

"I wouldn't either," Aelia answered, not looking away from the handsome tiger, even as her eyes grew damp. "I'm so sorry, Aaron. This happened to you because of me. And I have no idea how to undo it."

Ignoring the others, Aaron pushed himself to his feet and walked over to her, crouching in front of her. His face was serious, and the look in his eyes was a little dazed, a little shocked. She got it. She'd probably held a similar look after her first drowning. "Stop," he said quietly. She frowned, not understanding what he meant. "Stop blaming yourself. Stop feeling guilty. I'm not entirely sure how I feel about being immortal—and the fact that I had my throat ripped out before I came back to life kinda proves I am—but you're missing one key detail here."

She shook her head, frowning harder. "What detail?"

He dropped his voice to a quiet murmur. "You've been worried about losing everyone. I can't be lost now."

That was actually a good point, and one she hadn't considered, but it felt wrong to be happy about that fact. "Still, you didn't have a choice."

Aaron shrugged. "You didn't either. And a lot of things happen without choice. We don't choose who and what we're born as, what advantages and disadvantages we have in life, or who we fall for. This is just another of our choices. I'll deal with it."

"I'm still sorry."

"While I know you two are having a heart-to-heart over there, I'm still a little out of the loop," Kara called.

Hecate added, "I have a few questions of my own."

Aaron straightened and offered a hand to Aelia. Though she was exhausted both from the emotional turmoil and the wounds she'd sustained, she took it and rose, wincing as the movement pulled at her wounds. Part of her felt like she deserved the pain and human slow healing, but she asked, "Hecate? Before I answer your questions, could you please heal me?"

"Of course." The goddess walked over and touched Aelia's stomach, instantly making the pain vanish. It took a few more moments before the wounds sealed. She'd still be tired from blood loss, but that was okay. Rest would fix that.

"What are your questions?" she asked, grabbing a water from her bag.

"I have no idea how this other immortal managed to transfer something so powerful, but how did you become immortal to begin with?"

They had started with the one question she wouldn't answer. Aaron knew, and that couldn't be helped, but the gods were the ones most likely to be able to find wherever Grovek had hidden the tablet. "All I can say is that there will never be more than two immortals. Grovek ensured no one else would suffer like this again." Although if Blanche was right, there were actually four immortals. Sort of. A different brand of immortality, but the result seemed to be the same.

"So this Grovek guy knew all about this immortality thing?" Kara asked. "And who is he, anyway?"

"The Lemurian god of wisdom," Aelia answered. "And he knew about it, but I don't know if he knew everything about it. Why?"

Kara shrugged and stretched her legs out, leaning back and bracing her hands behind her. Despite the fight, she seemed relaxed now. "Because if he knew enough, maybe he knew how to reverse it. I mean, personally I don't want you guys to get rid of that, because I kinda like having you both around. Added to that, without your immortality, I never would have met you, Aelia. But it's not my choice."

"I've lived long enough, Kara," Aelia answered quietly. "And I think if Grovek had known how to undo this, he would have told me."

Aaron really hated hearing Aelia talk like that. He'd thought she'd started to move past it the last few days, but obviously he'd been wrong. Personally, he wasn't hating the idea of the two of them still being around in a few thousand years. Together. He could try to convince her, but he couldn't make the decision for her, not if it made her this unhappy. He just hoped someone else tried to make her realize she still had something to live for, because he was struggling with the idea that he'd just died and come back. It took a lot of his brainpower, because it shouldn't have ever been possible, but Aelia staying alive was more important. And not just for him.

But as Kara had said, it wasn't his choice.

"Didn't you say all this happened just a day or two before Lemuria went down?" he asked, hating himself even as he spoke.

"Yeah..."

"So maybe he just didn't have time to tell you the finer points of your immortality."

"Maybe he did, but you saw his journal. There wasn't much in there about this."

"I know Vazi hates the idea of there being so few Lemurian gods, but has he tried to figure out where the others are and bring them back?" Kara asked.

The idea had Aaron torn. Grovek might be able to give her what she claimed she wanted, but he also might help give her a new reason to stick around. Hell, maybe they could team up. Grovek engaging her mind, Aaron taking care of her body. And, if he was lucky, her heart. It was an idea worth considering, for sure.

"I know I'm not on Lemuria as often as the three of you, but I'm not sure he has," Hecate said. "Looking into it means potentially finding out that there's no way he can bring them back. As long as he doesn't try, he can have hope. Hope is an exceptionally powerful thing, and it takes a great deal of bravery to risk having that hope shattered."

"Maybe," Aelia began slowly, "it's time we looked. Every spell, every curse, has a counter. Even divine spells."

Hecate smiled. "That they do. If something can be done, it can be undone."

"Then can we trouble you to retrieve our things from our hotel room, and for a ride back to Lemuria? We have a god to talk to."

The goddess's smile widened. "I absolutely can. The world hasn't been quite as bright since Lemuria fell. It would be nice to see it shine again," she told them before teleporting them all to Lemuria.

CHAPTER 16

It was night in Lemuria, which was fine with Aaron. It meant fewer people around. Not that there were many on Lemuria, but he still felt extremely off from having died. Honestly, all he wanted at the moment was to take a shower and crawl into bed. Preferably with Aelia. Unfortunately, he knew it wasn't time for that yet.

Dying really did suck, and not just for the obvious reasons.

"I'm going to go now, but let me know if there's anything I can do to help," Hecate told them, resting a hand briefly on Aelia's shoulder.

"We will," Aelia promised. "Thank you, Hecate."

The goddess hugged Aelia, whispering something to her before she disappeared, their bags resting on the ground where she had stood.

"Let's get to my house before we call Vazi," Aelia suggested, picking her things up and starting in that direction.

"Works for me," Kara said, nodding. "There are chairs there."

"Can you give us a few first, Kara?" Aaron asked, watching Aelia's face and body language closely even as he picked up his own bags.

Kara looked between them for a moment before she nodded slowly. "Sure...I'll head home and grab some food. Just text me when you're ready," she said, turning to head for her house.

Aaron started walking toward Aelia's house, and she fell into step beside him, saying nothing, but giving him curious looks. It wasn't until they were back in Aelia's house and the door was closed behind them that she spoke.

"What did you want to talk about?" Aelia asked, slipping her pack off, setting it down, then turning to face him.

His bags were dropped unceremoniously before one of his hands cupped her cheek and the other slid into her hair, gripping it firmly. Her eyes widened slightly and her lips parted. Perfect. His head bent, and he kissed her the way he'd wanted to since he'd come back to life. He devoured, he plundered, and he gave form to all the emotions churning in his chest with that one kiss. The fear he'd felt when dying. The shock and confusion upon reviving. The horror of knowing his brother was a killer. And the way he felt for the woman who was currently melting against him.

When the kiss started to get out of hand, he forced himself to pull back, but he couldn't release her. He needed to be touching her.

"Um...wow. That...you didn't want to talk?" she asked, her hands on his chest, and he liked to think it was because she needed to touch him, too.

"I do," he said, wondering what she'd do if he pulled her in for a hug. Kissing she could pass off as sex. Hugging? That was affectionate, emotional. "First, it was hot as hell watching you kick ass to protect me."

She looked a little embarrassed by that, but didn't look away. "You're such a man."

"That I am," he agreed easily. "But I also wanted to tell you that I understand you a little more, now."

Her head cocked and her brow furrowed lightly. "You do? How so?"

"Dying? Coming back? I know the actual act isn't your biggest issue, but it's definitely major. And it's not something most people can understand. It's...weird as fuck." Which was the world's worst understatement, but how could he describe how it had felt to have his neck snapped? To have the world go gray around him and feel his heart stop? Then to come back, free of all the pain, but drained as though he'd been treading water for a full day with a full pack? Not to mention the disorientation. Maybe that went away after a few deaths, but maybe it wouldn't.

Her face went grim. "It only gets worse. The first is bad, maybe the worst, physically, mentally. It's when you keep coming back, but have fewer and fewer people around you that it really starts to wear on a person."

Before he could offer any sort of response, she stepped back and called out for both Vazi and Seth. Even as she was speaking their names, she grabbed her phone, no doubt texting Kara. He wished she had given them a few more minutes, but understood—reluctantly—that she probably needed some emotional space.

What in the hell was it going to take to get inside this woman's shell? At least he now had the whole of eternity to work on it. As long as she didn't find a way to reverse her immortality. If she did, if the worst happened, he still wouldn't give up on her. He wasn't sure he could. Besides, they were Arcane. Nothing was impossible.

Seth appeared first, but Aaron expected that. The man knew most of what was going on, and had been worried about them.

"Everyone okay?" he asked.

"Mostly," Aaron answered. "But let's save the Q and A for when everyone's here."

Seth didn't look pleased to be made to wait, but nodded.

Vazi appeared a moment later, frowning. "This had better be important," he said, folding his arms over his chest.

"It is," Aelia assured him.

"Trust us, you want to be here," Aaron added. "Just need to wait for Kara."

Vazi, ever the impatient, grumpy god, just huffed and waved a hand. Kara popped in, a sandwich in her mouth, mid-bite. She chewed and swallowed, then glared at Vazi, correctly guessing who was responsible. "What the hell, Vazi? A little warning would have been nice."

"Apparently this is important, and I didn't want to wait," he said, shrugging. "What's going on?"

"Hopefully, restoring Lemuria," Aelia said. "But you need some backstory first." Not that she looked happy about it. Still, she laid it all out. The nightmares, finding James in Sozu, tracking Navid, and everything that had happened in Norway, right up to the point where Hecate had brought them back.

Both gods turned their attention to Aaron, which he'd expected. "Yeah, I don't stay dead either. But that's not the point."

"Then what is the point? Because as interesting as all that is, it could have waited until morning," Vazi said. Then he frowned at Aelia. "And you should have told us about the nightmares."

"So you could kill the Ekklesia?" she retorted.

He shrugged nonchalantly. "Probably. What's wrong with that? I protect my people."

"They hide the Arcane from humanity. It's an important job!"

"Which means it should be handled by people who aren't going to abuse their position," he said, giving her another shrug. "But I ask again, what's the point if it's not that we have two true immortals on Lemuria?"

"We need to ask you something, Vazi, and you're not going to like it," she answered, and he could hear the suppressed irritation in her voice.

He gave a deep sigh and gave a go ahead gesture. "I generally don't like being asked questions, but that's not going to stop you."

Taking a bit of the heat off Aelia, Aaron was the one to do the asking. "We need to know what happened when Lemuria fell. To you. To the gods. Anything you can remember, however small."

Vazi's eyes narrowed, and a breeze began to swirl about the room. No one looked surprised. It was just what happened when Vazi was truly worked up. As long as a tornado didn't form in the house, they were safe. Probably.

"Why?" he asked darkly. "It's not exactly a pleasant topic."

"Because if we're going to try to bring the other Lemurian gods back, we first need to know what happened to them," Aelia answered.

Her words made him go still in a way very few beings could manage. It was like he turned into a statue until his gaze slid to Seth, then back to Aaron and Aelia. "Do you really think that's possible?"

"Aelia said it best, and Hecate agreed. Everything that's done can be undone. Every spell has a counter," Aaron said, shrugging. "So we don't see why not? Besides, I'm fucking tired of everyone thinking they can screw with us because we're such a small group. And that is *not* a dig about only having two and a half Lemurian gods," he said before Vazi could offer up a scathing remark.

"Three," Vazi snapped. "She might have some Greek in her, but Rhea isn't a problem. Some of her kids are, but she isn't, and Dania isn't."

Aaron held his hands up in surrender. "Not saying otherwise. I like Dania. She's sweet. Kind of reminds me of my little sister."

Vazi's head cocked and he glared at Aaron. "You don't have a sister."

"The one I never had, then."

"Can we get back to the idea of bringing the other Lemurian gods back?" Seth asked. "Don't get me wrong, part of me is scared as shit they'll come back and kick my ass, but it'd be nice to have more people like Vazi back. I'd certainly worry less about people like Zeus and the Ekklesia."

"Could Zeus have told the Ekklesia to target Aelia?" Kara wondered. Every eye in the room turned on her, but she just rolled hers. "Is it really that wild of an idea? He tried to kill Tempest. Tried to stop us—or anyone—from finding Lemuria. Chained Dania up for thousands of years and loaned her to a psychopath. Is it really that much of a stretch that he'd have the Ekklesia torment Aelia? I mean, it could have been any of us, but I don't think any of the rest of us have ever met them in person, and it kinda sounds like Aelia has."

"I hate to admit it, but she could be right. Though I don't know how he would have connected Aelia to Lemuria," Vazi grumbled. "But whatever their original motive, Seth is also right." He sat in one of the chairs and, though he tried to keep his normal resting grumpy face, Aaron could see the strain on the god's face. "I don't know how much help I'll be, but if it gets more of the gods back, then I'll tell you what I can."

"Take your time," Aelia told him, sitting in another chair. Not directly next to him, but close, her face full of sympathy. Since they were the only two in the room who had known those gods, who had lived through Lemuria's destruction, he thought she was the only one who could even remotely understand what he was about to relive.

"I know it's been mentioned how we were fighting for a while before we disappeared and Lemuria disappeared with us," Vazi began, tracing his finger over his knee, the first sign of agitation Aaron had ever seen him display. "It started off small, just little disagreements, but it escalated quickly. Too quickly," he murmured, shaking his head. "It couldn't have been more than a week from when the first spats started until basically all-out war broke out. I honestly can't remember if there was anyone who wasn't involved." He gave Aelia a weak smile. "Grovek might have abstained. Especially if he'd been holed up in his little sanctuary. Whatever caused us to bicker might not have reached him if he had been there."

"He was," she confirmed, returning the smile with a tiny one of her own. "He really only left to study something or for the festivals. And half the time he had to be dragged out for the festivals."

"Yeah, that sounds right." He sighed and flattened his hand on his leg. "We were fighting, and I do mean a full-out battle. I'd like to say Zeus or one of the others was responsible for the sinking itself, but he wasn't. It was us. It was me. I created hurricanes and tornadoes, and Tryno only made them stronger. Marchanta caused tsunamis to slam into the island. Basically, all of our powers were being used against each other and the land itself." His brow furrowed. "I have no idea how any of the land survived, much less continued to be hidden to outsiders."

"Even gone, your pantheon's power remained strong," Kara said quietly. "And even under whatever influence, obviously you didn't actually want Lemuria completely destroyed. Didn't you have enough sense to take Tempest away and put her someplace safe? I'm sure the same thread of sanity held you all back, at least a little."

"It's a nice thought. I hope you're right. Whatever the reason, in the middle of that last fight, I felt a...pull. I don't know how else to explain it. It kept pulling me, getting stronger, and then I slid into darkness. I don't mean unconsciousness or sleep or anything. I mean literal darkness. Void is the best way I can describe it."

When Vazi hadn't spoken for several minutes, Seth walked over, rested his hand on his fellow god's arm. "What happened then?"

Vazi looked like the touch startled him out of a memory, and he nodded. "I wasn't out, but I wasn't fully there, either. Sort of like right before you really wake up, when you're sort of half there? No sensation, no sense of how much time passed, just existence." He glanced up at Seth. "When you killed Jalvas and replaced him, it was like I was jolted awake, and pulled to where you all were. I never really thought about why I didn't come back in the same place I'd been before I...disappeared." He shook his head. "I still have no idea how anyone managed to do that to our entire pantheon. Even if some of us were killed in the fighting, we still had quite a few gods still alive, and it's not like any of us were truly weak."

"No, you were the strongest pantheon," Aelia agreed. "It's probably why they wanted you out of the way."

"Likely, yes. And unlike every other pantheon, we didn't require worshipers to maintain our power," he said, getting to his feet and walking to the window to stare out it.

"What do you mean?" Kara asked. "About the worshipers?"

Seth answered for him, since Vazi clearly needed a minute.

"The Greeks, Egyptians, etcetera, they all gain power from those who worship them. Offerings help, but just the belief and prayer and all that strengthens them. If they lose worshipers or are forgotten, they lose power. Think of it like they have a battery, and their followers charge the battery. Lemurians don't need that external charge."

"Oh. Yeah, I can see how that might upset the other gods."

"Yeah, but they also didn't have the balance Lemurians do. Look at what happened to Jalvas."

"True," Kara said, nodding.

"Obviously we've all heard the stories growing up of the different gods, and there's definitely a lot of propaganda about who's stronger than who, but back then, who were the strongest individual gods? Lemurian or otherwise?" Aaron asked.

Vazi glanced back. "Several Lemurians topped the list, though almost all of us were strong. Outside of our group..." He considered for a moment, shrugged. "Ra, Set, Odin, An, Enlil...Zeus should probably be on the list, though I'm honestly not sure how much of his is real power and how much is bluster and manipulating others into doing his dirty work. And the Anunnaki, of course."

Kara frowned. "Who are they?"

"They're the ones who created the universe," Aelia answered. "They existed before anything else. They created literally everything." Glancing at Aaron, she offered, "Those four statues in the entrance of Sozu? The ones with the wings and snakes? They're statues of the Anunnaki."

Vazi nodded agreement. "There are four of them, and they're paired up, which is probably why we were created with the balance."

"But who are they?" Kara repeated.

"Ananke, Chronos, Tiamat, and Apophis."

"Wait a sec. The creators of everything are gods? I mean, I haven't heard of Ananke or Tiamat, but Chronos is a Greek god, isn't he? And Apophis is some big bad to the Egyptians?"

Vazi shook his head. "No. Other pantheons tried to claim them, to say they were Greek or Egyptian, but they're not gods. They're more than gods, stronger than any of us. They are true embodiments. Ananke *is* fate. Not a god of fate who can see and alter it. She is the actual embodiment of it. Chronos embodies time, Tiamat is chaos, and Apophis is the void. All four were needed to create the universe."

Aaron frowned at the explanation. Vazi had described the place he'd been in as a void, and one of the Anunnaki was the embodiment of the void. Could the two be related? He wasn't sure, and it wasn't an immediate concern, so he asked, "Have either of you asked these Anunnaki about the other Lemurian gods? I mean, it sounds like you know them."

Seth shook his head. "I've never met them. I only knew a fraction of what he just said," he answered, looking to Vazi.

Seeing the powerful Lemurian god of the sky looking sheepish was amusing, even with the circumstances.

"I haven't, no," he admitted.

"Maybe we should ask? I mean, even if it's harder to get in touch with them than with a god, isn't it worth a try? The creators of everything should be able to at least give some insight, right?" Aaron suggested. "Hell, shouldn't they have the power to just snap their fingers and bring the other gods back?"

"The power, yes, but I don't know if they can bring the others back. As for contacting them, it's easier than with a god, actually," Vazi said with a shake of his head. "I don't know if they'll help, but I can see if Ananke or Chronos will join us. No one had seen the other two for years, even before Lemuria sank. I don't know if they're active again or not." His voice dropped to a murmur full of sorrow. "There's a lot I've been neglecting, it seems." That said, he closed his eyes, and Aaron was surprised to realize he was watching a god pray. Not something he ever thought he'd witness.

Within a minute, two figures appeared, and Aaron straightened his back, suddenly nervous about meeting *the* creators.

And here he'd thought dying was going to be the biggest shock of his day.

CHAPTER 17

Aelia wasn't surprised by the way the Anunnaki looked. As she'd told Aaron, there were statues of them, and currently, they very closely resembled those statues. Which meant she was looking at Ananke and Chronos, wings and all. There were no snakes at least, though serpents had never really bothered Aelia. At least not that she could recall.

Ananke was tall, with a curvy figure and long, curly blonde hair. It was wild, but in a way that suited the woman in a simple white dress. Her eyes and wings were easily her most striking features, as both seemed to be all colors at once. Not quite like opals, as the colors shifted even when she didn't move, but it was the closest Aelia could think to compare them to.

Chronos was just a little taller than his companion, but where she appeared to be around twenty, he looked like he was in his fifties. Both his shoulder-length hair and beard were black speckled with white, but like Ananke, the hint of wildness suited him. And where Ananke's wings matched her eyes, his matched his hair, white and gray feathers sprinkled in among the black.

She wondered if it was intentional, or if this was truly how they looked. Even with the gods, it wasn't always easy to tell, and these were the people who had created the gods.

"We were wondering if you were ever going to reach out to us," Ananke said in a smooth, warm tone that felt like the aural version of a hug, even as she actually slid her arms around the sky god. "You've been back for months, Vazi."

Again, the god looked sheepish as he returned the embrace. "We've been a little busy."

"That's no excuse for ignoring us," Chronos said. "We are, for all intents and purposes, fifty percent of your parentage."

Vazi sighed. "I know, and I'm sorry. But it's just Seth and me—and now Dania. There are so few on the island, and so many trying to destroy us. That had to be my focus."

"We understand, and we're not angry," Ananke said, stepping back and resting a hand on his shoulder. "I have to say I'm surprised to see you're still yourself. Both of you," she said, her gaze sliding to Seth. "Without your counterparts, we weren't sure just being light and dark would help."

"If there were more of us, it might not," Vazi said, shrugging. "But it's not like this has ever happened before."

"No, it hasn't," she said sadly, drawing her hand back. "And I'm sorry it happened this time, but it was fated. And unfortunately, I do not believe that the two of you will be able to balance each other for much longer," she warned.

Aelia wasn't sure which part of her statement worried her more; that Lemuria was always going to fall, or that Seth and Vazi were going to go crazy. The last thing Lemuria needed was for their gods to go insane. Again.

"Do you know how long we have?" Seth asked, brow knit in concern. "I have a wife and new baby. I don't want to do anything that would put them at risk."

Chronos was the one to answer this time. "A few more months. Six at the most."

"But you didn't call us to talk about your balance," Ananke interjected. "We're happy to see Lemuria is alive again, but what is it you need?" she asked, looking around.

When her gaze landed on Aelia's, her breath caught. She'd been around powerful people before, including dozens of gods, but none had been able to pack this kind of power in a simple glance. It truly felt as though the mistress of fate was poking around in her mind and soul in a way that should have felt intrusive, but didn't. It did scare the shit out of her, though. Throughout her life, she'd thought and done things that she wasn't exactly proud of. Some of them to survive, some when she was lashing out in her anger at not being able to die, and some out of desperation. Was Ananke seeing them all now? Was she judging her?

Vazi spoke, drawing Ananke's attention back to him, and the pressure in Aelia's mind and heart eased, just a little. "Actually, that isn't too far off," he admitted. "The balance, I mean. Obviously, it's possible for us to come back from wherever we were sent, otherwise I wouldn't be here, but I don't know where I was or how exactly I got there. We were hoping you might be able to help us bring the other gods back," he said, his voice and demeanor more humble, more respectful than she'd ever seen him. Not that it should surprise her.

These were two of the most powerful beings to ever exist, matched only by the other half of the Anunnaki. A little respect was wise, even if they did appear to view Lemurians as their children. Beloved children at that. Or at least they viewed Vazi that way.

The Anunnaki exchanged a look, and neither looked particularly happy. Instead they looked worried, which also scared the crap out of her.

"Unfortunately, it's impossible for us to simply bring your brothers and sisters back," Ananke said gently. "As I said, the fall of Lemuria was fated to happen, and I cannot just undo what was fated." Vazi's face fell into stony resignation, but she smiled. "That isn't to say it's not possible for your pantheon to be restored, sweet boy."

"How?" Seth asked, stepping up beside Vazi. "Please, if there's a way to do that, to give us both balance so we don't turn on those we've brought here and made family, we'll do it."

"It won't be safe or easy," Chronos cautioned. "The power required to send every Lemurian god away was substantial and required a great many blood sacrifices. Thousands were killed in order to harness the energy needed for such a monumental task."

Aelia was sure her expression was as horrified as everyone else's. Had Zeus and his cohorts really killed so many people just to take the strongest pantheon off whatever game board he was using?

"Can you define not easy?" Kara asked hesitantly.

"The ritual needed to bring the gods back is likely to kill whoever performs it," Ananke said, getting right to the point. "Even if you were to perform it, Vazi. A sacrifice to undo a sacrifice. But," she added quickly, "while a sacrifice is needed, it isn't certain that death will be the result. Some things are hazy even for us."

"If death isn't required, then what kind of sacrifice are we talking about?" Seth asked.

"It may simply be a great deal of pain. As I said, it isn't certain. Nothing like this has been attempted before."

Vazi shook his head slowly. "I don't know that I like this, but if we're going to seriously discuss this, then *all* Lemurian gods should be here," he told the group before he disappeared.

"A few months ago, we discovered that a half-Lemurian, half-Greek goddess had been left here on Earth when the rest disappeared," Seth explained. "She's living here now. Partially to hide from her half-brother."

Chronos nodded. "Zeus, yes. He does have some...unpleasant habits," he said, grimacing like the name had left a bad taste in his mouth.

"That's an understatement," Kara muttered.

"You can't do anything about him?" Aaron asked.

Chronos shook his head. "Unfortunately, no. Besides, if we were to do something to everyone who ever did anything wrong, there would be almost no one left on the planet, and most of them would be very young children."

"Good point," Aaron agreed with a sigh.

Vazi teleported back in, Dania at his side, though as soon as they materialized in Aelia's living room, Dania stepped away to an empty section of the room. The poor woman was still having trouble trusting people. Not that she could be blamed. Thousands of years of being enslaved by Zeus would do that to anyone. And as long as Aelia had lived, even she didn't know an easy and sure way of helping someone work through their trauma.

Now that all three current Lemurian gods were present, Vazi quickly ran through what the Anunnaki had told them. Dania's brow furrowed delicately. "I'm not sure why I'm here, though."

"Because you're Lemurian," Seth answered.

"But I'm half Greek."

Vazi shrugged. "You're still Lemurian," he argued. "And if we're going to seriously consider this, then we all need to be in agreement. I don't take the idea of someone being sacrificed lightly, but I don't think we should just dismiss it."

"You're all forgetting one very important fact," Aelia said, speaking for the first time since the Anunnaki had appeared. Every eye in the room turned on her, but she kept her chin up and back straight.

"What fact?" Dania asked, and Aelia realized the woman honestly might not know about her. The Lemurians gossiped like anyone else, but they also seemed to know she was a private person.

"I may die, but I don't stay dead," she answered. "So we can do the ritual and not permanently lose anyone. There won't be any reason for anyone to feel guilty."

"Hold on one fucking second," Aaron snapped, narrowing his eyes at her as he stepped closer, though he refrained from touching her. "Yes, she comes back from the dead, but you said sacrifice. Could this kill someone who's been unkillable up to this point?"

Chronos cocked his head and studied them both, saying nothing for a minute. Like Ananke, having his attention on her—on them—was intrusive, but where it had felt like Ananke was looking into her soul, now it felt like Chronos was scrutinizing her life. If he was the embodiment of time, it was possible.

"Very little is guaranteed in this world," was his eventual answer. "Whoever does the ritual may not die, but it might also permanently kill even someone who has cheated death over and over again. There is no way of knowing before it is done."

"Then we can't just assume everyone would be all right," Dania said, nodding. "Is it worth bringing the other gods back, then? Trading a life for a life seems wrong." Her voice dropped to just above a whisper. "It seems like something Zeus would do."

Those last seven words made everyone pause except for Aelia. She actually wanted to do the ritual. Not just because she desperately wanted Lemuria back to something resembling what it had been, but because it might give her the fresh start she wanted. She could see her family again. All of her families, because she hadn't just wed once, had children once. She'd tried several times before closing herself off.

"Before you make your decision, perhaps you should know all of it?" Chronos suggested.

"There's more?" Kara blurted.

He smiled. "There usually is, yes. In this case, you should know that this ritual will not be one life for one life, it will bring back *two* gods for each ritual."

"Wait, what? How?" Seth asked.

"For the same reason that when you became a god, you inadvertently brought Vazi back. The ritual will bring pairs of gods back. If you tried to bring Pyra back, you would also bring Caron. Debern and Kizza would come as a set, Machelis and Scuris. It will always be a set, not just a single god—except if you're trying to bring back your counterparts," he said, nodding to Vazi and Seth. "But that being said, no one can decide whether it's worth the sacrifice except for the person who chooses to perform it," he added, his gaze sliding back to Aelia.

Had he already seen her performing it? Or was it just wishful thinking on her part? She had no idea, but didn't think Aaron would take well to her asking. Instead, she focused on the details.

"What exactly is involved in the ritual?" she asked, ignoring Aaron's low growl of displeasure.

"First, it must be performed on the half moon. You're bringing back both a light and dark god, so that part is absolute," Ananke explained, sinking down onto a seat, her wings disappearing as she leaned back. Handy. "Second, you will need an object that was significant to one of the gods you're attempting to bring back. Something that holds at least a hint of their essence. And I don't mean physical essence, though that would certainly help. I mean emotional essence."

"Like a piece of their soul or magic?" Seth asked before turning to Vazi. "Like that bracelet you made for Tempest, maybe? It definitely has your magic, and you were intent on protecting your friend, so it's gotta have emotional essence. That might be why you were brought back instead of one of the other gods."

"That would certainly work, and your theory is a good one," Ananke agreed, nodding. "Once you have this object, it must be flooded with divine energy. From all three of you, since you are the only Lemurian gods still in existence. And if the ritual is done again, at least three of you will need to do it each time. Once you have the charged object, take it to the home of the gods, hold the object in full view of the moon, and chant." She glanced at Chronos, who nodded and looked at each person in turn. When it was Aelia's turn, she felt a small jolt, and words settled in the back of her head. She couldn't quite make out what they were, but had a feeling that if she performed the ritual, she'd know the words to speak.

"And what happens if someone does perform this ritual but botches it?" Aaron asked, a growl still in his voice, despite who he was speaking to. Neither Anunnaki seemed to take offense, fortunately. He might be overbearing at times, but she didn't want to see him killed by the Anunnaki—and they would likely be able to make it permanent.

Ananke shrugged. "I don't know," she told him simply. "Again, nothing like this has ever been done before. It might be that nothing happens. The ritual fails, no harm done. Or it might kill the one doing the ritual, or everyone in proximity to that person." Sorrow slid over her face. "Even the Anunnaki aren't infallible or completely omniscient. We know much, but we aren't perfect."

"One more thing you should know," Chronos began, focusing on Seth. "If you do go through with this ritual, it will be time for you to repay your favor."

Seth frowned and shook his head. "I'm sorry? What favor?"

Chronos smiled mischievously, and his form abruptly shifted. His wings disappeared, his hair and beard lengthened, and he seemed to age a good thirty years until he looked like a stereotypical old man.

Aelia didn't understand the reason behind the transformation, but Seth's eyes widened and he sounded like he was choking. "You?" he gasped.

"I don't understand," Kara said, looking between the two men. "What's going on?"

"Just after I killed Jalvas, remember I told you that a guy I called Father Time shifted me back to just before we stepped on Lemuria? So I could save everyone?"

"Yeah? Oh. Oh! That was you?" Kara asked Chronos.

He chuckled and nodded as he returned to his earlier appearance. "There are things we cannot do, but occasionally we can help out just a little."

"Hey, you kept me from being killed. I'll take it!"

He just smiled at her enthusiasm.

Seth, finally recovered from his shock, asked, "How do you want me to repay the favor? Not that I can ever really repay it, but what is it you want?"

"The first set of gods you bring back—again, if you choose to do this at all—is your choice. But the second set must be of our choosing."

"Which pair are you thinking?" Vazi asked, just a hint of suspicion in his words.

Ananke smiled sweetly. "Which pair are you thinking to begin with?"

To her surprise, Vazi looked at Aelia and nodded slightly. She supposed it made a kind of sense. It was her quest that had brought all of them to the surface, and Vazi tended to be fair, even if he was often grumpy. "Grovek. And since it would bring back his counterpart..." She sighed. "Telia."

Kara raised her hand. "For those of us who didn't know all these gods back in the day...what exactly is Grovek's counterpart? I mean what is she the goddess of?"

"Insanity," Vazi answered flatly.

"Oh. Yeah, I guess that makes sense," she mumbled, but she looked as pleased as Aelia felt.

Chronos just smiled and nodded. "A sound choice, actually. The second set should be Ocoina and Inanis," he answered, before looking to Kara and adding, "Birth and Death."

"Why those two? Not that I mind either of them. They'd be good to have around," Vazi said.

Both the Anunnaki looked like they were hiding something before Chronos answered, "They will be needed in the future. Ideally, all the Lemurian gods will be back by that point, but I cannot guarantee how long we have. The only benefit is that while there's only twelve or thirteen full or new moons in a year, there's a half moon twice a cycle."

Aelia hadn't considered that. If she did survive the ritual, that would be very handy. Within a year, Thelaria—the Lemurian home of the gods—could be bustling again.

Seth frowned. "What will they be needed for?"

Ananke shook her head. "All you need to know for now is that what you are doing now—rebuilding Lemuria, growing it, allowing the land and people to thrive again—is helping. And we are very, very pleased to see life on it again." She smiled wistfully. "We have a fondness for it, given this is where we created our first children."

"That's all we can do for now," Chronos said, walking to stand beside Ananke, resting his hand on her shoulder. "But we do wish you luck." Again, he looked directly at Aelia—no, both her and Aaron—and smiled. "We'll see you soon," he added, before the Anunnaki disappeared.

CHAPTER 18

When the idea of bringing back the gods—especially Grovek—had first come up, Aaron had been all for it. More Lemurian gods, someone else Aelia cared for, it was really a win-win. Then the Anunnaki had to go and put more *bad* ideas in Aelia's head. Of course she'd volunteered to potentially sacrifice herself.

Right now, he hated the creators of the universe.

"Why in the hell can't they just snap their fingers and bring the gods back? Or at least tell us for certain if anyone actually has to die?" he snapped, starting to pace.

Vazi sat on the arm of Aelia's couch and cocked his head, watching Aaron stalk back and forth across the room. "As I said before, they're literal embodiments of necessary elements to the universe. They cannot go against their natures. It isn't a choice, it's...biology," he explained. "It would be like expecting a fish to live in the clouds, or a bird to survive in the deepest parts of the ocean. They could try, but they wouldn't succeed. And given that Ananke is the embodiment of fate and inevitability, she truly can't prevent something that is fated to happen."

"But Chronos is time, right? Why can't he just look into the future and see what's going to happen?" Seth asked. He sounded a little baffled and overwhelmed, but calm. How could he be so fucking calm? Aaron was on the verge of shifting, barely clinging to his human form.

Aelia chose to answer this question, and he actually paused to look at her, though he was sure he didn't have the friendliest expression on his face. "The future isn't set. And before you ask about how fate works with an uncertain future, consider this; someone might be fated to, say, defeat a great evil. That could be seen by a prophet or someone like Chronos, but the method could change, or which evil, or even the interpretation of what's evil. It's why most prophecies are so vague. Each decision a person makes alters their future, even if the roads should all lead to the same destination."

"Exactly," Vazi agreed. "Like before you met Tempest, you might have had a million possible futures. Then you decided to go on your expedition, and it removed, say, seventy percent of those possibilities. You decided to help her, removing another half. You accepted Aaron's help, removing ninety percent of what remained. And you accepted Chronos's offer to go back in time, removing all but one."

"But if what Aelia said is true, shouldn't I have always ended up with Tempest?" Seth asked.

"Not necessarily. If you were fated to end up with her, then yes. If it was just a possibility? You could still be an archaeologist, fighting with Aaron over who got the next big discovery. It's difficult for most of us to say what's fate and what is simply an event that occurred."

"That's great and all, but have any of you guys considered that bringing more gods back might put a bigger target on our backs?" Kara asked. "I mean, Zeus went apeshit when he thought it was just one Lemurian, and Tempest wasn't even a god. Now we have three gods, almost twenty mortals, and the Ekklesia has been going after Aelia. What will they do if we have more gods?"

Vazi smiled, and it was vicious. All of them had reasons to dislike the king of the Greeks, but he had the biggest beef—after Dania. "They can try whatever they want, but they won't succeed. I'm powerful, but I'm just one god. Seth is powerful too, but he's still new to his powers. Dania?" He glanced at the goddess and smiled. "She can do amazing things, but she's still adjusting to Lemuria, on top of dealing with…everything she went through. But if we have other gods with my strength and experience?" He shook his head. "They won't touch us. They won't be able to. Not again."

Kara didn't look convinced, and Aaron actually agreed with her.

"They said the ritual needed to be done in the home of the gods. I'm guessing that means Thelaria?" Aelia asked, and he noted she was watching him like he was a trapped animal. Fitting, since he felt like he'd been backed into a corner.

"I can't think of anywhere else it could be," Vazi answered.

"Then are you willing to take others there? I know historically mortals weren't permitted there. You and the other gods just came to Lemuria to visit."

"For this? Absolutely. Besides, I've come to know everyone who lives here. I trust each of you."

And yet they were still skirting around the big issue, and Aaron was sick of it. "None of that matters, because the Anunnaki couldn't even guarantee that doing this wouldn't kill someone. And don't," he added, pointing at Aelia, "offer again, because they didn't know if you'd come back this time." Lowering his hand, he fixed his gaze on Vazi. "Is bringing your old friends back worth risking one of your new ones? Especially when it's a woman who was instrumental in bringing people back to Lemuria?" he demanded. "If it weren't for her, Tempest would probably have died before she ever realized Lemuria existed, which meant Seth never would have killed Jalvas, and you'd still be wherever the fuck you were."

"Remember who you're talking to," Vazi snapped, rising to his feet, a gust of wind slapping Aaron's face, but he was gratified to hear a note of defensiveness in the god's voice. Good.

Not backing down an inch, he just glared back at Vazi. "I'm talking to a man who is considering letting a woman kill herself to get him what he wants!"

"I have to think of more than just one person! It's not just about her, or me, or anyone here."

To Aaron's way of thinking, it was absolutely about Aelia. "No? Then what in the hell is it about?"

"The gods returning could help the entire world. Not just me."

"Fuck the world!"

Aelia was suddenly between them, a hand on both their chests. Aaron hadn't realized he'd gotten up in Vazi's face, and he still didn't want to back down, but the pressure of her hand had him glancing at her. She looked as unhappy as she felt.

Voice firm, she glared at them both. "You need to stop. This is my choice, not either of yours. If I want to risk my immortality to bring back a pantheon I admire, to help restore a land I love, then it is *my* choice," she said, moving her hand from Vazi's chest to thump against her own.

Vazi clenched his jaw, but took a step back. Aaron wasn't so easily pacified. "Everyone leave," he ordered. "I want to talk to Aelia alone."

Her glare was back, but the three gods and Kara quickly left the house, leaving him alone with the most infuriating, wonderful woman he'd ever known. Except he wasn't sure what words he could use to convince her to at least stop and think about what she'd already offered to do.

"This is my choice, Aaron," she said, retreating a step and folding her arms over her chest. "I'm okay with whatever the outcome may be. If I live, great. If I die?" She gave him a smile so sad he wanted to wrap his arms around her. "I'd finally get the chance to do what everyone else does. I'd go to the underworld and see the people I've lost again. Or maybe I'd be reincarnated. Perhaps both. Either way, it would be a fresh start."

"What's so wrong with the life you have now?"

She sighed and dropped into a chair, rubbing her hands over her face. "I've seen everything, Aaron. Been everywhere, tried everything that interested me, and lived hundreds of lives. I'm not living anymore, I'm surviving. Trying to help others live, so I have a purpose, but it's not enough. There's no joy in life. Not anymore. Not since I realized that there's nothing new left for me to do, and that I'll always end up alone."

It took every ounce of self-control he had to stay where he was. He wanted to convince her, but he wanted to do it by changing her mind, not by making her think there was no other option. "Honey, have you considered that the joy isn't there because of depression, not because there's an actual lack of joy in your life?" he suggested gently.

"Of course I have," she answered simply. "But it doesn't change anything. That's the problem. Nothing will change. That's why a fresh start is so appealing. I'll forget that I've done everything. It'll be new again. Fun, exciting."

"There are ways to get fresh starts beyond suicide missions, Aelia. Like...a memory wipe," he said, hating that he'd even suggested it. The idea of her forgetting him crushed him. "Everything would be new again."

She shook her head. "I've done it before," she admitted. "As soon as I die, my memory is restored along with my body. And it's only a bandaid in any case. I still lose people."

There had to be something he could say to make her want to live again, but he wasn't sure what. He wasn't a talker. Oh, he'd been known to sweet talk women out of their pants on multiple occasions, and he was good at it, but his job was digging, researching, translating. When a politician needed convincing to issue a permit, one of his team took care of that. So how could he make her see what he did?

All he could do was try.

"Before, maybe, but think of the friends you have now, the people you know."

"Aaron..."

"I'm serious," he insisted. "Vazi, Seth, and Dania are literal gods. From the most powerful pantheon to ever exist, according to you. Tempest? She's a real Lemurian, who could potentially live forever. Don't forget you seem friendly with Hecate, and who knows what other gods. There are plenty of people who could live until the sun goes supernova. You're only as alone as you choose to be."

She frowned, watching him curiously. "Why does this matter so much to you? I don't understand why you care so much."

How could she not know? Did she think he gave flowers to every-one? That he followed after them to other fucking realms? Or sat on the beach watching auroras with every pretty woman he saw? He wasn't a man given to romantic gestures, and had never wanted to be...until now. Until her. So how could she not know what was going on in his head?

He'd tell her, since she'd missed what he felt was obvious, but he'd also make sure she wouldn't be the one to risk her life. No matter how she reacted to what he had to say.

"Because I fucking love you, Aelia, and I'm not going to stand around and watch you die. Especially not when I don't know with absolute certainty that you're going to wake up. Because let me tell you, it crushes me every single damn time I see you die. Even knowing that you can't stay dead, part of me worries, every single time, that this time? This time it's going to be different. That you're not going to open your eyes. That this time, you're just going to stay dead."

Her eyes widened and her lips parted in shock, and he didn't know whether that said more about her, or about him. But he wasn't done.

"The whole point of doing this ritual is for you to bring back Grovek, which does no good if you're dead. So if you're set on it being done, then *I* am going to be the one performing it." And it wasn't a ploy, either. He absolutely fucking meant it.

This couldn't be happening. Aelia wasn't sure which part of his speech scared her more, but she couldn't believe he'd said any of it aloud. Her own death? It didn't scare her in the least. She'd lived long enough that part of her truly did welcome it, but the thought of him dying? Terrifying. But was it more or less frightening than this man being in love with her?

He clearly saw the fear in her eyes, because he took a step toward her. "Which part is scaring you, baby?" he asked, his voice a sympathetic murmur, though his eyes were as intense as she'd ever seen them. "Me loving you, or me doing the ritual?"

"I..." She had to pause, licking her lips and drawing in a desperately needed breath as she tried to figure out what to say. Then she stopped thinking and just let the answer come. "You doing the ritual."

Aaron moved closer, stopping just out of reach. "Me dying?"

She gave a single, slow nod.

"That's the same fear I've been dealing with since we found out about this ritual. But if you think your life is worth so little that you're okay with risking it for something that may or may not work, then I'm an even better option."

"What? Why? That doesn't make any sense!"

"It does," he argued. "I don't have your experience, your knowledge, or your selflessness. I'm just a tiger who likes to go find buried treasure. You're an immortal sorceress who has seen most everything and studied damn near the rest of it. And saved Lemuria. So if we're doing this ritual, it will be my hand holding the object. My lips speaking the spell. My life on the line."

Aaron joked around a lot, and often gave off the appearance that he was never serious about anything. He was absolutely serious now. The image of him dying back in Norway forced its way to the front of her mind, but what if he hadn't revived? No, she couldn't stand the thought. Before today, she'd known he would die, as everyone did, but not for hundreds of years, not until he was old and had lived a long, fulfilling life. Not in a few short days during a ritual that was her doing.

The longer she looked at him, the more her fear for him grew, until she realized that she couldn't lose him. Not to death, and not to her own hangups and fears. By pushing him away, she was forcing herself to accept the fate she'd been fighting for thousands of years. She'd found the one thing that scared her more than living. Losing this brave, sexy, stubborn man.

Aelia hurried the two steps to him and leapt at him. He caught her and shifted his grip to her ass, allowing her to wrap her legs around his hips. Her hands cupped his face, and she kissed him hard as she tightened her legs, wanting as much contact with him as she could manage. She doubted she'd be able to touch him enough to satisfy her, to calm both her fears and her desire.

Growling, he turned and stalked over the wall. Her back hit the surface a little harder than expected, but it didn't bother her. Nothing could hurt right now, not as long as he kept touching her. One of his hands left her ass and slapped against the wall beside her head and he leaned in, grinding against her. The friction was nice, but it wasn't enough.

Knowing he wouldn't let her fall, she let go of his face without breaking the kiss, tugging, tearing at his shirt until she got it up enough for her hands to slip beneath. When she drew her nails down his back, he snarled and bucked his hips, causing her to gasp at the pressure against the part of her that most needed attention.

"Careful," he whispered as he slid his lips along her jaw to her throat. "I'm on edge right now."

"So?" she asked, before moaning when he set his teeth above her pulse and bit. "You don't scare me."

Aaron lifted his head, one brow arched, a feral smile on his mouth. "No?" The single purred word made her pulse catch for a second before resuming, faster than before.

She could only shake her head, since she looked forward to every second of whatever he had in mind. Aaron had her complete trust, especially when it came to sex.

He reached back and tugged his shirt over his head, tossed it aside, then allowed his hand to partially shift as he leaned his upper body back, keeping her pinned to the wall with his hips. But she still didn't fear, even when he extended one razor-sharp claw toward her and set it lightly against her skin. She felt the fabric of her shirt tug, then heard it tear as he sliced through it, leaving it gaping open.

"Good, because I don't want you scared," he told her, using the tip of that claw to tug at the clasp of her bra until it came undone, baring her breasts, her nipples already tight. "I want you more turned on than you've ever been in your life. I want you wild. I want you hot. I want to see you lose all control." Claws receding, he traced the pad of a finger down a nipple. "And most of all? I want you to scream my name when you come."

"Yes," she moaned, grabbing him again and pulling his face down for another kiss. He gave it to her, but pulled one of her legs from around his hips and set her on her feet, only to take a step back. Not far, but she hated the space between them, even as she worked on kicking her shoes off and getting her pants off, frantic to have the cloth out of the way so she could have him. So he could have her.

Smirking, he dealt with his pants, too, though he didn't try to take them off, just opened them enough to free his cock from confinement. That was enough. Neither of them wanted to waste a second.

Her breath caught and her eyes fixed on something that hadn't been there the last time they'd been together. A silver bar that went through the thick head of his shaft. How had she missed that when he'd stripped and shifted the other night? And why was it so hot to think about him having a pierced cock?

His hand wrapped around his shaft and stroked slowly, her gaze following the movement of that bit of jewelry.

"When did you get that?" she asked, voice thick with need.

"Do you really care?" he asked.

She lifted her eyes to meet his and slowly shook her head. "I just want it inside me," she told him, finally getting her pants off and stalking toward him. Her hands slapped against his chest and pushed him back. He complied until his legs hit the side of the couch, but another push from her and he fell back. Climbing over the arm of the couch, she straddled him, hissing in a breath when the underside of his shaft rubbed between her legs. Instinctively, her hips rocked, sliding him over her, causing her eyes to partially close with pleasure.

"Now," he growled, hands gripping her hips and yanking her a few inches upward.

"Now," she agreed, reaching down for his shaft. He growled when she gripped him, his hands tightening, and she stared into his eyes as she positioned him against her then thrust down onto him. The sensation of him pressing into her made her head fall back, and she gasped his name, loving the way it felt. The way he felt. Then he bucked, driving him even deeper, and she let out a low whimper, but he wasn't done. One hand moved to the couch, shoving him partially upright, and he wrapped an arm around her waist, keeping her pressed to him when he twisted. Sitting on the couch rather than sprawled on it, he kept his hold on her and began rocking up into her.

Not content to be a passive participant, Aelia met each movement with her own, lifting up as he pulled back, then shoving down when he arched up. Her arms wound around him, crushing her breasts against his chest, but she craved more contact. Pressing her face against the curve of his throat, she held him as she realized she didn't want to let him go. Not now, and certainly not to death. This man had gotten under her skin in a way no one had in centuries. Maybe ever.

And she was done fighting her draw to him.

Leaning back so she could look into his eyes, she opened her mouth to say something, but he wasn't having any of that. Kissing her to cut off her words, his arm tightened and he shoved them forward until he landed on his knees on the floor.

"Not yet," he told her as he loosened his hold, sliding out of her as he lowered her body until she was on her knees as well.

"But—"

He cut her off again, turning her around and pressing against her back. But she hadn't climaxed yet, and having his cock digging into her ass only reminded her of that fact. Making a low sound, she arched back against him, but he only gripped her hair and bent her forward. All too eager to comply as long as it meant he'd keep going, she did, and when she turned her head to glance back at him, he let her, giving her a hot look that was more beast than man.

She liked it.

One smooth thrust and he'd joined his body with hers again, forcing another sound from her throat. "Whatever you want to say..." He drew back, then slammed in, hard. "Can wait..." Another almost vicious thrust. "Until you come for me." And with that, the slow movements and consideration went out the window. Holding onto her hips, he pounded in again and again, fast, frenzied, and in a way that made her happy she was already on all fours, because her legs would have buckled otherwise.

The man was relentless and seemed to have an endless supply of stamina, because he didn't stop when the first release hit her like a train. Nor did he stop when the pleasure built again and made her lower her upper body to the floor, unable to support herself any longer.

It wasn't until he fucked her to a third orgasm, one that had her weakly whispering his name, that his rhythm faltered and he stopped fighting his own climax. Growling her name, he wrapped an arm around her chest and lifted her up until her back was pressed to him, letting him hold her as he ground into her, coming while she trembled in his arms.

She could do nothing but lean her head back against him and moan.

It only took a minute before his energy disappeared as well, but he managed to control their fall so neither was hurt. Lying on their sides, he kept his arms around her, and made no move to withdraw. She got it. She didn't want this moment to end, either.

For the first time in thousands of years, she wondered if immortality actually had an upside.

CHAPTER 19

They didn't move for a long time, nor did they speak. Whatever Aelia had been about to say, either she'd forgotten about it, or—more likely—she'd rethought it. Aaron wondered whether he should be happy or disappointed about that.

Absently tracing random lines over her belly with the tips of his fingers, he decided not to worry about it too much, not when she was letting him hold her like this. It was as good as the sex, in all honesty. That had been amazing, if entirely too short, but she'd never allowed him this kind of thing before. At least not when he was awake. Which meant he was going to stay quiet and enjoy it for as long as it lasted. And since he'd admitted that he loved her before it all began, he really didn't expect it to last much longer.

She acted like she was going to say something a few times, but he just continued to lazily stroke his fingers over her skin, doing nothing to spook her. Finally, she sighed and shook her head. "I wonder if the ritual can be shared."

He seriously doubted she'd struggled so long with that statement, which made him think her true thoughts had been more personal. But still, he wasn't going to scare her off if she was on the brink of some revelation. Especially if it was a revelation that meant she'd live. "What do you mean?"

She hesitated, then twisted around until they were face to face. Their bodies weren't as close, but he rested his hand on her hip, still wanting the physical connection. "Some things, some spells, only one person can pay whatever price it requires. But I've heard of some rituals or sorcery or whatever where, if multiple people do it together, it splits the load. It's how some powerful rituals can be done by less powerful sorcerers. Instead of needing one super powerful person, you use, say, five semi-powerful people. It adds up to the same burst of power, it just has five sources instead of one."

This might not have been what he wanted to hear her say, but he wasn't unhappy with the idea either, assuming he was following her train of thought correctly. "You mean like this ritual, instead of one person doing it, and the ritual probably killing them, if two people did it, they might both survive? Or at least have a better chance of it?"

"That's the idea. I just don't know if the theory applies to something like this," she admitted. "That's the problem with new sorcery. It's just like science. Until it's tested, you can have an idea of what will happen, but you won't know for sure. There's always an element of chaos to it. Especially since magic doesn't always follow the laws of physics. But it does make sense. Two gods brought back into this world, two sorcerers doing it. It has a balance, and the Lemurians are all about balance. So are the Anunnaki, in a way."

It did make sense, but he couldn't be sure if that was just wishful thinking or the truth. "Then let's find out." She frowned and shook her head slightly, so he explained. "Let's get decent, then see if the

Anunnaki will respond to us, too, or if it's just the gods they pay attention to."

Her expression cleared and she smiled. "All right."

Given what they'd done together, they took a quick bath—he was getting used to bathing in a pool, though part of him really missed showers—before getting dressed. Instead of returning to the living room after that, they went out into Aelia's garden. The moon might still be too dim to provide much light, but it was a nice night, and he thought Aelia needed the fresh air.

"Ananke? Chronos? We would be honored if you would join us again," Aelia called out, her voice respectful. Not that he blamed her. As scary as the gods could be, it was even more terrifying to be in the presence of those powerful enough to create all those gods along with the world they lived in.

As soon as she'd spoken the last word, the two Anunnaki appeared in front of them. Fortunately, neither looked irritated at having been summoned again.

"Thank you both for coming back," she told them, offering a smile and a polite bow of her head.

"Of course," Ananke said, smiling back at them. "It isn't often anyone calls for us anymore. As you know, most just think of us as part of the Greek pantheon, and even then, most don't believe in the gods anymore."

"We absolutely do," Aaron assured them. "Of course, it's kind of hard not to when we've got gods for neighbors."

Ananke laughed softly and inclined her head to him. "That would help, yes. But what can we do for you two?"

"We discussed the ritual, with the others and separately," Aelia began. "I know you said you don't know exactly what will happen if we perform this ritual, but do you know if the price—the sacrifice—could be shared? Aaron and I are both immortal, and we're thinking that maybe, if the two of us perform the ritual together, it would give us a better chance of either not dying or our immortality saving us."

Ananke's smile widened and she nodded. "Yes. If you are both in contact with the object and speak the spell in unison, then the spell will pull from you both equally." The smile dimmed and she sighed softly. "I cannot say if it will absolutely be enough to save you, but it will greatly increase your chances."

"Before you decide either way," Chronos said, his eyes on Aelia, and he waited until she was looking at him before continuing, "you should know that there are much, much worse things than living."

Smiling kindly at her, both he and Chronos disappeared.

"I'm getting a little tired of everyone giving me their opinion," Aelia muttered as she turned and stalked back inside, but Aaron was happy to have the assist. Especially from someone with more clout than...well, anyone else. Ever. In the history of the world.

"We should go find the others, tell them what we learned," he said as he followed her.

"Mind if we walk? I think I need a minute before dealing with anyone else."

"That's fine." Especially since the others were probably at Seth's house, and it was a bit of a walk. They'd taken Tempest's original house, which was up on a cliff. More wind, she'd explained, which made sense for an air elemental. Besides, he could use a few minutes himself. Except his mood got a huge boost when her hand brushed his, then, when he didn't say anything, she linked her fingers with his. About time she started to give in. It might look like a small gesture, but it meant a lot to him. It was progress he wasn't sure she'd ever achieve.

They never got to Seth's house. As they neared the square, he saw what looked like almost every Lemurian sitting where they normally had their dinners. It wasn't hard to figure out what they'd been talking about, since all conversation stopped when they noticed Aaron and Aelia approaching.

"Everything okay?" Seth asked when they got closer.

"It's better," she answered. "We talked to Ananke and Chronos again."

Vazi arched a brow. "You did? I'm surprised they showed up."

It took her a few seconds, then she said, "I think they're lonely."

Sorrow filled his eyes and he nodded. "Yes, I imagine they are."

"What did they say?" Dania asked before looking stunned that she had spoken up in front of so many people. It was a huge step for her, and he was happy she was starting to open up.

Since he wasn't as angry as he had been earlier, he offered her a comforting smile, but let Aelia take the lead on explaining.

"If two people do the ritual in unison, the risk can be split between them. Which means the risk of dying—or staying dead—is less. So we think we should do it," she said, motioning to Aaron.

Tempest frowned. "I can understand why you want to do it, Aelia, but not Aaron." She gave him an apologetic smile. "No offense to you, but if the risk is that great, shouldn't it be someone else immortal? Even if it's not in the same way Aelia is?"

Those who had been in the room when Aaron explained what had happened in Norway all went still. There wasn't really any point in hiding it since they'd all find out at some point. He had never aged like a human, but now he was never going to age again. Which was still a kick in the ass. "That's why I'm going to be the second person," he said, smiling faintly, though he was sure it looked more like a grimace than a smile. It was going to take a while for the events in Norway to really sink in. "As it turns out, Aelia isn't so unique after all."

"What?" she asked, as shocked as he'd been. Honestly, he understood her reaction since Aelia had always been secretive about her condition. "How did that happen?"

"I thought that wasn't possible," Cyrus—a fire elemental who'd only been on the island for a few weeks—mused aloud.

"Long story, and kind of not the point," Aaron pointed out. "Let's just say I've joined the club of having died and come back to life, and it's as unfun as Aelia has told us. And if the two of us do the ritual, that's the best chance we have of getting the gods back without losing anyone."

"And you're both sure you want to do this?" Seth asked.

Aaron glanced at Aelia, but she wouldn't meet his gaze. She also didn't answer immediately, choosing her words carefully. "The world needs the Lemurians. If it isn't us, then people will die attempting it. How would that make us any better than Zeus?" she asked, her gaze flicking to Dania, who inclined her head in return.

He cocked his head, a little surprised by her answer, but he gave her hand a squeeze. "If she's doing it, I'm doing it," he told Seth. "Like she said, it's the best chance we have of everyone coming out of this alive."

Seth and Vazi looked at each other and seemed to have a silent conversation, before Vazi nodded and looked back at them. "If you're certain, then I thank you."

"Before this whole thing is decided on, I have a question." It came from Veronica, another of the new arrivals. She and her husband, Ezra, had brought their daughter Kelly to the island right before Tempest had given birth. They were starting the first new farm on Lemuria, so had been busy, not really giving him the chance to get to know them well.

"Ask away," Seth told her.

"If more of the Lemurian gods are back, are people like us still going to be welcome here?" she asked, moving closer to her daughter.

"Of course," Vazi said immediately. "You would have been welcome when they were all awake. Elementals and sirens are our children, after all. Besides, the Lemurians—other than the gods—are all gone aside from those of you who live here now. We need you as much as we need the gods. And it will take years to bring them all back."

Veronica relaxed and smiled at him, nodding as she wrapped her arm around Kelly's shoulders. "Thank you."

Cyrus called out, "If we're doing Q and A, then do we know what state their minds are going to be in after so long?"

"If we're using me as a baseline? Then they'll be a little disoriented, but they should be just as sane as they were when they went...wherever they are. It took me a minute to realize the island was empty, and I needed the others to catch me up, but I was perfectly sane." Seth snorted and Vazi gave him a dirty look. Then Tempest let out a little laugh, and he arched a brow at her. "You too?"

"You might have been sane—mostly—but you were also a grump," she told him without any trace of apology.

He just harrumphed and turned his back on them. "Since it does affect everyone," he called, ensuring everyone could hear him, "then I want to know if anyone has any objections to our doing this. The first pair of gods we intend to bring back are Grovek and Telia, the god of wisdom and goddess of insanity." He turned and jabbed a finger in Seth's direction. "Not a word," he warned, even as Seth burst out laughing. Vazi's eyes narrowed, then Seth choked, the laughter cutting off. After the immediate shock passed, he glared back at Vazi, and the ground rumbled beneath their feet.

"Vazi," Tempest warned.

He huffed. "Fine." Seth sucked in a breath, but since his wife laid her hand on his arm, he said nothing. "After that," Vazi said pointedly, looking back to the other Lemurians, "we've been asked to bring back Ocoina and Inanis, the goddesses of birth and death. Well, Ocoina is the goddess of birth and rebirth, but you get the picture. Then we'll work on bringing back both my and Seth's counterparts, since we're currently out of balance."

There were murmured conversations between friends and families, but Aaron remained where he was, content to wait and hold Aelia's hand. Aelia was going to do everything in her power to see this ritual done, no matter what the majority said, and he had a feeling Vazi knew that. But after everyone had weighed in, every Lemurian had agreed.

"This ritual has to be done on a half moon," Kara said, her phone in her hand. "Which is in six days." She glanced up and smiled at Aelia. "Are you going to have this ready by then?"

Aelia's lips hinted at a smile as she nodded. "We're starting with Grovek," she answered. "Finding something that holds his essence won't be a problem. We'll be ready."

Aaron agreed. It should be easy since the entirety of Sozu had to hold parts of him. They could pry a stone out of a wall and it would probably work. Not that Aelia would allow them to use anything that basic, he was sure. Better to go for something obviously personal than something just created by the guy.

"Sozu?" Vazi asked her, his thoughts clearly mirroring Aaron's.

"Yeah," she agreed.

"Do you need a spring, or did he give you some secret way of getting in?"

She smiled. "I have my ways, yes."

The god hesitated a moment. "I want to go with you. I was a little...distracted...the last time I was there." The grumpiness Tempest had mentioned was gone, replaced by a longing Aaron could understand.

"I'd like to go, too," Seth said.

"Maybe you guys should wait until morning to get started," Kara said, her eyes fixed on Aelia's face. "It's already late, and they've had a long day. Especially since Aaron died not that long ago."

He could have kissed her. Dying had taken a lot out of him, then he'd exerted himself further with Aelia. Not that he regretted it.

Vazi's voice couldn't have been more reluctant when he said, "Fine," but at least he agreed.

That seemed to be the cue for everyone to start heading home. Before Seth left, he walked over, waiting until most of the others were gone. "How are your nightmares?" he asked Aelia quietly. "Did you have any last night?"

She blinked in surprise, then gave her head a slow shake. "Actually, no. Olivia is a miracle worker."

"It's only a temporary measure," he cautioned. "She can't focus every night on someone else's dreams. Will you let me talk to the Ekklesia?"

She scoffed and shrugged. "You can try, but they aren't going to stop until I'm dead, crazy, or they've gotten what they want. And since I'm not giving them a single fact about Lemuria, the last option is out."

"They will if they learn there's a geas preventing you from speaking of Lemuria."

"But there isn't any geas," Aaron argued. "Don't they have ways of verifying that? I mean, they're not gods, but they're pretty damn resourceful. And for all we know, they're friendly with gods. I mean, we are, so why can't they be, too?"

"So we make it truth," Seth said casually. "It's not like she's going to betray us either way, and if it's worded right, it shouldn't affect any day-to-day business."

"And how are we going to do that?" Aelia asked.

"We do have a very nice goddess of witchcraft as a friend, and she knows quite a bit about that sort of thing," he pointed out. "Besides, if the geas doesn't work, I'll just send Vazi after them. I won't let him kill them, but I think he can be persuasive...in a scary way."

Aelia was silent for a moment, but clearly she was praying to the goddess, who appeared right away. "Don't tell me you've already tried to bring the Lemurians back," she said in lieu of a greeting.

"No, though we've figured out how," Seth answered. "We've got a more immediate issue we're trying to deal with that we hope you can help with."

"You know I'm always happy to help where I can. What do you need?"

"Can you put a geas on Aelia? One to prevent her from talking about Lemuria to the Ekklesia or anyone working for them?"

It was almost amusing to see the confusion on the goddess's face, but Aaron took pity on her. "They've been harassing her dreams. We want to give them a reason to back off without killing them all." Though if it didn't work, he'd go with Vazi to 'chat' with the Ekklesia.

"And you're all right with this?" Hecate asked Aelia.

Aelia's answer sounded as tired as she must feel. "I'm willing to do anything if it means I get to sleep at night. Besides, Seth said it best. I'm not going to give them what they want, so having magic preventing it won't be a hardship to me."

Hecate nodded and offered a hand. Aelia took it, and both women closed their eyes. Aaron wasn't one of the rare shifters who could smell magic, but he swore he could see it, weaving itself between the two women, like snakes coiling back and forth down their arms. After less than a minute, Hecate released Aelia. "It's done. I hope it helps."

"Me too. Thank you, Hecate."

"Of course." She turned to Seth. "Am I correct in assuming you're going to talk to them now?"

"Yep."

Smiling, she said, "I'd like to come with you."

"Probably a good idea. If they piss me off, I might collapse their secret hideout. On accident, of course."

The two gods disappeared and were almost immediately replaced by Kara and Tempest, the latter holding Katrina.

"Okay, we're kidnapping Aelia," Kara told Aaron. "No guys allowed. Shoo," she said, waving both hands at him.

His lips twitched, but he had no problem bailing so she could get some girl time. True, he wouldn't have minded going back to her place and picking up where they'd left off, but he was honestly still exhausted and more than a little worried about her mental state. Kara was perpetually upbeat, and Tempest level-headed, so they should be good for her. And the baby was pretty damn cute, too.

"Sure thing," he told them before looking at Aelia. "Come by my place when you're done?"

She hesitated for a moment, then shook her head. "Not tonight. I will tomorrow, after Sozu."

Not what he wanted to hear, but it made sense that she'd need a little time. It seemed like everyone else had known how he'd felt about her, but it had genuinely looked like a surprise to her. And maybe not an entirely welcome one. So he'd give her the time, the chance to relax and talk it out with her friends. It didn't stop him from squeezing her hand and kissing her cheek, though. "All right," he agreed. "But what I said isn't going away," he added in a quiet voice that was for her alone.

"I know," she whispered in return.

"Night," he told them all before leaving to head to his house, alone. It was one of the hardest things he'd ever done, but as they said, this wasn't a sprint, it was a marathon. He wanted more than just random nights of sex. He wanted forever.

CHAPTER 20

Aelia watched Aaron go, conflict bubbling in her belly, but she knew if she'd accepted his offer, she'd just have fallen into bed with him again. Maybe more than just fall into bed. She needed to think about everything that had happened in the last twenty-four hours before she made a decision about any of it. Except the ritual. She was a hundred percent in on that, but the rest? It was all so much, and it all felt so permanent. It was also a hell of a lot of pressure. There was no way she was going to let herself make a snap decision.

"So where are you kidnapping me to?" she asked Kara and Tempest, hoping she could distract herself, at least for a little while.

"Your house," Kara answered, hooking her arm around Aelia's. "Sounds like we've got a metric shit ton to talk about."

"You have no idea," she muttered.

"Ah, but we do!" Kara replied cheerfully, starting to tug her in the direction of her house, Tempest and the baby settling into step on her other side. "I mean, I was there in Norway. I *saw* Aaron die and come back to life. I saw the shit with his brother. I heard all about the ritual. And girl, if you don't know that you have I-just-had-sex eyes, then you don't know how to look in a mirror."

"I have what eyes?" Aelia asked, startled.

"You obviously took a bath, so mussed hair didn't give you away, but your eyes have that dreamy quality to them that says you were well satisfied," Tempest answered. "It's the same look mine get after Seth gets a hold of me," she added, smiling smugly.

"Well...gods. I didn't know it would be that obvious."

"Aelia? I love you, and you're normally a freakin' genius, but it sounds like you were literally the only person in the room who didn't know you and Aaron were going to end up naked when he told us to leave," Kara said, shaking her head sadly.

"Considering that just before you left I was breaking up a shouting match between him and Vazi? No, I didn't know."

Kara paused, pulling her to a stop as well, and gave her a funny look. "You've lived how long, and you don't know that when a guy's temper gets heated like that, it's going to lead to either fighting or fucking?" she asked. "And since he was alone with you, fighting was definitely *not* going to happen."

"Aaron's not normally that hotheaded, though," Aelia argued as she started walking again. "Yes, he's sarcastic, and will absolutely give someone a verbal lashing—"

"And is a major, major flirt," Tempest interjected.

"Also true," Aelia allowed, "but I've never seen him fight when it wasn't something important. Like when that cetus attacked us."

"Do you really think you're not important to him?" Kara asked, her voice surprisingly somber.

Her brow furrowed as she tried to figure out how to answer that. "I didn't mean that kind of important...but after you left, he..." She sighed and shifted one shoulder in a shrug. "He did tell me he loved me," she admitted, surprised that her voice sounded both resigned and pleased. She didn't know she could express both emotions at the same time.

She was further surprised when there wasn't a squeal or other exclamation from Kara. Instead, the woman was just grinning. Though after a few seconds of staring, she asked, "What?"

"I expected more of a reaction," Aelia admitted.

"It's not exactly news," Tempest told her. "He's been in love with you for a while."

"Basically everyone knows. Even the new people," Kara added.

"I didn't," Aelia grumbled, and seriously hoped that didn't mean they'd all been talking about her. Unfortunately, that was almost certainly what it meant.

"I think you did, you just didn't want to admit it," Tempest said, shifting Katrina in her arms so she could open Aelia's door.

"Which brings me to my big question," Kara said as they walked inside and found seats. "Why didn't you want to admit it? I mean, he's hot, he turns into a big, powerful tiger, and he'll go toe to toe with one of the most powerful gods in existence for you. If it were me, I'd have jumped him back when we first started picking out houses. Maybe sooner." Comfortable in Aelia's house, she took her shoes off and drew her legs beneath her, her elbow on the arm of the chair, her chin resting on her hand.

"I have to admit to wondering the same," Tempest told her, shifting Katrina to lay against her chest, her tiny head resting on Tempest's shoulder. The baby hadn't stirred once since Aelia had joined them. It was late, but Katrina was also just a good baby.

How much to tell these two? Aelia knew they were genuinely concerned for her, and she appreciated it. She knew they thought of her as a friend, and that scared her almost as much as Aaron's confession had. Even she couldn't fully explain it. When Kara had first reached out to her claiming to have a Lemurian, it had been the first time in far too long that she had felt anything resembling true happiness. Searching for, then locating Lemuria had added to that. For a while, she'd been able to forget about her past. Right up until she'd started getting close to these people. But the fact was that she *had* gotten close to them. Not just Aaron, but these two women and everyone else on the island.

Dammit.

"Actually, we jumped each other back when we first started picking out houses," she admitted, unable to prevent a faint smile from curling the corner of her lips.

"You bitch!" Kara exclaimed, which made Katrina stir and make a noise, so she quickly lowered her tone. "I can't believe you kept that from us," she continued in what a generous person might call a whisper.

"I'm a private person," Aelia explained, shrugging.

"And we understand that," Tempest said, gently patting Katrina's back to calm her down. "We're just trying to figure out why you're so unhappy lately. We've all seen it, we just weren't sure why or how to help."

It was now or never, and though it might be smarter to close up, she decided to let them in. At this point, what did she have to lose? "Short version? Depression."

Both women's faces showed sympathy, and it was in Kara's voice when she spoke next. "And what's the long story?"

"Immortality has the severe drawback of losing everyone I care about. Friends," she said, gesturing to both Kara and Tempest. "Family. I've been married, had lovers, had children and grandchildren. I've outlived them all, human and Arcane both. It's hard. So much harder to deal with than dying."

"And losing just one person can absolutely send a person into depression, much less multiple people," Kara said, nodding understandingly. "I can also see how it would make you hesitate to jump Aaron, and why you might be conflicted about him loving you. If you let yourself love him back, it means you can be hurt if you lose him."

That statement reminded Aelia that Kara wasn't just a fun-loving halfling, but a smart, capable woman. "It's also why I tried not to like the rest of you."

"Except some of us are long-lived. Maybe not truly immortal like you, but we can't die of old age," Tempest pointed out with a little smile. "And Aaron is now as impossible to kill as you are. You can't lose him. Unless you choose to."

"Nothing in life is certain," she murmured, remembering what the Anunnaki had said when asked about the ritual. "Can we talk about something other than Aaron, though?"

"Of course. How about I go grab some wine and whatever snacks you've got in your kitchen, and we just chat and get a little drunk?" Kara grinned at Tempest. "Sorry, you'll have to stick to snacks."

"I'd like that," Aelia decided. She'd never had a proper girl's night, and after the last few weeks, she could use a bit of relaxation.

"Be right back!" Kara hopped up and hurried toward the kitchen.

"I wish you'd felt comfortable talking to us about all this," Tempest said once they were alone. "I get why you didn't, but I'm technically even older than you are—even if I missed a few hundred decades—and I'm extremely well-protected. My husband's a god, my best friend's a god, and I think Hecate has a soft spot for me. And if I'm in danger, I can turn into air. It's not exactly easy to harm the air."

"No, I guess it isn't," Aelia agreed. "But when I first came to Lemuria—before it was destroyed—it was with a Lemurian witch. She should have been difficult to kill, too."

"Selana," Tempest said, nodding understandingly. "Except that was a unique circumstance. I can guarantee that if you and Aaron are able to bring the entire pantheon back, they'll be more on guard for...outside influence. And from what I'm told, few of the gods today have the same level of power they did back then. They don't have the worship they once did. When the Lemurians are back, they'll be as strong as they were the day they disappeared."

"That's true," she realized. "A few of the pantheons have a sort of worship again because of books and movies featuring versions of them, but I don't think it's quite the same. People might love the depictions of Zeus or Loki they see on screen, but it's not the same as worshiping the actual god."

"No, I don't imagine it is. But I have to wonder if there's something more going on."

Aelia frowned, but Kara returned then with a tray. Two glasses and a bottle of red wine, a glass of water, and white cheddar popcorn that had been dumped into a big bowl.

"Your snacks suck," Kara told Aelia, setting the tray on the coffee table. "Don't you ever just binge junk food like a normal person? This popcorn was literally all I found. You didn't even have cheese and crackers!"

"I don't really have people over, and...actually, that's all I've got. Just no guests to stock up for."

"I'll be fixing that. I've got some chips, chocolate, and ice cream at my place," Kara said as she poured wine into the glasses and handed her one. Tempest got the water, and Kara took the popcorn. "Now, what were you two talking about?"

"Tempest was just saying she thought there was something more going on, and I was about to ask her what she meant."

"I've spoken to several people since Seth woke me. Not just Lemurians, but the people who came here for our welcome home party," she began, shrugging and reaching across for a handful of popcorn. "Maybe it's just me, but it sounds like a lot of odd things have happened in the last few years."

"What do you mean?" Kara asked, frowning. "I mean, finding Lemuria is definitely odd, but that's just because there was no way for anyone to find it until Seth found you. We had to have a Lemurian to find it, and you were the last one."

"Actually, that wasn't true," Aelia corrected.

"What?" Tempest asked, her eyes widening.

"There was another immortal before me. He's the one who made Aaron immortal. Passed it from himself to Aaron, if you want to get specific. But he was Lemurian."

"What was his name?"

"Navid."

Her brow furrowed and she shook her head slowly. "I remember hearing about a man called Navid, but he disappeared a few years before Lemuria sank. Not unusual, since we were exploring the world, just like every other group at the time."

"Apparently he disappeared because he became immortal. Eventually...I think he went insane. But can we get back to the odd things?"

she asked, not wanting to think about the man or the repercussions from her quest to find him.

"Of course," she agreed, though she still looked disturbed. "Lemuria is one of them, because the odds of anyone finding me weren't exactly good. And the wolf and demoness couple? Samara and Wade? They met because there was a portal from a demon dimension that opened. It allowed a powerful demon to come to Earth with the intention of enslaving us. Julian and his wife just happened to discover the pieces of an ancient relic? That doesn't sound likely. And then the Miasma, a substance that everyone had forgotten about, was infecting people inside the Athenaeum? It just sounds like a lot in a very short period of time. Now, maybe it is all just coincidence, that events aligned to allow them all to happen at once, but could it be more?"

"When you put it that way, it sounds really freakin' bad," Kara admitted. "But like you said, it could just be coincidence? I don't know how they could be related. One or two, maybe. But all of them? Just doesn't make sense."

"And I could be completely wrong," Tempest agreed easily. "I just think we should be paying attention to the rest of the world. Harder for us to do since we don't leave Lemuria often, but the rest of you have connections with people in other countries."

"Have you told Seth about your theory?" Aelia asked. "As a god, it would be easier for him to listen for other unusual occurrences. And I know he has a lot of connections thanks to his former job."

"Don't call it former," Tempest warned, rolling her eyes. "Don't get me wrong, he loves rebuilding Lemuria, and is getting a kick out of being a god, but he really misses his old work. And it'll be awhile before he really has time for it. He's a little jealous that Aaron's been able to fit in a few expeditions. But no, I haven't mentioned it to him yet. We've both been concerned about you." She gave Aelia a sheepish smile. "He told me about the nightmares."

Aelia wasn't really surprised, so just shrugged. "Husbands and wives share most things. But Olivia—a woman from the Athenaeum—made sure I didn't have any last night. I'll need to figure out how to repay her for that."

"I wish you'd mentioned it sooner, Aelia," Kara said before sipping at her wine. "I don't know if it would have worked, but I could have tried to put a ward around your mind. Might have kept someone from fucking with your dreams. And I know Seth or Vazi would have done something."

"That's what I was worried about," Aelia admitted.

"Mmm. Vazi can be a little act first, think later," Tempest agreed. "But he is the god of the sky. When has the wind ever been constant? People talk about water being changeable, but wind is just as unstable. That said, don't you remember how the gods treated the Lemurians?"

Aelia nodded. "More like children and friends than subjects."

"Exactly. And Vazi wasn't any different. It's why we were friends even back then. If you'd gone to him, explained, and asked him not to attack the Ekklesia, he would have complained, but he would have listened."

Now she felt ashamed, because Tempest was right. She hadn't given him enough credit. Hell, she hadn't given anyone enough credit. Starting with Vazi and ending with Aaron. It always ended with Aaron, it seemed. "I'll need to apologize to him, too."

Kara shook her head. "Nah. I think we—and by that I mean the first of us—know you've had a rough time of it. And Vazi might not know about the depression, but he likes you. I also think he thinks of you as an honorary Lemurian—the real kind—since you were actually here back then."

"I actually thought for a while that you and he might end up together," Tempest said with a quick grin. "Obviously it's not going to happen, but he did like you from the start."

Aelia smiled, but shook her head. "I can't deny he's an attractive man—gorgeous, even—and I do like him, but I can't say I was ever drawn to him like that."

"Probably because you met Aaron first?" Kara asked, grinning impishly.

"Oh, shut up," Aelia said, but the words were spoken with a laugh.

"See? She laughed. That means I'm right," Kara said smugly, leaning back in her seat and lifting her wine in a toast.

Tempest smiled and shook her head. "As much as I'm enjoying this and think we should make this a regular thing, I really should get Katrina to bed. She's sleeping now, but if she's not in her bed soon, she's going to wake up and *not* go back to sleep."

Aelia was actually disappointed, but she understood and nodded. Babies took priority. "Of course. Thanks for coming over, though."

"Anytime," Tempest assured her, getting to her feet. "But make sure you let me—or someone—know if you need anything else? Even if it's just to talk for a little bit."

"I will."

"I'd like a promise. I know you take those seriously."

She did, but she wasn't sure she liked being known so well. Except…it was kind of nice. "I promise."

"Good." She walked over and, after shifting Katrina, bent down to give Aelia a one-armed hug. "Good night," she offered to them both before she left.

"Are you leaving too?" Aelia asked Kara.

"Nope," she said, shaking her head. "If you don't kick me out, I'm staying the night. I'm still worried about you, even if Olivia's watching your dreams."

Yes, it was nice, being cared about. And honestly, the trouble came when she cared about others. Too late to stop that now. "No, I'm not kicking you out." She picked up her wine and drank. "How about we drink too much wine, talk, and just have a little fun until we're so drunk we pass out?"

Kara laughed and again toasted with her glass. "Sounds like a plan!" She drained the rest of her wine and reached for the bottle. "About time you cut loose."

That was something Aelia couldn't argue with.

CHAPTER 21

W hile Aelia was being comforted and Aaron was stewing, Seth and Hecate went to complete their task. Though Seth wanted to go straight to the Ekklesia and leave Vazi out of it, he knew the other god had a soft spot for Aelia. Then again, he had a soft spot for everyone who had been on Lemuria at its height. And Seth wouldn't hear the end of it if he went with Hecate and left Vazi behind. And he had a feeling Vazi would be able to hold a grudge for years.

Transporting both him and Hecate outside of the Ekklesia's base in Italy, he sighed. "Give me a minute. Need to let Vazi know what we're doing."

She arched one dark brow. "Is that wise?"

"Probably not," he admitted, "but I don't want to have him rag on me about it for the next century."

She smiled and nodded. "That's fair. He can be rather vindictive."

"Tell me about it," Seth muttered before he mentally summoned his fellow Lemurian.

"You couldn't have told me you were doing this before you left Lemuria?" Vazi asked dryly when he appeared.

"Just be glad I called you at all." He narrowed his eyes. "No killing them all. The Arcane need them."

"But killing one or two is acceptable?" Vazi asked, brightening marginally.

Seth only rolled his eyes. "Remember, we just want to keep them from going after Aelia. She has a geas on her now—and she agreed to it, before you start bitching—so we can use that."

"And I'm going in disguise," Hecate told them. "It's unlikely a certain someone keeps tabs on his entire pantheon at all times—there are just too many of us—but better safe than sorry. And some of the Ekklesia are Greek worshipers."

"Whatever you need to do."

She nodded and her form shifted. Her dress turned into charcoal slacks and a deep green shirt. Inky black hair turned curly auburn, and her skin darkened just a little. No one would look at her and mistake her for the goddess of witchcraft, not right now.

When she nodded that she was ready, Seth looked at the castle the Ekklesia had claimed a good thousand years ago. Inside he could sense the eleven councilors that made up what most called the ruling body of the Arcane, though it wasn't really true. They didn't rule in any sense of the word. They had exactly two roles; hide the Arcane from humanity as a whole, and judge if someone had committed a crime so heinous that they were to be imprisoned in the magical prisons the Arcane had been using for about as long as Lemurians had been missing from the earth.

Clearly, they'd forgotten their purpose.

Taking them inside, they appeared in a large room. There was a huge stone fireplace at one end, big enough for Seth to walk right into, and several windows looking out over the sea, but it was the round wooden table that dominated the room. The eleven councilors sat around it, a mixture of men and women, each of them a different race.

The first to spot them—a woman that Seth sensed was a shifter—half rose from her chair. "How did you get in here?" she demanded, her tone both shocked and angry.

A gust of wind knocked her back into her chair as the rest of the Ekklesia looked at them. "Do you not recognize gods when you see them?" Vazi drawled, sounding way more relaxed than Seth knew he was. If there was one thing Vazi hated—aside from Zeus—it was people fucking with those he'd decided to protect. Which meant every person on Lemuria, or who had helped the Lemurians.

The Ekklesia glanced amongst themselves, and he was certain there was telepathic conversation going on, before a man—vampire, this time—spoke, though he didn't dare rise from his chair. "We recognize your divinity, but not your identities. Who are you?"

Since Vazi had gotten the first attack, however minor, Seth took this one, letting the earth beneath them rumble. Before he could speak, Hecate did, but he thought that worked in their favor. Keep the councilors guessing.

"You should know better than to question gods, no matter their identity," she warned in a voice frostier than he'd heard from her before.

"Might we ask what it is you wish from the Ekklesia?" a woman—gargoyle, he thought—asked.

"That you can ask," Seth said, strolling toward the table and beginning to circle it. He kept a light vibration moving through the stone floor beneath their feet, just to keep them off balance. It was the least they deserved for what they'd done to a woman who helped basically anyone who needed it. "We're here because it has come to our attention that you have been...trying to persuade someone into giving you information."

"Information that you neither need nor are entitled to," Vazi picked up, and he followed Seth's lead, letting a breeze flow around the Ekklesia. Calm for now, just something to gently move through hair and over clothing, but it was a promise that there could be more.

"What information do you refer to?" the vampire asked.

"That isn't the important question," Hecate said, folding her arms over her chest. "You should be asking who that someone is."

"They really should, shouldn't they?" Seth said absently, pausing behind the elemental councilor. "But since they didn't, I'll help them out." He leaned in between two councilors and noted they went dead still. Okay, it was kind of fun being a god. "You need to leave Aelia alone," he said, slowly letting his gaze move around the table, meeting the eyes of each one.

A dark-haired woman rose, despite the implied warning. This had to be the jinn, since it was the one represented race he'd never encountered before. It was also the race he knew the least about. "We know the woman you speak of, and she has been a...private contractor...for many years. It is her duty to give us information when we ask."

She was bold, he'd give her that. He might even appreciate it if it wasn't his friend's sanity on the line.

"Is it also her duty to be tortured nightly by one of your min-ions?" Vazi asked darkly, the breeze kicking up.

"We have the right to punish our employees however we see fit," she said, lifting her chin.

In a blink, Vazi was in front of her, lifting her off her feet without laying a finger on her. "She's not your employee, and you will cease all contact with her—physical, mental, magical, or through any of your other employees."

To her credit, the jinn remained calm despite Vazi's treatment, but Seth doubted this was going anywhere. Time to switch tactics.

"He's correct. She's not your employee." He straightened and resumed his walk around the table, doing nothing to curb Vazi's actions. "She's also completely useless to you now."

"What do you mean, useless?" the witch councilor asked, his brow furrowed.

"Simple. We've put a geas on her that prevents her from telling you absolutely anything." A small fib, but he didn't feel the least bit of remorse. "So unless you want my friend to kill you all for being sadistic fucks, you're going to leave her alone."

"And you're going to start leaving her alone right now," Vazi warned.

Seth almost missed it, and it was only his new divine senses that allowed him to catch the whisper. "Do you think she's the only one with a geas?"

He fought not to look at the one who had spoken, because he was sure none of them were supposed to hear it. "Do we have your agreement?" he asked, letting the ground rumble harder.

There was another of those exchanged looks and silent conversation. "I suppose there is nothing to be gained by pressing her for more information," the jinn said, still calm though her feet were a good six feet off the floor.

"And the rest of you agree?" Vazi asked.

They all gave their assent, though none of them sounded particularly pleased about it.

The jinn was lowered back into her chair. "If she has even one more nightmare that can be traced back to you. I will ignore the fact that the Ekklesia is supposed to be important and kill all of you. Am I understood?"

Another round of assent came from the eleven councilors.

"Good," Seth said, moving back to Hecate's side. "Don't make us come back."

He took them all back to Lemuria, frowning as soon as they were out of sight of the council.

Hecate resumed her normal appearance and smiled. "I have to say, it's been a while since I've seen you work, Vazi. Or seen a group like that put in their place."

"It was entertaining," Vazi admitted. "You know the Ekklesia better than I do. Do you think they'll keep their word?"

"I do, actually," she confirmed with a nod. "You took away the one thing they were hoping for. They have absolutely nothing to gain by tormenting her further, and everything to lose if they ignore your warning."

"I hope you're right," Seth murmured. "I know she was able to sleep last night, so she looks a little better than she has, but she still looks like crap. And do *not* tell her I said that."

"She did look tired," Hecate admitted. "I've seen her in rough shape before, but even without a wound she looks like she's suffered more than then."

"Physical wounds are sometimes easier to heal from than mental ones," Vazi said. "And I do hope they listen, but I wasn't kidding.

They keep using her dreams to cause her pain, and I will make sure the Arcane are in need of eleven new councilors. A fresh start might be a good thing in any case if they've become so corrupt."

"Or they could be replaced by people even worse than they are," Seth pointed out.

"Which is one of the reasons why I didn't just suffocate everyone in that room," he said on a sigh. "They're at least a known evil. I just wish we knew what else they were up to, because there is no way that poking at Aelia for information on Lemuria is all they're doing."

"Hell, it's probably not even the worst thing they're doing."

"The gods mostly stay out of the Ekklesia's affairs, but I can do some digging—discreetly, of course—and see if I can learn anything useful," Hecate offered.

Vazi smiled at her. It was a tiny smile, but it was the best he normally got. "You are a very good friend, Hecate. I know Aelia was instrumental in getting Tempest and Seth to Lemuria, but from what they have told me, you were as well."

Hecate shook her head. "I didn't do that much."

Seth scoffed and shook his head. "You healed me and Tempest, magically taught her English so we could communicate, and convinced Aaron to help us. You definitely helped, so don't sell yourself short."

She smiled. "I may be Greek by birth, but I've always loved your people." The smile disappeared. "I mourned when they disappeared. Helping the last Lemurian reclaim her home was the least I could do."

"As far as I am concerned, you will always be a friend to the Lemurians, and welcome here," Vazi told her. Something he knew the god didn't say lightly. Yes, there were a few gods who had the ability to visit Lemuria—Rhea, of course, and Hephaestus—but Vazi was very particular about who had the ability to visit his land. Seth wasn't much better, not after the rough time they'd had finding it.

"I appreciate it, and as far as *I* am concerned, the ability to come here when I like is repayment enough." She sighed. "But I should probably leave. I love visiting, but I don't want to draw any further attention to you and your people. I'll let you know when I know something more."

She disappeared and Seth looked back to Vazi. "Did you hear that whisper after I told them about the geas?"

Vazi's expression darkened. "I did, and I don't like what it could mean."

"Neither do I." But it was, unfortunately, a problem for another day.

CHAPTER 22

Like all Lemurian gods, Vazi had spent his fair share of time on Lemuria. Not in disguise or meddling like other pantheons had with their worshipers, but actually spending time with his people. Since returning a year before, he'd spent even more of his time on the island. Thelaria was empty now but for him, and he found he disliked feeling lonely, so he chose to be around the new Lemurians. It wasn't so bad, really. Tempest was a true Lemurian, as was her daughter, and most of those who had moved to the newly rediscovered land had Lemurian blood. And the only other Lemurian gods chose to live on Lemuria rather than Thelaria, which gave him another reason to visit.

But today he was concerned about the single human who lived among them. Not only could she be considered a Lemurian as one of the few people still alive who knew and understood the Lemuria of old, but she had been instrumental in the land being inhabited again. While he preferred to spend his time with true Lemurians—gods or otherwise—she had become one of his favorite people. So, as much as he wanted the other gods back, he was having doubts. That was why he brought himself to Seth's front door this morning.

He didn't knock. There was no need. Instead, he sent a thought to the other god. It was more efficient than what the others had. Doorbells, they called them. Inefficient things, really.

Seth opened the door looking grumpy, his hair rumpled, and Vazi deduced that he'd woken the man up. Too bad. There was a lot to be done that day, and this conversation needed to come first.

"What in the hell do you want that can't wait?" Seth asked, leaning against the door frame and yawning.

"We need to talk about this ritual."

Seth frowned and scrubbed a hand over his face, trying to wake up. "What about it?"

"You know that no one wants the other gods back more than I, but…I don't know if we should let Aelia and Aaron do the ritual."

Seth's frown deepened, and he shook his head. "Okay, I'm still waking up, but I thought we'd decided on this last night. If they do the ritual together, they're less likely to die. And if they do die, they're both immortal now. Their chances of coming back are good."

Vazi shook his head, frustrated with the situation. "Chances. Less likely. There's no certainty there, and the Anunnaki couldn't offer us any."

"So what do you want to do? Shelve the idea of bringing the other gods back?" Seth asked, sounding confused.

"No, but I think we can do better than having two of our people risk their lives."

Rubbing a hand over his face again, Seth straightened. "Okay, first, it sounds like no one knows Grovek like Aelia, so she's most likely to be able to find an object to use to bring him back. And honestly, even if she hadn't requested him in particular, I would have. Having the god of wisdom helping out can only be a good thing with all the shit going on."

"If we can get him out of his library," Vazi grumbled, folding his arms over his chest.

"I doubt that'll be a problem, based on what I've heard of most of the other gods. Second, if you're thinking of doing it yourself, remember the Anunnaki said you'd probably die, too. Hell, I think you have worse odds than Aelia alone, much less her and Aaron together. And," he continued when Vazi started to say something, "what do you think would happen if you did do the ritual, it failed, but it killed you anyway? Instead of going from three gods to five, we'd drop to two. And look at the two! I've got a decent control over my powers, but I don't know most of our history. And I've never gone head to head against another god. Well, not as equals, anyway. And not only that, but what if it comes to a fight between us and another pantheon? Dania and I won't stand a chance alone."

"But we're supposed to protect our people, not sacrifice them for our own ends!" Vazi snapped. "We're not the Greeks or Aztecs, who sacrifice their own for an extra iota of power. We created them and loved them. We *still* love them. And the Greeks? Their first attempt at creating a person with power resulted in them literally splitting the entire race in half. I will not be like that."

"Neither will I," Seth agreed easily, though there was a question in his eyes. "But we also can't take the choice away from them. Aelia and Aaron volunteered. Aelia was extremely adamant about it, in fact. Do I like the idea that they might die? Fuck no. But I have to believe they'll be okay if we let them do what they have chosen to do. And

Vazi? They are probably the only people on the entire planet who are literally immortal. Except maybe the Anunnaki."

Vazi sighed and took a step back, feeling defeated. "I know, but I don't have to like it."

"Neither do I. Unfortunately, we all sometimes have to do things we don't like."

"You should tell Tempest goodbye or whatever you need to do, so we can go find Aelia. If she's going to go through with this, I'm going to make sure she has the best chance of surviving that we can give her. Give them."

"How?"

"Helping her find the right object. She might know him better than I did, but I don't know if she can sense his essence in an item. I can."

Seth nodded. "I'll meet you at her house in ten," he promised.

"Thank you," Vazi said, before disappearing into the air to head for Aelia's house.

Though Aelia had told him flat out that she wasn't going to come by, it still bothered him that she'd followed through with that. Not just because she'd basically left him on read after he had told her he loved her, but because he was worried that the time alone might have planted more doubts in her mind. He knew her initial reason for wanting Grovek back was to try to reverse her immortality, and he still wasn't sure how to change her mind. There was a chance he already had, but he wasn't sure he could risk everything on a chance.

How in the hell did he save the woman he loved? To give her a reason not to die, but to live?

That precise question had kept him from sleeping more than an hour or so the night before, and was why, not long after dawn, he was heading to Aelia's house. Vazi and Seth had beaten him there, and were already knocking on her front door. "Were you two worried, too, or just eager to get started?" he asked, unable to prevent the bitterness from seeping into his voice.

"Worried," they answered in unison. He wasn't sure that made him feel any better, though.

The door opened, but it wasn't a gorgeous blonde on the other side. It was an impulsive brunette.

"Hi guys," Kara answered on a yawn. "Aelia's in the bath, but come on in," she said, stepping back and pulling the door with her. "You hungry?" All of them answered in the negative as they filed into the house. She just shrugged. "I'm still going to bring coffee. It's too freakin' early to do anything without coffee."

"Coffee I'll take," Seth told her.

Kara had brought out cups for everyone—including Aelia—by the time Aelia joined them. She didn't look surprised to see three men in her living room, just took her coffee and gulped it down while she surreptitiously watched Aaron over the rim. He noticed, but said nothing. That could wait until they were alone.

"Are you still wanting to go find Grovek's item today?" she asked.

Instead of answering, Vazi asked his own question. "Are you still certain you want to do this?"

Her gaze flicked to Aaron, then remained there as she nodded. "I do, as long as Aaron's still willing."

He almost smiled. Maybe he'd started to get through to her. If she only wanted to go through with the ritual as long as he did it, then she wanted to give life a chance.

Unless she just thought it was the greatest chance of bringing the gods back, but he opted for optimism. For now.

"Yeah, I'm willing," he confirmed.

"And you said you had an easier way of getting there than going to the hot springs?" Vazi asked after no one else had spoken for a moment.

Aelia sipped again and nodded. "I do. And I think I know what item will work, too. Though I'm guessing you're going to want to check it before we bring it back."

"About that," Seth said, half-sitting on the arm of the couch. "Vazi told me about his trip to this place with the Athenaeum. He said there was some rule about not taking anything out of that place. Sounded like it was magically enforced."

"She's special," Aaron said, smirking at his former rival. "Though I wouldn't recommend any of the rest of us attempting to do it."

"It wouldn't hurt you," Aelia assured him. "It just wouldn't work." She looked over to Vazi and smiled. "Even for you."

"Both are good to know," Vazi said, inclining his head toward her. "Are you ready?"

"I am," she said, setting her cup down.

"Wandering around some mega-library is definitely not for me, so I'm gonna bounce, but good luck," Kara said, pausing to give Aelia a quick hug before she left.

"I'm very interested, so ready to go whenever you're ready," Seth said, standing.

Aelia stepped in front of them, offering her hands out. "I need to be touching you to take you," she told them. Aaron took one of her hands, and the gods laid their hands on her arm. That done, she murmured something and the world around them changed, taking them once more to Sozu, back to the platform where they'd appeared the first time.

"Okay, this is cool," Seth said as he turned in a circle, trying to take it all in.

"Before you get excited, can one of you see if you can sense any other life besides the four of us?" Aaron asked. "Last time, we ran into my brother and two of his friends, and they killed Aelia. I'd rather avoid surprises like that this time."

Vazi cocked his head for a few seconds, then shook his head. "Lots of magic, but no one is here except for us. And..." He took a step off the platform, causing the image of Akila to appear and give her greeting again. "And her," he said sadly. "Thank you, Akila. We're fine for now," he told the apparition, causing her to disappear.

"That was a little eerie," Seth said quietly.

"Kind of, but now that I've met them, that's eerie too," Aaron said, nodding to the statues he now recognized as Ananke and Chronos. The other woman must be Tiamat, and the man Apophis.

"That brings up another question," Seth said, moving closer to the statue of Tiamat. "Like they said, some of the other pantheons adopted them, tried to claim them as just part of their pantheon. But Grovek put statues of them here. Where everyone would see them." He glanced back at Vazi. "Did the Lemurian gods worship them?"

Vazi shook his head. "Not in the way you mean, no. They were our parents. No, they didn't birth us in the way you probably think of when you think of parents, but they still created us, cared for us. People today put up portraits of their parents and other family. This was just Grovek's version of that. Or I would assume, anyway." He smiled wryly. "He never told most of us about this place. Just his apprentices, it seemed."

"It wasn't that he didn't trust you," Aelia began, but Vazi waved that off.

"I'm not offended. He just chose people who would most appreciate this place, I think."

"Yes," she agreed. "Come on. What I've got in mind is this way," she told them, heading for the doorway.

"What are you thinking?" Aaron asked.

"His journal."

"Don't get me wrong, I know his research was incredibly important to him, but you don't think there's an object that would be more personal or whatever than that?" Seth asked. "The Anunnaki said it needed to hold the god's essence."

"I really don't. Yes, some of his research is in there, but it was more...his experiences as he gathered other research. Like you might have detailed how you got to Tempest's tomb, how you got in, all that. Not just what you found, but how you felt, what you did, the importance of it to you. How you hoped it would end, what you were scared you'd find. It's not just hard facts."

"Gotcha. Yeah, that might work. Especially since he was the god of wisdom."

Aaron and the others followed her into the office, and she went right to the table where she'd left the journal.

"That doesn't look like a journal," Seth said, frowning, when Aelia ran her fingers over the lashed together sheets.

Vazi scoffed and asked sarcastically, "Did you think it would look like a journal from today?"

Seth shrugged. "I guess I did. I hear journal, and I think of a book, not a couple of sheets of...what is that, papyrus? Held together with cording?"

"Covered books came a little later," Aelia told him, picking up the journal carefully. "Will this work?" she asked, offering it to Vazi.

Aaron watched Vazi take the item with as much reverence as Aelia had shown. He let it rest in his palm, his other hand hovering above it. It took him only seconds before he nodded. "You're right. Though honestly, everything in here feels like Grovek. Every stone, every chair, every page."

"Because it was created with his magic?"

"Exactly."

"Except the Anunnaki said it basically needed to be a piece of his soul," Seth pointed out. "The journal might feel like him, but was it special enough to be considered part of his soul?"

"I honestly cannot think of anything else he cherished more. Anything else he put more of himself into," Aelia told him. "Remember, he was the god of wisdom. If Ananke is all about fate, Grovek was all about learning, expanding his mind and knowledge. This is the embodiment of what he stood for. But if you want to check for something else, then I'd still stick to this room. There are bedrooms, but none were his. They were just used for sleeping and bathing, not for living. If he wasn't out exploring and studying, cataloging and learning, then he was in this room."

"It can't hurt to check," he suggested, shrugging at Vazi.

Vazi and Aelia stared at each other for a long moment before he shrugged. "No. It will all feel like him. If Aelia says this was his most prized possession, then I don't see how the rest of us can say otherwise."

Seth didn't look reassured. "Sorry, but that just feels way too easy. Like this part is simple, just to set us up for failure later on."

While he didn't exactly disagree with Seth, Aaron tried to be logical. "This one may have been easy, but I have a feeling not all the others are going to be," he said, leaning against the door frame. "I'm not going to claim to be an expert on the Lemurians or how things were back then, but what are the odds that we'll have someone so familiar with each of the gods? Like the birth and death gods. Aelia, Vazi, were either of you close to them?"

She shook her head while Vazi frowned. "Not really," he admitted. "Enough to speak with them, of course, but Inanis spent most of her time in the realm of the dead. Ocoina did too, actually, when she wasn't attending births."

Aaron gestured at Vazi as he proved his point. "Then, unless Grovek or the insanity goddess know something, we'll have to hunt to find an object to work for that pair, and we'll only have two weeks to find each object. So try not to overthink this and make more work for us."

"Easier said than done," Seth admitted. "But if we're happy with the journal, maybe we should head back to Lemuria, grab Dania, and do the whole filling it with magic thing? If that goes wrong and this gets fucked up, I want to make sure we've got plenty of time to find a replacement."

"That's not a bad idea," Aelia admitted.

Vazi still held the book as they made their way back to the portal. Before they stepped through, Aaron caught Seth leaning toward Aelia and whispering, "You can bring me back here sometime, right?"

She smiled faintly. "If this works, it's not me you're going to have to ask," was all she said before stepping through and back to her house.

"Just to ensure everyone is safe, let's go to an uninhabited part of the island for this next part," Vazi said. "Get Dania and join us?" he asked Seth.

"Be right there," Seth said before disappearing.

Vazi didn't ask Aaron or Aelia if they were ready, just popped them to another part of the island. It was mildly familiar, but a lot of parts of the island looked the same to Aaron. Unless there were houses or unusual features, or it was near the village, it was all just 'Lemuria' to him. This particular part of Lemuria was atop a hill, with no trees or buildings nearby. Perfect for attempting risky magic. Honestly, Aaron was a little surprised Vazi hadn't tried to leave him and Aelia behind. Until he remembered they were both immortal.

Damn, that really was going to take some time not just to adjust to, but to start remembering. But it did have some advantages. There were places he'd wanted to excavate in the past that he'd had to pass on because they were too dangerous, even for the Arcane or with modern technology. That wasn't really an issue anymore. Flooded caves or tombs? No problem. Once he got used to dying, he thought he'd be willing to risk it. As long as he didn't get trapped, he would be good.

Just as he was starting to explore those possibilities, Seth and Dania joined them.

"I know you had said you were going to look for something to-day," Dania said, her eyes widened with surprise. "I didn't expect you to find something so soon."

"Aelia knew Grovek well," Vazi explained. "Do you understand what we're going to do?" he asked, glancing at Seth, almost as an afterthought, it seemed.

"I think so," she answered.

"You explained it to me a few dozen times," Seth said dryly. "I think I've got it by now."

Vazi nodded and looked at Aaron and Aelia. "You two should step back. This should be completely safe, but I'd rather not hurt you two if we can avoid it."

Aaron nodded and hooked an arm around Aelia, pulling her back a few steps. "Do you understand what they're doing?" he asked her in a low tone, watching as the three gods stood equidistant from one another. Vazi held out the journal, and it hovered in the air in the middle of them. Holding out both hands, pale, iridescent magic streamed from all three of them and into the delicate pages.

Aelia nodded. "God magic is unique. They've all got their specialties—sky magic for Vazi, stone magic for Seth, and storm magic for Dania—but they also have basic god magic. That's how they teleport, hear the prayers of their worshipers, and so on. Like how elementals can all control their particular element, and witches have the varied abilities they're known for. But like every being that has magic, there's a well of it inside them. They're directing magic from that well into the journal. Not magic to do anything particular, just raw magic. Basically adding parts of themselves to the part of Grovek that's in the journal.

My guess is it helps act like a tether or lifeline to Grovek and Telia, guiding them back to the gods of their pantheon."

Magic was kind of weird, he decided, happy he was a shifter. He changed form, and that was it. Nice and simple.

The flow of magic only lasted for a minute, but when it stopped, the journal continued to hang in the air, except now it glowed faintly. Not with light, but with magic.

"That's it?" he asked.

"That's it," Vazi confirmed, reaching out to take the journal. "I'll keep it safe in Thelaria until the half moon. Since we have to go there to perform the ritual anyway, it seems best. And we can ensure it's kept safe there."

"And you'll bring us there for the ritual?" Aelia asked, watching him with mild suspicion.

"I don't like it, but yes," Vazi said on a sigh. "I know at first I was just excited about bringing the others back, but I don't like risking our own people."

"Who else would take the risk?" she asked simply.

"I just wish there was another way. That Chronos could take us back to before Zeus did this to us, maybe. And it's still damn insulting to think that that weak, moronic rapist could manage to do this to us!"

"Didn't sound like he did it on his own," Aaron reminded him.

"Still. For the entire pantheon to have been shunted to some other dimension or wherever we were... When the others are back, I'm going to make damn sure it's not allowed to happen again."

"It won't," Dania said quietly. "You're on alert now, and he seems to be a coward unless it's one on one."

Aaron had never heard the word 'he' spoken with so much derision, but if anyone had the right to hold such anger toward Zeus, it was her. Even Vazi—who definitely had a justified issue with the head of the Greek pantheon—didn't have as much right. Especially when he added in the fact that it was her half-brother who had abused her for so many centuries.

"That he is," Vazi agreed before taking all five of them back to Aelia's house. "You have a few days to decide if you want to change your mind," he told him and Aelia before disappearing.

"Good luck," Dania said quietly, before she, too, left.

Seth, however, lingered. "You should know, he showed up at my place this morning. Vazi, I mean."

"Okay?" Aaron said, unsure where Seth was going with it.

"He was half convinced we were either going to shelve this whole ritual thing, or do it himself. He may be a grumpy ass motherfucker, but he really does care about the Lemurians. The current Lemurians as well as the ones he lost."

Aelia nodded and smiled. "I've noticed that. It was just Tempest at first, but I think that was just familiarity and her being...an original, I suppose. But especially with no other gods, and no chance of bringing the ones who died back, we're all he's got. Or were."

"True, but I don't think it's just because you're all he's got any-more." Seth shrugged and shoved his hands into his pockets. "He's adapted, and that's not an easy thing for gods."

"Most gods," Aaron corrected. "You're not exactly standard issue."

Seth grinned and cocked his head. "Half the time I still forget I'm a god. I'll go to walk somewhere and remember I can just pop my ass over there. Or when Tempest was having pregnancy cravings? She'd start getting upset and I'd start freaking out, then realize it would be easy for me to get whatever weird-ass thing she wanted."

"Works for me. I like having a god who doesn't act like I'm beneath him."

"Be fair," Aelia chided. "Vazi doesn't do that." She barely paused before adding, "All the time."

"Hell, he does it to me sometimes," Seth admitted. "But I want to go fill Tempest in. Try to stay alive. Both of you."

"Always my goal," Aaron assured him before the god disappeared.

Now they were alone, so he just needed to figure out where Aelia's head was at, and how to get her on the same page as him.

Honestly, the ritual sounded easier.

CHAPTER 23

Aelia wasn't sure what to say once the others had left. Aaron had made a huge confession, and she'd shut him out for the rest of the day. He couldn't be happy about that, but she'd needed both the time and the space to try to figure out how she felt about it.

"Are you hungry?" she asked for lack of anything else, turning to head for the kitchen.

"Not really," he admitted. "But I do think we need to talk."

She stilled but didn't look back at him. It was easier when she couldn't see his bright blue eyes staring into her. No matter what emotion was in them, they struck her each time. Anger, grief, affection, arousal. They all affected her, regardless of what she tried to tell herself. "About what?"

He huffed out a breath and her head turned slightly toward him, but not quite enough to let her see him. "The fact that I love you. What you're going to do if you survive the ritual. What you're going to do if we do bring Grovek back. I've got a list, so you can take your pick. But what I really want to know," he continued, walking toward her until he could take her arm and turn her until she was faced with those blue eyes, "is if you're going to keep trying to find a way to become mortal."

Why couldn't he understand just how hard living was for her? Yes, he was immortal now, had even died and revived, but he'd only been alive for a few centuries. He had no idea what it was like living through everything she had. How little life seemed to hold for her now. Some people talked about days blurring together, but for her it was centuries. Faces she'd once cherished had blurred in her mind, and she couldn't find it in herself to hope for the future.

"I am," she told him, unsurprised when his eyes narrowed and a little growl came out of his throat. He might be composed when he was working, but he really was an emotional man. Not a bad thing, she admitted, except for now, when she wanted him to be logical, and she decided to tell him that. "You need to think about this rationally."

The growl deepened, then disappeared as his face smoothed as he apparently calmed. She didn't trust it. "You want rational?" he checked.

Uneasy at the abrupt shift, she nodded slowly. "I do..."

"Okay. Here are two very rational reasons for you *not to* try to die of old age in a couple of decades." Releasing her arm, he lifted a hand, index finger extended. "First? Odds are this ritual will kill anyone who performs it, and the only chance we really have is two immortals performing it simultaneously. Correct?"

Again, she nodded, not sure she liked where this was heading.

"Then if you're mortal, you're either condemning the Lemurian gods to stay wherever the fuck they are, or condemning the people who aren't immortal who are still willing to take the chance and perform the ritual."

"That's not fair!" she snapped.

Unfazed by her anger, he shrugged. "You didn't say you wanted fair, you wanted rational," he pointed out. "You can't deny that it's a very valid point. It's not how I wanted to convince you, because guilting a woman is definitely not my thing. But since you're also talking about unfairness, I can point some of that out, too, if you want."

Aelia caught her jaw clenching and forced it to relax. "No. Stick to rational," she said, voice clipped. "But you can't put something like that entirely on me."

"Like I said, I didn't want to, but you wanted rational, so I'm trying to be rational. The safest way of bringing the gods back is both of us." He smiled a little too sweetly. "Which brings me to point number two. If you become mortal, you'll be putting immortality entirely on me. I'd be the only one, since Grovek made sure no one else could use that tablet."

"That's not true. If it works on me, it'll work on you, too," she insisted.

"That's true. If it works on you, I'd have an escape clause," he allowed, nodding. "But I don't know if I want that. Life is an experience, Aelia. I have all of Lemuria to explore. And maybe I'll find other places I thought were myths, too, like Atlantis or Mu. I'll be around when humans finally figure out how to colonize space, and maybe I'll get to visit other planets, talk to aliens, and see some of the weird ass shit that's out there. I want to do all those things." His voice gentled, his eyes softened, and he cupped her face. "But I want to do them with *you*, Aelia. I know you said you've seen it all, done it all, but you haven't, baby. And you have to admit that doing something with someone is a hell of a lot different from doing it on your own. Being able to share things—good and bad—with another person makes them better. You've been on your own entirely too long."

The shell she'd fought to keep over her heart fractured. She shook her head repeatedly. "Don't," she said, hating how her voice cracked. "Don't manipulate me like that. It's not fair."

His voice remained gentle and low, and using the hand still on her arm, drew her in until he could embrace her. It felt so good, so warm, even though part of her wanted to draw back, to run away from his sweet words. "It's not manipulation. It's truth. I do want to do those things. I do want to do them with you. And I really do think you've been lonely for too damn long. I would die thousands of times if it made you realize that the future doesn't have to be like the past, because that would hurt a hell of a lot less than seeing you die for good."

Again, she shook her head and tried to pull back, falling back on the same argument she'd been using for centuries to avoid getting close to others. "I can still lose you, Aaron. I lost them all."

"No, baby. The only way you can lose me is if you refuse to let me in." He bent his head, but slowly enough that she could have dodged the kiss if she'd wanted to. She didn't want to. Her emotions felt too close to the surface, and she wanted nothing more than the balm she knew his kiss could be. He delivered. It was long and tender, softening her resolve, though he stopped before her emotional walls could collapse. "And there's one thing I don't think you've considered."

The fracture cracked a little more, began to widen. "Just one?" she asked weakly.

Aaron chuckled softly and nodded. "Just one. If you were still set on becoming mortal and dying, you should have asked the Anunnaki to help with that when they were here. You didn't, so I have to wonder if part of your insistence on becoming mortal is now more habit and stubbornness than anything else." Another kiss, this one short and sweet. "Don't let fear get in the way anymore. Don't make me suffer the way you suffered all these years. Let me in," he begged.

The shell disintegrated completely, leaving her raw and completely helpless to the offer of love in his eyes. Maybe he was right. She had suffered so long, and he was offering her what she'd always wanted. Someone she couldn't lose. Except that wasn't why she was caving. It also wasn't his annoyingly rational point about the gods. The fact that he was immortal helped, yes, but that wasn't why she felt what she did for him. If he'd been a different sort of man, she might have been content to just have an immortal friend, but Aaron? He could be an immortal love. Except love was always a risk. He might never die, but he could still leave.

But she didn't think he would do that. And if tried...maybe she could fight for him. It had been a long time since she'd fought for someone.

"Okay," she whispered.

He leaned his head slightly to one side, brows lifting. "Okay?"

Drawing in a deep breath for courage, she nodded. "Okay. I..." She let out a little laugh and dropped her forehead against his chest. "Gods, Aaron. It really isn't fair that you can affect me like this. I'm not entirely sure I like it." Lifting her head so she could look up at him, she smiled, just a little. "I couldn't keep you out, and believe me, I tried. You're the first person I've loved in more than eight hundred years."

A smile grew over his lips and he tightened his hold on her, lifting her to her toes before he kissed her again. Though it was soft and loving, when it was over, he whispered against her lips, "If you don't want me to tear those clothes off, you've got thirty seconds to take them off."

Aelia laughed. If she'd expected him to change how he acted toward her just because they'd confessed their love for each other, clearly she was wrong. And honestly, if she thought about it, he'd never touched her just like it was sex, not even the first time, almost a year ago. He'd always touched her like she mattered. No, like she mattered most. Before, she'd just refused to acknowledge it. Now that she'd accepted what he felt for her, and what she felt for him, there was no need to hide from it. She could embrace it.

"Fuck the clothes," she told him, sealing her mouth to his again. She did kick her shoes off because they weren't exactly easy to tear off, but he made quick work of the rest of what she wore with those claws. Not once did he so much as nick her, but she'd expected nothing less. He might be half-feral, but he'd never intentionally hurt her.

When he'd brushed the scraps of fabric off her body, she smiled against his lips. "My turn."

Aaron arched a brow and grinned wickedly. "Do your worst, honey," he purred.

She might not have claws, but she'd started learning sorcery more than six thousand years before. At first she'd focused on useful spells, but of course she had also made a point to learn a few fun ones. Speaking the syllables in a silky tone, everything he wore disintegrated—except for that intriguing piercing of his.

"You have got to teach me that spell," he told her as he grabbed her ass and lifted her easily against his body.

Winding both arms and legs around him, she slowly rocked, teasing them both. "Gladly," she promised, as he started to walk back toward her bedroom. Each step caused him to rub against her, and she paid him back by setting her teeth against his earlobe and tugging. He growled and walked faster, which only heightened the sensations.

He stopped by the bed, his hands tightening, to rub her against him, making the warm metal of his piercing slide over her clit. She gasped and dug her nails into the back of his shoulders. "Don't think I'm gonna make this easy on you," he warned.

"Same goes," was all she could manage, since the constant stimulation was starting to make a climax begin to build within her.

"Oh, I think I want to experience that." He set her on her feet, holding onto her for a few seconds to make sure she didn't fall. When she was steady, he stretched out on the bed, perfectly at ease being at her mercy.

This was a surprise. Clearly, her lover was a more complex man than she'd given him credit for. Given that he'd always been so dominant in bed, she never would have thought he'd be the sort to not just allow the woman to take charge, but to eagerly encourage it. That made him even sexier.

"Good," she said absently, letting her gaze slide over him. He really was so gorgeous. He kept himself fit and strong, giving him a body she genuinely loved in every way. And his face was ruggedly perfect, especially with his sly grin and eyes full of both love and desire. He might not be perfect, but he was exactly what she needed.

Climbing onto the bed on all fours, she moved over him, letting her breasts brush against his chest. There was one more spell she'd learned for fun that would work here, and she debated for only a moment before deciding to use it. He trusted her, and she wanted not just to push him to the point where he lost control, but beyond it. She had a feeling they'd both thoroughly enjoy it.

Kissing his lips, then his throat before making her way down his chest, she whispered the words she'd learned long ago. His arms drew up above his head as though pulled by bindings, which then held his wrists against the pillow. His legs were bound just as easily.

Surprised, Aaron tugged at the invisible bonds. When he realized he couldn't escape them, he just gave her another hot smile. "You're full of surprises, baby. I love it. Have your fun. Enjoy me."

Smiling, she bit gently at one of his nipples, and he hissed. "I plan to."

And she did, taking her sweet time in moving down his body until she knelt between his legs. Her fingers slid around his shaft and she stroked slowly until her thumb brushed the piercing. "Should I ask why you decided to get this?" she asked, watching as he twitched in her grip.

"I was thinking ahead."

She grinned and bent down, letting her tongue flick over the tip of his cock. "You certainly were."

He barked out a short laugh and shook his head. "I was hoping I'd be back in this amazing woman's bed, and knew she'd seen a lot and done a lot. Figured I might have to do something to…pique her interest."

"Oh, I'm definitely interested," she admitted. "I've never been with a man who had his dick pierced." Another lick, this one slower. "I think I like it."

"If I promise to get a fucking ladder, will you stop teasing me?"

She pretended to consider that for a moment before smiling sweetly. "No." But she did indulge herself, sliding her hand down, until just her thumb and index finger remained around him, allowing her plenty of room to lick him like the most delicious candy.

He groaned and tried to arch up against her mouth, but the spell prevented that, too. Until she released him or lost focus, he was at her mercy. "You really want to torture me?" he asked, his eyes hooded as he watched every stroke of her tongue against him. She made a sound of agreement, but didn't stop. "Then use your other hand to touch yourself while you play. I want you to be as turned on as I am."

That sounded like a damn good idea to her. Spreading her knees, she slid her hand between her thighs and stroked over her already slick sex. She sighed against him, and his arms jerked against the spell's bonds.

"That's it, honey," he murmured. "But don't make yourself come. Save that for me."

"You think you get a choice?" she asked, circling one damp finger over her clit.

"I think you want the same thing I do."

She did, but wasn't going to tell him that. Not yet. Instead, her lips trailed up his length then parted, taking him into her mouth. He growled, encouraging her to keep going. The metal against her tongue was a little odd, but the way he reacted when she toyed with it made it worth it. And still she teased. She moved, but slowly. She sucked, gently. Not enough to push him over the edge, but neither did she do enough to push herself to orgasm. This was just the warm-up act. And a way of apologizing for putting him through hell the past week. It had been difficult for him, she knew that, but she also didn't think any other chain of events could have led to her giving in like she had.

And giving in was also worth it. Not just in the short-term, she hoped, but for her entire long life.

His growls grew more frequent, and her own breathing quickened, both her fingers and mouth affecting them both, but he hadn't broken yet.

He would.

Drawing him deeper, he groaned and fought against her magic, trying to push even a fraction of an inch more into her mouth. He'd only have it when she was ready. So she drew back, then pressed down, giving him almost enough twice more before she sat up. If her mouth couldn't give her the reaction she wanted, then she'd find it another way.

Moving up his body, she settled over his hips. This had driven her crazy earlier, so maybe it would do the same to him now. Rocking her hips, she slid her aching core across his shaft, pausing only briefly when she pressed against his sensitive head.

Oh, that was doing it, she realized almost immediately, the muscles in his arms and stomach straining. But rather than watching as she moved over him, his eyes were fixed on her face, while he wore an expression so hungry it made her inner muscles clench. But still, she didn't stop, didn't give in, just rubbed against him over and over, until he thrashed and snarled, so close to the edge she could feel the need radiating off him.

"Aelia! Godsdammit, stop teasing me!"

Shifting, leaning forward until he was positioned at her opening, she kissed him lightly, then pressed down, filling herself with him. At the same time, she released the spell holding him in place. In only a breath his arms were around her and he rolled them, not stopping until her back hit the bed and his hips arched into her, making her cry out.

"You're going to pay for that," he growled, but the words weren't angry. They were an appealing mix of heat and humor. Holding onto him was her only option as he surged into her repeatedly, holding nothing back. She might have bruises from the rough loving later, but she didn't give a damn. It felt so good she knew it would be worth it.

The teasing had been more than enough foreplay, so the fierce, rapid thrusts rocketed her to her first climax. It was just as fierce and powerful as he was right now. She screamed his name as she wrapped her legs around him, not to help her move against him or try to hold him still, but because she needed the anchor. The release was powerful enough to make her believe the euphemisms about leaving one's body.

"Not enough," he whispered against her ear, not stopping, even when she clenched around him. "I'm going to need an eternity before I'm done with you."

She loved the sound of that and pushed against his chest, just enough so she could stare into his eyes as he rocked into her. At least until the second climax forced her lids to close, blocking out everything but the waves of sensation that poured through her.

But his control was far from inexhaustible, and feeling her spasming around him that second time sapped what little he had left. There was no snarling, no growling, just a look of almost painful bliss as he slammed into her one more time, then finally gave in to his body's demands, emptying himself into her.

With the last of his strength, he nudged one of her legs off him then rolled them onto their sides, not yet ready to let her go. She was okay with that. It had been far too long since she'd let herself savor lovemaking and just hold a lover. And Aaron was more than just a simple lover.

Kissing his shoulder, she sighed, her entire body relaxed and loose. "Thank you," she said softly.

She felt more than heard him chuckle weakly. "Start thanking me for fucking you senseless, and I'll get an ego," he teased her.

Lips curving, she shook her head. "You've already got an ego, but that's not what I was thanking you for." Forcing her eyes to open and settle on his face, she explained. "Thank you for not letting me give in to the depression. For pushing until I leaped despite my fear."

"Thank you for not giving in," he said sincerely. "I meant everything I said, baby. But I'll repeat the most important part, just in case you missed it." When her head tilted questioningly, he grinned. "I love you."

"I love you, too," she told him, smiling. Because he was right. It absolutely was the most important part.

CHAPTER 24

They'd spent the rest of that day, and most of the next, making up for lost time. Not just in bed, but talking. There were brief breaks for food or rest, but even the meals were interspersed with learning about one another. They'd been friends for almost a year, but friends didn't share the kind of things lovers did. He loved learning about her and her life just as much as he loved the sex. She'd been to so many places, experienced so much of history. He could honestly listen to her stories for years. Fortunately, they had those years.

Neither could say they were sated the day after that, even after Aelia had woken Aaron, her soft, naked body sliding across, over, and onto his. Afterwards, when they were sprawled out on the bed, she had promised him a surprise. Honestly, the sexy alarm clock had been surprise enough, but he wasn't going to turn down anything she wanted to give him. When she'd admitted her plan, he'd been a hundred percent on board.

He was going back to Sozu. This time they weren't searching for an object that was important to their people, or trying to save Aelia from nightly torments. This time, he could explore. Next to making love with Aelia, it was his favorite thing to do.

Once they were back in the pocket dimension Grovek had created, and they'd been greeted by Akila, he took Aelia's hand and started for the stairs. "So how big is this place?"

"Now? Six levels, including this one. But I heard from other apprentices that it began as a single room," she told him as they began climbing. "As Grovek either wrote or found things that belonged here, he expanded it. One room became one level. One level became two, and so on. It was sometime around when he created the third level that he began bringing apprentices here."

"Makes sense. Needed someone to help catalog it all."

"That was probably part of it," she agreed, nodding. "But he genuinely did enjoy teaching others and sharing what he'd learned. Even better was when one of his apprentices was able to teach him something."

"Really?" he asked with no small measure of surprise. "A lot of the professors I had would have hated it. One tiny correction, even if it was a misspelling or something, and they lost their shit. They were the teachers, so they didn't like being shown up by students. Always thought it was stupid."

She shrugged as they reached the landing, then started up the next flight of stairs, curving their way upward. "Not all professors are like that. There are some absolutely amazing teachers out there, who don't care where new information comes from. Besides, Grovek isn't a professor, though. A teacher certainly, but remember, he's a Lemurian god. They're not like the others. Thoth and Athena and the other wisdom gods might all be intelligent, even geniuses, but Lemurian gods are a little more like the Anunnaki."

"How do you mean?"

"They're more embodiments of whatever they're god of instead of just having the powers. Not to the extent the Anunnaki are, but it's there. It's why Vazi can go from happy and laughing to furious and violent, just like the wind can change from a cool breeze to a hurricane. Or why Seth is so strong and steady."

"Jalvas wasn't exactly strong and steady," he reminded her, remembering his brief encounter with the former god of mountains.

"He also wasn't balanced," she pointed out. "Once, he was as steady as stone."

"I don't know if that's really a good thing, though, since we're going to try to bring back the goddess of insanity in a couple of days," he said, grimacing.

She laughed and shook her head. "She'll be balanced, and insanity is...complicated. It can mean a lot of things. Hallucinations, delusions, erratic behavior, yes, but also being just crazy enough to do something like, say, performing a ritual that could kill us just to strengthen Lemuria." She shrugged again. "But honestly, while I was close to Grovek, I never met Telia. You'd have to ask Vazi if you want to know more about her."

"I think Monday will be soon enough," he decided, especially since he had this entire place to explore. "So where are we going exactly?" he wondered.

Aelia glanced up at him and smiled slyly. "You can wait another minute to find out. I promise you'll enjoy it, though."

"You're teasing me again," he said, giving her hand a squeeze. "Don't you remember what happened the last time you teased me like that?"

Her smile went hot and smug. "I really, really do. Think I'll get a repeat of that?"

Though they were halfway up the stairs, he tugged her to a stop, cupped her chin with his free hand, and kissed her hard. "Anytime you want, honey. Just say the word."

"I'm tempted to say it now, but not here," she said, sighing regretfully.

"Then you better hurry and get us to wherever we're going," he warned. "I know there are beds back downstairs."

They went up to the fourth level, and she guided him out the arch and to the first room on their left. What Akila had called the north side of Sozu. "You're going to want to get very comfortable with reading Lemurian very fast," she told him, making a gesture for him to go ahead.

This room was like the others he'd seen. Shelves and cubbies lined the walls, full of tablets and sheets, with a table and chairs in the middle for working. "Believe me, I know. It's frustrating not to be able to read something when I pick it up," he told her, going to the first set of shelves.

"And I'd say everything in here is written in Lemurian, but Sophia claimed they found some texts written in newer languages. Greek, Sumerian, things like that. Akila may have translated some of it," Aelia admitted as she went to a different shelf and started to poke through the items there, clearly searching for something. "But I think you'll find this interesting," she said after a few minutes, pulling out a thin stone tablet, about six inches by ten inches.

"Why?" he asked, though he joined her at the table, where she laid it down gently.

She didn't answer, just pointed at the hardened clay. Frowning, he bent over it and started working on deciphering it. Some words were easy, but Grovek—or his apprentices—hadn't been content with just using common words. Lemurian might not be the most complicated language he'd ever encountered, and it might have that familiarity, but it still wasn't a simple thing to learn.

Maybe his sorceress girlfriend knew a cheat spell? It was worth asking. Later.

He struggled through the tablet, then shook his head and glanced up at her. "I don't get it. What's so important about this?" From what he could tell, it just detailed a group of Lemurians who had decided to leave their home en masse. Not because they were unhappy, but to explore and settle elsewhere. Spreading Lemurian influence, maybe. They'd gone to what Grovek had called the other side of the world, near where another civilization was starting to form.

Saying nothing, she gently turned the tablet over, and he saw it had words on that side, too, along with a crude map. Not that maps written in hardened clay could be as intricate as modern-day maps, but that was okay. It was still interesting.

Cocking his head, he resumed working through the language of swirls and straight edges. Between the words and the map, he was guessing the other civilization might be the Sumerians, except it looked like the map wasn't indicating that part of the world, but a point to the west of it. The Mediterranean, maybe? It fit the marks on the map. And then his eyes narrowed. "Aelia? Where exactly did these people settle?"

She smiled at him and pulled out a chair, settling into it. He'd never seen her looking smug outside of sex, so the fact that she had that look on her face now had him intrigued. Pointing, she said, "These are the Tigris and Euphrates rivers." He nodded, as he'd worked that much out himself. "The Mediterranean Sea," she continued, sliding her finger left of the rivers, then circling it lightly with the tip of one nail before she tapped on it.

"You're going to have to lead me a little more here, my beautiful nerd. There are a hell of a lot of islands in the Med, and a lot of them have been inhabited for a lot of years."

Shaking her head, she pointed to a line he'd mostly been unable to translate. "It doesn't say specifically, and certainly not using any name you'd know, but if I remember correctly, in one of those," she motioned to the shelves, "Grovek mentioned that this group was mostly witches and elementals. From what I've read about this group, I've always wondered if they didn't go for some sort of alternative living situation. Especially once rumors of Atlantis started spreading. I know everyone associates water with the mers, but it's not the only possibility." She shrugged and sat back. "It's only a theory, and there may be something here that disproves it, but you mentioned wanting to find Atlantis and Mu. From all accounts, Atlantis probably wasn't around when Lemuria sank, so you're probably not going to find anything concrete here, but it's a lead, isn't it? I've never heard of a Lemurian settlement on land in that part of the world, so either they failed, moved on, or, like I said, went for an alternative living situation."

Aaron went still. He'd never gone looking for Lemuria. He'd heard of it before Hecate had asked him to help Tempest and Seth, but only in passing. At the time, he'd thought it only a myth. Atlantis? Everyone had heard of that, and he was inclined to think that Plato hadn't been completely full of shit. Even myths were generally based on something real. Hell, Bigfoot had gotten started because of a shifter in their half-form had been spotted by humans. The Ekklesia had apparently had a hell of a time spinning that around until humans just thought it was something drunk or crazy people saw.

Looking back down at the tablet, he reread every word he could decipher, then studied the map again. "You think Atlantis is real? And that they were Lemurians?"

"I don't know," she admitted, "but I know we both like learning and exploring. And I've never been there." She smiled, and it was almost shy. Somehow, it made him want to kiss her until she got that dazed smile he loved so much. "It would be kind of nice to go somewhere I've never been before."

"First, we can do that anytime, especially since neither of us can die. We can hit some of those places humans say are too dangerous to go. Second?" He gave in to the urge, cupped the back of her head, and kissed her, taking his sweet time about it. He didn't plan to go further than that, not now, but she had definitely earned that kiss. "I absolutely fucking love the idea of exploring the world with you. The thought of finding Atlantis with you is even better." He released her and straightened, pleased to see she had a sappy smile on her lips. "But if Sozu is older than Atlantis, then you're right. We probably won't find much here." Dropping down into another chair, he smirked. "Think the Athenaeum has anything on it? They're only like ancient Greece old, right?"

Aelia smiled and nodded. "Just after the Alexandria Library burned."

"Which time?"

Her smile widened. "I do love a man who knows his history. Even if he can't know it as well as I do."

"Yeah, well, none of us lived through it like you did. Which time?" he repeated.

"Fifth century BC," she answered. "So yes, they might have something. The harder question is whether Sophia will allow us to look."

"Hey, we helped her save the place. Shouldn't that get us a library card or something? Especially since I offered to help them find shit to stash there?"

"It might," she agreed. "Especially since it's just about Atlantis and not anything dangerous like the Miasma."

"Oh, fuck no," he assured her. "One world-ending goo from the beginning of the universe was more than enough for me."

"For me, too. But for now, why don't we see what else we can find? We've got a few hours before the island dinner."

He cocked his head, relieved that she didn't sound like she was dreading the dinner. He'd seen her for the last two, and she'd interacted as little as possible. And that last time? The time he'd followed her? She'd looked like she'd rather be burned alive than sit there and converse with people who had become both friends and neighbors. Now she looked like she might actually look forward to it.

He was going to make damn sure it was a dinner to remember.

CHAPTER 25

Aaron and Aelia had spent several hours in Sozu, even taking a break for lunch, before they'd gone back to Lemuria. They'd bathed before she prepared her contribution to the meal, and she'd picked up their earlier conversation while she cooked.

"You know, you don't have to wait to find Atlantis before you can see someplace old and forgotten."

"I don't?" he asked. While he wasn't horrible in the kitchen, he was admittedly a typical bachelor-type guy who was better with a grill than anything else. So he was basically playing sous chef for her. It was oddly pleasing. Working together in the kitchen, talking, moving in sync. More than that, it didn't feel like playing house, it just felt...natural. He'd have to see what other everyday things they could do together.

"Nope. Remember how you said I lived through history?"

"I do. And hell, I've seen your library. You even had statues of Lemurian gods. I've never seen them anywhere else before we got here."

"I do," she echoed. "And I've made notes throughout the years. Time may have buried a lot of places, and people forgot, and I'll even admit to having forgotten a lot, but there are some places that I still remember that no one else does. If we survive the ritual..."

She trailed off, but he didn't have to ask why. Like her, he was willing to go through with the ritual, but he honestly didn't want to stay dead. And it seemed she'd finally come around to his way of thinking.

Shaking it off, she continued. "When we survive the ritual, I'll show you some of the places I remember. You've probably even heard of some of them."

Some of them? "You really know some places that there are no records of?" he asked, not trying to hide the excitement that caused. It was hardwired into him. A lot of people thought everything had been discovered, but he knew better. Not just Lemuria, but even other archaeologists were still finding new sites and information. Major ones that rewrote parts of known history.

Aelia shot him an amused look. "I know I do. So does the Athenaeum. Not every culture left records, or if they did, sometimes they were left in a form that didn't survive the centuries, like papyrus. And some of the records that did survive, ones I found, I gave to Erasmus or his predecessors years ago. Or they were in languages that humans believe are indecipherable." She bumped his hip with her own. "Don't worry, I'll take you to all sorts of fun places."

He set down the knife he was using to cut carrots, and wrapped that arm around her, pulling her in for a quick hug and kiss to her cheek. "And I'll take you to some beautiful places where you can relax and not worry about having to do anything." Wanting her to smile—and meaning it—he grinned and added, "Except me, of course. That's not negotiable, because you won't be as relaxed otherwise."

"Of course," she said dryly, though she was smiling. "But for now, we need to finish cooking."

So they did, and he again thought how he didn't mind cooking so much when he was helping her do it. Then again, he thought he'd enjoy most anything if she was involved.

When dusk fell, they took their contributions and made their way to the square, unsurprised to find others were already there. Moving to Lemuria had been a major adjustment for everyone. They'd all come from countries where it was easy to jump in a car and drive to the store or to a friend's house. On Lemuria, everything needed to be grown, made, or imported, and there were only a few dozen other people to befriend. For the most part, he and everyone else enjoyed it, but there were some very social people on the island—like Kara. They needed this weekly dinner to recharge the part of them that craved contact.

Aaron had to admit to being one of those people. When he wasn't lost in work, he needed people, so he was happy the place was growing.

"Haven't seen you two in a while," called a voice. Of course it was Kara, already sitting in a chair, grinning at them like she'd just won a prize.

"We've been busy," Aelia responded with a smile.

The grin widened. "Oh, I don't doubt that one bit. All I gotta say is, about freakin' time!"

Aaron couldn't help it. He smiled. Smugly. And quietly agreed with her.

"About time for what?" Logan, the only vampire on the island, asked, looking like he'd just woken up. He probably had, since the sun had only been down for twenty minutes.

Kara lifted a hand and wiggled her finger in their direction. "For those two to finally get together," she explained.

Logan looked over at them, then nodded. "Agreed. He's been mooning over her for months."

"Am I really the only one who missed that?" Aelia asked, setting the dish she carried down and settling into the chair beside Kara.

As Aaron sat on her other side, he nodded and rubbed her back. "I really think you are. But it's okay. You're cute when you're clueless." She only rolled her eyes, but he noticed she couldn't quite keep a smile off her face.

The others showed up fairly quickly, and it still surprised him that the gods joined in. Not Seth. Because of Tempest and his mortal beginnings, that made sense, but Vazi and Dania had been unexpected. The former spent most of his time in Thelaria or learning what parts of Lemuria still remained, and Dania...well, no one would have blamed her if she'd needed more time before being around a crowd. Then again, maybe she felt safer with others around. He didn't know, and he wasn't going to poke at her trauma.

After getting Tempest and Katrina settled, Seth came over to them, bending down so he could speak without projecting to everyone present.

"I went to talk to the Ekklesia the other night."

A wrinkle appeared on Aelia's forehead as she looked up at him. "How did it go?"

"They weren't super happy, but they seemed to believe me about the geas. Not sure that would have done it, though. They seemed pissed. One of them was bitching about how you were an employee who *had* to obey them," he said, shaking his head.

"Does that mean they're going to keep coming after her?" Aaron asked, wondering if he could talk Seth into taking him to the Ekklesia's headquarters.

Seth shook his head. "Nah. Between that and having a couple of pissed off gods warning them off, they gave up."

"Do I want to know what warning you gave them? And did you really take Vazi with you?"

He smirked and shrugged. "Just a warning. And I took Hecate, too, but couldn't not take Vazi. I can be scary as a god, but he's got way more practice at it. Besides, I never would have heard the end of it if I hadn't."

Aelia pushed out of her seat and threw her arms around him. "Thank you so much, Seth!"

Seth smiled and patted her back. "Hey, gotta keep my people safe, don't I?"

"And you do it very well," she said, releasing him and going to give Vazi the same treatment, though to Aaron's amusement, he looked resigned at the grateful affection. Or at least he pretended to, because Aaron could see the god was pleased by the attention.

"Seriously, thank you, man," Aaron told Seth, his eyes never leaving his wonderful woman.

"Totally worth it," Seth admitted. "I doubt it's just the Ekklesia, but I haven't seen her this...relaxed...since I met her."

"No, not just the Ekklesia. I kind of browbeat her until she decided to live. And realize I was damn good for her."

Seth laughed and clapped a hand on his shoulder. "Don't know about that, but I'm glad for the first part. Congrats," he said, before returning to his wife and daughter.

They ate, talking, laughing, and sharing stories about renovations that had been done, or new bits of the island that had been found. It was like a big family dinner, and Aaron loved it. He'd grown up in a large family. True, he just had the one brother, but holidays had meant aunts, uncles, cousins, and grandparents all getting together for loud, wonderful meals. Which meant this felt like the happiest times of his childhood.

When the food was nearly gone and conversation picked up more, Vazi stood, a breeze swirling through those gathered to get their attention. Who needed to clink a spoon against a glass when you were a god?

Once all eyes were on him, he spoke. "I know most of you have heard what we're planning on doing. What Aaron and Aelia are going to do for us," he began, glancing in their direction, and most eyes followed his. "Only a few of you know what it was like when my fellow gods were here, but I tell you that all of our lives will be better when they are back. We will be safer. We will have the knowledge and resources to continue growing."

He smiled, a warm, true smile, one of the few times Aaron had seen him do such a thing. "If all goes well, that will begin at our next dinner. If all goes well, we will be joined by two more gods next week!"

The cheer that rose from the Lemurians was small, but no less enthusiastic for the lack of volume.

"Let's celebrate!" Kara said, pulling out a portable speaker. A few taps on her phone, and music began to play. Though Vazi looked aggrieved that she'd stolen the attention, he didn't complain, just sat back down with a huff Aaron wasn't sure was genuine.

He needed to get the stick out of his ass, but overall, he really was a good guy.

"Come on, let's dance," Kara said to Aelia, tugging her out of her chair. Laughing, Aelia allowed herself to be pulled into the middle of the square, and they started to dance to the upbeat music. In almost no time, they were joined by several more people. Tempest handed Katrina to Seth, but that didn't surprise him. Aelia, Kara, and Tempest had gotten close since their all too eventful trip here. Delilah drew her wife, Rose, out, both looking more at ease than they had when they'd first arrived on Lemuria. Even Seth's dad and Cyrus went out there.

Most of the dancers had more enthusiasm than talent, but that didn't matter. They were having fun, and honestly, Aaron couldn't think of another island dinner that had held such an air of…happiness, he guessed was the right word. There had been dinners full of relief, especially after new people had joined them, and certainly dinners full of welcome or relaxation, but this one was different. He didn't even know if it was just the prospect of the gods returning, either. It was more like it was an excuse to be happy. Like it was a sign that Lemuria was growing and going to be all right.

His eyes followed Aelia as she whirled and dipped, lifted her arms and laughed. It was definitely going to be all right now. It had to be. He hadn't gone through hell to get Aelia only for it all to go to shit.

As he continued to watch her, thoughts of the future slipped out of his head, taken over by her. She'd consumed him almost since the instant they met. Certainly since she'd first spoken. Her physical beauty had been what had caught his eye, but it was her knowledge, her spirit, her stubbornness that had captured the rest of him. Just like she was doing now. She was only dancing with her friends, something she'd probably done hundreds of times, something he'd watched other women doing hundreds of times, but this time was special, just like the dinner was.

He'd never seen a woman dance with the skill and grace she displayed now, and her openness only made it that much more appealing. Not that she needed to do much more than exist to appeal to him.

The faint light from the moon and the flickering orange from the torches played over her skin like another kind of dance, and he felt himself rising from his chair. He knew the others were still chatting, but he didn't hear them, entirely focused on the ancient survivor who laughed and spun.

Mid-spin, her gaze landed on him, and she faltered before regaining her balance. Smiling like the sirens of legend, she extended a hand to him and crooked a finger. He was helpless not to respond, walking toward her, though he wasn't a dancer. As a tiger, he had the grace, was light on his feet, but he'd never had the time to learn how to put those to use on the dance floor. He didn't care. They weren't showing off tonight, they were enjoying the companionship and moonlight.

When he was closer, she twirled and brushed against him, using the music, the dance, to seduce him. Except he'd been seduced months ago, and doubted that would ever change.

As his body responded, he dimly noticed the music changing. Instead of a fast tempo and bright beat, it slowed, the tone heavy and deep, so he could feel it in his bones. Tugging her into his arms, he began to move with her, their bodies swaying, pressed together intimately.

He loved seeing her face in the light of the crescent moon, free of worry or sadness. Like this, happy and free, she was even more beautiful than ever.

"I have someplace I want to take you," she murmured, just barely over the music.

"Okay," he said without hesitation, knowing he'd let her lead him anywhere.

Smiling at him, she stepped back, her hand trailing down his arm until she could link her fingers in his. When she started to leave the square, he didn't even look back. They walked away from the village, through the darkness, and into the forest. Saying nothing, he only walked beside her, anticipation—sweet rather than sharp—building with each step.

Eventually he saw a small pool he'd not found before, but it was beautiful. Surrounded by the trees, it should have been dark, but there was an opening that let moonlight play over the water and the flowers whose color had been sapped by darkness. But it didn't matter. The beauty was still there.

Neither said a word as they undressed each other and sank to the soft grass beside the water. Sighs and moans were their music now as they loved each other, skin sliding against skin, hands and mouths caressing even as they aroused. And when he slid into her, it felt like the last piece to link them together forever clicked into place.

They spent hours there by the calm pool, and the only words spoken were each other's names. No other words were needed. Not with their hearts linked, their bodies joined.

Aaron had never been a man who thought much about romance, choosing blunt honesty and desire over gestures, but he couldn't deny that he was extremely moved by what he could only refer to as an interlude. Not that he was going to give up the primal anytime soon.

He'd slept outside before, even nude after a shift, but this was the first time he'd done so with a woman curled up beside him. But as she drifted off, her head resting on his bicep, he trailed his fingers up and down her arm, wondering when they could do it again.

CHAPTER 26

Aelia remembered falling asleep beside Aaron next to the pond, so when awareness returned, she smiled and reached for him, except the spot next to her was empty and cool. And while the grass had been soft the night before, now it was dry and crunchy.

Opening her eyes, she struggled to process what she was seeing. The pool was gone, and all she could see was an endless field of dead grass. Frowning, she pushed herself to a sitting position, one hand still on the ground to support her as she tried to figure out where she was.

"Did you really think that we were just going to bow to your godly friends and let you off without any repercussions?"

The angry woman's voice sounded familiar, but Aelia wasn't able to place it until she turned and saw the woman behind her. Shit. It was Daria, the jinn councilor. Arguably the most dangerous member of the Ekklesia.

"Did you really think I was just going to take your nightly tortures without responding?" Aelia shot back, getting to her feet. She wasn't sure what kind of jinn Daria was, but she didn't want to be at a disadvantage in case the woman decided to attack. But her own words made her pause and frown. This had to be another dream, despite the promise that the Ekklesia was going to leave her alone. There was no other explanation for how she'd gotten from Lemuria to this barren plain. If gods couldn't manage it, then it should be impossible for the Ekklesia.

"Actually, I expected you to give us what we demanded," Daria said, sauntering closer. "We've protected you for centuries, Aelia. You owe us."

"No," Aelia said firmly, "you protected yourselves. I'm not Arcane, but I could get humans asking too many questions that you didn't want asked. That's why you protected me. It was self-serving. Since it's just the two of us here, don't even try to pretend otherwise."

Daria shrugged and continued advancing, and Aelia noticed the grass starting to catch on fire in the woman's wake. Definitely a fire jinn. Hopefully she wasn't an ifrit—though it would explain more than a few things. "Whether it helped us or not is irrelevant. Without us, you would have suffered a great deal more than you did."

"I think you made up for that in the last few weeks," Aelia said, fighting to keep her voice neutral. Daria had to know how much suffering she'd caused, but it didn't mean Aelia had to make it easy to see.

"And the nightmares will stop," Daria assured her, the fire starting to spread outward, instead of just following in Daria's footsteps. "As long as you remain in hiding like a coward, we will not contact you again."

Aelia didn't trust that promise for a second. Daria and the other Ekklesia had to have something up their sleeves. "What's the catch?" she asked bluntly. She was already on the Ekklesia's bad side, so there wasn't any point in trying to suck up to them now.

Daria smiled cruelly and continued closer as the flames started to circle them both. Aelia grit her teeth because she knew just how painful flames could be, but she refused to show an ounce of weakness to this woman. Not easy, because she really, really hated being burned alive.

"The catch? Is that I am going to ensure you regret crossing us and choosing your pitiful friends over us." Slowly she lifted her arms out to her sides, palms up. The flames rose with the movement until they were taller than either woman. "Don't worry, I don't plan on killing you for long," she assured Aelia in a sickeningly sweet voice. "That would just shorten the suffering."

Her hands clenched into fists as she pulled them toward her chest. In a rush, the flames filled the circle, covering Aelia. She desperately tried to wake up, to hold in her scream, but she failed at both. As the fire began to eat away at her blackening skin, she screamed, curling in on herself as she tried to escape the flames that followed her.

Over the roar of the fire and her own pain, she heard Daria's laughter and prayed for it all to end.

The warmth of the morning sun drew Aaron out of his dreams of Aelia. She was still curled up against him, and he tightened the arm that was draped over her waist as he nuzzled the back of her neck.

The night before had been amazing. Not just the sex, though he'd never argue against that, but the way she'd actually opened up at the dinner. She'd talked, danced, and laughed without reservation, simply enjoying herself. He hadn't seen any of the sadness that had veiled her face for so long.

Sighing against her hair, he thought about waking her, but as his fingers lazily stroked over her belly, she tensed. Not just a twitch like if he'd accidentally tickled her, but a tightening of every muscle he could feel. Sitting up, he gently rolled her onto her back. Her eyes were still closed, but it didn't look like she was sleeping peacefully. Frowning, he gently shook her shoulder. "Aelia?"

She didn't respond, which reminded him of the nightmares she'd been having. The Ekklesia had agreed to back off, and if they hadn't, wouldn't Olivia have been monitoring Aelia's dreams? Unless Seth had told her it wasn't necessary any longer.

He shook her again, said her name louder, but she still gave no response. Then her skin began to redden, then blister, which did *not* remind him of the earlier nightmares. If he didn't know better, he'd think she was being burned—she even smelled faintly of fire and scorched flesh—but he didn't know how that was possible. And fixing it was definitely not in his skill set.

"Seth! Vazi! Dania!" he yelled, barely finishing the last name before Aelia's mouth opened and an agonized scream filled the air. "Aelia needs help!"

A lot of help. If this was the Ekklesia, he was going to kill them.

Dania showed up first, wide-eyed and a little unsteady. She turned toward him, flushed, and averted her eyes. "What's wrong?"

He'd forgotten that both he and Aelia were nude, and he was sorry to have unsettled Dania, but apologies would need to wait.

"I think she's having another nightmare, but somehow it's affecting her physically." Aelia let out another scream, and he had to move his hands away to prevent himself from hurting her as his nails shifted to claws. "It looks like she's being burned."

That distracted Dania from her embarrassment, but before she could move or speak, Vazi and Seth showed up, only a single second between them. Neither reacted to the lack of clothing, though Vazi did give Dania a quick look.

"What happened?" Seth asked as Dania knelt beside Aelia.

More than half of her body displayed signs of burning, and now she began writhing in agony. He could only imagine what she was feeling, based on the much smaller burns he'd received in his life-time.

"I woke up and a minute later she tensed up. I tried to shake her awake, but it didn't do any good. Then she started screaming and looking like..." Aaron trailed off and just motioned to the angry blisters and skin that was starting to blacken and split.

"Shit." Seth shook his head and looked at Vazi. "Can you do anything?"

"I can heal her, but I don't know if I can pull her from the dream," the elder god said, kneeling and resting his hand on Aelia's an-kle—one of the few places still untouched by the chimerical flames.

Aaron watched Aelia's skin, fighting the urge to touch her and hoping Vazi's healing would be enough. The progress of the burns seemed to slow for a moment, before resuming at a pace that terrified him. People could die from burns. Infection, shock, and gods only knew what else. And even asleep, it obviously was hurting like hell.

Dania placed a hand beside Vazi's, adding her powers to his, but again, it only looked like it helped for the first few seconds.

"I'm going to get Olivia," Seth told them before he disappeared.

"How can they do this? How can they make something she's dreaming become reality?" Aaron asked, torn between terror and fury, while he felt helpless to actually do anything useful.

"Dreams aren't my realm of expertise," Vazi said, shrugging as he continued to pour power into Aelia, his brow furrowed with worry.

It was difficult for Aaron to hear him over Aelia's screams, and he couldn't take his eyes off her face which was contorted with pain. Fur began to spread over his body, and the only thing preventing a full shift was the knowledge that she'd need him as a human when she came out of this. She had to come out of this.

Seth returned, Olivia at his side, looking frazzled. "What the hell?" she asked as she looked up at him.

"Aelia's burning in her dream. Get her out of it. Now," Aaron said, knowing he was snarling at the woman, but unable to help it.

"What?" She looked down at Aelia and spat out what had to be a curse. Dropping to her knees beside Aelia's head, she grimaced as her eyes slid over Aelia's face, then she gently rested her fingertips on the writhing woman's temples. Her eyes closed and she exhaled slowly.

Every second felt like an eternity as Olivia worked. Why was it taking so fucking long? She was a nightmare. This was literally her specialty, so why was Aelia still trapped in her own mind and burning in reality?

A soft hand touched his shoulder, and he looked up to see Dania, her face full of concern and empathy. "She'll be okay. She has you and the rest of us. She'll be okay."

He was shocked she'd willingly touched him—especially since he was nude—but could only nod. Any words he spoke would be full of what he was feeling, and even now he didn't want to scare her.

The wordless screaming changed to a wailed, "No!" that brought Aaron's attention fully back to the woman he loved. Her eyes were open now, and he'd never seen such pain in them, nor so much fear.

"You're okay," he quickly assured her, hating that he couldn't touch her yet. "Don't move. Let them help you."

Olivia quickly lifted her hands from Aelia's skin, and all three gods placed theirs on the least injured places they could find while she trembled and silently cried. This time, their healing had an obvious effect. As soon as her hand was free of damaged skin, he grabbed it, making sure his claws didn't prick her. Her fingers tightened on his with more strength than he'd known she had. She didn't scream, but he saw her jaw was clenched so hard her teeth had to be grinding together. Both the clenching and death grip on her hand began to lessen as the gods healed more and more of her damaged body, until all he could see was smooth, lightly tanned skin.

It was only then that it occurred to him that she was naked around four people who weren't her lover. Dania must have caught on at the same time, because a Grecian-style gown appeared on Aelia, and he felt clothing settle around his body as well. No dress this time; she'd put him in jeans and a tee-shirt. Not that he cared what he was wearing.

"How do you feel?" Dania asked, voice soft. "Did we miss any-thing?"

Aelia's arms wrapped around herself protectively as she shook her head wordlessly.

Unable to resist the urge to comfort her any longer, Aaron pulled her into his lap and held her close. At any other time, it would have delighted him that she curled into him, but now he just wished he could do something to erase the last few minutes from her memory.

"Let's give them a few minutes," Seth suggested, his voice also quiet. "Call for us when you're ready," he added to Aaron before all four disappeared.

Aaron didn't say anything at first, just rubbed Aelia's back as she trembled and tried to calm down. He knew she needed a few minutes, and she'd talk when she was ready.

The tremors gradually subsided and her hands began to loosen, though she didn't try to pull away. Still, he just stroked and held until she drew in a deep, not quite steady breath and tilted her head back so she could look up at him.

"Are you okay?" he asked, brushing her hair out of her face.

"No," she answered, surprising him, since 'I'm fine' was her normal go to. "But I will be."

"Want to tell me what happened?"

She considered for a moment, then nodded. "But I don't want to have to go through it more than once."

Aaron nodded and called out for the gods. The fact that all three and Olivia appeared within seconds told him they'd just been waiting.

"How are you feeling?" Vazi asked.

"Like I was burned alive," Aelia answered, letting her head fall against Aaron's shoulder. "I do not recommend any of you try it."

"Aaron said you were having another nightmare," Seth said. "Olivia got you out of it."

"I was. And thank you, Olivia. Again."

"No problem. Your nightmares before were bad, but this one was a particularly nasty one," Olivia said, and though her voice was mild, he could see the disgust and anger on her face.

"It was," Aelia agreed.

"Was it the Ekklesia again?" Aaron asked, arms tightening around her.

"Not all of them, but yes."

"Who do I need to kill?" Vazi asked, his tone darker now. "Or can I just kill all of them?"

"Stand in line," Aaron growled, but Aelia shook her head.

"You can't kill them all. They're needed."

"Fuck that," Olivia said, eyes narrowed. "How can we trust them to protect us when they do this?"

Dania cleared her throat quietly, and when she had the attention of the others, suggested, "Maybe we should let Aelia tell us exactly what happened before we start making plans to kill people?"

"Yes, you're right," Vazi said. "Aelia?"

"It was Daria." Like Aaron, the others didn't seem to know who that was, and the confusion showed on their faces. "She's the jinn representative."

Vazi and Seth looked at one another, and Aaron noted they both looked even more pissed than they had a minute before. "Why is that significant?" he asked them.

"She was mouthy and had no respect," Vazi answered in a snappish voice. "For Aelia or for us."

"And it seemed like she was in charge," Seth added. "But what did she say?"

"Fuck what she said. I want to know what she did," Aaron grumbled, running a hand over Aelia's arm, in a spot that just minutes ago had been burned to a crisp. The fact that it was smooth and unmarked now didn't erase the memory. Her screams were going to haunt him for years.

"She was...upset...that the Ekklesia wouldn't be able to use me anymore," Aelia told them, head still on his shoulder. "She even said the nightmares were done, that they were going to leave me alone, but clearly she wanted to punish me. So she burned me."

The last four words were said with almost no emotion, and the urge to kill this jinn rose up again.

"I don't know a lot about jinn other than they're either made of air or fire, but how in the hell was one able to burn her in a dream and have it actually burn her physical body?" Seth asked.

"Is she an ifrit?" Olivia asked.

"I don't know," Aelia said with a small shake of her head. "I've never really been that close to the current Ekklesia."

"Ifrit are the most powerful—and often the most evil—of all jinn," she explained. "An ifrit teamed up with a powerful dreamwalker or nightmare could possibly do this. I've heard of physical injuries transferring to reality, but magic being used like this is a new one. Still, it makes sense."

"I'm going to find and kill that dreamwalker," Aaron snarled.

"I'll help you," Olivia said, her eyes narrowed. "It pisses me off when people do shit like this. It's why nightmares have such a bad reputation. And dreams aren't even our only powers!"

"If you think I'm not going to be involved, you're both sadly mistaken," Vazi said.

"It can be a group lynching," Seth said dryly, but Aaron felt the slight vibration in the earth beneath him, proving that the god was more affected than he was letting on. "But first, we have the ritual tomorrow, and Aelia probably needs to rest after dealing with this bullshit. Afterward, we'll show the Ekklesia that they do *not* want to fuck with Lemuria."

Vazi looked like he was struggling to hold off, but Seth had effectively doused most of Aaron's anger. Aelia did come before anything else. "Can one of you gods pop us back to Aelia's house? And Olivia, do you think you could keep an eye out for more people fucking with Aelia for a day or two? Just to be safe?"

Olivia nodded. "I was planning on doing that anyway."

"Thank you," Aelia said.

Vazi sighed. "I'll send you home. But I want you to let us know if they try anything else. And I do mean *anything*. It's not just to protect you—though that's important—but to make sure all of Lemuria is safe from their machinations."

"I will."

He nodded and waved a hand, sending both Aaron and Aelia back to her house, setting them on the bed. Except other than getting her some place familiar, where he hoped she'd feel safe, he wasn't sure how to help her. "What do you need?" he asked.

"A bath," she answered without hesitation. "They did a good job of healing me, but I can still feel it. Smell it."

"Whatever you need," he told her, lifting her and carrying her into the bathroom. And though she protested that she could bathe herself, he carefully washed every inch of her, then simply held her some more in the warm, fragrant water. And given that the ritual was planned for the next night, spent the rest of the day pampering her in every way he could think of. If this was going to be their last full day, he wasn't going to let her spend it dwelling on the past.

CHAPTER 27

The last few days had been the happiest ones Aelia had experienced in ages—the visit from Daria aside—and eventually she realized she wasn't scared of what the future held, not anymore. Oh, her depression wasn't magically gone, nor was the anxiety that went hand in hand with it, but they were both a little muted now. It wasn't just that Aaron was immortal, or that she'd accepted that she loved him. No, it was that she felt she had purpose again. It was always good to be needed, especially by those who cared for her.

The ritual had her a little apprehensive, though. She intended to go through with it, felt it was important, but the risk of dying and staying dead was a deterrent now, not a lure. But she had to hope that having Aaron at her side, sharing the price with her, would make a difference. And to give themselves the best chance of succeeding, they'd even worked on being able to recite the spell in unison. It wasn't as difficult to be in sync with him as she'd thought it would be.

But while they prepared for success, they also planned for failure. They'd spent the first half of the day of the ritual together and alone, neither speaking of how the moon was in the correct position for the ritual. All too soon, Vazi, Seth, and Dania showed up for the ritual, though a few hours earlier than she'd expected. Before going anywhere, Vazi wanted to make sure they were certain they wanted to go through with it.

"I am. We are," she said, glancing up at Aaron. "The world needs the Lemurian gods back."

"And we both think we've got a good chance of coming through it if we do it together," Aaron added, but the playful and sexy tiger was gone, replaced by a serious man who knew exactly what he was risking.

"Then I think you both deserve something few others have gotten to experience," he decided, and both Seth and Dania nodded their agreement.

"Like what?"

He smiled faintly. "How do you feel about hanging out in Thelaria for a while before the ritual? There are a few hours until the sun will set. You can spend it here if you want, but we all thought you might like to see the home of the gods."

Aelia hadn't really lied when she told Aaron that she'd been everywhere, but she'd never actually managed to make it to the home of any of the pantheons. So, the chance to see the original realm of the gods excited her in a way little did anymore. "Are you serious? Don't toy with me, Vazi. I've got some very unpleasant spells that will work even on you," she warned.

Seth chuckled as Vazi shook his head. "I'm not toying with you. We talked about it. There's not a lot we can do to show our appreciation for what you're doing. If this goes badly, no gift will matter, and no words will be remembered. But this? We can give you this, and the promise that no matter what happens, your name won't be forgotten the way our names were."

"They weren't forgotten," Aaron said, shaking his head. "Aelia remembered. Akila did for a while. Someone always remembered you."

Vazi inclined his head in agreement. "That's part of why we want to do this, though." He stepped closer, eyes fixed on her. "You remembered us. You helped Tempest come back, helped bring me back. Don't get me wrong, Lemuria's going to remember Aaron's name—more's the pity—but you? You're going to celebrated, regardless of whether more gods come back or not. You're the reason we're all here. You're the reason Lemuria has a chance to thrive."

Aelia wasn't sure how she felt about his words, though they were technically true. She knew for certain that she was uncomfortable with the expression on his face, and the appreciation that basically rolled off the other two gods. It also touched her to have such a surly man giving her sincere appreciation for her actions.

Aaron must have sensed her discomfort, because he slid an arm around her shoulders and kissed her head. "Sometimes," he whispered just for her, "having gone everywhere, studied everything, can have a very big impact." Another kiss, then he grinned at Vazi. "Beam me up, Vazi," he said, shattering the air of solemnity. She could kiss him for that.

"Beam you up?" Vazi asked, looking confused, which made Seth and Aelia laugh.

"Remind me to introduce you to classic TV when this is over," Aaron said, shaking his head in disgust.

Vazi scowled, but said nothing, just taking them all to Thelaria.

Most divine teleportation was as smooth as silk, but something about going to Thelaria left her queasy and a little lightheaded.

"Just rest for a while," Vazi said, helping her to sit, while Seth eased Aaron to the ground.

Unable to do anything else, she just nodded and bent over, putting her head between her legs until the sensations passed. "Why did it feel like that?"

"There's a reason we very rarely brought our people here," Vazi explained. "This place feels like home to us, as comfortable as a mother's embrace, but for those who aren't Lemurian gods, it can be a little...overwhelming. But it gets better, and it's only when you first arrive. So when you feel better, look around. Drink from the stream, eat the fruit. It's all safe for you to enjoy without consequence."

Mention of those things had her finally paying attention and getting her first look at Thelaria.

Her first impression reminded her of Lemuria —a tropical paradise. There were trees and bushes and flowers, filling the area with color. Not just a few, either. Green was prevalent, of course, but she saw blossoms and leaves in every color she'd ever seen. The area they were in was a clearing surrounded by all that flora. She could see a mountain beyond the trees, with a tall waterfall spilling over it. Gaze following the flow down, she saw the water from it snaked toward them then split into two, so the twin streams circled the clearing.

It wasn't all natural beauty, though. She was actually sitting at the top of an open amphitheater. Tiered seating had been carved into the very stone, leading downward, with a fifty-foot circle at the bottom. Judging by the size of it, a few hundred people could sit on the bench-like seating.

"What is this place?" Aaron asked, sounding as awed as she felt.

"It's where we met to discuss...whatever we needed to discuss," Vazi answered. "Some pantheons opted for thrones or great halls. We preferred being here, outside. And equal. Some of us might have held more power, but all members of our pantheon were important."

"Nice system."

"We thought so. Hopefully, it will be the same when we're all back."

"I don't see any temples."

Vazi snorted, and even Aelia smiled. "Have you seen a single temple anywhere on Lemuria?"

"Huh. No, guess I haven't," Aaron conceded.

"We have houses here, scattered around Thelaria, but even if we were the sort to go for temples, I already said we didn't bring our people here, so what would have been the point?"

"Good point."

Feeling better, Aelia pushed to her feet and walked over to the stream, kneeling and trailing her fingers in it. Cool, but not cold. It would feel good to take a dip in, but for now, she couldn't resist a taste. Bending, she cupped her hand, bringing some water to her lips. The taste of it made her smile and close her eyes. "I haven't drank water like this in centuries."

"Hell, I never had until Vazi brought me here," Seth admitted, plopping down on the top tier.

"Almost no one has anymore, even in the Arcane."

Aaron joined her, though he was more hesitant to take that first drink. Understandable. Even when he'd been born, there was already industry and a growing population that had tainted most water, though not to the degree it was today. Watching, she saw the surprise on his face, and he took a second handful. "Fuck me. This is good. I mean, the water on Lemuria's pretty clean, but not like this."

"Because it's on Earth, and even though Lemuria is untouched by humans, it still shares the sky and sea with the rest of the world," Vazi said.

"Try the fruit," Dania said, voice still quiet and shy. "It's even better here, too."

Aelia chose a simple apple, biting into it as she walked back to the amphitheater and sat. Like the water, she hadn't tasted an apple like this in centuries.

"Do you spend much time here?" she asked the goddess. She was less skittish than she had been, and seemed somewhat comfortable around Vazi and Seth, though she'd been told that at first Dania had been terrified of men. Oddly, she also seemed comfortable around Aaron, though at the dinners she watched every other man with some measure of suspicion.

"Some," Dania answered, looking startled to have been addressed. "It's nice here, but it's nice on Lemuria, too. Sometimes there are too many people there, so I come here instead. And it feels like home."

Guilt flooded her. She understood trauma, and should have been there more for the goddess, especially when she had still been so uncomfortable around men. Yes, she'd tried to step back so Dania and Rhea could get reacquainted, but that was just an excuse. Though if Dania thought two dozen people were too many, perhaps it had been best if she'd stayed away. Or maybe that was just a weak justification.

"Have you chosen a home here or there?" she asked, deciding to start doing better here and now, vaguely aware all three of the men were paying attention.

"There. My mother can't come here, since she's Greek, so I chose to live there so she can visit me." She smiled, though it was small and unpracticed. "It's nice that she can visit."

"She's a lot less scary than I expected," Aaron said, sitting down next to Aelia, but she noted he put her between him and Dania. "You hear about the goddess of motherhood, and you think she'll be a major mama bear."

Dania frowned and shook her head. "She's not a bear."

Aaron chuckled and shook his head. "It's a phrase. It means a woman who is overly protective of her children, much like bears are of their cubs."

"Oh." She processed that for a second then nodded. "That's accurate, but she's not irrational. She knew you weren't a danger to me."

"Why would he have been a danger?" Vazi asked, giving Aaron a dark, suspicious look.

"He ran into me in the forest, and when *Matera* showed up, it was just the two of us," Dania explained. "She knows that I...She was just concerned that I was alone with a man, but since I wasn't afraid, she wasn't a...mama bear." Her lips curved into an impish smile. "Of course, that could be because I made a mistake when offering him clothing after he shifted."

"Oh!" Seth said, laughing. "Was this the day you showed up at my house in a dress?" he asked Aaron.

"You went to Seth's house in a dress?" Aelia asked, stunned, amused, and sorry she'd missed it.

Unperturbed, Aaron nodded. "She put me in a dress, and since it covered everything it needed to cover, I didn't see why I'd need to change it to something else. And I only went to Seth's because that was the day you were babysitting Katrina."

"Think you could do that again?" Aelia asked Dania, smiling.

"No," he told her firmly, though he gentled when he looked at Dania. "They're just trying to tease me. No need for a dress right now. Especially since we don't know how the ritual is going to affect us. If I go down, I might flash everyone. Wouldn't bother me, but I don't think the rest of you want to see that."

"I second that," Vazi said dryly. "No one needs to see that."

"Thirded," Seth added.

"I need to see that," Aelia said in an innocent tone.

"What kinky shit you get up to in your own free time is fine, but not where my virginal eyes can see it," Vazi said, and everyone, including Dania, gave him a look of disbelief.

"Virginal eyes?" Aelia asked, shaking her head. "You forget, I was around back in the day. I saw some of the festivals. You're as virginal as Aphrodite!"

Vazi just shrugged, but he clearly knew better than to try to argue. Which was good. She really had seen him wander off or teleport away with more than one lady. A couple of times, it hadn't been only one woman he'd left with, either. It might be good to be king, but it was obviously better to be a god.

"While we have a few, I should probably share something from our visit with the Ekklesia. With all of you," Seth said, glancing at Vazi, who scowled and nodded once, sharply.

"Don't tell me they've fucked with someone else like they did Aelia. It's bad enough they told you they were backing off and then burned her in her dreams," Aaron said, his expression now similar to Vazi's, which amused her, despite the apprehension Seth's words stirred.

"No, everyone else is okay," Seth confirmed, nodding slightly. "But they said something when we visited them that's been bugging me since then. I mentioned it to Vazi, and he caught it too."

"And I don't like what it implies," the other god said darkly.

"Can you stop with the foreplay and just spit it out?" Aaron asked. "Do we need to expect another attack?"

"You know how I was going to use the geas as an excuse for them to leave her be?" She nodded, as did Aaron, and Seth continued. "I told them about, and like I said at the dinner, they were irritated about that, and for a while I thought it wouldn't be enough to get them to back off. Then I heard one of them whisper to another, wondering if it was just you who had the geas," he said, looking at Aelia.

She understood his meaning instantly. "They might have another source on Lemuria. Someone else they're torturing to find out about us."

Vazi nodded once. "That's what it sounded like to us."

"Do you have any idea who?" Aaron asked.

"No," Vazi ground out.

"We know it's not us," Seth elaborated. "Tempest definitely would have told me if she was having nightmares, and Kara isn't exactly known for holding in her feelings. And she would have said something to me even if she didn't feel comfortable sharing it with anyone else."

"That's for damn sure," Aaron said, a hint of amusement showing through the irritation.

"I can't see that my dad would keep quiet, either," he continued. "But that does leave multiple people."

"It's probably not the children," Aelia mused aloud. "They'd be the easiest to...convince...but they're also the least likely to have any useful information. And I would hope that the Ekklesia would have better morals than to torment children."

"Yeah, but we thought they were above blackmail and dream torture, too," Aaron pointed out.

She couldn't deny that. "True."

"So how do we find out?"

"Julian's wife is a powerful telepath. She might be able to help," Seth suggested.

"Unless it's someone who's helping them willingly and who is shielding their mind," Vazi said, crossing his arms as he shook his head. "We tried to ensure only those who would be loyal to Lemuria were allowed on the island, but the Ekklesia do have resources, and they've had thousands of years to accumulate methods of hiding their actions."

"It is their whole reason for existing," Seth agreed. "They're masters of suppressing memories and hiding things.

"Exactly."

Aelia considered a moment, then offered, "Grovek might have some ideas of how to figure it out." That was kind of his reason for existing. They hid, he learned.

Vazi brightened, though she wasn't sure what she thought of the glee in his eyes. She'd need to remember never to get on his bad side. Though from what he'd said before, it sounded like she had a few thousand free passes before he actually retaliated in any way. More, if she did manage to help bring the gods back. It was good to be a god, but it never hurt to have one as a friend.

They shifted away from serious topics and continued talking and joking for the next few hours. Dania came out of her shell more and more, right up until the sun set and the moon started to glow in the sky. She was a little surprised that it seemed to operate the same as it did on Earth, but supposed it was mirrored. Thelaria was another realm, but why would the gods have created a vastly different home than the one created for their people?

Staring up at the perfect half-circle as it hung almost directly overhead, she sighed, uncertain if she felt excitement or dread at the sight. It didn't really matter either way. She looked at the gods, then over at Aaron.

"It's time."

CHAPTER 28

T he mood of fun and friendship shifted, and the eyes of the others lifted to the moon. "Are you two ready?" Vazi asked, lowering his gaze to them.

"Can you give us a few minutes real quick?" Aaron asked.

"Of course," Seth said, he and the other gods moving away to give them some space.

"Are you still okay with this?" Aelia asked him, but he pulled her into his lap, wrapped his arms around her, and buried his face against her neck.

Since he seemed to need the contact—and honestly, so did she—she didn't press, just hugged him tight and closed her eyes, savoring what could be their last embrace. On this side of the veil, anyway.

"I'm okay," he murmured. "Nervous, and I'm really hoping this works out, but I've risked my life for a lot less in the past." Lifting his head, he brushed her hair back. "Part of me still hates that you're risking yours, too."

"That's mutual."

He nodded. "Then give me two things before we do this?"

"Anything," she said, honestly meaning it. She'd give this man anything in her power to give.

"Kiss me and tell me you love me. Just in case."

The easiest things in the world to give. That was all he was asking for. "I love you," she said, voice strong, thick with emotion.

"I love you, too. So fucking much," he said, sliding a hand into her hair, though his touch was gentle. Giving in, she tipped her face up and kissed him. She didn't want it to end and lingered over it. To their credit, none of the others interrupted, giving them as much time as they needed. Except now she wasn't sure she'd ever have enough time. Gods, she hoped they lived through this so she could have lifetimes of kisses and his surprising moments of sweetness.

"We should stop," she said after reluctantly drawing back.

"Probably. I don't care about an audience, but even I've gotta think twice about getting naked and sweaty where the gods meet," Aaron whispered.

It made her smile, as she expected it was meant to. "Yeah, Vazi might love us right now, but he might draw the line there."

Aaron helped her to her feet, then rose. "We're ready," he called to the gods.

As a group, they walked down to the bottom of the amphitheater. When they reached the center, Vazi lifted a hand, the journal appearing in it, and he offered it to them. "Don't screw up. You've grown on me." He arched a brow and focused on Aaron. "Even you, despite you being a pain in the ass."

"Trust me, I plan to live to be a pain in your ass for the next couple thousand years," Aaron said, accepting the journal. All three gods backed away, probably so they didn't interfere with the spell in any way. Then he turned to Aelia, holding it out so she could wrap her fingers around it as well. "You ready?" he asked, taking her free hand in his.

Aelia nodded, drawing in several slow, deep breaths. She'd performed hundreds of spells, including powerful ones, but never anything this important. "Remember, we have to speak in unison," she reminded him, despite their earlier practice.

"On three?"

"On three."

His eyes remained on hers as he began counting. "One. Two." They both took a breath before he said, "Three," then began the chant.

It only took a few syllables before energy poured from the journal and into them both, stronger than she thought she could bear. Her words tried to falter, but she couldn't screw this up. She couldn't risk Aaron's life because she had fumbled the spell. She wouldn't. With each sound, it became harder to speak, but she managed to match her words with Aaron's.

Pain followed the pure energy, and as one they fell to their knees, unable to remain upright. Even kneeling was difficult, but they seemed to support one another, preventing them both from falling and breaking contact with the journal. She felt moisture sliding down her face and from her ear, but didn't need to wonder at the cause, not when she could see blood trickling from Aaron's eyes, nose, and ears. The red haze that clouded her vision only proved that her eyes bled as well.

The Anunnaki hadn't been exaggerating when they said the spell would take a toll. Even in pain, her brain fogged from both it and the magic using her body as a conduit, she realized bleeding like that meant that something was very wrong. Every part of her wanted to stop, to do anything if it meant the agony would cease. Death would be preferable to this, but still, she refused to be the cause of Aaron's demise, especially if it might become permanent. It was hard enough seeing the strain on his face as more and more blood poured out of him.

There was a ringing in her ears now, and she didn't know if it was internal damage or something external, but she couldn't even hear her own words. The only way she knew she was still in time with Aaron was by the movement of his lips. And the pressure. Gods, the pressure. She'd been deep below the surface of the ocean before, felt it pressing in on her from all sides, crushing her more easily than she could ball up a piece of paper. That had been a pleasant sensation compared to what she was experiencing now.

Her vision started to go spotty, but she forced herself to speak the last few words. As soon as she did, the world exploded with light, before it all disappeared into darkness.

Since Dania had been born, she'd known she was a goddess. She might have forgotten that while she had been under Zeus's control, isolated from others. But that meant she hadn't been around gods for most of her life, so she was unused to magic like this. Her own powers? Yes, absolutely. She'd been forced to use them on numerous occasions for her captor, so knew every nuance of how to create destruction. This was something on an entirely different level, and it scared her. But if this succeeded, then her father might be one of the gods they were able to bring back. Having her mother in her life again was wonderful, and she treasured every moment she spent with Rhea, but it had reminded her of the time she'd spent with her father when she was a child, learning to use her powers, how to enjoy them. She could see his face again, and she missed him.

And yet, watching the human and tiger so obviously suffering was bringing back memories of times she'd been tortured for refusing to do as her half-brother had commanded. And though men—most men, she corrected—still frightened her, she found herself easing toward her fellow gods. They were safe. Seth was so obviously enamored of his wife, and Vazi had done everything he could to make her feel comfortable. Even Rhea had assured her neither would harm her, so now, when she was fighting off her own painful past, she reached out for a hand, not caring whose she grabbed.

Vazi caught it and squeezed, but didn't look down at her. "They're going to be okay," he whispered, staring at the couple just like she was. "They have to be okay."

His words sounded desperate, and she understood. It was a hard thing they had asked the pair to do, and it was astonishing that they'd not just agreed, but volunteered. That didn't make it any easier to watch, knowing they could do nothing to help. Knowing that this could kill them. That this could be the last time anyone ever saw them alive, sacrificing themselves for Lemuria.

She could see the power swirling out of the journal and toward them, building stronger and stronger with every word they spoke. When they dropped to their knees, she took a step toward them, but Vazi held her back, even when blood masked their features.

"If we get too close, we might disrupt the spell, which could be fatal," he told her quietly. "We can't interfere until they're done. Their best chance is if we let them finish."

Aelia and Aaron swayed, and her hand clamped down on Vazi's, not caring that she was starting to cry in sympathy for what they were dealing with. Then there was a light, bright enough to blind even her vision. Lifting an arm to shield her face, she bit her lip to avoid embarrassing herself by making a frightened sound. When the light dimmed, she cautiously lowered her arm, then gasped.

The couple she'd come to like—though she knew Aaron better than Aelia—was sprawled on the ground, completely covered in blood, now. From where she stood, they looked dead, their eyes open but unfocused. They weren't alone. Next to each was another body, one man, one woman. They were still as well, but somehow they looked to be sleeping rather than gone.

Dania wanted to rush to the two who could be her friends, but the appearance of the other two honestly frightened her. True, it was more the man than the woman, but she knew neither one.

"It worked," Vazi breathed.

"But at what price?" Seth asked, rushing forward without hesitation and dropping to his knees beside Aelia and Aaron. For now he ignored the other two, but since he was checking on her friends, she joined him. It took only seconds for them to search for signs of life and realize that the ritual had done just what the Anunnaki had warned them about. They were dead.

"They're gone," she whispered, crying without shame. Aaron had been so kind to her, even when she'd messed up and put him in woman's clothing. And Aelia had always seemed so sad, at least until the last few days, but she'd been just as kind. Seeing them gone injured her already battered heart. She manifested a cloth and bowl of water. Maybe she hadn't been able to help them, but she could clean the blood from their faces.

"They might come back," Seth said, voice thick, and she glanced at him to see he was just as affected as she was. It astonished her to see a powerful god with tears in his eyes, but he didn't seem to notice.

"Do you really think so?"

"I have to." Drawing in a breath, he looked over at Vazi. "Are the other two alive?"

Vazi nodded and glanced up from where he knelt beside the man. "They're just unconscious. I guess this ritual is harder on a god than whatever brought me back."

"Is it the two we wanted? Grovek and...insanity girl?" he asked.

"Telia," Vazi supplied. "And yes."

Hand on Aaron's shoulder, hoping that it would move beneath her fingers, she actually looked at the gods these two had brought back. Telia was tiny. Not quite as small as a child, but shorter than her, and maybe a little slimmer, too. It was hard to tell. Her blonde hair was partially obscuring her face, but it looked a little wild, and not like it was just a result of her falling. It was long, though, partially covering her upper body.

The man—Grovek—was much taller. Close to Vazi's six four, she estimated, and with a similar athletic build. His hair was black and around shoulder-length, so she could see his face better than the woman's. His skin was tawny where the woman was fair. Then his eyes opened, proving they were brown.

Grovek's eyes landed on Seth first, and his brow furrowed with obvious confusion. "Who are you?" he asked in Lemurian, and it struck her that it was the first time she'd heard the language spoken since she'd been released from captivity.

"I'm Seth," was the answer in the same language. "You don't know me, but I think you know him," he said, pointing to Vazi.

Pushing himself into a sitting position, Grovek looked over and nodded. "Vazi. Yes." He lifted a hand to his head and rubbed at his temple.

The woman woke a little more quickly. Her eyes—blue, Dania saw—popped open and she shoved herself upright. "There are strangers in Thelaria," she said in a voice more dreamy than confused. "Why are there strangers in Thelaria?"

"Telia," Vazi said, waiting until her focus shifted to him. "I'm not a stranger."

Her head cocked, bird-like, and she made a small sound in her throat. "Sky boy. Yes, I know you. Why are there strangers here?"

"This is Dania. She's a half-Lemurian goddess. Her father is Tryno."

Her lips curved into a smile that was half-pleased, half...crazed? "Ahh. I like him. He makes storms."

"And the man?" Grovek asked, though he still sounded like he was acclimating after his...was journey the correct word?

"He's the new Lemurian god of mountains," Vazi explained.

Telia scrambled to her feet. She swayed like a drunk and shook her head so strongly that her hair flew about. "What happened to Jalvas? Jalvas is the mountain king."

Feeling protective of Aelia and Aaron, even though they might never wake again, Dania leaned slightly over them as she continued to wipe at the blood, but Telia didn't even seem to notice they existed.

"You and all the other gods had disappeared except for Jalvas, and he lost his balance," Seth explained, voice calm and patient, almost like he was speaking to a child. "He tried to kill the last Lemurian woman, and I had to kill him in self-defense. And," he added when she started to growl and took a step toward him, "if I hadn't, then none of you would be here right now. Me becoming the new god of mountains brought Vazi back, which helped lead to you and Grovek being back."

Abruptly—because everything the woman did was abrupt—she calmed. "Pity. I liked Jalvas."

"Is...Is that Aelia?" Grovek asked, staring at the body of the woman with a mixture of hope and horror.

"It is," Vazi confirmed, looking just as torn between emotions. She could even guess which ones. Excitement about there being more Lemurian gods, and sorrow over the deaths that had been required to do it.

"Aelia," he said on a sigh, moving to kneel beside Seth, carefully pulling a strand of hair from her face, then gently wiping some of the blood from her cheeks. When it did little, he waved a hand, all the blood disappeared from both Aelia and Aaron, leaving them clean, but cold and still.

"You knew she was immortal?" Vazi asked.

Grovek nodded. "I did, and it's my fault."

"How so?"

"She wasn't the first. I brought the cause to my sanctuary, but then I brought her there. She found it and..." He made a helpless gesture toward her. "I was looking into what could be done for her—and the other—then I was..." Frowning, he looked up at Vazi. "There was a void for a while, then I was here. What happened?"

"Shouldn't they be coming back?" Dania asked, caring less about the history lesson than she did for the two still lying lifeless on the ground. "How long does it take?"

"I've only seen it happen a few times, but it seemed to take a couple of minutes. But those were normal deaths. Drowning, shooting, things like that. This was definitely not natural." Seth glanced at his watch, and his concern deepened, making her think it had already been longer than normal.

Did that mean they weren't coming back?

"The Anunnaki did say it would be difficult. Maybe it will take longer to recover from so much power?" she asked desperately trying to find any strand of hope she could cling to.

"Maybe," was all Seth could offer her.

"Hello," Telia said in a singsong voice, drawing the word out. "Anyone going to answer book boy?"

Vazi didn't go far, but he did sit. He explained about Zeus and other gods inciting them to fight, how it had caused them to destroy a large part of Lemuria along with a great many of their people. How somehow they'd all been sent elsewhere, in some kind of stasis, while the remaining Lemurians had been killed off until only Tempest remained. Seth picked up the story there, telling them how he'd found Tempest and, with the help of the Aelia, Aaron, and Kara, had rediscovered Lemuria, fought Jalvas, and begun rebuilding. Vazi slid in then, explaining about the ritual and handing Grovek back his journal, though the god didn't seem to care much about it. Odd, since Aelia had sworn he cherished it. Maybe he liked Aelia at least as much as she'd started to? Certainly not as much as Aaron did, though.

Dania truly hoped they woke up. Love wasn't something she understood well, but it was clear these two had it, and it seemed wrong for them to lose each other as soon as they'd found each other.

"So how long were we gone? Did I miss anything good?" Telia asked.

"More than six thousand years," Vazi answered, and she blinked at him, not seeming to comprehend. "A lot has changed while you were gone. Those of us here? We're the only Lemurian gods on this plane of existence. And while there are thousands of witches, shifters, sirens, and elementals, there are only two true Lemurians. Tempest—who you might both remember—and a daughter she had not long ago. Only about twenty people live on Lemuria now."

Crazy or not, even Telia looked horrified at the summation.

"You are free to go for now, but we're keeping a low profile right now," he warned her. "There are too few of us to go up against the other gods right now. And I mean it, Telia. Don't harass the other pantheons until we're stronger."

She made a 'pfft' sound while wagging both hands in the air. "Fine. Spoiling my fun. I'll be good. For now." Then she disappeared.

Grovek looked more concerned and kept looking between Vazi and Aelia. "I can't say I'm surprised Zeus became a problem. From what I learned about him, he was extremely ambitious and jealous of those who had more power than he did." He asked Dania, "You said something about these two coming back. Can I take that to mean she's still immortal, and he somehow has the same ability?"

She nodded, but was uncertain quite how to answer otherwise, and looked to Vazi, then Seth, for help.

"They found Navid. I guess he was the first immortal?" Seth asked. When Grovek nodded, he went on. "From what they told us, Navid ended up hating being immortal and found a way to transfer it. He had tried it on quite a few people, unsuccessfully, before he managed to do it with Aaron a few days ago. That...That's why they did this ritual."

The god of wisdom frowned disapprovingly. "You knew they would die?"

"Don't judge him—or us—too strongly, old friend," Vazi said quietly. "First, they both volunteered. Second, the Anunnaki were the ones who gave us the ritual to bring you back, one pair at a time. If just one person, even an immortal like them, did the ritual, there was almost no chance of survival. Aelia wanted to do it from the start, even knowing it might be her last death. But the Anunnaki said if two immortals performed it together, there was a chance they would survive."

"How long have they been in this state?"

Again, Seth glanced at his watch. "It's been about ten minutes now."

Too long, Dania thought. If it had only taken a few minutes before, it was too long. Too much change. Too much loss. She prayed to her mother that she was wrong, but her abilities all focused on natural disasters. She could do nothing to help them. But she would stay and watch over them, for as long as it took.

Grovek nodded and lightly touched Aelia's hand. "Then we will wait longer, and see if they need to be honored as fallen heroes, or celebrated as the ones strong enough to begin rebuilding our pantheon."

No one argued, just moved the limp bodies until they were on their backs, side by side. Settling around them, two on each side, they waited, and they hoped.

CHAPTER 29

Dying, at least for Aaron, was nothing like what people described. He'd seen a white light this time, but it wasn't a beacon to lead him to the other side. There had been pain, but it hadn't faded just before he'd died. Instead, it all built until everything had disappeared. No floating, no visions of lost family, no glimpses of the afterlife, just...nothing. Then, abruptly, he was back. His body ached, and he wasn't sure where he was or what had happened.

Groaning, he went to lift his arm, but it was heavy and took a lot of effort to move even a little.

"Take it easy," a soft woman's voice said. "You've been dead for a while."

Unable to place the voice, or quite understand what she'd meant, he opened his eyes. No bright light now, just a soft glow from the half moon overhead. Two faces hovered over him, and it took several seconds before their identities clicked in his mind. Seth and Dania.

Thelaria.

The ritual.

Dying in agony.

He remembered it all now. "Aelia," he breathed and tried to sit up, but that, too, was difficult. Dying really took its toll on the body, and it wasn't until Seth helped him that he managed.

"She's right here. She's waking up, too," a different voice said, and he turned to see Aelia lying beside him, Vazi—the one who had spoken—and a dark-haired man he didn't recognize on her other side.

Forcing his body to cooperate, he grabbed her hand, squeezing as hard as he could at the moment. "Aelia," he repeated.

"We came back," she told him, and he hated how weak and pained her voice sounded. She probably felt like he did, but he didn't like that she was suffering.

"We did," he said, willing her to open her beautiful violet eyes.

She did, and they found his before she smiled tiredly. "You're alive," she breathed, squeezing his hand in return. He barely felt it, but that didn't matter. She was alive, and she'd get stronger. They'd both get stronger. They were alive, and everything else they could fix. "Did it work?"

Aaron was reluctant to look away from her, but he did, to look at the stranger. "Not sure. You Grovek?" Normally he might be a little more respectful of someone who might be a god, but he didn't have the energy to care. Besides, if this was Grovek, he very literally had paid for the god's presence with his life. He definitely owed Aaron a little leniency.

The man nodded. "I am, yes."

Aelia's head turned, and he heard a soft catch in her breathing that made him look back down at her. Her eyes were damp, and she reached up with her free hand toward Grovek, which he caught. "You're back. It worked. It really worked," she said, voice thick.

For a second, Aaron felt the sharp pang of jealousy, but he forced it away. This man had been her mentor. He was a partial reason why she'd still been alive for Aaron to meet. And with everything Aelia had said when referring to him, he'd never gotten the slightest hint that she'd ever been romantically or sexually attracted to the man. She was just relieved, which was understandable. This had been a long shot, and they'd not only survived, they'd achieved what they intended.

"How are you feeling?" Dania asked.

Unbelievably tired, he laid back, but kept his hand in Aelia's. "Dying really fucking sucks, but I'll be all right." He hoped. "Thought it was supposed to bring back two gods, though."

"The other one left," she explained. "You two have been dead for a while now."

"Close to an hour," Seth confirmed.

"I'm glad you're not dead anymore."

Aaron smiled faintly. "Me too."

Vazi and Grovek pulled them both to a sitting position, though Aaron wouldn't have minded lying there for a while longer. Then Vazi did something that made him feel better. Maybe not a hundred percent, but the ache lessened and the weariness no longer went right down to the bone.

"I want to thank you both," he told them, as serious as Aaron had ever seen him when he wasn't pissed off. "I know this wasn't easy for you, for either of you. Not just deciding to do it, but we could all see how much you suffered in the actual doing. And it's...huge. What you've done for the Lemurian gods is huge."

"It is," Grovek agreed, his face solemn. "I had a sense something was wrong, but no more than that while we were in that void. Still, it is good to be back."

"It's good to see you back," Aelia said, smiling at him as she leaned into Aaron. Releasing her hand, he wrapped his arm around her, comforted by the feel of her against his side, alive and warm.

"I will give you a few minutes, but then, if you do not mind, I would like to talk to you."

She nodded. "Of course. I know this has to be jarring for you."

He smiled wryly and nodded slightly. "That would be an understatement, yes."

"How about if we give them a little space?" Seth suggested, straightening. The others agreed and while Dania decided to leave, Seth, Vazi, and Grovek moved to the top of the arena, giving them some privacy.

"How do you really feel?" Aaron asked, shifting until he could wrap both arms around her.

"Exhausted, even with whatever Vazi did, and it feels like every muscle and joint aches. And my head," she admitted, relaxing against him.

"Same. It didn't feel this bad when I got killed in Norway." And it felt unbelievably weird to be talking about dying so casually. Maybe one day it would become normal, but right now he doubted it.

"Not all deaths feel the same when you come back," she explained. "Quick deaths take less of a toll afterward. Lengthy or especially painful deaths? They'll leave you more drained. Deaths that...don't leave you mostly intact will take longer to come back from. But you'll always be healed of whatever killed you. And I do mean whatever."

He hated to think of what she might have recovered from, especially knowing history like he did. The options were damn near endless. And horrifying. "So in a little while we'll both feel good as new?"

"I don't know how long it'll take, but yes. I can't say I've ever died doing a ritual like this." She paused, then glanced up at him. "I didn't think I had any firsts left," she said, sounding bewildered and a little awed by the fact.

"We'll find more firsts," he promised, hoping he could hold himself to that promise.

"Like Atlantis?"

"Oh, definitely Atlantis." He could actually think of multiple ancient sites that the humans were clueless about. He'd love to discover the truth of them with her.

They said nothing for a few minutes because, honestly, he was just so damn happy they were still alive. But then she sighed. "I want to go home and sleep, wake up, eat, bathe, then sleep some more."

"Same. With some celebratory sex tossed in somewhere."

She laughed, as he'd intended, though he wasn't really kidding with that. Not that he'd ever needed a reason to want to get her into bed.

"Let me go talk to Grovek, then we'll do just that. Including the sex. I vote for bath sex," she said, working on getting to her feet.

Aaron helped her before doing the same. "Sounds like a plan," he said, taking her hand as they started up the arena. The gods saw them coming and met them near the bottom, moving much quicker than they were.

"You could've just yelled for us," Seth told them.

"Yeah, because yelling at three of the most powerful gods on the planet is a smart idea."

Seth shrugged. "Nothing you haven't done before."

"True." And he realized just how comfortable he'd gotten around Seth and Vazi. Grovek might take some time, if only because he seemed stuffier than the other two. Vazi might have a temper and be unpredictable, but he wasn't normally stuffy.

"Are you feeling well enough to talk?" Grovek asked Aelia, just ignoring the byplay.

Definitely stuffy.

Aelia nodded. "I am, though lengthier conversations will need to wait until I've rested and eaten."

"Understood." He looked to his fellow gods. "If you will excuse us?" he said before both he and Aelia disappeared.

"What the fuck?" Aaron asked, his hand suddenly empty. He didn't like her being out of his sight so soon after they'd both died.

Vazi cocked his head for a second, frowning. "I can't sense either of them, so I'm going to assume they went to Sozu."

"A little warning might have been nice," Aaron muttered.

"Try to give the guy a little leeway," Seth suggested. "This is probably even more jarring for him than it is for you. You knew what was happening when you died and came back. He just lost six thousand years of his life."

It was a good point, but that didn't mean he needed to admit it. Or like it.

"Can you let him know we'll be back on Lemuria? Not sure how long they'll be, and I really do need to eat and get horizontal for a few hours."

There was another pause, then Vazi nodded. "Done."

"I'll take you back. Your house or Aelia's?" Seth asked.

"Aelia's. It's where she's most comfortable."

He nodded, and in the blink of an eye, he was back in Aelia's house.

"Call if you need anything," Seth told him before he left.

He did need food, but it really did sound like too much work. Sitting down on the couch, he tilted his head back, closed his eyes, and prepared to wait.

In just a minute, he was asleep.

Aelia wasn't surprised to see Sozu when the world reformed around them. Still weary, she sat on the edge of the platform, then winced when Akila's image appeared. If she'd known he hadn't intended to talk there in Thelaria, she would have warned him. Instead, she looked at his face and saw the tightness, the sorrow, as he listened to Akila's welcome.

"She is gone as well?"

Aelia nodded. "Until a year ago, Jalvas, Navid, and Tempest were the only Lemurians of any kind still alive, and Vazi had essentially put Tempest in stasis for that entire time. I lost contact with Akila many, many years ago. I'd held out hope she'd survived until some Arcane managed to find this place thanks to clues she left in her tomb."

He nearly smiled. "She would leave clues. Properly difficult, I hope?"

"Probably. I wasn't there, but I think they said Vazi was."

He nodded and stepped off the platform, looking around the room with a sigh. "I am pleased to see this place is intact."

"I couldn't bear to come here after Lemuria was destroyed, but it sounds like Akila continued to come here until her death."

Frowning, he turned back to her. "This is the first time you have been here in thousands of years?"

"No, I was here last week." She briefly explained the issue she'd been having with nightmares, finding James, and admitted to taking the unicorn horn to find Navid.

He waved off her pilfering of ingredients. "I was obviously not using it, and it sounds like if you had not taken it, I might not be here. That is how your companion also became immortal, and two immortals were needed to restore me to this world."

"True."

"I am sorry to hear about Navid, though. He was once a fine man. However, I am pleased that you have managed to remain as you were."

"But I haven't, not really," Aelia admitted, shaking her head. "I might not have gone on a killing spree like he did, but there were times when I sought mortality and a final death. It's actually what prompted...everything that's happened in the last two weeks." She smiled. "Aaron didn't want to let me go."

"I take it immortality has not been kind to you?"

She sighed and shook her head. "Grovek, I've died thousands of times, and most of them were extremely unpleasant. I stopped letting myself get close to people because everyone kept dying. I can't even count the number of people I've had to bury." He looked guilty, so she offered him a smile. "It hasn't been all bad, though. If I hadn't been immortal, I couldn't have helped Tempest get back to Lemuria, prompting the return of you, Vazi, and Telia."

"And you would not have been alive to meet the man I met in Thelaria?"

"Aaron, yes," she confirmed, nodding. "He's good for me, Grovek. I love him. And he shares my love of history. Fortunately, he loves me for me, not because I lived through much of the history he likes to study."

He nodded and began to wander the room, his hands clasped behind his back. It made her smile and lightened her mood. She recognized this as his being deep in thought, something she'd seen him do hundreds of times in the year she'd been his apprentice.

Eventually, he made his way back to her and cocked his head. "After I realized you had become immortal like Navid, I began working on a way of reversing the effects. Can I assume that doing so is not something you desire any longer?"

That was a huge part of why she'd wanted to bring him back, but she couldn't say she wanted that now. As Aaron had said, if she truly wanted death, she would have asked the Anunnaki. "A week ago, I would have begged you to find a way. I would have helped you. But now?" She shook her head. "I can't lose him. No matter what else happens, I can't lose him. That matters. It's not why I love him, but it matters. And he makes me see things as though they were new again. Helps me to find new firsts, things to make life...worth living, I guess." She laughed softly. "Besides, if Aaron and I become mortal again, then you and the other gods will have a hell of a time getting the rest of your pantheon back."

"Mmm. That is a factor I had not considered, but a very important one, yes. More importantly, I am pleased you want to stay. I just have one more thing before I take you back to Lemuria. The new god—Seth, I believe his name is—took Aaron back to your house."

"Yeah, there are about twenty of us living on Lemuria now," she said. "Seth, Tempest, and their daughter are the only true Lemurians, but it's a start."

"It is," he agreed. "Are you still wishing to be my apprentice, Aelia? Your mind does not seem to have dulled in the years since I last saw you, and you were always very eager to learn."

As soon as he asked, it clicked that she'd been hoping for that very thing. She'd loved learning from him, hypothesizing with him, experimenting with him. "Of course. I might even be able to teach you some things now."

He smiled. "I am actually counting on that. Much can happen in a single year, and I am told it has been more than six thousand. I am sure there are many things I will need to learn."

She couldn't help it; she laughed. "There really, really is. I won't get into any of it now, but just so I can get your wisdom juices interested, remind me to start with computers and the fact that the Miasma was almost released into the world a few months ago."

His brows shot up, but he nodded slowly. "When we reach that point, can I request you start with the Miasma?"

"I figured that would be your focus. And yes, I'll start there. But I think you'll find the computer a fascinating invention. I would wager money that you'll have one very soon after you understand what they are."

"Intriguing," he murmured. "But you need rest now. Can you think of the place that is now your home? I will send you there while I ensure everything here is how it should be." She nodded and pictured her house. He smiled and touched her arm lightly, which was his version of showing affection. "Be safe," he told her before sending her back to her house.

Aaron was already there, asleep on the couch. Tired, just wanting him, she laid down, her head in his lap, and let herself join him in dreams.

CHAPTER 30

Light streamed in through the windows when Aaron woke, the aches in his body gone. Groggy, he was certain he'd only closed his eyes for a moment, and he'd been sitting up. Now he was horizontal, with a gentle weight pressing down on him. Blinking his eyes open, he saw a familiar blonde head on his chest.

That was a good way to wake up. Not wanting to disturb her in case she needed more sleep, he remained still, though he couldn't resist a stroke of his hand down her hair. Apparently she was stirring, too, because she made a small sound of pleasure and shifted atop him.

"Morning," he murmured, his voice still rough from sleep.

Tilting her head back, she looked up at him with still-blurry eyes and gave him a sweet, lazy smile. "Hey."

Since she was awake, he ran his fingers down her back, then up again, and she stretched like a kitten. He wanted to ask how she was, but thought it better to do after they'd both fully woken. He didn't know about her, but his brain was still fuzzy. "Coffee?"

"Gods yes," she breathed. Before she got off him, she gave him a light kiss, and he instantly regretted his suggestion. His body didn't seem to care that he'd died, not when he'd woken up with such a sexy sorceress draped over him like a blanket. Forcing himself to ignore his erection, he got up, and neither of them spoke until they'd dealt with the necessary morning tasks and had a cup of coffee each in them.

"How are you feeling?" he asked, following her out into the garden. The sun was well-overhead, showing that the morning was already gone.

"I'm okay," she told him, sitting on one of the benches.

"Really?" he asked, settling beside her, knowing she'd understand he didn't mean physically.

She nodded and leaned into him. He loved how casual she was with him now, especially with the small things. Sex was easy; it was basic. Genuine affection and intimacy were harder, especially for someone with her past. "I really am," she promised. "I'm not going to lie and say I'm cured, because that's not how it works. The future is still scary, and it weighs on me, but it feels like my immortality has a purpose now, which helps. It's like all these years I've had to suffer through were just the price that needed to be paid in order to bring back the Lemurians."

"That's one way to look at it," he said, nodding slowly.

Smiling, she shifted her coffee to her other hand so she could lace her fingers with his. "It's not just the Lemurians either," she said. "You help, a lot. And I can't say I love you because you're immortal, but I think it's why I was able to admit it. Like you said, I *can't* lose you, and that matters. And..." She hesitated, clearly struggling with the right words. "You know how you said you'd die a thousand times for me?"

He nodded. "I did, and I mean it. Dying sucks, but you're worth it."

She blinked rapidly for a moment, and he saw her eyes shining with unshed tears. While he didn't like the idea of making her cry, he wasn't against making her feel so strongly. "I think I've already died a thousand times for you," she said quietly.

Damn, but he hadn't thought he could love this woman anymore than he did, and he ignored the stinging of his own eyes as he bent his head and captured her mouth in a long, deep kiss.

"If I have my way, you'll never die again," he told her quietly. "And I know I can't make the future less scary, but I can take some of the weight. We've still got those firsts, like Atlantis. And we'll find other things that excite you."

"Actually, aside from the idea of finding Atlantis and being with you, I do have something else that excites me," she admitted.

"Good. What's that?" he asked, stroking his thumb over the back of her hand.

"Grovek." Again there was that spurt of jealousy, but he beat it back. "He wants me to be his apprentice again. And to teach him."

"The stuff he's missed while he was gone?" She nodded. "No better person to help him with that. Especially on Lemuria. You're the only one who's lived through it all."

"And I'm the only one who understands, at least a little, how his mind works." She smiled. "It'll be nice, learning again. I know I've learned a lot on my own, about the human world, the Arcane world, the natural world, but I know there's still a lot he can teach me."

"Did he always have two apprentices at once? Like how he had both you and Akila?"

"Generally, yes. Especially since we assisted as much as we learned. Why?"

He grinned. "Because he's down an apprentice and I have even more to learn than you do. Though I don't know if I'd be anywhere near as good a student as you are."

She laughed. "Not all of his apprentices were like me. Even Akila was more...outgoing."

"So he's not going to zap me the first time I ask what the fuck he means?"

"Not the first time. And I can definitely ask if he'll consider teaching you. I think it's a possibility. Remember, other than me, he only ever taught Lemurians. They're not exactly easy to find anymore, and I don't know if any of the others would be interested."

He nodded and gave her hand a squeeze. "So with all this, does that mean you plan on sticking around for the next few centuries?"

"Right now I plan on sticking around for the next few millennia," she admitted. "You were right. There are still things to discover and learn here, and we're getting close to exploring space." She smiled. "And I'm more than a little rusty with relationships, so I'll need to relearn how to do that," she teased.

"We'll both need to learn how to be in a relationship with someone who's never going to die," he agreed before he set his coffee aside. He wasn't really a guy anyone could consider traditional, but he could fall back on the classics when it was something that mattered. She definitely mattered.

Sliding off the bench to settle on one knee, he took her hand in both of his. Her eyes went wide, and she blindly set her cup down, lips parting as he heard her breathing quicken.

"Aelia, I can't say I'm perfect. Anyone who knows me knows that's a fucking lie. I'm impulsive, kind of crude, have a temper...the list really goes on and on. But I'm also completely fucking loyal to those who matter to me, and you matter more to me than anyone else ever has."

"Aaron," she breathed, but he squeezed her hand and continued.

"I know you were pissed when you realized Navid passed his immortality onto me, but I'm not. Not because it means I have time to explore like I wanted, but because it means more time with you. I may make you want to kill me sometimes, but that's okay because I'll always come back, and I'll always say I'm sorry. I may be kind of crap with romantic gestures, but I'll always make sure you know I love you. So Aelia...even though I screwed this up by not having a ring...will you marry me? Be my wife for the next few thousand years? And the thousands that come after that?"

Aelia was the sort who was never without something to say—usually something wise—but it took her a few tries before she managed to get a single word out, and he hoped that was a good sign.

"What about children? Do you want children?" It wasn't the response he'd expected, but it wasn't an outright no, so he would take it. Especially since he understood why she was asking. Losing a husband was hard enough, but he couldn't imagine how badly it had hurt when she'd lost her children.

"I wouldn't mind kids," he admitted. "I can't say I've been around them a lot, but I like the idea of raising a little Aelia. That said, it's not a deal-breaker for me either way. If we never have kids, that's fine. If we do, that's fine, too. But I do need to point out one thing."

"What's that?"

"From what I understand about Lemurians, shifters were originally Lemurian, right?"

She nodded. "Right."

"And if I'd been born on Lemuria, I'd have been as immortal as Tempest, right?"

"Right," she repeated.

"So if we had kids, and if they were born on Lemuria, they'd also be as immortal as Tempest? I mean, they'd be half shifter."

Her response was slower this time, but she nodded again. "They should, yes. Halflings still have the Lemurian blood of their Lemurian parent."

"Then if we do have kids, we'll make sure we have them here. It might not be our kind of immortality, but they'll also have two parents who aren't afraid to literally die for their kids. But I really am okay either way. I just want you, however I can get you. I'd say I don't even care if it means we just stay together but never get married, but I want that commitment. I want us to stand up in front of our friends, our family, and make those vows to each other."

"And you won't resent me if I can never get past my issues and never want kids?"

He shook his head and tried to think of the right words to convince her, because nothing had ever been as important as getting her to say yes to this one thing. He'd compromise on just about anything else, but he needed her to say yes. "I promise I won't. If I ever get baby fever—though I'm pretty sure that's a woman-only thing—I'll just make sure I'm the cool uncle Aaron and play with everyone else's kids. I have a feeling there are going to be plenty of them on Lemuria pretty damn quick."

"You would make an excellent uncle. And an excellent father," she decided. "But if you're absolutely sure...then yes. Yes, I'll marry you."

He surged up, dropping her hand so he could wind one arm around her back, the other hand gripping her hair as he kissed her. Her answer had been the one he'd hoped for, but he hadn't been certain it was the one she'd give him. Between that and the fact that they were both still alive, he wanted to celebrate it. He wanted to show her what it meant to him that she loved him enough to face her fears. Big romantic gestures really weren't his thing, but for her, he'd try. Later. Now, he preferred to show her in the best way he knew.

Pulling her off the bench and onto her knees, he pulled her shirt up, then off, tossing it back onto the bench where she'd just sat. He quickly undid her bra and set it with her shirt before he laid her down in the soft grass. She'd looked beautiful in moonlight, but somehow the sunlight enhanced that beauty further. She was meant for sunlight.

His eyes held on hers as he removed her shoes, then slowly undid her pants and began drawing them down her legs. When she was completely bare to the sun, he sat back on his heels and let his gaze slide over her. "I don't care how many years we live, you are always going to be the sexiest woman I've ever seen. And I don't care how many times I have you, I've always going to want you again."

She made a low sound of pleasure and lifted her arms, beckoning him to her. With one hand, he pulled his shirt off and discarded it, before he braced himself on one hand and bent down to kiss her. Though it would be easy to lay himself over her, to feel her breasts against his chest, he kept some separation between them. Otherwise, he wouldn't be able to hold out long enough to show her how much he cared for her.

She had other ideas.

"Stop being so sweet," she whispered, propping herself up on an elbow. She nipped at his throat, even as her hand moved between his legs, cupping him in a way that made him growl. "You can be sweet another time. Right now, I want my wild tiger." She bit again, squeezed just shy of too hard and made his cock throb. "Make me yours. We can say all our vows later."

"You are so fucking perfect," he groaned, brushing her hand away so he could undo the button of his pants and pull the zipper down. Before he could do anything else, she yanked his pants down just below his ass. But as much as he wanted to be inside her, he refused to rush it and hurt her.

Hooking his arms beneath her thighs, he lifted her to his mouth. When she moaned at the first touch of his tongue, his hands tightened on her legs, but he didn't stop. Even when she squirmed against him and fought to touch him, to grab him, he continued to lick, to brush against her clit, using nothing but his mouth to push her to her first climax.

As she cried out, he lowered her back to the grass, then quickly flipped her over onto all fours. He didn't give her time to truly process the shift in her position, just grabbed her hips and thrust deep. Their groans mingled together, though feeling her still tight from her orgasm nearly ended it then and there. He'd woken up wanting her, and that need had only grown stronger with every word they exchanged.

Sliding a hand up her spine, then around to her throat, he pulled her back, so she was pressed against his chest. "Tell me you're mine," he growled, punctuating his words by drawing his hips back, then slamming into her again.

"I'm yours," she moaned, her head dropping back against his shoulder, one hand lifting to his forearm, the other covering the hand still on her hip.

Another thrust, a little harder. "Say it again," he demanded. She wanted him to make her his? He'd absolutely fucking comply. He'd make every inch of her body his, and give her every inch of his own.

"I'm yours!"

Bending his head, he bit her shoulder, just hard enough to sting. "Forever?" he purred against her ear.

She didn't hesitate as he'd expected, just breathed, "Forever."

That was all he needed to hear. He rolled his hips up against her, smooth, fast, and hard, claiming her with his body. She cried out, the sound sweeter than any music, but he demanded more. His hand dropped from her throat to her breast, while the hand on her hip slid around to her belly, helping to draw her back each time he thrust forward.

"I'm yours. Forever," he told her, fighting to hold off long enough to say what he needed to say. "I'll love you every day. Physically. Emotionally. Every. Fucking. Day. I'll never leave." Then he gave in to his tiger instincts, bending his head and setting his teeth firmly against the back of her neck.

The sound she made was almost a sob, but it was followed by her clamping down on him so tightly it made his eyes flutter closed with pleasure. "That's it, baby. Come for me," he purred as he released her neck, even as he stopped fighting and let himself join her as he came so hard it was almost painful. After all they'd been through, and knowing she'd agreed to be his, it just made it so much better. And he'd try every day to make her feel as amazing as she'd just made him feel.

Drained in the best of ways, he half fell forward, one hand hitting the grass and preventing them both from faceplanting on the ground. Slowly, he lowered her down, then let himself fall beside her, rolling onto his back as he waited to catch his breath and his heart to slow.

When he felt her fingers brush his, then her hand wrap around his, he smiled and turned his head to the side so he could see her. Her lips were curved in a soft, happy smile, her eyes half-lidded. "Just so you know," he began, waiting until she looked at him. "As far as I'm concerned, those vows are just a formality. You said you were mine. I said I'm yours. Your husband." As her eyes widened, he lifted the hand he held to his lips, kissing her knuckles tenderly.

Rolling onto her side, she propped her head up in one hand and let her other arm drape across his chest. "You're very pushy, did you know that?"

Aaron couldn't help the grin that appeared on his lips. "I haven't heard you complain about that before. Well, except when I was trying to convince you that living was a good thing."

"No, I didn't say it was a bad thing. Mostly," she said, giving him a poke in the stomach. "But as it happens, I don't disagree. Though I still want the vows, and the wedding."

"Oh, you're getting that," he assured her. "Do you really think I'd miss a big party where I get to tell all of Lemuria that we belong to each other? I mean, the alternative would be biting you a little harder next time and being pushy until you wore your hair up so everyone could see."

Aelia rubbed the back of her neck, but she didn't seem bothered by the imprint of his teeth that was still in her skin. "I don't think everyone understands shifter mating habits."

"Eh. Not all shifters give in to their instincts." He leaned over and kissed her again. "But we'll have the wedding, just as big as you want it, however you want it. Just don't make me wait too long, okay?"

Aelia smiled and moved closer, and he happily wrapped his arms around her, pulling her over him. "I won't. I've waited too long to have you. I'm not waiting anymore."

He closed his eyes and couldn't stop smiling. Never before had such a rocky start ended with such a fantastic outcome. And he was going to spend every day making sure she never regretted it.

And while she planned her dream wedding, he'd make sure the Ekklesia could never hurt her again.

CHAPTER 31

Seth and the other gods gave them the rest of the day and the morning after before they interrupted Aaron and Aelia's private celebration by knocking on the door. Fortunately, while they were lying in bed naked, they'd also finished a few minutes before the first knock, so it was annoying, but not horrible.

"I'll get it," he told Aelia, giving her butt a pat before he got out of bed and pulled on a pair of sweats. He didn't bother with a shirt as he went to the door and opened it. Seeing Seth, Vazi, Grovek, and Cyrus there, he arched a brow. "Do I even want to ask?"

"I'm surprised you have to ask," Seth answered. "Didn't figure you'd want to wait before we figured out what we wanted to do about the Ekklesia."

"No, I really don't," he said, waving them in. "Let me go tell Aelia you're here," he said, turning to head back to the bedroom, knowing they'd make themselves at home.

"Who was it?" Aelia asked with a smile when he walked into the room, sitting up and stretching.

"The gods and Cyrus. They're here about that jinn bitch."

The softness that good sex had given her dropped away. "I'd almost forgotten about Daria," she murmured before she rose and pulled her clothes on.

Since he wasn't sure when they were going to act, he put on his own shirt and shoes. "I hadn't. I hope they've got a good plan for dealing with her. Maybe a nice, simple one. Teleport to wherever she is, kill her, come home. Easy, done, problem solved."

"Except we still have to worry about the dreamwalker," she reminded him, but she didn't say a word about his wanting Daria dead.

"Good point." When she was dressed, he followed her out to the living room. Seth and Vazi were sitting, looking perfectly relaxed. Cyrus stood off to one side, looking serious, while Grovek wandered, looking at the various items Aelia had collected over the years. "You guys got a plan?" he asked as he sat on the couch next to Aelia.

"I'm personally in favor of showing up at their castle and making an example of the jinn, forcing the others to tell us where to find the dreamwalker, then making an example of them as well," Vazi answered coolly.

"I like the way you think."

"And if the others don't know where to find the dreamwalker?" Cyrus asked, folding his arms over his chest. Aaron didn't know him well, as he'd only been on the island for a short time. He was just shy of six feet, with a runner's build, but something about the man had always warned Aaron not to underestimate him. With his curly, shoulder-length black hair and dusky skin, he looked like he had Sumerian ancestors, but Cyrus didn't really share about himself. And Sumerian or not, the amber-colored eyes were unusual. He'd seen shifters with eyes that color, but never an elemental. Maybe it was a mark of how powerful his fire magic was?

Aside from what he was, all Aaron really knew about the man was that he was working on building a ranch so they could bring over horses. Something they were all looking forward to, since they'd unanimously voted to keep cars off the island. They'd need the horses to fully settle the island.

"I really doubt this Daria is the only one who knows about the dreamwalker," Seth said, though he frowned.

"Didn't you say Julian's wife is a telepath?" Aaron asked, sliding his arm around Aelia's shoulder.

"I did," Seth said, nodding slowly, "but if there's any risk, I doubt she'll agree to help. She's pregnant."

Aelia immediately shook her head. "We already know Daria's a powerful fire jinn."

"Which is why Cyrus is here," Vazi said, inclining his head to the man. "He's a powerful fire elemental."

"I've never gone up against a jinn," Cyrus admitted, scratching at his close-cropped beard, "but I don't think I'll have an issue with one, either."

Aaron cocked his head and studied the man. Oddly, he believed the man's confidence was genuine, but he wasn't sure why. He doubted jinn were anything to sneeze at.

"Is it possible the witch representative is the dreamwalker?" Seth asked, directing his question to Aelia.

"He's a witch, so yes, but I can't tell you anything more than that," she admitted. "I tried to avoid them whenever possible, so didn't learn as much about them as I might have liked."

"Given how they've treated you, I can't say I blame you. But is there any way of telling for certain?"

"There is," Grovek said, contributing to the conversation for the first time as he walked back to the others. "Magic can do literally anything. A simple spell can force this witch to speak the truth. Or the jinn."

"Olivia said she wanted to come as well," Vazi pointed out. "A nightmare may be able to recognize a dreamwalker. Their powers are similar."

"I'd forgotten that she wanted in on this," Seth confessed. "Let me go get her," he said before disappearing.

"So what's the plan?" Aaron asked. "You guys take us to their place, we find the jinn, Cyrus deals with the fire while we question her and make sure she's not going to fuck with anyone else, then find the witch?"

"If the jinn says the witch is the dreamwalker who tormented Aelia, yes," Grovek said, nodding. "Though I doubt they'll be alone. From what you've said, these don't appear to be the sort of people who take chances with their safety."

"I disagree," Vazi said, smiling darkly. "They defied multiple gods. That's taking a huge chance with their safety."

Grovek only inclined his head, conceding the point.

"And you're absolutely okay with helping with this?" Aelia asked Cyrus.

The corner of his mouth twitched, but he didn't quite smile. "Lemuria took me in, gave me a home. We're a small community, but we have to look out for each other. From what Seth and Vazi told me, this woman has greatly overstepped the bounds of what she promised to do by joining the Ekklesia. The way I figure it, going with you, I'm not just protecting my new home, I'm also ensuring she can't do this to anyone else. Because I'm certain that if she's done that to you, she's hurt others, too. People like that don't stop, not after they learn that it works."

"No, they don't," she agreed quietly.

Seth returned then with Olivia, again covered from the neck down. It was odd, but he wasn't about to question anyone's fashion choices. Especially not a woman's. He knew better.

"Why are you just sitting there? I thought we were going to kick some jinn ass," Olivia asked, arching a brow as she looked around. "And who are the new guys?" she added, looking at Grovek and Cyrus.

"That's Cyrus. He's a fire elemental who's going to help us with the jinn," Seth explained, nodding to the man. "And that's Grovek. The Lemurian god of wisdom."

Olivia's eyes widened and her lips parted in surprise. "There's another one of you wandering around? How in the hell did that happen?"

"There are actually two more of us," Grovek answered. "My counterpart, Telia, is back as well. And it's largely thanks to Aelia. Her and Aaron."

Olivia's gaze slid to the couch, and Aaron only shrugged. "I'm giving the credit to Aelia," he told her, and was happy he'd done so when Aelia's hand rested on his thigh and squeezed.

"Huh. Well, awesome." Olivia looked back to Grovek. "Glad to have you back. The Lemurians have been missed."

"Not by everyone," the god said.

"And on that note...is everyone ready to go make sure this jinn doesn't abuse anyone else?" Seth asked. When they all easily agreed, he pulled them out of Aelia's house, and into a darkened room on the other side of the world.

Aelia grimaced as she looked at the room she knew all too well. She'd never visited the Ekklesia's castle voluntarily, but she'd been here multiple times in the past. And like it was now, it had always been full. Every chair at the table held a representative, and whatever conversation they'd been having trailed off as they noticed the intruders.

She spotted Daria instantly, and wasn't surprised to find that she recognized most of the other representatives. Unlike some so-called ruling bodies, the Ekklesia continued to 'serve' until they died or retired. Clearly, none of the current representatives wanted to give up their power, as the newest representative seated at the table had been 'serving' for more than three hundred years.

None of them looked happy to see seven people standing in their private chambers, but Aelia couldn't find it in herself to care. They had taken what had once been a useful, necessary group and abused it. Oh, they still hid the Arcane from humanity, but they had become just as large a threat, because Cyrus had been right. If they'd done this to her, how many others had they gone after in order to secure their power base?

Daria rose from the table, her fingertips resting on the table, eyes narrowed as she focused on Aelia. "What are you all doing here? We permitted one intrusion, but this is beyond what we can tolerate."

"And we find that using dreams to torture our friend, including burning her in the waking world, is beyond what *we* can tolerate," Vazi said darkly.

"She was our employee, and she failed us. It's our right to punish her as we see fit."

"Employee?" Aaron asked with a low growl. "That's what you call blackmailing someone? Then trying to force them to reveal information you have no right to know? You really are a power-hungry bitch, aren't you?"

"What right do you have to speak to any of us like that?" a man asked. The witch councilor, she noted, unable to recall his name at the moment.

"Gods," Seth answered, sending a rumble through the room, and the gargoyle representative winced.

Grovek skipped all the byplay and got right to their task. He spoke words even Aelia couldn't recognize, then looked at the nearest representative, a vampire. "Were you a part of torturing Aelia in her dreams in order to force her to provide you with information on Lemuria?"

"No," the man said, his voice tight, like it had been forced from his throat.

Vazi nodded and flicked a hand at the man, who disappeared.

"What did you do to him?" the shifter representative demanded, shoving to her feet.

"Sent him home," Vazi answered with a shrug. "We have no desire to punish those who are innocent of wrongdoing. Something this group could learn. *Will* learn."

Grovek then went around the table, asking each person the same question. Only two others were able to say they hadn't been part of her torment—the fae and gargoyle councilors—and were sent to their homes like the vampire had been. Every single one of the others had been complicit. She wished she could have said she was surprised, but she wasn't.

Power corrupted, and these people had held absolute power for far too long.

The remaining eight showed a mixture of fear, arrogance, and fury, protesting the treatment and discussing the current situation amongst each other.

"Do you really think you're going to punish us for giving Aelia some bad dreams?" Daria demanded.

"Oh, we really, really are," Seth told her. "You went way beyond your fucking purpose, and we're tired of you abusing your position."

"We're doing what is necessary!" the witch said, slamming a fist onto the table. Given Grovek's spell, he had to truly believe that.

"How the hell is trying to force her to tell you about Lemuria necessary?" Aaron snapped. "It's hidden from humans better than you could ever manage. You're trying to get more power. Power that you don't need to do your fucking jobs!"

His nails were lengthening into claws, and Aelia rested a hand on his arm. Not to stop him, but to reassure him she was okay. They'd hurt her, she couldn't deny that, but she was all right. That wasn't going to keep him from killing Daria, she knew that, but she'd long since gotten over being squeamish about death when it was necessary. Preventing a group this powerful from harming others counted as necessary.

"And I have one more question," Grovek said, his voice as calm and bland as it might have been discussing basic math problems. "Who is the dreamwalker—or nightmare—who was responsible for getting into Aelia's dreams? Whose magic was used."

Even before anyone spoke, she saw two sets of eyes flick toward the nightmare representative.

"That one is mine," Olivia said in a soft, dangerous voice.

No one argued with her.

"I'd like to say something," Aelia said, speaking for the first time since they'd arrived.

"I think we've heard enough from you," Daria sneered, but the Lemurians—and Olivia—didn't object.

She took two steps forward, not truly afraid of this group. Not anymore. They couldn't kill her, and they wouldn't be able to get into her head after today. "When the Ekklesia first found me, I thought you were wonderful people. Helping not just the Arcane, but people like me who lived on the fringes of the Arcane society. Sorcerers and people who brushed against magic, even if they didn't hold any themselves. And for a little while, you were. I was happy to repay the help the Ekklesia had given me."

Her gaze slid to Daria. "But you've changed. You still hide the Arcane, but only because it serves your own interests to do so. Now you just want power. Not to protect the Arcane, but for your own selfish purposes. And to gain that power, you're hurting the very people you're sworn to protect. I don't know how you could have possibly thought you'd be able to continue that indefinitely. The more people you hurt, the more people who can band together to have you replaced." She smiled, just a little, but she didn't really feel it. "You thought I was just a human who couldn't die. You thought I was alone. That I was vulnerable. That I would be an easy target who would roll over and give you all the information you wanted on Lemuria."

She took another step forward, putting her just within reach of the siren councilor. "Lemuria is none of the Ekklesia's concern. It's none of anyone's concern except for the Lemurian gods and those lucky enough to live there. Something I hope those who come after you will remember. Because I? Will *never* give anyone the tools they need to harm the land or its people."

Daria's patience broke, or maybe her fury took over, because she stopped listening and attacked. Her body was engulfed in bright orange flames that immediately set the table she touched on fire. She lifted her arms and sent a stream of flames directly toward Aelia. Even as she braced for them to hit, for the pain she knew they'd cause, the streams separated and circled upward, splashing harmlessly on the stone ceiling.

Cyrus. It had been a damn good idea to bring the elemental.

That was all it took for hell to break loose. The entire room shook as Seth unleashed his power, and part of her worried the whole castle might collapse around them. She didn't feel the wind of Vazi's power, but that was good. It would have only fed the flames.

She heard a snarl and saw a flash of black fly past her, slamming into the shifter councilor. The woman changed form even as she was tackled, turning into a huge crocodile. Aelia fought not to be concerned or to help. Aaron was strong, and he was immortal now. Whatever happened, he'd be all right.

The room was quickly filled with flames and shadows, and it took only a glance to see the shadows were due to the two nightmares battling it out. Neither moved, and there was no physical fight, but they had to be doing something for the darkness to be so pervasive, even with the flames from Cyrus and Daria. Except...the flames weren't all yellow and orange. The initial ones, the ones from Daria, had been, but Cyrus's fire was white. She'd never seen anyone—elemental or jinn—whose flames were anything but shades of gold and red.

Vazi, Seth, and Grovek seemed more than capable of handling the councilors who weren't already engaged. The elemental? Controlled air, which meant he was no match against the Lemurian god of the sky. The elf? Was actually trembling in his seat, and being left alone for now. Or maybe he was being held there. She didn't know and right now she didn't care. The mer was lying on the floor, neck at an unnatural angle. The siren was clawing at her throat and chest, and she had to assume Vazi was depriving the woman of air. The witch had the dubious honor of trying to go against Grovek. He might not be known for his magic, but she was well aware of just how much sorcery he knew. He at least rivaled the skills of Isis and Hecate, and exceeded the knowledge of Odin.

Aaron, still in his tiger form, stood over the still body of the shifter councilor, blood pooling around her body. He looked at Aelia before turning toward Daria—still fighting with Cyrus—and roaring.

Aelia wasn't worried about the siren or elf, but she was done letting others fight this particular battle. Yes, the Ekklesia had been doing wrong for a while, and she wasn't the only one Daria had hurt, but this confrontation? It was about her, and she wasn't going to sit around watching.

Daria was starting to look scared as she was battered by white flames. Cyrus was definitely more powerful than she'd realized if he could scare a fire jinn like that. The problem was they were filling the room with fire and smoke, making it harder for the rest of them. This needed to be ended quickly, or Olivia was going to be in danger.

"You did this to yourself, Daria," she called over the roaring of the fire.

"Fuck you!"

No remorse, not that she expected any. But Daria wasn't going to be defeated by fire. Fortunately, Aelia had learned much in her long life, and knew one thing Daria couldn't defend against.

She looked around the room and saw a side table with decanters and glasses. Hurrying over, she dumped the contents of one on the floor, then broke a second. Aaron snarled a protest, apparently figuring out part of what she intended, but she ignored him. Using one of the broken shards, she cut the back of her forearm, wincing at the pain.

"What the hell are you doing?" he asked, suddenly back in his human form. Nude, of course, and she ignored that, too.

"Ending this before we're all burned alive," she told him, coughing as she inhaled too much of the smoke. "Get the gods to get Olivia out of here as soon as she's done with the nightmare."

He didn't look happy, but went to do as she asked. She sat down to escape the worst of the smoke and worked on breathing as shallowly as she could. Resting the decanter in her lap, she dipped her finger into the blood from her arm and started to draw on the glass's surface. It was an intricate symbol she was forming, and she had to get it exactly right or it wouldn't work.

The Seal of Solomon was something many people had heard of, but so many 'facts' about it were wrong. For one, Solomon had adopted the seal as his own, but its origins were much older. And it had nothing to do with demons, but it did affect jinn.

"No!" Daria screamed as Aelia drew more of the symbol onto the decanter, its stopper still resting on the table. The jinn tried to split her focus, shooting a blast of fire toward Aelia. She felt the heat, smelled burning hair, and her body tensed at the pain, but Cyrus quickly diverted the flames away from her. It still took a minute for her to recover enough to continue drawing without fear of a shaky hand messing up the sigil.

"Hold her for just a little longer," Aelia yelled to Cyrus. He didn't respond, but she did feel a breeze. Confused, she looked up and saw all three gods standing between her and the jinn. It was likely Vazi could deal with Daria by himself, sucking the air from around her and smothering her flames, but he was giving Aelia this chance, and protecting her while she took it. Something she greatly appreciated. This had started with her. It should end with her, too.

Breathing slowly and deeply, she drew the last lines of the sigil. Daria obviously felt its pull, but the symbol itself wasn't enough. Getting to her feet, she held the decanter in one hand, took the stopper in the other, and turned toward Daria. She pushed between Grovek and Vazi until there was no one between her and Daria. Fighting not to choke on the smoke, she chanted the thankfully short phrase in Sumerian that would ensure Daria wouldn't be able to hurt anyone else. And honestly, it was a worse punishment than death.

She deserved it.

Daria began screaming curses directed at Aelia as her human form began to fall apart, flesh and bone replaced by fire. Cyrus's flames died down, and out of the corner of Aelia's eye, she saw confusion on his face, but she kept her focus on Daria as she became living flame.

"I didn't know jinn could do that," Aaron said, frowning as he watched.

"They...can't," Vazi said, sounding as confused as the others. "Wind jinn can, but not fire jinn."

If that messed with them, what was about to happen was going to blow their minds. The problem was, she couldn't enjoy the looks on her faces, not if she wanted it to work.

Keeping focused on what she was doing, she watched the flames that were Daria as they writhed and jerked in her direction. Then, they began to flow through the air toward her. Not smoothly, but in starts and stops, like a rope in tug of war. She saw Cyrus make a gesture toward them, trying to block the flames from her, but she shook her head. "Don't."

He hesitated, but Grovek said, "Listen to her," and he subsided.

This part didn't scare her, but depending on exactly how strong Daria was, it was dangerous. This was a battle like the rest, but this one was a test of wills, not magic or physical strength.

Aelia kept fighting to pull Daria's flame form toward her, but Daria was struggling just as hard. The others might not know what was going on, but there was no way a jinn hadn't been warned about this exact situation. It didn't matter that most people had forgotten about this particular spell, it was still a jinn's greatest weakness.

Pulling on Daria was quickly draining her, but she didn't stop. Daria might be powerful and pissed, but Aelia had centuries of practice focusing her thoughts and performing sorcery. It didn't mean it was easy, but it did give her an edge. The fact that she had suffered greatly at this woman's hands didn't hurt.

Sweat beaded on her forehead and rolled down her cheeks and nose, and the hands holding the decanter and stopper began to tremble with the mental effort it took. But Daria's flames inched toward her. It might be at a snail's pace, but it was progress. Then, like Daria had given up or lost the energy to fight, she darted forward.

Aelia heard sharp intakes of breath, but the jinn didn't hit her, she flowed into the glass vessel she held. As the flames entered the decanter, they compressed and swirled, but she had to wait until all of Daria was inside. The second the fire had disappeared into the container, she slammed the stopper in place. It wasn't airtight, so the physical container wouldn't normally contain fire, but the sigil, already dry on the glass, would. As long as no one broke the decanter or took the stopper out and spoke the right incantation, Daria would be trapped in the vessel. Forever.

But the payment for doing such a thing was due, and she couldn't put it off any longer. "Take it," she said, shoving the decanter behind her toward the gods and Aaron. She felt someone take it from her just before the magic took its toll and she lost consciousness.

Aaron's body ached, and he had scratches and one nasty bite from the crocodile, not to mention he was sweating like he was in the middle of the Sahara at noon in summer and his lungs burned from the smoke, but none of that mattered when he saw Aelia's eyes roll back and her body start to drop.

He was glad Seth had grabbed the bottle, because it meant his hands were free to catch her before she hit the stone floor. "What happened to her?" he demanded of the gods.

"Probably magical exhaustion, but we should leave," Grovek told him.

Vazi glanced at the windows and with a quick gust of wind, broke several, then used his magic to clear the smoke from the room. "We should decide what to do with him first," he said, nodding to the elf.

"Leave him. He was so scared of us he pissed himself. You got Olivia out, she's safe, so can we get back to Lemuria and take care of Aelia?" Aaron asked.

"The Ekklesia will have a hard enough time rebuilding with only four left," Grovek said.

"Remember this if you decide to fuck with Lemuria again," Vazi told the elf councilor before he took them all back to Aelia's house.

Aaron picked Aelia up and laid her on the couch, then looked at Grovek. "Fix her," he demanded.

Grovek didn't complain about receiving orders from him, just knelt beside the couch and laid a hand on Aelia's forehead. While he did whatever he was doing, Aaron felt something settle over him and glanced down to find he was clothed again.

"Got tired of looking at your bare ass," Seth told him, but it wasn't snarky. Probably going easy on him until they found out if Aelia was all right. He might bitch about that later, but not now.

Aelia drew in a deep breath, then sighed and opened her eyes.

Grovek drew his hand back and rose, letting Aaron take his place. "Aelia? Baby, what happened?"

"Paid the price," she mumbled.

"Okay, but what did you do?"

"Trapped her."

Grovek chuckled softly and looked at the bottle Seth still held. "You truly do have a lot to teach me. I knew of jinn, but I didn't know a way had been devised of imprisoning them. Is it permanent?"

"'less the decanter breaks...or someone knows the spell."

"Am I understanding this correctly? That jinn is trapped in a whiskey decanter until the end of the universe?" Vazi asked.

"Yep," Aelia said, sounding exhausted. Aaron gently helped her sit up and sat beside her to support her.

Vazi laughed, a little too joyously. "That's perfect," he said, taking the bottle from Seth. "Anyone mind if I take this and set it on my mantle? I don't have a mantle, but I'll create one just to put it on."

"You're kind of a sick man," Seth said, shaking his head.

"She caused a lot of trouble, and that's just considering the things we know about."

"Never wanna see her again," Aelia said, resting her head on Aaron's shoulder.

"Excellent." The decanter disappeared and Vazi smiled. "But how are you, Aelia?"

"Tired. She's strong. Fought hard. Just need to rest."

"And that's my cue to say thank you and kick all of you out," Aaron said, and though he was grateful to all of them, he meant what he said and let it show in his voice.

"We understand. Let us know if she needs anything," Seth said, taking him and the others out of the house before anyone could argue.

As soon as they were alone, Aaron looked down at Aelia. "Are you really okay?"

"Yeah. Really just tired. I'll be okay after I sleep. But what about you? I didn't fight a crocodile."

Honestly, he should have asked one of the gods for a heal, but he was more worried about Aelia. Besides, he'd suffered worse and survived without a heal. And he hadn't been immortal then.

"I'm okay," he told her, even though he planned to clean and patch himself up after she was in bed. Since his injuries were currently covered, she didn't need to know about them until she'd slept. "But let's get you in the other room so you can get some sleep."

"I won't argue," she said, getting to her feet with his help. She was still unsteady, so he scooped her into his arms and took her back to the bedroom, setting her on the bed. She sighed and smiled at him. "It's over," she murmured.

"It is. Now you just need to plan the wedding."

Her smile widened. "I do."

He bent down and kissed her gently. "Remember, don't keep me waiting too long."

She laughed softly and brushed her fingers across his cheek. "I won't," she promised, before closing her eyes and giving in to the rest her body demanded.

For a minute he only stood there watching her, unable to believe how his life had changed in the last year. He wasn't sure which was more unbelievable; that he was immortal, or that Aelia was his, and he was hers. All he knew was that he was going to spend the rest of eternity making sure she never felt alone again.

EPILOGUE

One month later

Aaron had asked her not to make him wait too long, and she'd easily agreed. It had been a month since they'd brought back Grovek and Telia. In that time, Aaron had moved all of his things to her house, and it had been surprisingly easy to adjust to having someone else constantly in her space. Surprisingly—to her at least—having him beside her when she went to sleep and again when she woke had improved her mental state, too. She still had days when the depression pulled at her, but it was a little easier with someone else to help shoulder the burden.

Grovek had agreed to take Aaron as an apprentice as well, which had thrilled her new husband. Together, they'd spent at least part of every other day in Sozu, and she'd been pleased when Grovek had admitted that Aaron was an excellent student.

As she'd predicted, Grovek had loved computers when he'd understood them, and was working out a plan for how they'd be incorporated into Sozu. Aaron was helping with that.

Two weeks after Grovek's return, they'd gone back to Thelaria. Grovek had known Ocoina—the goddess of birth and rebirth—well enough to know what object to use to connect to her; the blanket she'd wrapped the first Lemurian baby in after birth.

Like with the first ritual, the second had resulted in a painful and lengthy death, but they'd revived once again, and the number of Lemurian gods had increased to seven. All of Lemuria was rejoicing as their numbers continued to expand, though those who knew of Seth and Vazi's first visit to the Ekklesia were worried. None of the Lemurians seemed to be guilty, but neither could they come up with an alternative explanation for the Ekklesia's question as to whether Aelia was the only one under a geas.

And throughout it all, Aelia had planned her wedding. With the help of several of the Lemurians, of course. Big wasn't really her thing, but she had invited all of Lemuria, as well as friends from outside the island. Sophia, Erasmus, Lucas, and Olivia from the Athenaeum. Seth's friends who had been to the 'housewarming' party not long after they'd found the island. Hecate and Rhea, of course. And Aaron's parents. Each and every one had happily agreed, though his parents had been interesting. They'd been stunned to learn about Lemuria, and had been horrified to learn what their other son had done. But, after the shock had worn off, with prompting from their son and new daughter-in-law, had decided to join Lemuria's growing population, bringing the total—including gods—up to twenty-seven.

They'd chosen the square to hold both the wedding and party to follow. Vazi had offered to officiate, just as he had at Tempest and Seth's wedding, and to her delight, Grovek had insisted on walking her down the aisle, after he'd been informed of modern wedding customs.

Not that they were doing things completely modern, but instead mixing Lemurian customs with those Aaron was more used to. So while she would be wearing a white dress and escorted by a father-figure to her husband, the joining would be done more in the Lemurian style.

It was perfect to her, though Aaron had chafed at spending the night before at Seth's house, while Kara, Tempest, and Sophia had stayed at Aelia's. To be honest, she'd chafed, too. She'd become very accustomed to having him in bed beside her at night, and spending the morning with him. But she had been able to handle a single night without him, especially with the three women there to keep her distracted.

And now she was standing at the end of an aisle in her gown, a bouquet of flowers in her hand. Her hand was on Grovek's arm as she looked out at all of Lemuria and their friends, with Aaron—in an exceptional tux—standing at the far end beside Vazi, Seth, and Kara. The best part was just how happy she was in that very moment. Oh, the depression tried to cling to her like honey, but it couldn't overshadow the way Aaron made her feel.

"Are you ready?" Grovek asked, his expression thoughtful, like he was viewing this all as a research project. She wasn't offended. It was just his way, and she knew he was happy for her, which was enough.

"Absolutely," she told him, though she didn't take her eyes off Aaron.

He guided her through the rows of friends, then passed her hand to Aaron.

"You look so fucking beautiful," Aaron whispered. Then, despite it not being time for it yet, kissed her. It was brief—more than either of them might have liked—and she heard some of the guests laughing.

"Save it for later," Vazi said dryly.

"Why waste time?" Aaron asked with an unrepentant grin.

Aelia could only smile. She wouldn't change a thing about the man she already considered her husband.

"Can we at least get to the joining now? I got a sample of the food earlier, and I can't eat it until I finish this," Vazi complained.

Now she laughed, because she knew Vazi was joking. Mostly. "Yes, we can get to it," she told him.

"Friends and family of Aelia and Aaron, I am pleased to have you here, and to have the honor of joining these two together."

The rest of the ceremony passed by in a blur, with her and Aaron replying at the appropriate moments. Instead of exchanging rings, Vazi wrapped a blue ribbon around their hands and wrists, tying them together. Then, finally, Vazi pronounced them joined, and Seth leaned in to whisper, "That means you can kiss her now."

"Yeah, I got that," Aaron told him, using his free hand to cup her face as he kissed her, lingering over it this time. It wasn't enough, especially when he ended it and brushed his cheek against hers, until he could whisper, "You're stuck with me, now. Nothing, not even death, can separate us."

Too swamped with emotions to reply, she could just wrap her arm around him, hugging him tightly. No, nothing could separate them now; neither of them would allow it. But he was wrong about one thing. She wasn't stuck. She was exactly where she wanted to be.

About the Author

Meg M. Robinson is a fantasy author who lives in north Georgia with her husband, cat, and three dogs.

She's obsessed with crows, mythology, and Halloween. And, of course, books. When she's not focused on either reading or writing a book, she enjoys going for motorcycle rides with her husband, archery, and baking.

www.megmrobinson.com

Please consider leaving a rating or review for this book. Reviews are extremely important for authors, but especially indie authors like me! Believe me, we appreciate it!

www.ingramcontent.com/pod-product-compliance
Lightning Source LLC
Chambersburg PA
CBHW021341310726
48971CB00001B/230